About Doris

"Doris Elaine Fell has become one of America's favorite storytellers."
—**Karen Kingsbury**, USA Today and New York Times best-selling author of more than 40 novels (over 15 million copies sold), 10 of which have hit #1 on national lists

"Doris Elaine Fell writes with a tender heart. You won't want to miss this one!"
—**Angela Hunt**, Christy Award-winning author of more than 100 works, including The Tale of Three Trees and The Note (also a Hallmark movie)

"Doris spins an intriguing tale."
—**Robin Jones Gunn**, Christy Award-winning author of over 70 books, including the Glenbrooke series, the Christy Miller series, the Sierra Jensen series, the Katie Weldon series, and the best-selling Sisterchicks® novels

"A tightly woven contemporary story of political intrigue and spiritual redemption that pumps the adrenalin and brings peace to the heart. The names and places jump out of today's headlines, but the deceit goes all the way back to the Garden of Eden."
—**Stephen Bly**, Christy Award-winning author of more than 100 books, including The Long Trail Home, and television/radio speaker (Focus on the Family and others)

"A plot that could well have been taken from today's headlines…a thought-provoking page-turner you won't want to miss."
—**Deborah Raney**, best-selling author of 19 novels that have won the RITA Award, HOLT Medallion, National Readers' Choice Award, Silver Angel, and been chosen twice as Christy Award finalists, including A Vow to Cherish (which inspired the award-winning World Wide Pictures film) and Remember to Forget

"A compelling and timely read! A contemporary war story that will engage readers while reminding them of battles fought beyond our normal lives. The characters are great, and the story, engaging."

—CINDY MARTINUSEN, best-selling author of 10 books, including *Orchid House*, *The Salt Garden*, *Winter Passing*, and *North of Tomorrow*

"With equal parts mystery, romance, and intrigue, it's a book you don't want to miss."

—JAMES SCOTT BELL, former trial lawyer, best-selling suspense writer of over 20 books, including *Try Fear* and *Deceived*, as well as Christy Award-winning novels *Final Witness*, *Circumstantial Evidence*, and *Blind Justice*

"Seeps into your soul. A modern-day saga of tragedy and triumph, grit and grace."

—KATHY HERMAN, best-selling author of 22 novels, including The Baxter Series, Seaport Suspense Series, Phantom Hollow Series, Sophie Trace Trilogy, *Poor Mrs. Rigsby*, *The Last Word*, and *A Fine Line*

"Doris Elaine Fell is a masterful storyteller who emblazons her literary landscapes with unforgettable characters…and exotic locales. *Blue Mist on the Danube* is a delicious reading experience, whetting the appetite for more."

—CAROLE GIFT PAGE, best-selling author of over 40 books, including *Becoming a Woman of Passion*, *The House on Honeysuckle Lane*, *Cassandra's Song*, and *By the Beckoning Sea*

"Strikes the reader right between the eyes. With up-to-the-minute insights into realistic characters caught up in the twists of fate in our present war, this author makes the battle personal for each of us. An award winner for sure."

—HANNAH ALEXANDER, author-duo of numerous novels, including *Hideaway*, *Safe Haven*, *Double Blind*, *Fair Warning* (all Steeple Hill), *Sacred Trust*, *Solemn Oath*, *Silent Pledge*, and *A Killing Frost*

"Intrigue and betrayal, love lost and found, denial and faith...all played out in exotic settings where nothing is as it seems. Prepare to lose some sleep!"

—**STEPHANIE GRACE WHITSON**, best-selling author of *A Claim of Her Own, Secrets on the Wind, A Garden in Paris,* and *A Hilltop in Tuscany,* as well as two-time Christy Award finalist, winner of the Inspirational Reader's Choice Award, and *ForeWord Magazine's* Book of the Year

"A story filled with living, breathing characters who remain in your heart long after the last page is turned."

—**DIANE NOBLE**, award-winning novelist of more than 27 titles, with a quarter million books in print, including as lead author of the popular Guideposts series Mystery and the Minister's Wife, The California Chronicles, and *The Brides of Gabriel* (Harper Collins)

"International intrigue, secrets from the past, and a delightful romance make *Willows on the Windrush* a fun read. Another wonderful book by Christy nominee Doris Elaine Fell."

—**GAYLE ROPER**, award-winning author of more than 40 books, 3-time Christy Award finalist, RITA Award for Best Inspirational Romance, 3-time Holt Medallion winner, the Reviewers Choice Award, the Award of Excellence, and the Golden Quill, for novels such as *Spring Rain, Summer Shadows, Autumn Dreams,* and *Winter Winds*

"International tension, family secrets, and God's steadfast provision...a gripping, timely story."

—**NANCY MOSER**, award-winning author of 21 novels, including Christy Award-winner *Time Lottery, Washington's Lady,* and *John 3:16,* as well as *How Do I Love Thee?, Crossroads,* The Sister Circle Series, The Steadfast Series, The Time Lottery Series, and The Mustard Seed Series

Novels
by Doris Elaine Fell

SAGAS OF A KINDRED HEART
*Experience the romance,
the adventure, the intrigue....*

Blue Mist on the Danube
Willows on the Windrush
Sunrise on Stradbury Square

THE EUROPEAN CONNECTION
Fast-paced international romance thrillers

Assignment in Paris
Encounter in Zurich
The Spanish Connection
The Phoenix of Sulzbach
Deception in Prague
Conspiracy on Corfu

☙ THE EUROPEAN CONNECTION ☙

ENCOUNTER IN Zurich

DORIS ELAINE FELL

OAKTARA

WATERFORD, VIRGINIA

Encounter in Zurich

Published in the U.S. by:
OakTara Publishers
P.O. Box 8
Waterford, VA 20197

Visit OakTara at
www.oaktara.com

Cover design by David LaPlaca/debest design co.
Cover images © iStockphoto.com/ Joe Cicak, background/Edyta Pawowska, father and daughter/Zbindere, mountain/Nikontiger, leaf

Copyright © 1994, 2010 by Doris Elaine Fell. All rights reserved.

ISBN: 978-1-60290-023-3

Encounter in Zurich is a work of fiction. References to real people, events, establishments, organizations, or locales are intended only to provide a sense of authenticity and are used fictitiously. All other characters, incidents, and dialogue are drawn from the author's imagination.

For Bobbie

Well done, dear friend.
You have tasted eternity and
will go on savoring it forever.

Prologue

Ingrid von Tonner loved the charm and coziness of the Schweizerhof dining room and the faint ring of the cowbells on the lower meadows. But she hated waiting for the stranger. Discreetly, she drew back the lace curtain. Her gaze swept over the Alpine fields, her thoughts twisting like the serpentine trails that coiled their way among the Swiss chalets. She allowed her gaze to rise with the steep mountain slopes toward the jagged peaks capped with powdery plumes of snow.

A thunderstorm had darkened the sky at the higher elevation, pelting those peaks with rain and leaving behind a mantle of mist arced with miniature rainbows. The Alps dwarfed the village and momentarily weakened her anger. She let the curtain slip back in place, one ringed hand drumming on the tabletop. The more she tapped, the more the melting candle flickered.

The waiter came, squinting as the late afternoon sun filtered through the window. "Does the Baroness wish another candle?" he asked.

She smiled up at him. "Later, Garret. Perhaps when Mr. Williams arrives. Has there been any word from him?"

"None. Would the Baroness care to order now?"

"I'll wait awhile longer." *An hour at most,* she thought.

She slipped a deutsche mark across the table. He bowed politely and backed away, the money tucked in the palm of his hand and her table secured for the evening.

The stranger had ordered Ingrid's favorite table for two—revealing to her that he knew far more about her than she cared to admit. On the telephone he had called himself Smythe Williams, an art dealer. Intuitively, she knew it was not his real name. Nor did she believe that he was interested in the purchase of an original Rembrandt or Renoir.

Ingrid's attention turned to the chugging groan of the cabled train pulling into the station, beating the arrival of twilight. Would it bring her unknown dinner companion? Or a Swiss policeman? For several minutes, she studied the people plodding up the hill—men in lederhosen and green feathered hats, women in dirndls and buckled suede shoes. Tourists and foreigners milled slowly into the dining room—couples and families and four handsome Austrians in their Trachten charcoal-gray suits. But not the stranger who would dine with her this evening.

As the Austrians passed her table, it pleased Ingrid that they took notice of her flamboyant attire, her sleek figure, and the expensive jewels that magnified her polychromatic personality. At fifty-three she had a flawless complexion and the impeccable grace and charm of a socialite. She returned each man's gaze with a sultry warm smile that said, *Sorry, my evening is already taken.*

Glancing around, she recognized Sigmund Valdemar at a nearby table. Sigmund, thirtyish, an artistic, tight-lipped young man with murky brown hair, nodded reassuringly—a truculent rawness to his smile. In an almost imperceptible signal, his clay-cold eyes shifted to the man approaching her table. Ingrid saw him then—the stranger who called himself Smythe Williams. *The game of wit begins,* she thought.

For days she had pictured a short, pudgy man, bald and demanding. Instead, a tall, silver-haired gentleman cut across the room toward her, his shrewd black eyes glancing furtively at the diners around him. He walked ramrod straight, pensively stroking his goatee as though it were new and annoying.

Half-amused, Ingrid smiled as he reached her. His thick black eyebrows gave him away. His hair was obviously dyed. But why? He was sixtyish, older perhaps, but well-preserved. Men his age dyed their hair black or blond, not a shimmering gray like her own.

"Mrs. von Tonner?" he asked politely.

"Yes. You're late," she said as he sat down.

"I missed the earlier train."

"Did you?" she challenged. "When it went past seven, I considered canceling the reservation, Mr. Smith."

"Smythe Williams," he corrected.

"I didn't take that for granted. I checked. I do have my sources. Your name is really Harland C. Smith, a Parisian businessman. You've been in self-imposed exile ever since your private jet exploded. Hiding from the French and Americans, I believe."

"Yes, they forced me into hiding months ago," he admitted, surprising her. "I'm alone—without my family." The bitterness in his tone was brief. With control, he asked, "Did you order dinner?"

"No, I waited for you."

He adjusted his thick-rimmed glasses and requested a French menu. "The evening special—*saumon fume,* then *medaillons de veau doree,*" he said to the waiter, his French tainted with a Brooklyn accent. "For dessert, cherries jubilee for two."

He glanced at Ingrid. She considered opposing him. Instead, she lit a cigarette, her first one in months, and forced a smile. "If you insist," she said.

"Wine, sir?" Garret asked, pointing to the bottle of Liebfraumilch on their table.

"Later," Smith told him. "Evian, for now."

When they were alone, she deliberately blew a puff of smoke into his face. He turned away. "You didn't just invite me to dinner, Mr. Smith," she said, crushing the half-smoked cigarette in the ashtray. "Let's get to the point. What was this business deal you had in mind?"

With a precise flick of his wrist, he unraveled his napkin and placed it on his lap. Lowering his voice, he said, "I understand that you deal in priceless art pieces, Mrs. von Tonner."

"I've sold a few."

"At a fair market value?"

She toyed with his question. "Any business is for a profit."

"You do very well in yours, but you could do better."

"I'm listening."

"I'm interested in meeting your associate."

"Someone in particular?"

"Your Los Angeles contact. Drew Gregory's wife."

She slipped tapered fingers around the glass. "Miriam? You know Miriam Gregory?"

"I know her husband."

Her ex-husband, she thought. Aloud, she said, "They're not in touch. They've been divorced for years."

"I know that, too," he said calmly. "I'm interested in the art treasures that pass through Miriam's Art Gallery."

"The store in Beverly Hills?"

"That's the one. Drew Gregory funded the shop."

In her mind, she questioned Smith again. *He's guessing, or did he know that Miriam had invested years of Drew's alimony checks and inheritance into the gallery?* Tongue-in-cheek, she said, "Miriam is a shrewd businesswoman."

"Clever, like you, Mrs. von Tonner? Aren't you using Drew Gregory's wife for a profit of your own—selling frauds to an unsuspecting public?"

"I'll take that wine now."

"No, let me finish—"

She slid a crystal glass toward him. His hand held steady as he poured—a gentleman's hand, the nails neatly filed, his fingers ringed with diamonds and an onyx. "You seem interested in more than art, Mr. Smith."

"I'm interested in destroying Drew Gregory."

"I think Miriam already beat you to that."

He put his hand firmly on her wrist before she could light another cigarette. "Smoking annoys me. And so does your banter. I need your help. Otherwise, your profitable art exchange with Mrs. Gregory is going up in smoke." He dabbed his thick lips with a napkin. "I know about those 'priceless' art frauds that you pass through Mrs. Gregory's gallery. I represent one of those angry customers."

She shifted uneasily, hoping Smith was bluffing. "Every painting we sell is certified—licensed properly."

"Ah! The certificate of authenticity," he mocked. "So easy to forge, so necessary to impress the customer. Before contacting you, my dear, I made serious allegations to Mrs. Gregory's lawyer."

"You what?"

"I contacted Aaron Gregory, Drew's half-brother. On behalf of my client, we've threatened a lawsuit over one of those sales."

She knew the painting would be a Rembrandt or one by the

French Impressionist Renoir; Sigmund Valdemar specialized in copying these. Had Smith arranged for its purchase and sounded an alarm? She pushed her empty glass toward him, allowing herself time to sort out the scenario that motivated him. *Miriam's gallery,* she decided, *has been under his scrutiny for some time. But why?*

"We've stirred up some ruckus in Washington at high levels, my dear. And at the Langley headquarters in Virginia."

She swirled her wine glass. *Not a CIA connection! Drew in the CIA? Impossible.* She watched Smith, baiting him, certain that her silence irritated him.

His mellow tone rose in annoyance. "Aaron Gregory took the threat of a lawsuit personally, as though he were somehow involved in your operation, Mrs. von Tonner. He seemed so anxious to protect your friendship. Your affair, perhaps?"

The crimson began at the nape of her neck and moved to her cheeks. She resisted the urge to slap Smith's face and storm from the elegant Schweizerhof. They sat in silence, waiting catlike, until the waiter brought their dinners. Smith seasoned his food with garlic pepper in the same precise manner in which he had placed his napkin. His angry gaze matched hers.

"Baroness, I need Miriam Gregory and her daughter Robyn in Switzerland at once. That will bring Drew Gregory out in the open."

"Drew is of no concern to Miriam. As far as she knows, he makes his home somewhere here in Europe, living like a rich vagabond. Thanks to his family inheritance."

"Aaron Gregory will know where he is."

"And if I refuse to help you?"

"Then your nice lucrative art empire will fold."

"I am Miriam's European buyer. That's all."

He wiped his fingers meticulously on the napkin and then stroked his goatee. "You're more international than that, my dear. You're quite knowledgeable about the Dutch masters, thanks to your second husband's heirlooms. But you're having difficulty selling them publicly. I have contacts—potential buyers around the world—that would be of interest to you and the baron."

"Maybe to me," she said. "The baron is elderly and ill— confined

v

to a medical clinic. I handle his legal affairs."

"And spend his money? You speak so lightly of your marriage."

"My *former* marriage. It was a business arrangement. Perhaps you mistook my butler for the baron. They're both ancient."

Another hint of bitterness flashed in his cagey dark eyes. "Unlike you, I miss my companion. That's why I want to rescue Monique and the boys from Paris and have them here with me. But until Drew Gregory is out of the way—"

"That again?" she asked. "I still won't help you."

"I think you will. I've heard about that hoard of old masters that you keep in the von Tonner mansion. Some of them frauds, no doubt. But all worth a pretty sum on the open market."

"I told you—they're family heirlooms."

"Yes, they've passed from generation to generation. My dear, I've looked into your background. *Thoroughly.* I am well informed about the art vaults beneath the mansion and the young artist who duplicates the old masters for you. These are more than rumors."

Smith was guessing again, but good guesses. What else did he know about Sigmund Valdemar? She allowed her gaze to circle the room. Valdemar frowned, a savage tightness to his mouth. She turned back to Smith. "So what do you want from me?"

"Weren't you listening? I want Miriam and Robyn Gregory in Switzerland. Once they are here, Drew will come looking for them, especially if he thinks they're in danger."

"He won't even know they've arrived."

"That's where brother Aaron comes in."

"And what do I tell Aaron? That you're waiting to destroy his brother? He won't care. There's no love lost between them."

"Just dazzle Aaron with those beautiful dark eyes of yours. He's no doubt used to it. Or tell him I'm on to your art capers." Smith pushed back his chair. "I'll be in touch. *Auf Wiedersehen.*"

"There's no need to use German with me. The baron is German, Mr. Smith. Not me. My first husband—God rest his soul—was French. I speak French fluently. I prefer that...or English."

Smith gave a click of his heels and mocked her with a bow. He made a commanding figure as he walked away. At once Sigmund

Valdemar was on his feet following Smith out of the dining room.

Ingrid lit another cigarette and with gusto blew endless puffs of smoke at Smith's empty chair. There wasn't a man alive that Baroness Ingrid von Tonner couldn't charm and use for her own purposes.

So he wants Drew Gregory, she mused. *He can have him. And if my little art world is collapsing, I must salvage my own interests. I'll phone Miriam and Robyn on Sunday and urge them to come to Switzerland for an overdue visit. I must know what they know—what they suspect. And I must warn Aaron so we can turn our business channels elsewhere. What will it matter if Drew Gregory gets caught in the crossfire?*

But Ingrid's curiosity tantalized her. What had Drew done that so threatened this stranger at the Schweizerhof?

One

Robyn Gregory brushed a wisp of auburn hair from her face as she scrutinized her mother's latest acquisition, a newly discovered Rembrandt. She squinted at the painting, trying to shut out the muffled, angry voices in the glass-enclosed office. A door slammed shut, cutting off her mother's words.

Balancing the Rembrandt on a display easel, Robyn blew a speck of dust from the corner of the frame and then stepped back to study the painting again. Something about the style and the brush strokes in this picture troubled her, a nebulous uncertainty as to its authenticity. For a week she had kept these concerns to herself. Without proof, she would only stir up already troubled waters. It was, after all, Miriam's plush impeccable shop, not her own.

Robyn took pride in her mother's success—an art gallery located on the south end of Rodeo Drive in Beverly Hills— in the same town with Battaglia, Giorgio, Chanel, and Tiffany's. Miriam was fast becoming an artistic legacy. Like Gucci and Giorgio, her shop had a worldwide reputation.

As Robyn walked away from the easel, she felt out of place in these posh surroundings. The clientele of movie stars and retired oil barons from the gated estates on the canyons above Sunset Boulevard belonged to her mother's frilly world. Robyn felt plain and undistinguished, too casual, her features average in comparison to the glamorous customers who frequented Miriam's gallery. Sometimes she was convinced that her only assets were her shiny auburn hair and a shapely pair of legs. She didn't have her mother's slim, graceful figure, her sophistication, or her calculated business aplomb. But the customers liked Robyn, mostly for her sincerity. She never rushed nor pressed them for a sale. She let them browse freely.

Her attention turned to the couple window-gazing outside. They made a handsome pair—she fair, he with jet-black hair. The girl looked close to Robyn's own age, twenty-six. She was slim and beautiful, her expression animated, her eyes blue like a cloudless day. And her dress! Surely it bore a Lina Lee or Fred Hayman label. She wore it with poise, enhancing the color of her eyes and fair peach complexion. For a moment Robyn caught the reflection of her own pudgy nose and ordinary face in the gallery window and felt a startling sense of envy Robyn's own name-labeled suit, taupe in color and stylish, looked now like it came from the bargain basement.

The young woman gave her companion a provocative glance, her chin tilted up, her smile persuasive as she pointed toward one corner of the window display.

The van Gogh painting, Robyn decided.

The ruggedly attractive man towered above her, shaking his head. But moments later they made their way into the shop, the melodious chimes announcing their entrance. Still smiling, the girl tugged at his hand, urging him on.

"May I help you?" Robyn asked as they reached her. "You seem interested in the van Gogh in the window."

"Well, not exactly," the girl said. "It was the owner's name that caught our attention."

"Miriam Gregory is my mother. Did you wish to see her?"

The girl touched Robyn's arm. "Then you must be Robyn?"

She felt herself frowning. "Yes, I'm Robyn Gregory."

"I thought so. I'm Andrea York—I mean Andrea Prescott—and this is my husband, Sherm."

"Guilty." The handsome face was all smiles now.

"Newlyweds? Are you looking for a painting for your home?"

"No more paintings," he said. "Our walls are covered."

"With old wallpaper," the girl teased back. "Actually, Robyn, you're the reason we came inside. We know your father, Drew Gregory."

Sherm nodded. "I had dinner with him in London last week."

Robyn's legs buckled. She placed one hand on the nearest easel to steady herself. "My father? Did he send you?"

The man's voice mellowed his words. "No. He warned us against coming. He didn't want us to stir up painful memories for you."

"Then why did you?"

"We came because your father cares about you."

Anger tempered her words. "He has an odd way of showing it. He walked out on my mother and me sixteen years ago. We haven't heard from him unless you count the alimony checks to Mother. I didn't even rate a letter. He's like a stranger to me."

"Then don't you want to know about him?" Andrea asked.

Robyn tried to ward off the longing inside her. All her life she had wanted to know more about him. Her childhood memories remained scattered fragments. Many times she had dreamed of seeing him again—of running up to him and throwing her arms around his neck, asking, "Daddy, why did you go away?"

She pulled back as Andrea stepped closer. "It's too late. My father is the one who went away."

The melodious doorchimes rang as another customer entered. Now half a dozen visitors browsed among the paintings, their voices soft like the decor.

Some of the fire left Andrea's face. "Please give me a chance to tell you about him. If it weren't for your father, I might not be alive today."

Sherm slipped an arm around his wife. "Andrea witnessed the assassination of the American ambassador in Paris several months ago. Your father was assigned to the case."

"Is that the job of an embassy attaché?" Robyn asked.

"Drew was on loan from there. He followed Andrea when she fled from Paris to Canada with the wrong man."

"Your father risked his own life to protect me." Lightly Andrea added, "More than once Drew told me I reminded him of you."

Robyn chortled. "How? Because of our striking resemblance, Andrea? Or my warm personality? Your features are so delicate, so lovely, and mine are like—"

Andrea tilted her head and studied Robyn's face. "You're warm and pretty beneath your scowl. You do remind me of your father. He cares about you. I know it."

Robyn wavered, wanting to believe them. Unruly wisps of hair slipped down on her forehead. She left them there, her gaze defiant as she stared at the Prescotts. "You walk in here and, just like that, expect me to welcome my father back into my life?"

Andrea's fingers pressed gently on her arm. "Forgive me. I can't even imagine how you must be feeling. My dad was always there for me. Please, Robyn, let me tell you about Drew—he's much more kind than you remember."

"Not here, Andrea." Robyn glanced anxiously toward the back office as the door opened. "Not here."

"Then where, Robyn?"

Miriam Gregory stood in the doorway, glancing back at the person inside. "A lawsuit would ruin me, Aaron," she said.

Robyn still heard anger in her mother's voice, but Miriam was in control as she made her way toward them. "Mother and my uncle have been quarreling again. You'd better go. Please."

Sherm took his wife's elbow, but Andrea resisted. "Where can we meet then, Robyn? We must talk, really. What about lunch?"

Curiosity lit in Miriam Gregory's deep-set eyes as she reached them. She was elegant in frills and lace, her reddish-brown hair swept back seductively into a chignon, her ivory face sculpted like one of the paintings on the wall. She surveyed the trio with a patronizing gaze, her lips parted in a precise half-smile. "Is Robyn helping you find what you want?"

Sherm smiled politely as he took Miriam's hand. "We're the Prescotts. Your daughter tried to interest us in the van Gogh in the window, but we're more interested in the owner of the gallery."

The arched brows lifted, the smile was still detached. "In me?"

"Mrs. Gregory, we're in town on business, but Andrea insisted on a quick trip to Rodeo Drive."

"How nice." Miriam's words hung in the air, inquisitive and uncertain as she appraised Andrea. She turned back to Robyn. "Is something wrong, dear? You're so quiet."

"I feel a bit faint."

"Then why don't you take an early lunch? I'll have Floy come up front and help me with the customers."

"Lunch with us," Sherm offered. "At Chasen's or the Tribeca. You can tell us about the merits of the van Gogh while we're eating."

"Yes, Robyn, and a bonus for you, my dear, if you sell the van Gogh to the Prescotts." Miriam's alert eyes were laughing now, particularly at Sherm.

"Will you be all right, Mother? You and Uncle Aaron?"

There was an uppish tilt to Miriam's chin. "Aaron? He left."

"Out the back door? Without saying good-bye to me?"

"Even you, my dear, could not improve his mood. He's outraged over some of our shipments from Europe."

Robyn's gaze strayed to the Rembrandt on the easel and the customers standing before it. She couldn't risk asking more, not in front of the Prescotts. She brushed Miriam's cheek with a kiss. "Mother, try and sell the Rembrandt while I'm gone."

The half-smile formed again. "We'll hold off on that one for now—Aaron's orders. But don't worry, Robyn. I can handle your uncle. Go on. Enjoy your lunch."

Outside the air was brisk against Robyn's face. She sucked it in, smog and all, as they walked to the restaurant. All she could think was, *Why, Daddy? Why are you coming back into my life after all these years?"*

&

Drew Gregory eased into the leather chair in his basement flat on the outskirts of London and stretched his lanky legs on the worn hassock. His quarters were cramped and spartan, but the furnishings were ample for his needs. He enjoyed the seascape above the fireplace, a gift from the previous renter who had found life too dismal to go on. Hours after the man had committed suicide, Drew moved in without waiting for the owners to repaint the rooms.

He liked the added caution of barred windows. In his line of work it was a safety feature. It freed him to open the windows at night for fresh air and sleep soundly and untroubled. Of course, someone could toss him a Molotov cocktail while he slept, but lately terrorists weren't into eliminating embassy attaches. He'd had thirty-plus years with the CIA—not a bad record except, he mused, for that clerical blunder that compromised his code name and doomed him to a desk job in London, a boring existence at best. He wondered how much longer he'd have to wait for Porter Deven, the Station Chief in Paris, to put him back into the thick of Agency work At the rate it was going, he'd drop dead first. Or—and that thought appealed to Drew—Porter might put him in the ranks of the retired.

Drew sank deeper into the chair, listening to the downpour outside as it splattered the windows and drenched the London streets. He pushed his empty plate and a half-cup of cold coffee aside and dropped his silk tie there. The insipid meal consisted of leftovers—the last of the lamb, mixed veggies, stale coffee, and fruit. The neighbor had given him the spongy red apple with a coy smile and a, "Good evening, Mr. Gregory."

He had wondered even then what was good about it, but she seemed kindly and kept his flat cleaned on a weekly basis. As the clock chimed, an object whizzed through the open window, past his face, and ricocheted off the stone fireplace. As it landed, he realized with terror that it was a crude hand grenade. He dove for the floor and yanked the lamp cord from its socket, plunging the room into semidarkness. Cursing the dying embers in the fire, he shielded his face.

As the grenade dud sizzled out, Victor Wilson's raucous laughter exploded. "Drew, unbolt your prison. It's wet out here."

It took ten minutes before Drew's temper cooled, and he found a measure of humor in the younger man's arrival.

Drew faced Vic now, his legs back on the hassock. "Your jokes will get you killed, Vic. If my revolver had been loaded, you wouldn't be standing there with a smug grin."

Vic's cocksure smile broadened. "Just keeping you alert."

In the semidarkness Vic looked over Drew's collection of buy-backs and secondhand books and picked one from the shelf. "Do you really read this stuff?" he asked.

From where he sat, Drew recognized the torn copy of *The Rise and Fall of the Third Reich* in Vic's hand. "If you think that's weighty, I'll loan you the six volumes of Gibbons' *The History of the Rise and Decline of the Roman Empire.*" *Or any other empire,* he thought wryly. "Right now, I have more British dates and facts at my fingertips than the man on Downing Street."

"What good does it do you?"

"It fills my time. I'd rather be out making history. But, thanks to Porter Deven, I read it instead. Forget the books for now, Vic. Put another log on the fire and sit down." As the log crackled, he continued, "I didn't hear your car, and you're not a man who likes to walk in the rain—so what brought you here at this hour?"

Vic leaned back in his chair, his hands behind his neck. Drew studied the man in the light of the rekindled fire. Vic had a pleasant enough face in spite of the sharp, angular features. And nice eyes, gray-green and daring. Women liked his carefree style. In his thirty years, he had flitted through two marriages and several brief affairs.

"You ought to settle down, Vic," Drew said, his thoughts once again on his own broken marriage. "And get out of this line of work. You're too impulsive. It's going to get you killed someday."

"That's part of the business."

"Are you on official business tonight?"

"Unofficial. Look, we've been friends for a good while."

"That's why I'm telling you to get out of the Agency."

"It's too late, Drew. I like living on the cutting edge."

"And you've got battle scars to prove it!"

"Yeah, like last month's broken ribs."

The fire crackled. Vic shifted, wincing as he did so. The humor was gone, his voice serious as he said, "Drew, I'm here to warn you that you're in trouble. Porter Deven is in town. Over from Paris. If he gets wind of my being here, he'll have my head."

"Better your hard head than mine. Is he here on the Harland Smith case?"

"Hardly. He's too busy studying your files and records, Gregory. This time he has enough to hang you."

Inside, Drew bristled. "Go on."

"Whatever else you are, you're honest. So you deserve a break on this one. They're trying to frame you with your wife's problem. She's being investigated for art fraud."

Drew swung his legs off the hassock and sat bolt upright. "My ex-wife in art fraud? Never."

"It's international in scope. She has a European buyer."

"And what is the buyer selling?"

"Copies of the old masters—some through your wife's gallery."

"Miriam has an art gallery of her own?"

"An exclusive one with expensive paintings. It's in a good location—right in the heart of Beverly Hills, California."

"Miriam can't afford that."

"That's what Langley headquarters is saying. They're digging for mud on this one. They think you funded the gallery, Drew."

"On what? My salary? Besides, Miriam and I aren't in touch."

"The Deputy Director of Operations isn't bothered by that little detail. The Agency doesn't want art scandal linked with its name. So, over the weekend, Porter is to find any reason—or invent one—to ground you before the investigation breaks."

"I'm already grounded at the embassy."

"It'll be worse Monday morning. You'll be asked to clear your desk and fade into oblivion. At least for a while."

"And what about clearing my name?"

"You'll have to clear your wife's first."

"My ex-wife. There's no way she could own an art gallery in some elegant district. And there's no way she'd do anything fraudulent. She's squeaky clean. There's got to be a mistake."

"I hope so, Drew, because rumor is thick that you put up the money for the gallery when you signed over a goodly portion of your inheritance to her."

"I expected Miriam to give our daughter the good life."

"She's got it."

Alarmed he asked, "My daughter's not involved?"

Vic shrugged. "She works at the gallery."

"More scuttlebutt from the directorate at Langley?"

"Actually, the DCI has a pretty good source of information. Some lawyer in upstate New York, but the lawyer's pointing the finger at Mrs. Gregory, not your daughter."

Drew slammed his fist against the palm of his hand. "My half-brother, Aaron?"

"That's the way it was riding when I left Porter tonight."

"When is Porter calling me on this?"

"My bet is on him going back to Paris and calling you from there. He's not much on confrontations with you."

"I'm still a big challenge to him, eh?"

"He relishes what's going on, but he won't dirty his own hands. For the good of the Agency, someone else will ask you to clear your desk and go quietly. No questions asked. None answered."

"Wrong. Porter would never miss this opportunity. He'll be waiting for me bright and early Monday morning. And after he gives me the boot, I'll get in touch with Miriam."

"If you contact her now after all these years, the Agency will throw the book at you. Wham. Dismissal. Dishonor. No pension. They're just waiting for you to make a false move."

Drew loosened his collar. "A catch-22 right from the Company?"

"I'm sorry. I couldn't let you walk in blindly."

"It's a risk for you, Vic, if they find out you came here."

A self-satisfied smile crossed Vic's lips. "My cousin Brianna lives a few miles from here. I'll overnight there. She's my excuse for not being home this evening in case Porter asks. Besides, no one believes that she's really my cousin. I stay there often. She's all the family I have left."

It was Vic's longest speech on record. He seemed almost vulnerable, not his usual brusque self. "Thanks, Vic, for the warning."

Vic stood and tugged at his wet raincoat. "No problem."

Drew frowned. Was it part of Company policy to trick him into trusting Vic? Or were they trying to distance him from the Harland C. Smith files? "Vic, contact Miriam for me."

"I'm not up on art, but you might try Baroness von Tonner, your wife's old friend. She's the European supplier for the gallery." Vic pulled her address from his pocket. "If she's not there, she usually stays at one of the Schweizerhofs in Switzerland."

"Socializing with the elite of Europe?"

"Probably. If I learn anything new from Porter, I'll call you."

"Will I be free to leave once my desk is cleared?"

"Langley figures you'll contact Miriam, and then they'll have you both. They're convinced she's in the thick of the art scheme."

"What do they care?"

"They wouldn't if you weren't a Company man. They shy away from international scandals. So once they connect you with Miriam, the DCI will put out rumors expressing disappointment in a good officer gone greedy. Langley will look good. You'll be wiped out."

Drew walked Vic to the door. "I'll take my luggage with me. Once I pick up my personal belongings and the Harland Smith file at the office, I'll be on my way. My rent's paid up for a month."

"Drew, do you have an extra set of car keys?"

"Are you planning on going with me?"

"Why not? I've got some vacation time. Porter wanted me to delay it so the Agency could assign me to keep an eye on you. I fought that one. I told him I was overdue for holiday leave, so I'm heading for the Riviera—no known address."

"So what's with my car, Vic? I'll need it."

Vic grinned. "They expect you to take off in your own car, but if they can't find it, you'll be a step ahead of them. Taxi to the embassy Monday. I'll pick up your luggage here and park your car at Brianna's place. We'll meet at Heathrow."

"No, Miriam needs me. I'm not going to let her hang for false allegations, no matter how big the Agency paints them."

"Would your wife thank you for showing up in Beverly Hills?"

A tic threaded itself up Drew's neckline, throbbing wildly. Vic gripped his shoulder. "The von Tonner woman has been under surveillance for some time. Word from Swiss Intelligence places her in Switzerland three days ago. She's been ordered to get your wife and daughter to Zurich—we assume to protect herself."

"Why Zurich?"

"We don't know. So far there's no indication that she has contacted your family. Until we have something definite, I think the best way to help your wife is to check out the von Tonner woman. If Miriam is receiving fraudulent shipments, they came from this end, maybe even from Zurich. Are you with me?"

"I'll still go it alone."

"You need me. We'll catch a flight to the Riviera. If no one tails us, we turn north by car and drop in on von Tonner."

"You're determined to go with me? Your idea or Porter's?"

"Somebody's got to keep you alive, Drew."

The door closed soundly behind Vic. Drew checked the fire and then headed for his bedroom. It was a compact room, difficult to maneuver. He still wasn't certain whether Vic was on the level or obeying Porter's instructions—feeding Drew false information to lure him to Zurich.

Drew flopped down on the bed and stared up at the ceiling. On and off for years, he had envisioned a reunion with Miriam and Robyn, but he hadn't counted on putting their lives at risk again.

Two

Robyn sat across from the Prescotts, barely spooning her broccoli soup. "I grew up in a lopsided home in upstate New York," she said pensively. "A house without a dad, a one-parent home. Sometimes it makes me angry that my mother is still in love with him."

"Is that so wrong?" Andrea asked.

"He ran out on her. Packed up and left—just like that."

Sherm lifted his fork. "Did she ever say why?"

"Not really. Mom rarely talks about it. She won't let me say anything against him, either. We have war every time I do."

Andrea's thin brows arched. "Families were meant to be together."

"Even mine, Andrea? Should my parents and I pretend to be a triple-braided cord? You know—love, honor, and loyalty?"

"No, no pretense. What happened between them? Was it their age difference? Your mother looks much younger than Drew."

"She's eleven years younger, but that didn't bother Mother. They met at the Metropolitan Museum of Art where Mother spent her summers lecturing on the Dutch masters. One Thursday my father—a confirmed bachelor—barreled through those sacred halls."

"I didn't know he liked art," Andrea said.

Robyn threaded her answer with smiles. "That wasn't his thing. He was on assignment from Washington, tracking down a Russian agent. Mother told Dad not to disturb the tourists. He was embarrassed by her reprimand—or so taken by Mother's beauty—that he stayed for her lecture and almost lost the Russian."

"Makes a good story," Sherm said.

"My classmates liked it."

"You're like him, Robyn," Andrea said. "In the way you laugh and lift your chin. Come to Europe while we're there. We'll arrange for you to see your dad again."

Sherm looked annoyed. "We'd have to check with Drew first to see if he's free. But if you have a message for him—"

"For my father? Why? He's never had any for me. Don't worry, I won't show up in Europe and spoil your vacation."

His tone turned apologetic. "We're not on vacation. I'm on business for the Kippen conglomerate. I oversee our investments abroad, mostly in an advisory capacity."

She mellowed as well. "Doesn't the European Community frown on foreign investments—with no room for outsiders?"

"That's true. They're big on a shared heritage, but Kippen had its foot in the door years ago. We have five offices abroad, all staffed by Europeans. We'll be in Brussels this visit. It's rapidly emerging as a center for the European Community, so we're reorganizing there, putting a greater emphasis on Belgian control under the Kippen label. It should prove more successful that way."

"Won't it still be a Kippen empire?"

"A nice choice of words," he teased.

"Perhaps I'm envious. I've tried to convince Mother to invest in an art gallery in Europe. I've always wanted to live there." She heard wistfulness in her own voice and tried to cover it with a shrug. "We specialize in the European paintings—so the idea isn't totally foolish, Sherm."

"You don't just arrive in Europe and start an art gallery. You'd have a language barrier and cultural differences."

She felt his rebuff and considered answering him in fluent German. Instead, she said, "I minored in foreign languages and majored in art appreciation here at home and abroad. I learned the hard way that I'm not an artist, but I have an eye for good art."

"And a sensitivity for the customers?" Andrea asked.

"Yes, I enjoy helping them select the right pictures for their homes. I was in college when Mother moved west and started the gallery. I never planned to get involved, but Mother and I have come to terms lately. An equal footing almost. Mother is grossly efficient—shrewd, polite, businesslike. I spent months in the European museums studying the great paintings and even the fraudulent ones, so I'm useful in the business, too."

"You're prosperous here, but to establish yourself in Europe you'd need contacts and foreign capital."

Again Robyn sensed Sherm's disapproval. "We have a European buyer, one imbued with social graces and charm itself. Actually, Ingrid von Tonner is more than that. She and Mother have been friends for years, ever since their early days at Radcliffe."

She hesitated, reflecting briefly on Ingrid's untimely exodus from college, but she kept silent about that, saying, "I don't like her personally, but she's savvy politically and well-connected in the art world. She could help us incorporate there."

"Could she help you access land and property?"

Robyn had a sudden mad frenzy to prove herself to Sherm. "That's where Ingrid comes in. She owns a fabulous countryside manor in Germany and a villa on the Riviera. Her marriages didn't last, but her husbands left her well-situated as far as property goes."

As her gaze settled on Andrea's delicate features, envy struck again. Robyn forced herself to go on. "If we worked it right, Ingrid might let us use one of her properties to start an old world art shop. Uncle Aaron could help us with the legal matters. Mother could take out a loan on our assets here."

"Whoa. Don't sell yourself short on this end. Check out the possibilities in Europe and then confirm the financing."

"I did get carried away," she admitted. "But you've done what I want to do, Sherm. You've established yourself in Europe."

He nodded. "After we established ourselves here at home."

Andrea pressed Sherm's hand. "Don't squelch her dream."

"I'm just being practical, Andrea."

She winked at Robyn. "Don't let him fool you. He takes risks, too. He married me! And he plans to promote my fashion designs at ski resorts all over Europe—one of those Kippen enterprises. But he knows I won't stop there. I have plans to expand my career."

Robyn shot a glance at Sherm. His face clearly showed displeasure as though they had argued this decision before. To ease the tension, Robyn said, "We were going to discuss the merit of van Gogh's paintings over lunch, not our cloud-nine projects in Europe."

"Well, don't quit dreaming, Robyn," Andrea insisted as she excused herself and left for the powder room.

In her absence, Sherm asked, "And van Gogh? Do I look like a man who should have a van Gogh painting in my office?"

For seconds the van Gogh in the gallery window and the Rembrandt on the easel nibbled at Robyn's conscience.

"Well, Robyn?" he asked.

"A portrait of your lovely wife would please you more."

His dark eyes smiled back, his good humor returning. A practical man, Andrea had called him. Not someone steeped in legalese like her uncle; but a successful businessman, she decided. She assessed his handsome good looks and the expensive cut of his charcoal-gray suit, his straight-collared Burberry shirt, and the neatly knotted tie with its pheasant design. An Yves Saint Laurent tie, she was certain. She tried to imagine Andrea dictating his attire, but the thought fell flat. Sherman Prescott was his own man, somewhat conservative, but well-dressed and clearly defined.

She squirmed under his unrelenting gaze. *What would he say if he knew that we display Ingrid's paintings at the gallery with no questions asked? That those that don't sell go on an auction block to the highest bidder at private sales?*

The waiter filled her water glass, allowing her time to form an excuse to break away from lunch before Andrea came back—to leave her father's friends while she was still an enigma to them.

"Robyn," Sherm said, calling her back from her troubled thoughts, "let's not end our visit in silence."

"I'm tired," she said lamely. "It's a busy season at the gallery. We have constant shipments coming in from Europe."

"That's good for your business, isn't it?"

"That's what my uncle says." She flushed.

"Was he the man arguing with your mother at the gallery?"

When she didn't answer, he pressed gently, "I didn't mean to eavesdrop, Robyn, but I heard your mother mention a lawsuit that could ruin her. Can she trust your uncle?" He sighed when she wouldn't look at him. "Robyn, as your father's friend, can I help in some way?"

She hated defending Aaron. "No need. My uncle is a criminal

lawyer from upstate New York. He can handle the problems for us. He visits us frequently. And he's good to me, my father-figure, if I have any at all. He handled mother's divorce and still oversees our finances. If he says the European shipments are all legitimate, they must be."

"So what worries you?" he asked as Andrea joined them.

In her mind's eye, she saw the brushstrokes on the Rembrandt painting in the gallery. She *was* worried. Could Sherm really help her? She risked it, saying, "It's the paintings. Ingrid has a collection of her own, but she keeps coming across new works by the old masters to send to us. She finds them in odd places—at a villa on the Riviera, from the estate of an unknown Swiss collector, and one from a private auction. The most expensive one came from an unknown art peddler."

Robyn pushed her half-empty soup bowl aside and picked at her salad. She had said too much. "So, it's Europe for you two?"

"Yes, and Andrea's invitation is still open. Come to Europe and we'll check up on Mrs. von Tonner's new discoveries." Sherm's words were as penetrating as his gaze. "We came as your father's friends. We had no right to rush in unannounced, but your father did try to get in touch with you through letters."

She wiggled the numbness from her toes and again considered fleeing. For a frightening moment, she wondered whether her uncle or mother had held back her father's mail—just to shield her from pain. "No," she said with confidence. "There were no letters, just alimony checks. Mother cried every time she got one. She never stopped loving Daddy. She just couldn't live with him."

"But she allowed his brother to control all her funds?"

"This sounds like an inquisition, Sherm," she said lightly.

But her thoughts went deeper, darker. What information would the Prescotts carry back to her father? Should she send a message that would hurt him in the same way that he had wounded her so long ago?

"Sherm, my uncle is very meticulous with our financial records. It's his fondness for Mother that bothers me." She laughed, a strained falsetto that turned to tears. "Aaron is in love with my mother and—he'd be wrong for her." She looked away, fighting off the bitter tears. "Crazy, isn't it," she whispered. "I always wanted my dad to come back. Even now. I never, never wanted him to go away."

Sherm said firmly, "Then come to Europe and see him again."

She recoiled. She wanted to pound her fist against Sherm's chest, to lash out at him for being her father's friend. "Never," she cried. "He ran out on us. He should have taken us with him."

Sherm met her challenge honestly. "Not in the work your father does. When we met him, he was cooperating with Canadian Intelligence, tracking down an organization of terrorists that made millions, maybe billions, selling weapons to Third World countries. Your father saved my wife's life on the same bridge where one of the young terrorists lost his. I'll always be grateful to Drew for protecting Andrea."

Andrea's voice slipped to a whisper. "Your father didn't have to defend me. He had every reason to doubt me—but he's such a man of honor and integrity."

Robyn winced. Her father's promise when she was ten came winging back. "He didn't keep his word to me," she said softly. Tears cascaded over her cheeks, crooked rivulets streaking through her makeup. She made a futile effort to brush them away as the waiter approached with the dessert tray.

Sherm waved him off.

She twisted the pearl ring on her right hand. It had passed down from the Gregory side of the family, her link with her father. It had been removed by Miriam, if Robyn remembered correctly, from her Gramma Gregory's finger as she lay in her casket.

Unexpectedly, Robyn shared some of the emotions she had harbored for years. "When I was ten, I idolized my dad. I felt so safe with him. The last time I saw him, we went hand in hand into the den and squeezed into his mother's old Queen Anne chair together."

Her hand shook as she picked up the water glass. "I gave him my *Heidi* book and said, 'It's your turn to read, Dad.' He smiled and said, 'Not this one again, Princess. We've read it a hundred times.'

"That night he stopped reading in the middle of a chapter and said, 'Robyn, someday we'll climb Heidi's Alps together.'

"'When?' I asked him.

"He said, 'Someday, I promise.' Then he closed the book and said, 'Princess, I'm going away. I don't know when I'll see you again.'"

She shuddered, her body convulsing at the memory. "He was

always going away on business trips, sometimes for weeks at a time. I asked him, 'Will you be home for Christmas, Daddy?' He said, 'No, your mother and I won't be living together anymore.'"

Glancing at the Prescotts, she saw their compassion. "My world fell apart that day. I wondered what I had done wrong. Dad tried to tell me it was his job, that mother didn't like his long absences. When I started to run from the room, he said, 'May I keep this copy of *Heidi?*'

"I screamed back, 'I don't care what you do with it.'

"The last thing I heard my father say was, 'I won't forget my promise, Princess.'"

Sherm slid his handkerchief across the table to her.

"You think my father is so wonderful, but when I got up the next morning, he was already gone, airborne on an overseas flight. Mother said it was best that way. But he had packed his bags and left without saying good-bye."

"And you never saw him again?" Andrea asked.

"In my dreams, but even then, he was mostly walking away."

Softly Andrea said, "Maybe Drew has changed over the years. To us, he's been so special. He even flew in for our wedding."

"My father in a church?"

Andrea smiled. "It wasn't exactly a church—just a tiny chapel near my hometown in Index, Washington. Just room for twelve, including Drew. Afterwards, he stayed on for a visit with my grandmother—only weeks before Katrina died."

"Were you close to your grandparents?"

"Just my grandmother. My grandfather was killed in Normandy in World War II." Andrea's voice faltered. "And now Katrina's gone, too. I miss her dreadfully, but my grandparents are in heaven, together again forever. I really believe that."

Robyn shifted uneasily. "We're not very religious in my family," she admitted. "Although when I'm out jogging on Sunday mornings, I rest on the lawn of a little white church. Their music is so comforting."

"Why don't you go inside?" Andrea asked.

"No one ever invited me in." Robyn looked down, reflecting.

Andrea broke their momentary silence. "Next Sunday slip inside and sit on the back pew. Listen to the hymns. Or sing them. Even if you don't want to speak to anyone, that's okay. Just let the quiet comfort you."

Robyn glanced at her watch, not certain how to respond. She had thought about going inside that little church. Now Andrea was laying the responsibility on her. The thought was not offensive. She wished Andrea would stay on and go to the little church with her.

"Will I see you again?" she asked them.

"That's unlikely this trip. Sherm and I have to get back to the hotel and pack. We're flying out to Europe in the morning."

Sherm reached for the bill. "If you change your mind about Europe, get in touch with us through our Brussels' office."

Robyn didn't ask for the address, but as they stood on the street corner, Andrea pressed a card into her hand. "That's our hotel number in Brussels. Call us night or day. I don't want this to be good-bye, either."

"We really must go," Sherm insisted.

"And I must get back to the gallery."

With a hug, Andrea said, "We'll tell your father we met you."

And then she was off, trailing behind her husband. He slowed, reached out, and tucked her arm in his. Watching them, Robyn felt a terrible loneliness. She had seen Sherm look at Andrea at the lunch table, love and admiration in his gaze.

The Prescotts merged with the jostling crowd, leaving Robyn to face the awakening memories of childhood alone. Had her father really written to her over the years? she wondered. If so, where were those letters? Did Aaron toss them all away? Or had Miriam deliberately locked them in the family safe?

Robyn slipped the purse strap over one shoulder and turned resolutely toward Miriam's Art Gallery, her narrow two-inch heels tapping rhythmically against the sidewalk.

Three

On the last lap of her Sunday morning jog, Robyn sprinted ahead at a steady, even pace, her face to the breeze, her upturned nose peeling from the August sun. The usual laugh lines around her eyes felt taut and her expression was ridged to a frown as she cut through the city park.

Robyn heard the music as she crossed the street and ran up the sloping, manicured lawn of the small white chapel. She had a favorite spot near a massive shade tree with a trunk that bulged the topsoil—close enough to listen, distant enough not to be noticed.

Hands on hips, she bent forward blowing puffs of winded air. As her breathing eased and her heartbeat slowed, Robyn dropped to the ground and stretched on her side facing the church. She was later than usual, but they were still singing, a rather upbeat number this morning that seemed to be shaking the rafters. High organ notes burst through the open stained-glass windows, blocking out the words of the song.

Robyn split a blade of grass and chewed on it pensively as the hymn stirred a responsive chord inside her. Loneliness. Sadness. An emptiness that sought fulfillment. It seemed worse this morning. Only fragmented phrases reached her: "Because He lives, I can face tomorrow."

As the melody softened and the hymn faded, she considered taking Andrea Prescott's advice. But what would the people think of a stranger in white shorts and a midriff top? No makeup, no perfume, her body still sticky damp from the run, and her bare legs sporting a deep California tan. She propped herself up on one elbow, trying to visualize what it would look like inside. She'd only been to church a few times in her whole life—for weddings or funerals. Those visits were a blurred memory of flowers and solemn voices.

Then, suddenly, the pain of her father's broken promise was so fresh and searing that Robyn stumbled to her feet and tossed the blade of grass to the ground. She wanted to shove the memory of him back into the cobwebbed recesses of her mind. She burned with resentment against him—at the Prescotts really—for this awakened restlessness in her spirit, this dread of tomorrow.

The traffic in front of her had picked up—carloads of people, radios blaring, surfboards tied to the rooftops. Everyone seemed to be heading to the beach for one of those last picnics of the summer before the school bells started ringing. Robyn loved the sun and sand, but not the summer crowds. She needed space for her beach towel, quiet surroundings, and elbow room to follow her own plans. As she jogged along the sidewalk, she felt a growing dissatisfaction with any long-term commitment to the "orderly, well-established" life at Miriam's Art Gallery.

She had other options, like camp counseling at Big Bear. Or spending a summer at a forestry lookout in total isolation. She promptly dismissed it. The forestry dream was another eight months down the road, even if she applied tomorrow. What she really wanted was a career as an art historian in a museum.

She cut a sharp corner and ran the last two blocks to the house. It sat in the middle of a private cul-de-sac with copycat houses in pastel colors all around it. Miriam had insisted on an azure blue with white trim and a picket fence. Even here in this neighborhood, Miriam tried her best to impress others. An enterprising young man from Tijuana, with college in mind, kept the windows washed, hedges trimmed, flower beds weeded, and pansies planted along the walkway.

Robyn eased her pace as she approached the house, her frown returning. Floy Belmont's Chevy was parked in the driveway beside Miriam's sports car. Roj Stapleton's motorcycle leaned against the kickstand, leaking oil on the street. Miriam would be infuriated when she discovered it.

The gardener whistled as he patted the soil around the rosebushes. He brushed the dirt from his hands as she reached him.

"Hi, Gino," she said, "what's going on?"

"In there?" he asked, nodding toward the house. "There's one angry mother and three guests, including a lady who liked my roses.

And one missing daughter. That's you."

He clipped an Apothecary rose, a deep pink against his bronzed skin. The highly scented flower felt like velvet as he handed it to her. "This may get you safely inside. Give it to Mrs. G. It's one of her favorites. I didn't think I could grow this kind, but look at that bush."

"It's lovely." Robyn lingered, not wanting to face the trouble indoors. "We weren't expecting company. What happened?"

"I was having coffee with your mother when the phone rang. Mrs. G. said, "Hello," and then the words started flying. I don't know who it was, but I grabbed another donut and came back to my yard work. Then everybody started coming."

Robyn ran up the steps and then turned back. Gino was right behind her with another rose in his hand. "I was wondering—"

Don't, she thought. *Don't ask me again.* He had tried to date her twice. He was twenty at best, handsome, his rich brown eyes studying her. It seemed as though his broad hand caressed the rose. "It's still no," she said.

Miriam met her at the door. She took the exquisite roses with a chuckle. "Is Gino trying to win your favor—or mine?"

"Both, I think. But I'm the one he wants to date."

"That's good. He's too young for me. I hope you told him it would cost him his job if he dated my daughter."

"He's counting on you liking his rosebushes."

"Since when were they his?"

"Since the day he began working here."

Miriam nodded toward the living room. "I've been waiting for you. We have company. Where have you been, Robyn?"

"Jogging."

"For two hours?"

"I sat on the church lawn for a while."

"Isn't that getting to be a habit?"

"I like their music."

"Yes, you would like that, wouldn't you?" She brushed a lock of hair from Robyn's forehead, her hand unusually gentle. "We should go to church there someday."

"Don't tease, Mother."

"I'm not. I have problems. Perhaps going to church is the answer. That's what Floy always tells me."

Robyn's attention strayed to two cycle helmets lying near the door. "Did Julia come with Roj?" she asked.

"Yes, they roared in here right behind Floy."

"What's wrong, Mother? Gino said you're worried."

"I am. We're facing some serious allegations at the gallery."

"What?"

"We're in trouble, and I don't know why. If your uncle knows, he's not saying, but something insidious is going on in our buying-selling link in Europe."

"Ingrid?" Robyn felt sick, as though she were choking on something massive like an apricot seed. She wanted to ask, *Mom, it's not the Dutch masters—not the Rembrandt painting?*

"I don't have any answers. Not yet. But it can't be Ingrid. We're old friends." Miriam's crooked smile faded. "I need your help, Robyn. They're waiting for us in the living room. And please don't be surprised at anything I say. I'll explain everything to you later."

Robyn followed her to the living room door and paused to size up the guests sitting there. They stared back at her. Roj Stapleton knew the art business. Floy Belmont knew the customers and cared about them. And as much as Robyn disliked admitting it, Julia Lewan, with her come-on smile and her flirtatious ways, could always bring in the money at the gallery.

Floy offered Robyn and Miriam a reassuring smile. She was Miriam's close friend, a trusted employee. Floy was only six years older than Miriam, but she was matronly— plump and pleasant. Floy had slipped contentedly into being everybody's grandmother. She was widowed and witty, generous and gentle, a kindly woman with a jolly face and snow-white hair and facial wrinkles that crisscrossed in every direction. Robyn had the sudden urge to be cradled securely against that expansive bosom.

Julia, the youngest employee, was a shapely brunette, coquettish, with a lovely, oval face and wide eyes, deceptively innocent as she sat on one end of the sofa with Roj Stapleton. At twenty-nine, Roj was ten years her senior, suave, urbane, with flashing brown eyes and slick dark hair that grazed his crinkled shirt collar.

Roj took frequent trips to Europe to oversee the art selections for the gallery. He made points with Miriam by insisting that it was a man's job to open the crates when they arrived, to do the heavy work, to check the invoices, label the paintings, and discard the packing crates. To Robyn, he seemed overly aware of his own importance, or perhaps it was her mistrust of him. Miriam trusted him too much.

His eyes stayed on Robyn, shrewd and uncompromising, as she crossed the room and took the seat next to Floy. Floy patted her hand, the gesture conveying strength to Robyn. *Keep calm,* it seemed to say. *Miriam needs us.*

"Sorry to keep you all waiting," she said cheerily. "I lose track of time when I'm out running."

Miriam's pinched smile relaxed. "Robyn and I are leaving for Europe for a much-needed holiday. That means that the three of you will have added responsibilities at the gallery."

Robyn was too stunned to speak.

Roj, too, stared at Miriam in disbelief. "You're taking a vacation at the height of our season?"

"It's a business holiday, Roj. As you know, we've been charged for several shipments that never arrived. We have the copies of invoices, but no paintings."

The muscles around his mouth tightened. "Well—I had nothing to do with that."

"And you had nothing to do with the Italian painting that brought such a good price? You selected it. You and Ingrid. You catalogued it. Julia made the sale. It was returned last week, Roj, as damaged property Did you know that?"

"Of course. The canvas had been slit."

"Deliberately, according to the insurance investigator."

"Once it leaves the shop, it's not our responsibility"

"Mr. Stapleton, we guarantee both our paintings and our deliveries. We stand behind our paintings. Is that clear?"

He tugged at his watchband. "If there's a problem with the shipments, then it must be on the other end."

"Precisely. That's why we will be in Europe."

"Mrs. Gregory, I'm scheduled to be there myself in two weeks. We have an opportunity to bid for some paintings in Vienna. Mrs. von Tonner recommended them. She expects me."

"Mrs. von Tonner is not your employer. So I suggest that you cancel that reservation. Robyn and I will take care of the Vienna purchases while we're there."

He leaned forward as if to argue, but the laser-sharp gleam in Miriam's eye set him back against the cushions.

"Roj, you and Floy will be in charge, but all final decisions will be Floy's. Is that understood?"

"Miriam," Floy said, "I have no problem working with Roj. He knows the business end of the shop better than I."

A mellow smile crossed Miriam's face as she gazed at Floy, a look of trust for an old friend. "I will be most comfortable with you at the helm, Floy."

Robyn squeezed Floy's hand and whispered, "I'd stay home and help you, but I think Mother will need me more. She hates flying that far alone."

"Don't you worry. If things get hectic, I can handle that young man. And, if necessary, my daughters can come and help out. They're down there browsing all the time anyway."

Roj seemed calmer. "You know we'll do our best while you're gone. Can we count on Aaron if we have any questions?"

"Really, Roj, we're only going for a month. Besides, Aaron will not be available. He plans to meet us in Europe."

So it was more than lost invoices or a damaged Italian painting, Robyn decided. Was Aaron going as Miriam's advisor?

"Is anyone interested in when we are leaving?" Miriam asked.

Roj's expression remained indifferent. Julia placed a hand gently on his leg as she came out of her quiet mode, saying, "Floy told us you want to fly out Wednesday or Thursday morning—whenever we can get the best reservations for you. I'll help on that. Direct to Zurich, right?"

"Yes, and keep our return flight open."

Robyn shut the door behind their guests and faced her mother. "Why are we going away at a time like this? Missing shipments. Damaged paintings. And now Roj just told me that you're facing financial shutdown. He said someone offered to buy the gallery at a good price."

Miriam laughed out loud, a thing she rarely did. "Roj is suddenly so knowledgeable, isn't he? Perhaps he talked with Aaron. Roj is right. We are in financial difficulty, but I'm not ready to retire or sell. That offer is nothing but a hoax. I won't sell and that's that. But I am ready to fight."

"So what's really going on?"

Miriam's voice turned cold. "I have been accused of selling fraudulent paintings. If the pending lawsuits go through, we stand to lose everything."

⁂

Late Wednesday evening as Robyn packed, they were still arguing about Europe. "Mother, you are worn-out. We should just cancel this whole trip."

"No, Ingrid insists that we both come for a rest." Miriam massaged her fingers, her cheeks flushed. "I'm tired, Robyn, but I'll be all right. Europe will do us both good. You and Floy just have to stop worrying about my health."

She picked up one of Robyn's sweaters and refolded it. "Besides, they do have doctors in Europe if we need them."

"Mother, Roj claims that he never ordered that missing shipment. He was in Czechoslovakia with Ingrid on that date. What was he doing there?"

"Traveling on my expense account, no doubt. I'll ask him, but not until we get back. Floy needs his help while we're gone."

"You're so certain the answers are in Europe?"

"Yes, and if we're to salvage the gallery, we must go." Miriam ran her fingers along the edge of the bedspread. "Ingrid warned me that what we discover in Europe may be costly for both of us. Robyn, we may not want to face the truth."

Their gaze met briefly.

Robyn hesitated. "The truth about what?"

"It's about your father." Miriam's voice faltered. "Do you know that he's living in Europe?"

"Yes. I know."

"But you don't know that Aaron is convinced that Drew is trying to destroy the gallery."

"Don't say that. Not even as a joke."

"Your dad may not be the man we once knew, but don't ask me about him. Not now."

How could she not ask about her father? These days he was constantly in the back of her mind, especially as she thought about her visit to the land of Heidi and the Alps. Would he really attempt to destroy her mother's shop? She must hear the truth from him. She must face this man who could not keep his promises.

"I've missed having my father around," she said. "That was painful enough. Don't rob me of his reputation, too."

"Would you rather he robbed me of the gallery?" Miriam walked to the bedroom door and opened it. As she turned back and faced Robyn, her sigh echoed across the room. "Dear Robyn, it's hard for you to believe, but I loved your father once, too. Sometimes I think I still do."

The name that could never pass comfortably between them rose like the old Berlin Wall. Robyn's loyalties were split down the middle. "I have to finish packing, Mother."

"Don't stay up all night. Roj is picking us up at six in the morning. And please take your nicest clothes, Robyn. Ingrid plans some special events for us while we're there."

Robyn put a carefully folded sweater in the Weekender and snapped the lid shut. "I won't bother you and Ingrid in Europe. I'll stay at the hotel. You won't have to admit that I'm your daughter—Plain Jane Gregory."

"Robyn! You're the one who can't see your own beauty—no matter what clothes you wear. I've seen it all along." Miriam went quietly from the room, the door soundless as it closed behind her.

Left alone, Robyn piled the rest of her clothes in the Pullman in those neat little stacks that would please Miriam. Then she went to the bookcase and ran her fingertips along the book titles, finally finding the copy of *Heidi* she had bought to replace the one her dad had taken. A yellowed snapshot of her as a child on her father's shoulders was tucked inside its pages. Her tears brimmed over as she placed them both in her overnight case, out of sight, tucked under an assortment of cosmetics and scarves.

There was one thing left to do as she set the alarm for the brief three hours of sleep she would have before leaving for Zurich. She crept downstairs with her locked suitcases, entered her mother's office, and faxed a letter to Brussels—addressed to Sherm and Andrea Prescott.

Four

Drew Gregory scrawled his signature in the sign-in log and charged down the hall of the embassy, his gym duffel in one hand, his office key in the other. The door stood ajar. It didn't take math calculations to figure that the room was occupied by an uninvited guest—Porter Deven, most likely.

Drew paused in the corridor in his rain-soaked sneakers and faked an intense interest in a poster hanging on the wall.

Others pressed past him. One said, "Sorry, old chap." Another, "Good morning, Gregory." A third, "I see Porter Deven is in."

From the corner of his eye, Drew saw his secretary, Lennie, prim and proper, plodding toward him in her sensible laced shoes, two cups of steaming cappuccino in her hands. Reaching him, she whispered, "You have a guest, Mr. Gregory. Mr. Deven is a bit irate at missing his early flight back to Paris."

"I think he waited over to give me the boot."

Her rattled expression shattered even more, her gaze apprehensive as though the prime minister had invited himself for dinner. Drew touched her shoulder. "What's wrong, Lennie?"

"Mr. Deven made me empty out your desk. And he had someone change the locks on your file cabinet."

Drew suppressed his rage. "It's okay, Lennie. I'll take care of it. The embassy will keep you on."

She blinked back tears, drops of coffee spilling on the floor as her hands shook. "He asked me all sorts of questions."

"Just tell him the truth."

"I did. He didn't believe me."

Drew considered ducking into an empty closet and avoiding the confrontation with Porter. He wasn't sure he could feign surprise or keep a cool head in the interview. He smiled to reassure Lennie, but it did little to bolster his own spirits.

"Go on, Lennie. Give Mr. Deven his coffee."

"It's not *his* coffee," she said precisely. "It's for you."

He grinned. "But it's getting cold, so let him have it."

Drew brushed back his hair with his key and watched her go the remaining few steps to his office, a tiny trail of coffee marking her path. He followed, his damp sneakers squishing as he entered. Porter had taken over the desk, the chair—his unpleasant scent filling the room with stale tobacco and brilliantine.

Porter had the usual bulge at the neckline, the shirt collar too tight for his thick rolls of fat. He slurped another mouthful of cappuccino and put the cup on the desk—Drew's cup, Drew's desk. He glared at Drew with a wintery frost in his crystal-blue eyes.

"You're late."

"Am I?" Drew dumped his gym duffel on the floor, thrust open window louvers for air, and eyed his personal effects piled on the corner of the desk. "What's all the hurry, Porter?"

Porter's jaw dropped a visible half inch. "I'm due back in Paris this afternoon to meet with a Vietnamese delegation."

Vietnam was Porter's old stomping grounds, his personal war. He still wore the smell of smoke on his shirt sleeve, drank too much when he was alone, and carried the barbs of anger on his tongue. "Since when did you start entertaining the Vietnamese?" Drew asked.

"I'll interpret for them—the old MIA/POW issue again."

"After all these years? Well, you do speak the language fluently. So why are you wasting your time here in London?"

"I missed the morning flight to talk to you."

"You came all the way to London for a chat?"

Porter let the comment pass. "Sit down, Drew."

"You've got my chair."

"You won't be needing it. I'm relieving you of your duties."

"So it's straight to the point?" Drew sat down across from Porter and stretched his lanky legs, sizing up his old friend, his arch-enemy. Their friendship had died slowly in heated disagreements over Vietnam, the civil war in Yugoslavia, the closed files on Harland Smith, and their jobs with the Company. Porter's promotion to Station Chief in Paris and Drew's demotion to a desk job in London cut their friendship completely. Drew waited, reveling in his own irritating calm, knowing that his silence aggravated Porter.

Porter ran an emery board over his thumbnail. "When did you see your wife last, Drew?"

"My ex-wife. Sixteen years ago." Amused, he glanced at his watch. "Sixteen years, six weeks, and eighteen hours to be exact."

"The State Department thinks she may be en route to Zurich, Switzerland, with your daughter."

"They've traveled together before, but since when does Washington keep tabs on tourists like Miriam?"

"This tourist is different. She faces charges on art fraud."

"Whatever Miriam is, she is not guilty of fraud."

"She owns an exclusive art gallery."

"So I've heard."

"Three of her recent sales turned out to be frauds. Your wife's lawyer has been most cooperative with Washington."

"I bet he has. My brother Aaron is a criminal lawyer, a cagey type. But that doesn't explain Washington's interest."

"Gregory, your money paid for the gallery."

"Come on, Porter. Be real."

"They've checked. Your brother keeps detailed records."

"On what? My old alimony checks?"

Porter ignored him. "The paintings came from Europe. That makes it international fraud. Your wife—your money. As far as Langley is concerned, that links you to the problem."

"Art fraud? Ridiculous. How did Washington get involved?"

"Through Interpol." Porter studied his fingernails, then filed vigorously. "Your wife buys the art pieces from her old college friend Ingrid von Tonner."

Inwardly, Drew groaned. "Is Interpol interested in von Tonner?"

"They've been interested in the baroness and her friends for years, but nothing specific until now. In the last few months, several pieces of the missing von Tonner collection have surfaced."

"That happens in the art world, doesn't it?" Drew asked.

"Yes, of course, but this is one of the famous German collections stolen during World War II. Odd that it should begin to turn up now." He tweaked the corner of his moustache. "Some of the paintings appearing on the market are outright frauds, copies of the originals. At least three of them passed through your wife's gallery. Copies made with the intent to deceive the buyer are illegal. It's a nasty business. Langley won't tolerate one of its officers involved in an art scandal. They want you to just disappear."

"You'd like that, too, wouldn't you, Porter?"

The vessels in Porter's neck throbbed so wildly that Drew expected him to bleed out with an aneurysm. "Langley wanted to dismiss you immediately. I argued against it."

"So I'm shafted? I go in bits and pieces. The disgrace is the same." Drew ran the key back through his hair. "I have holiday time coming. I'm going to Zurich."

"I can't let you do that."

"Isn't my track record with the Company good enough? Thirty years ought to count for something."

"I'm just following orders. You know that."

"I know no such thing. Just assign me—"

Porter popped an antacid pill. "No assignments, Drew. You're on suspension, without benefits of any kind."

Drew reached across the desk toward his top drawer.

"What are you doing?" Porter asked.

"I need paper to write my resignation."

Porter gripped Drew's wrist. "You are not going to do anything that might blow my career. You will get no pay. No pension. No assignment. No vacation. And right now, no resignation. Pack up your desk and get out."

Drew shot a glance at his personal items. "You've already packed me up. And you haven't told me everything, Porter."

"Your ex-wife is in trouble. That's all you need to know."

"Deven, Robyn is not my *ex-daughter.* If she's in trouble, she may need my help."

They were inches apart now, Drew's fists doubled.

"Yesterday your wife made two reservations to Zurich. It seems an unusual time to vacation when your gallery has just been accused of fraudulent practices."

"My wife hates flying. I'm going to Zurich to meet her."

"Let it alone, Drew. Just lay low for a few weeks."

Drew started toward the file cabinet. Porter's words stopped him. "The files are off-limits to you."

"I have some personal folders in there."

"Including the one on Harland Smith? You're chasing ghosts."

Drew snatched up his pile of belongings from the desk and shoved them into his gym duffel. Then he stalked quietly from the room without looking back. He went straight to Lennie's desk.

She looked miserable. "I'm sorry, Mr. Gregory."

He winked. "Not your problem, Lennie."

He reached in front of her, pressed the intercom button, and listened. Porter had already placed a call. "This is Porter Deven. I just met with Gregory. He's out of here already."

There was a deep chuckle. "He's doing exactly what we expected. He'll be in Zurich before we can get a man there."

The secretary's lips parted. Drew signaled for silence. She complied, her face turning a ghostly white.

"Of course, he wanted the Smith file," Porter said. "Yes, I'll have him tailed. He usually parks in the same place. I'll have someone get on it right away.... Sorry about that. I thought it would take him longer to pack up."

Drew had heard enough. "Lennie, did Porter call out?"

"I don't know."

"Did he call Victor Wilson? Or long distance to Langley?"

"I don't know, Mr. Gregory. He placed the call himself." She inched a coffee-stained memo across the desk to him. "I'll have to make a clean copy for Mr. Deven."

"On Smith?" he asked.

"It isn't classified—yet." She looked away, busying herself with another file.

"You're a sweetheart," he said. He tucked the stained memo inside his shirt and dropped his keys and I.D. badge on her desk. "Turn those in for me, will you, Lennie? Give them to Porter on his way out." He gave her a reassuring smile. "You've been the better part of my being here, Lennie."

"I did my best, Mr. Gregory."

He left the building and deliberately headed for the parking lot, knowing that Porter could be at the window watching him. As he cut down the first lane of parked cars, an Audi-100 squealed to a stop beside him.

"Hop in," the driver said. "I'm Brianna."

Vic's cousin? He smothered his surprise, tossed his duffel in the back, and slipped into the passenger side. She leaned over, smelling of Arpege, and planted a kiss on his cheek. He pulled back, startled.

"Don't be a prude," she said. "I'm just following orders."

"Vic's or Porter's?"

She pressed her jeweled ankle on the accelerator and shot past the security guard. "I'm doing this for Vic. He's crazy, but I love him, so I do the foolish things he wants me to do."

Drew exhaled and went for his seat belt. "Where to?"

"Heathrow," she said cheerily.

He turned enough to watch her. Like Vic, she was thirtyish, but there was no hint of family resemblance. She had a nice profile, her face more youthful than Drew had expected, a sad melancholy to it. Her hair was shoulder length and brushed to a high sheen. The deep fuchsia gloss on her lips matched the flowers in her sweater. As she wove wildly in and out of traffic, Drew braked from the passenger side. "You'll be in trouble if the guard took your number," he warned.

"It's a car rental. I work for the company. An incoming passenger at Heathrow ordered an Audi-100, so I'm just delivering it. I'll drive Vic's car back home."

"You're as crazy as he is."

"Yes," she agreed. "We grew up together. We had such splendid times as children. We hated to grow up." Drew heard wistfulness in her voice. "Several months ago, I took the job in London. I like it here. It gives Vic a place to come home to now and then. He's like a little boy still playing a game of hide-and-seek while the world collapses around him."

She gave Drew a quick glance, the sadness in her eyes magnified by contact lenses. *They should have stayed in their happy childhood,* he thought.

He thumbed through Porter's memo en route to the airport. Nothing new. Nothing except the last notation: *Harland Smith last sited in Zurich.* Porter's initials were scribbled beside it.

As they neared Heathrow, Brianna said, "Vic lives hard, plays hard. It's as though he's crowding a lifetime into a few years."

"Don't worry. He's survived more close calls than I can count."

"I do worry. We're not just cousins. Vic and I are friends, confidants. I don't want to lose him."

"Am I to talk him out of going with me?"

"Oh, no. You're one of his only friends. Porter despises him, and women use him."

"I thought it was the other way around. I keep telling him to settle down with one woman."

"He tried that twice. They made a fool of him. After that, he ran free. It's those meaningless affairs that will kill him."

"Have you talked to him about it?"

Her laugh ended in a whisper. "Have you?"

"In a backhand way."

"He doesn't feel well, Drew. Have you noticed?"

"Broken ribs are painful, but it didn't affect his tennis game this morning. He beat me."

Brianna's laughter was softer this time. "He calls you the silver-haired swinger on the tennis court."

I'm not silver-haired, just gray-fringed, he thought. "He swings a mean racquet himself and wins all the games."

"But he has to work at it."

"He'll have to work at curbing his relationships."

"His first wife really hurt him."

Drew thought of Miriam. "That's no excuse."

"Will you talk to him, Drew? For me."

"As a silver-haired father?"

"No, as his friend."

"Is there anything I should know, Brianna? A serious illness could ruin his career."

Her knuckles went white as she gripped the steering wheel. "Is career all you Company men think of? I'm worried about his life. Just forget it...." She pulled smoothly to the drop-off curb for British Airways. "You're catching a flight to Nice in an hour."

"I thought it was the Italian Riviera."

"That's what Vic wanted Porter Deven to think. Be patient with Vic. He's trying to sort out things between the two of you. He'll want to spend some time on the beach at Nice."

"Why? I don't like men who waste time on wine and women."

Her gaze sharpened. "And Vic despises men who fall into disfavor with the Agency—and men who disgrace it."

She didn't give him time to question that one. "A few hours in Nice will do you both good. Pretty girls. Warm sun. It will seem like a real vacation. Besides, you'll get the car there." She brushed another kiss on his cheek. "You'll drive to Cannes first—to a medical clinic near there, then north past Monaco."

"A medical clinic for Vic?"

She smiled patiently. "There's an old man there Vic wants to see. If anyone knows about the von Tonner collection, this man will. Look, there's Vic now. Be careful, both of you. And take care of him, Drew."

Drew pulled his gym duffel from the back seat. "Thanks. I enjoyed your timid driving, Brianna," he teased.

She winked, blew a kiss to both of them, and drove away.

❧☙

Forty-eight hours later, the two men stood on either side of the car, conversing heatedly. "You and Porter had it all mapped out, didn't you?" Drew asked. "How come he didn't tell you the old man was confused? Baron von Tonner was pathetic, I grant you that. But we wasted time visiting with him."

Vic's grin was wiped clean, leaving the angular face gaunt and angry. "Did we? He was thrilled to death to have guests."

"But we didn't learn a thing."

"Then you weren't listening," Vic said wearily. "The ramblings of a confused old mind often speak the truth."

"You believed all that stuff about caves and tunnels."

"I believe the old man was lonely. I don't want to live that long or be that sick. And quit worrying about Porter." He pounded the roof of the Renault. "There's no friendship lost between Deven and me. If he weren't going for your jugular, Drew, he'd be on my case." Vic was already behind the wheel. "Come on; it's a long drive to Kaiserslautern and then halfway up the Rhine to Dusseldorf."

Drew squeezed into the passenger side, cramping his legs in the effort. "That's a roundabout route to Zurich."

"Believe me, we'll get there. By the way, I posted Porter a card at Heathrow. I told him we were heading to Greece for a holiday. He'll get my card in a day or two. When he stops cussing, he'll start looking for us."

"You wasted a postage stamp. He knows I'm heading to Zurich."

Vic whacked his forehead. "Thanks for blowing it." He cooled quickly. "Well, what do you think of Nicole's little buggy?"

"Pretty tight quarters."

"It's safer than a car rental and cheaper. Brianna's idea. Besides, Nicole and I dated for some time. She owes me one."

"A gal in every European community? That kind of life is going to kill you."

"Sounds like you and Brianna have been talking. She called Nicole and told her we needed transportation. For now we've got the car and no records of us renting one." He glanced in the rearview mirror. "And no one tailing us. So time's in our favor. We'll be in Zurich before your wife gets there."

"Did you arrange that, too, Vic?"

"Your trust level is down. If we're going to handle these next three weeks, we're going to have to come to terms. This is my vacation, and I have better ideas of where I could spend it, with Nicole for one. Get off my back, or you can strike out on your own, and I'll stay at the Riviera like I planned."

Drew slouched, his knees banging into the dashboard. "I don't have much choice, do I? Porter is expecting us in Zurich; I don't want to disappoint him."

"That's better."

"But if I catch you reporting to Porter, I'll forget we were ever friends."

"You'll break my neck?"

"Maybe just a few more ribs."

"Then I won't let you catch me calling him. Now get some shut-eye. You'll need it. You're going to spell me at this wheel when we hit the German autobahn at 140 kilometers an hour."

"Miles sounds better," Drew said.

"Either way, it's insanity."

"But you like danger."

Vic shrugged. "Not this kind, but it's the shortest route to the von Tonner mansion."

"Why there, if Ingrid is meeting my family in Switzerland?"

"The von Tonner art collection was presumably stolen during the Nazi regime. In recent years, some of it surfaced. Sotheby's handled two or three sales and then refused to take more."

"What's that got to do with my family?"

"When the collection disappeared from the market again, the frauds appeared. You saw the condition of the old man—he couldn't put the paintings on the auction block or order the copies. That means Mrs. von Tonner has the answers. Are you with me?"

"Ingrid isn't clever enough for that, either."

"She knows where that collection is—at the mansion perhaps."

"More scuttlebutt from Langley or Porter?"

"Part of the file that Porter showed me."

"So we storm the mansion and demand the answers?"

Vic chuckled. "I don't have definite plans. But if I had a chance to get inside and look around, that would please Porter."

"Whose side are we on, Vic?"

"No sides. Not yet. We're just looking for answers. If we can find where that art collection is hidden, perhaps—"

"It doesn't prove my wife's innocence."

"We may not be able to prove that, Drew. She may—"

Drew tried to rub the circulation back into his legs. "I lived with Miriam for a number of years. Whatever she has become, it is not a thief. Art was her whole world."

"But it didn't include you and your daughter?"

"She found room for Robyn. Miriam was a good mother. She may have put the art world in Robyn's mind when she was little, but at least she spent time with her."

"It left a deep impression. According to the file, Robyn studied art history. She's well-versed in it. That's another reason to question what's going on. She and your wife should be able to recognize a fraud, especially one of the Dutch masters."

"That was my wife's specialty."

Vic switched to the fast lane. "The frauds passing through Mrs. Gregory's gallery are all Dutch paintings. I don't know how to give it to you any easier."

Had sixteen years made a difference? Drew, in his usual monotone, asked, "Is there anything else I should know?"

"The von Tonner woman dined at one of the Swiss hotels, the Schweizerhof, the other evening—with an old friend of yours."

"I don't really care who she dines with."

"But it was her dinner companion who wanted your wife in Switzerland as quickly as von Tonner could get her there." Vic flexed his shoulder muscles. "Does someone six-foot-plus, a French-speaker with a Brooklyn accent and a crooked thumb ring any bells?"

Not Harland C. Smith? Hope for his family splintered like a burned-out log in the fireplace. "Does he have a name, Vic?"

"An alias. Smythe Williams according to the waiter, Garret, but the description fits Harland Smith. Porter doesn't agree."

"He wouldn't. He prefers Smith dead."

"There's less political embarrassment for him that way. I think he pulled you out of London, because you were too close to the truth. The way I read it, Smith may be in Zurich waiting for your wife's arrival. And yours. When we go in, we're not going to be on the front row waving."

"Why not?"

"I want to save your neck, Drew. I don't know why. You've been unbearable so far. I guess this wife reunion is getting to you. I've faced a couple of those myself."

Again Drew studied the narrow profile. How long had he known Vic and still not known him? "Any particular reunion?"

"The one with my Georgia peach. I really cared about her. Or I thought I did. I wanted to hold that marriage together, but she dumped me. Did you know that?"

"For any particular reason, Vic?"

"Yeah. I didn't want kids."

Five

Ingrid von Tonner roared her silver Mercedes Benz up the private winding road toward the house. She slowed on a steep curve, coming almost to a stop for a glimpse of the von Tonner mansion, an impressive stronghold of grayish-white stone glistening in the sunlight. The mansion sat on a cliff overlooking the Rhine where the river wended its way westward toward the Netherlands and the North Sea. It was less majestic than the medieval castles that dotted the velvety hillsides, but Ingrid never ceased to thrill at possessing it.

She hit the accelerator and shot full speed around the outer edge of the stone wall that encircled the courtyard. Albert Klee had already swung open the electronic gate to welcome her. The butler was aged like the baron, but unbent and alert. He and his wife, Hedwig, came with the house. They remained loyal to the memory of the baron but were wise enough to tread lightly with Ingrid for the sake of a roof over their heads.

Other men Albert's age seemed antiquated, but his agility and strength amazed her. He opened the car door for her, the scowl lines on his face deep and ugly. Bushy brows shielded the keen dark eyes; puffy patches bulged beneath them. His lips were thin, narrowing the appearance of a wide mouth, his teeth spaced and stained. "Should I get your luggage, Frau von Tonner?" he asked.

She waved him off with a flick of her gloved hand. "Have Hedwig do it. I'll need these clothes by morning."

He nodded and followed her up the steps at a respectful distance. The double doors stood open, the way he had left them when he hurried out to meet her. She stepped into the enormous entryway and gazed at the familiar surroundings—the gilt-laced chandeliers, the delicate rose-cut marble floor, and the valuable art treasures that hung on the white walls. Just ahead lay the sweeping staircase with its ivory balustrade. The baron's favorite painting, a masterpiece highly valued on the open market, hung above the landing,

Albert stood rigidly beside her with an expression of forced politeness as she surveyed her surroundings once again. Visible to his right was the living room with its massive stone fireplace and the striking eight-foot portrait of the baron with his sharp, well-chiseled features. Everything revealed Albert's scrupulous care, and everything in that room boasted the former wealth and power of the von Tonners—rich brocade tapestries, ornate carvings, and antique furnishings from the seventeenth and eighteenth centuries.

Meticulously, Ingrid worked the gloves from her hands, one finger at a time. She turned to the hall mirror. The reflection was shocking—her travel-worn face side by side with the baron's. *Someday,* she thought angrily, *I will tear that portrait from the wall and pack it* away. She sensed Albert's hostility, as though he were protecting the baron even from her thoughts.

"Is Herr Valdemar in the studio?" she asked.

"Yes," Albert said unhappily. "Should I tell Hedwig you will both be here for dinner?"

"No, that isn't necessary. I'll take dinner in my room this evening. I don't care what Valdemar does."

"Will there be anything else, Baroness?"

"No. I'm leaving in the morning. I'm bringing guests back—next week perhaps. Open the pink rooms and air the eiderdowns."

A frown puckered his brows. "The rooms with the connecting bath—the ones overlooking the river?"

"My guests would like that."

"Should we open the east wing, too, Baroness?"

A musty smell permeated the east wing. The baron had kept it sealed off and draped in dusty sheets to conserve heat, but they always aired it out for the annual von Tonner ball and the arrival of special guests. Ingrid occupied several rooms—the living and dining rooms, the master bedroom on the second floor, her private studio on the west wing, and the well-polished ballroom. She still held the annual von Tonner dance even though Felix had relinquished his right to the mansion and to Ingrid herself.

"Will your guests be staying long, Baroness?"

I hope not, she thought. *The sooner I get this Gregory problem settled, the better for me.* Aloud, she managed, "I'm not certain. Yes—open the east wing; make it all look lived in."

She waited for him to leave. Then she walked slowly toward the stairs, pausing briefly at the living room to look at the baron. Once again those sparkling eyes stared down at her, a mocking little smile at the corner of his thick lips. "It's all yours," he seemed to be saying.

All mine, she repeated. *All mine, Felix.*

She reached the foot of the stairs, her thoughts still on the baron. From the day she had met him, she had wanted his money and mansion. It was only after their marriage that she realized some of his millions existed more in his memory than in actual investments. The family inheritance had dwindled considerably with the baron's high living and self-indulgence.

For a while she had tolerated the marriage. She was not unkind to Felix; it was not her style to be unkind to any. man. She found him personable, gentle-hearted, and even humorous with his aging memory. His past wealth and family name gave him entry into some of the finest homes in Europe. She cultivated these friendships. In spite of the baron's failing heath, they threw parties and entertained and spent months in their villa on the French Riviera. Even so, she fretted that there would be little money left for her to squander unless she could connive a plan to turn the von Tonner property into a livelihood for her future.

She ran her hand over the balustrade, savoring the moment of discovery of the lost von Tonner art collection and the profitable business that had come from the art treasures. Again she stared up at the baron's favorite painting above the landing. She had taken it down once to sell, only to find Albert nailing it back on the wall. She decided against freshening up and went instead to find Sigmund Valdemar. Cutting behind the stairwell, she lifted the key ring from the hook and walked the narrow passage to the isolated studio.

From outdoors, this section looked like an addition to the house, constructed as an afterthought; even its roof seemed a richer slate-blue. The windows in the studio looked out on the countryside and down over the fast-flowing Rhine. Ingrid had been adamant about her right to the studio. Felix had bowed to her relentless demands but stubbornly refused to remove anything, not even the old bookcases that covered one wall.

She turned the knob and stood in the doorway, almost retching at the smell of paint and turpentine, yet touched by the strains of an Italian opera playing softly in the background. Sigmund went on painting, oblivious to her arrival. Her personal library stood on the far side of the room—books on art and world-famous artists. Sigmund rarely touched these, but he took great pleasure in her collection of operas in every language. The striped, king-sized sofa where Valdemar slept took up another wall. The last time Ingrid had offered to spend the night there with him, he had humiliated her, saying, "Not this time, Ingrid." Staring at the wrinkled covers and the decorative pillows on the floor where he had dumped them, she remembered.

Even now he sat at his easel—a striking, yet mulish man, calm and unhurried, his brushstrokes gentle against the canvas. His muscular, bare back was to her, his trousers stained with paint, his feet clad in scuffed moccasins. Light streamed through the windows, sending sun paths across the rug and giving an unusual glimmer to Sigmund's unkempt, murky hair. He was a magnetic composite: artist and musician; aloof and pragmatic; violent and passionate; remote, yet powerful.

Yes, she decided, Sigmund was out of step with the world, and the studio was out of step with the rest of the old mansion. They had made this room too modern for the generations of von Tonners who had lived here. She controlled the room but could not control the man whose copies of the Dutch masters would make them both wealthy. She cleared her throat above the strains of music.

He whirled around to face her, his eyes void of feeling.

"Ah, Mrs. von Tonner, you've taken flight from Mr. Smith?"

"Hardly," she answered. "Will you finish that Rembrandt soon?"

"Do you have a buyer for it?"

She ignored him. "I haven't seen you since you followed Mr. Smith from the Schweizerhof. You were going to get back to me."

"Was I?"

"You know that you were."

"Smith slipped away from me at the train station." He stirred paint on the palette. "Don't worry. He'll be in touch when the Gregorys arrive. They are coming, aren't they?"

"Yes, soon."

"Does Mr. Smith know?"

"Not yet. Miriam and I need time alone."

"To build bargaining leverage with Smith?" he challenged.

"The safety of my guests is important to me, Sigmund."

"As important as protecting your art franchise?"

"*Our* franchise. What else do you know about Smith?"

"He owned the Plastec Corporation in Paris until his private jet exploded over the Atlantic."

"But he's alive and hiding out in Switzerland. Why?"

Sigmund's eyes hardened even more. "I don't know."

"Then guess," she snapped.

"Drug-trafficking maybe."

"You don't believe that?"

"No," he answered. "He sold arms to Third World countries."

"You're certain?"

"The CIA and the French Sûreté are using his 'death' to cover up whatever happened. The scandal would have died months ago except for Drew Gregory refusing to believe that Smith is dead."

She cupped her trembling chin with a jeweled hand. "What am I getting into, Sigmund?"

"A death trap," he said calmly.

She felt the color drain from her face. "If Smith were reunited with his wife, would it protect the Gregorys?"

"It's worth considering. On the other hand, if something happened to the Gregorys, it might save your reputation, Ingrid."

She recoiled. "Don't be arrogant, Sigmund. Miriam and I are old friends. I wish her no ill. None."

"You should have thought of that before you cheated her."

"You act like I'm drowning in international waters."

"You are," he said. "Especially if American Intelligence traces Miriam's arrival in Zurich back to you. Her ex-husband is CIA, Ingrid.

The Stasi used to be interested in him."

"That's past history. The East German secret police went with the Berlin Wall."

"Did we?" he challenged. "Or maybe we're just waiting for the right moment to reappear."

"Don't be foolish, Sigmund. For three years, I've offered you the chance to make something of yourself, to be a gentleman rather than a beribboned militant."

His eyes burned like coals of fire that refused to go out. "An unknown artist," he said bitterly.

"Copying the old masters pays well, doesn't it?"

She walked over to him, self-assured again, and patted his face. "I've set you up in a comfortable lifestyle, darling. You're safe from your past—right in your own native land. No one knows who you are. Now I need your help, Sigmund."

He turned and stared at the canvas, the muscles of his back tightening. She lifted her hands to run her fingers over his shoulders, but the Italian opera had played itself out. Just as the music had stopped, so had the moment.

As he dipped the tip of his brush in the sorrel paint, she let her hands drop to her sides, her gaze fixed on his strong back. She hated the unrestrained emotions that raged inside.

"When will you finish the painting?"

Huskily, he said, "In a day or two. And then if you loan me your Mercedes Benz, I'll drive to Paris and bring this young and beautiful Madame Smith back across the border with me."

"And the Smith children," she reminded him.

"They weren't in the bargain."

"They are now." She thought of his recklessness. "You can use the Fiat," she said.

"There's no power to it."

"Then walk." She kissed his shoulder and turned to leave.

"Where are you going, Ingrid?"

"Riding with Monarch. Would you care to join us?"

"That's a wild stallion. I'd rather finish this painting."

"Afraid of horses?"

"No, of you. Go. Go now, before we both regret it."

Angry that he knew how she longed for him, she left the room.

He called after her, "We're business partners, Mrs. von Tonner, not lovers. Don't forget it."

He was laughing at her as the door closed. She leaned against it, trembling. Until now she could have any man she wanted—even this man wasn't born too late for her. She liked his rugged build and that bronzed, unsmiling face; she tolerated his blunt, unpolished manner and admired his sensitive feel for art. She remembered their first meeting on the snow-capped slopes of St. Moritz long after the fall of the Berlin Wall. It was a brazen public appearance for a Stasi agent still sought by the West Germans. He was an avid sportsman, skillful on skis and charming as he helped her to her feet She invited him back to the mansion for the weekend. It was then she had discovered his artistic gift and had cultivated that skill for her own purposes.

Mock me, she thought, *and I'll turn you over to the German polizei.*

Yet even as she considered it, she knew she wouldn't. He was still too valuable to her.

≈≪

Sigmund stared at the closed door, confident that Ingrid stood on the other side. He had not heard her walk away. He sensed his growing disfavor in her eyes. Ingrid the woman intrigued him. Ingrid the fool amused him. Beauty and vanity, power and ill-gotten wealth had blinded her. Even now, she did not know that he was using her. More than once his friends had sat around the massive dining table, drinking beer and making toasts to the baroness and her hospitality—saluting Ingrid for her contribution to the future Stasi organization. Albert Klee knew. Hedwig knew. They had seen Sigmund's friends come and go in Ingrid's absence, but they had kept quiet for their own safety.

He heard Ingrid walk away now, her heels tapping against the marble tiles. He listened until the hall was quiet. He thought back to the night he had met a former Stasi officer on the rubbled path where the Berlin Wall had once stood. There were others, he was told, waiting and planning their return to power. Sigmund had joined them, eager to stir up political unrest in the unified Germany—and to plant seeds of discontent in the minds of the unemployed and the hungry.

The studio door opened, and Albert stole in with a tray of tea and sandwiches. He put them down and left without a word to Sigmund. Albert despised him. Hedwig feared him. When the time came, Sigmund would dispose of the Klees by putting them in the vault in exchange for the rest of the famous paintings hidden there. Then he'd walk out of this mansion on the Rhine and free himself of Ingrid's miserable companionship.

But he would not go empty-handed. He was prepared to take over the von Tonner collection—and possibly the mansion itself. The collection, he knew, was valued into the millions, money that would fund the new Stasi movement and perhaps buy him a position of power. He stared at the painting on the easel, admiring his own skill. *Rembrandt,* he thought. *A brilliant mind. A great artist. But I have so much more to offer.*

There were loopholes. Ingrid's toppling art empire threatened his own plans. He knew little about the art market, but Harland Smith, this mastermind of intrigue, was a promoter of the black market. If for no other reason, Smith's ability to obtain weapons would be most useful to the Stasi movement. The paintings, no matter how valuable, would do Sigmund little good in the von Tonner underground. But Harland Smith could walk into the best of auction houses and sell the paintings before Ingrid or Albert or Hedwig even missed them. Smith would delight in deceiving even the best of the auction houses—Sotheby's or Christie's. Smith and Sigmund were well acquainted with the art of betrayal and duplicity.

Sigmund stirred the sorrel paint once more, the sun rays forming a rainbow effect on the colors. He'd work through the night to complete the painting, then leave in the morning. He would promise Smith the von Tonner art collection in exchange for weapons. As a guarantee, he might even offer to fly to Paris and bring Monique and her sons back to Switzerland.

A woman half Smith's age! Did Harland really deserve her?

~~

The chestnut stallion neighed before Ingrid even reached the stables. She passed the gelding and mare and stopped at the middle stall to wrap her arm around Monarch's long, well-muscled neck. He was a proud Persian Arab, a strong-spirited horse, his coat brushed to a shine. He nuzzled her, searching for a carrot or apple.

"I've got a special treat for you, Monarch."

He watched her with his wide eyes as she held the soft peppermints in the open palm of her hand. He took them and nibbled contentedly, nudging her for more. She marveled at his beauty and strength—a wide powerful chest, long sloping shoulders, an elegant mane, and a white star on his forehead. Monarch had been a gift from the baron. "A wild one like you," Felix had said.

It was true. Ingrid and the stallion challenged each other; they vied for dominance—a mutual friendship growing between them. "I missed you, Monarch, but I'll be gone again in the morning. I've got to get this thing settled with the Gregorys."

Monarch talked back, sounds that Ingrid recognized.

The stable boy sauntered over, a young man not more than eighteen, solidly built, cocky—the Klees' grandson. She doubted this, but the boy needed a job, and she needed a good groomsman for the five horses she still had. Once—so long ago—the stables had been filled with riding horses and show horses. In his day, the baron had been a commanding figure in the saddle. *So long ago.*

"Saddle him for you, Baroness?" Klaus asked.

"I'm tired. I just came back from a long trip. Would you mind—could you lunge Monarch for me?"

The lad cocked his head. "Could," he said, "but he looks like he wants a good ride. He's been missing you."

She ran her hand over the thick neck, rubbing with a loving gesture. "You've been tending him well?"

"Like always," the boy answered. "But he's a wild one for anyone but you. He tried to toss Albert while you were gone."

"Albert is never to ride him, Klaus. Where's the Hanoverian?"

"I let him out to grass. Should I bring him in now?"

"No, when you get back is fine." Ingrid glanced anxiously at her watch. She needed Klaus away from the stables for twenty minutes or more. She saddled Monarch herself, talking in soft whispers to the animal. "You're going for a good ride with Klaus," she said. She noted the agitation beginning and placed her head against Monarch's again. "Tomorrow we'll ride before I leave."

She handed the reins to Klaus. "Give him a good workout."

The boy frowned. "In the woods?"

"Why not?" she asked. It would give her time to enter the tunnels and check on the vaults. She waited as Klaus mounted and walked off, Monarch rebelling. Klaus was firm in his commands. He tightened the reins for a second, then nudged Monarch gently with his knees. Monarch responded, sprinting quickly from trot to canter. Rider and horse passed through the gate behind the mansion and reached the open trail at a gallop.

Ingrid raced to the other end of the stable, past the tack room with its saddles and bridles, and entered the foaling stall beside it. There hadn't been a birthing for years, so the foaling box had become another cluttered storage area—still off-limits to Klaus. Kicking the thick pile of shaving chips from the floor, she lifted two planks to expose the trap door. She swung it back, twisting her shoulder in her haste. Grabbing a lantern from the hook, she descended the creaky steps into the darkened tunnels. At the bottom of the steps she reached blindly for the switch and lit the cavern with a long row of forty-watt bulbs.

The tunnels spread out far to her right, but she had never explored their depths. She went left instead, the damp cement walls closing in on her. The isolation no longer frightened her, though. She had grown accustomed to checking the main vault periodically ever since Sigmund had discovered its location.

She worked the combination lock; then, with great effort she swung the door open and stepped into the steel-lined vault that held the Dutch masters. Everything was as she had left it, the paintings kept warm and protected by snug quilts. As she unwrapped one painting and examined it, she knew that the five years of marriage to the baron had been worth it. She had simply taken advantage of his growing senility, persuading him to sign over the rights to the property in their divorce settlement.

She remembered her relief when Felix entered the clinic on the Riviera and the joy as she began remodeling the studio. When she had ordered the rough-hewn floor-to-ceiling bookcases torn from the wall, Albert Klee's face had gone black with rage. In the thick panels behind them appeared the outline of a doorway. At the threat of firing Albert, Hedwig had given Ingrid the rusty key. She had jammed it in the lock as the Klees sulked beside her. Finally, it turned. The paneled door had creaked open, sending an eerie chill against Ingrid's legs as she walked down into the cold passage. It was then that she discovered the vaults tunneled deep beneath the courtyard. The largest room hid a collection of Dutch masters, statuettes, and other famous paintings that Hermann Goering had coveted during World War II. She drove at once to the clinic and tried to speak to Felix about her discovery. The baron had merely smiled, his memory dim.

"Were they stolen?" she had asked. "Were they Goering's?"

"Oh, no. It was a family collection." He seemed sure of that. "When the war came—" he frowned as though it were just happening—"my parents buried the collection beneath the house to keep it safe from the Nazi regime. And now I have kept them safe from you, my dear."

As she stood there, she saw him as nothing but an eccentric old man. He had delighted in hiding his treasures. She would never know why. She didn't care. Someday—when the baron died—she could go public and lay claim to the whole collection. Or should she wait that long?

It had been her last visit to the baron. As far as she knew, he still roamed the halls of the clinic, boasting about his family heritage, his victory over Goering—and her.

Now as Ingrid wiped away more cobwebs and sorted through the paintings, she sensed someone behind her. She tensed and turned, expecting it to be Klaus.

"I thought I would find you here," Sigmund said. He had come quietly on his moccasins.

"How dare you follow me!"

He smiled. "When the stable boy rode off on Monarch, I knew you had other plans than riding. Are you counting your wealth?"

"What do you want, Sigmund?"

"Something else to paint. I'm weary of Rembrandt and Renoir."

He thumbed through one of the cement containers, shredding the worn quilts in his excitement, his attention finally drawn to a Vermeer. He lifted the painting gently in his hands, his broad shoulders braced against the damp wall. Ingrid watched his eyes brighten as he studied the picture—a Dutch painter working diligently at his easel, a paintbrush in hand, his lovely model sitting demurely on a stool as he painted her.

"Put it away, Sigmund. You could never match Vermeer's color and design," she said impatiently.

"But I'd like to try."

Again she attempted to see it from Sigmund's practiced eye, noting the old-fashioned Dutch clothing, the gold chandelier, the thick drape pulled back, its colors dark yet detailed. "All right," she said, "take it upstairs to the studio. Paint it if you must, but remember, Henri Van Meegeren already copied Vermeer."

"And quite successfully," Sigmund said.

"Tragically," she countered. She closed the lid. "Sigmund, let's get out of here before Klaus comes back."

He followed her, the Vermeer painting in his hand.

Humor him, she thought as they made their way hurriedly back up the narrow steps. *I still need him. But can I trust him now that he knows about the stable entry into the tunnels?*

She felt a cold chill sweeping over her. Perhaps the baron had been wise after all—leaving the art collection hidden from a greedy world. He had refused to share it—had refused to let it destroy him. And now, already, it was destroying her. She stepped into the foaling stall first, then turned to wait for Sigmund.

"Hurry," she said. "I hear Klaus and Monarch returning."

Six

Sigmund stood by the manor window and watched Ingrid accelerate until her shiny Mercedes disappeared down the winding road. He was still standing there when an Audi squealed up the arrow-thin drive and screeched to a stop near the front hedge.

Aaron Gregory stepped out, bounded up the steps, and rang the doorbell impatiently.

Trouble, Sigmund mused. *He has been trouble since day one.*

He turned back to the easel, covered the canvas, and soaked the brushes. As he left the room, a faint smell of linseed oil clung to his clothes. He locked the door, then made his way round the circular stairwell to confront the American.

Aaron's long strides came to an abrupt halt as he reached Sigmund. In height they were about the same—five-ten, five-eleven at the most. Aaron had a studious, indoor face— pallid skin, thin lips, intelligent dark eyes; the lower part of his bleak face was insipid and lean. Sigmund thought of him as silver-tongued; clearly, his battles were won with words, not physical strength. Even the clothing added to this image— double-breasted navy blazer, well-cut gray slacks, and gold tie clasp—the look of the perfect gentleman, right down to the clipped nails and signet ring.

"Where's Ingrid?" he demanded.

Sigmund shrugged. "You passed her on the highway. She'd be hitting 140 kilometers by now."

"Where is she?"

"I told you. On the autobahn—speeding to Zurich."

"When is she due back?"

Sigmund shrugged again. "In a day or two. Next week. Whenever. I'll tell Albert you're here. He can make up a room."

"Don't bother. I'll see myself up."

To one of the guest rooms? Sigmund wondered. *Or will you head straight to Ingrid's suite?*

"I'll need the keys to the art vault, Valdemar. We have to get your paintings out of here."

"Nothing moves out of the mansion without Ingrid's say-so. You know that, Gregory."

It amused Sigmund, the slight change in Aaron's stance, the deeper blanch to the lips, the unsmiling, courtroom facade. Aaron's chin was cleft, but weak; his small jawbone drew the lower part of his face into a point. *It wouldn't take long,* Sigmund decided, *to break a man like this.* Aaron was used to being on the defensive, defeating someone else in a court scene, but he wasn't steeled to being the one on trial.

"Valdemar, we can't waste time waiting for Ingrid. We've got to get your copies out of here and destroy them."

Sigmund bristled at the thought of ruining his long hours of work "No, Gregory. We have buyers for them."

"You can't channel any more through Miriam's gallery. Now give me the key."

"The key to what?"

"The vault—wherever it is."

So Ingrid hadn't told Aaron about the exact location. Well, then, Sigmund wouldn't break the silence either. "Talk to Ingrid when she gets back," he said.

"We can't wait that long."

"Aaron, we're not destroying my copies of Rembrandt."

"Then hide them until this blows over."

Sigmund considered the art bunker beneath the mansion with its three-ton door leading into the steel-lined vaults. Von Tonner had built it to withstand earthquakes and terrorist attacks. So guaranteed—it was Aaron Gregory-proof, too.

"The paintings are in a safe place," Sigmund said. "I'll take care of them." He yawned, purposely emphasizing his boredom with Aaron. "Tell me, what do you hear from your brother, Drew?"

The eyes in the gaunt face flickered. Sigmund had pushed another panic button, but the panic quickly turned to anger.

"I don't keep in touch with him."

"Really? I thought you handled the Gregory business affairs."

"Mostly I'm Miriam's financial adviser. But I have a legal reputation to maintain. I won't let you and Ingrid ruin me."

Sigmund walked off, but Aaron's unexpected grip on his arm jerked him to a standstill. He whirled back and slammed Aaron against the railing. "Don't lay a hand on me again, Gregory. Selling the von Tonner collection was your idea."

Aaron twisted the fingers on his milk-white hand. "I suggested selling one or two of the paintings from the walls of the manor. I didn't authorize copying the originals. No, not copies," he repeated.

Valdemar felt nothing but contempt for the lawyer. "You didn't bow out when the frauds sold so successfully. You knew we had to do something. The reappearance of some of the von Tonner collection on the European market was not going well."

Aaron leaned against the banister, his arms folded. "Ingrid's approach was all wrong—calling Sotheby's and Christie's and pitting them against each other. It was stupid for her to say she'd part with the paintings under the right circumstances—for the right amount of money. She thought she could set the conditions, promising them a collection she couldn't produce."

"Oh, she could produce it all right," Sigmund said. "It's real and more fabulous than historical records indicate."

"Then why didn't the auction houses believe her?"

"They couldn't risk a scandal, not with the collection still listed in the International Art Loss Registry."

"I tried to warn her."

"We both did. She's more threatened by Pierre Courtland, the young friend of the baron's, who opposes the sale of any of the baron's paintings. He insists that the collection still belongs to Felix—that it wasn't spelled out in the divorce proceedings."

The corners of Aaron's mouth arced down, allowing his narrow chin to jut more. "Is there anything to that?"

"He convinced Ingrid to back off. Why make claims to something you thought was lost or stolen back in World War II?"

"Does the man want money?"

"According to Ingrid, Courtland is financially stable, even

borderline wealthy."

"But is he going to be a problem to us, Sigmund?"

"Maybe! He comes across as pleasant and easy-going—always whistling 'To All the Girls I've Loved Before.'" Sigmund shook his head. "But, believe me, he's no Julio Iglesias. He has Julio's build and dark hair. He's even attractive like Iglesias, but that's where it ends."

"Forget the rundown on his good looks. Is he a threat?"

Valdemar shrugged. "He's shrewd, that one. Looks harmless. He's the young executive type—in business in Geneva. But Ingrid has made no attempt to sell an original since he interfered. She'll leave the bulk of the collection hidden until the rumors die down, and Courtland backs off."

Sigmund picked at a paint stain under his fingernail. "That's when I appeared on the scene, paintbrush in hand. The way Ingrid figures it, we can still sell my copies of the collection until the baron dies. After that the paintings are all hers—all ours."

"And Pierre Courtland won't oppose it then?"

"If he persists in getting in the way, we can take care of him."

"Don't be a fool."

"You're not a German, Gregory. So you can't appreciate the historical significance of one of the best-known European art collections disappearing during the Third Reich. The baron kept his collection hidden from the Nazis—and from an auction market that would have made him a millionaire all over again."

"He's senile," Aaron said ruefully. "I warned Ingrid against announcing the discovery of the von Tonner collection too soon."

"The question is, why did Felix keep it hidden all these years? We'll never know where his sympathies lay during that war."

"Albert Klee might know."

"True. But Ingrid doesn't care. She will assume the role of one betrayed by the baron's family and left with fake paintings in the collection. Embarrassment. Apologies. She has social contacts who will rally to her support. She'll come out of this white as a water lily." He smiled, his own arms folded now as he stared eye-level at the American. "And she'll get by with it. I assure you, Gregory, Germany will not want the embarrassment of any of the collection being labeled a fraud. It's a point of honor. A famous family. Baron von Tonner may be cooped away in an asylum, but he's still highly respected. They'll grab at any reason to protect his name. So you see, Gregory, there's something to be said for artful deception."

"Miriam will not be so easily deceived. She's an angry woman. There's going to be a stormy confrontation with Ingrid."

"Don't forget, Aaron, no shipment left this country for Miriam's shop without exhaustive documentation."

Aaron pounded his fist. "Then why have three paintings been returned to the gallery as absolute frauds? Let's just closet everything. Washington is really moving in on this."

"That's your problem. They have no jurisdiction over me."

"No, it's our problem. I've cooperated with Washington enough to know that Interpol has had Ingrid under surveillance for months. If they can prove we sold frauds through Miriam's gallery willingly, frauds that originated from this end—"

"You're the one who suggested marketing the baron's paintings through Mrs. Gregory's gallery. *Our American contact,* you called her."

"I miscalculated there. I trusted you and Ingrid to channel some of the baron's collection through Miriam's gallery so some of the 'lost treasures' would be traced back to her. I never expected you to send fake paintings to her."

"I think you did."

"We're in trouble, Valdemar."

"No, I'm an unknown in Mrs. von Tonner's world—just one of her guests who dabbles in art. If my hostess took my reproductions of Rembrandt without my knowledge and sold them well…."

He watched Aaron's expression turn sour. Sigmund knew he would have to arrange a rendezvous with Harland Smith quickly. For now, the paintings were safe in the vault. Albert Klee would see to that.

Aaron extended one hand. "I need the key, Sigmund. We've got to take your paintings out now."

"That's out of the question. Ingrid has the only one."

"I'll find it." He turned, took the stairs on a run, pausing briefly on the landing to stare up at the Rembrandt hanging there.

"That's the baron's favorite painting," Sigmund called.

"Then sell it."

Sigmund watched from the bottom of the stairs, his fingers curled around the key in his pocket. *Sell it?* he mused. *Not until I have some copies made.*

Above him, Aaron rummaged around in Ingrid's room, banging drawers and stomping across the carpets. At the commotion, Albert Klee bulldozed through the kitchen door, his gaze menacing as he looked up the stairs.

"Aaron Gregory," Sigmund said. "The American. I'm leaving, Albert. Keep Aaron out of the studio and away from the vaults. He's not to take a thing from the premises."

Albert's hawk eyes turned on Sigmund, loathing in his gaze. But nothing that belonged to the baron would leave the mansion. That, Sigmund was sure of.

☙❧

Aboard the international flight to Zurich, Robyn felt Miriam stir in the seat beside her. In the dim reflection of the reading light, her mother looked weary, restless, her head pressed against the tiny pillow. Her hair was soft and loose, the way she wore it after a shower, her subtle touch of makeup washed clean. In that moment, Miriam seemed vulnerable, exposed.

The thought of her mother being anything but self-assured startled Robyn. She wanted to look away, to pretend that she hadn't caught her in that unguarded moment, but Miriam turned and smiled at her. "Do I look that bad?" she asked.

"No, just a little pensive and a bit rumpled."

Miriam adjusted her black pearl earring and fluffed her hair. "And do I look a bit worried about flying? I am, you know."

"I'm surprised you slept at all."

"It helps me forget we're skimming fleece-lined clouds."

The man behind them shifted and shoved his knees into the back of their seats. He would snore again any minute.

"It's more like a drugged sleep with that man's jowls flapping behind me."

Robyn smothered a chuckle. "He'll be rested when he arrives."

"We won't. I'm going to sleep for hours once we get to Zurich."

"Impossible. When you and Ingrid get together, you talk."

"It may not be the same this time." She glanced at the book in Robyn's lap. "Sweetheart, what are you reading?"

"Heidi."

"Darling, that's a child's book."

"I know, but I'm enjoying it." She closed the cover, keeping one finger in place. "It's a nice story. Sweet in a sad little way."

In the semidarkness Miriam's eyes seemed a deeper brown, her voice sad as she said, "You and your father were always going to climb Heidi's Alps together. Do you remember that?"

Robyn's thoughts tumbled over her words and muffled them. "Were we? I guess it just didn't work out"

Miriam's hand pressed gently over Robyn's. "It seemed so far away then, so impossible. But your father meant to keep his promise. I'm sure of that."

Miriam retreated, her fingers no longer resting on Robyn's hand. "You need to get some sleep," she whispered. "We both do."

She closed her eyes and tried to doze again, her head drifting toward Robyn's shoulder. Robyn opened the book, but the words blurred. Miriam rarely spoke of Drew and here—only moments ago—she had spoken of him kindly.

An unexpected rumble came from the belly of the plane, a sudden jolt as they hit an air pocket. Miriam's eyes flew wide. She struggled to wiggle life back into her flight-weary body. "What happened, Robyn?"

"The pilot didn't say. I don't like the turbulence either."

"Small comfort. I think I'll just keep watch with you."

"Another four hours and we'll be there."

"If we make it, I'll never want to leave again."

"Are you up to staying near Ingrid?"

"I hate confrontation. Maybe we'll find her gone."

"Mom, when will you tell me what's really going on?"

"Let me work it out first. I don't want to worry you."

"I'm already worried."

"Me, too. Ingrid and I have been friends for years. I can't imagine her deliberately sending me fraudulent paintings."

"Someone did."

"When we get there, she'll be able to explain."

"Sure, Mother. She always has an answer for everything."

Tiny worry lines popped out around Miriam's eyes as though she had purposely arranged them with an eyebrow pencil. "I wish you liked her better. Aaron does. At least he keeps defending her."

"Why did Uncle Aaron fly to Zurich ahead of us?"

"That's one of the things I intend to find out. He wanted to pave the way for our arrival—whatever that means. He tells me he wants to protect me, and then he goes off without us."

"Protect you from what?"

"From art fraud. Can you imagine, Robyn? Me, guilty of fraud."

"We'll get to the bottom of it."

"I hope so—and soon. Right now I have this eerie feeling that someone may have boarded this plane—just because we did."

Robyn reached out and squeezed her mother's icy fingers. "Whatever do you mean?"

"If the government believes that I am deliberately deceiving my customers with fraudulent paintings—as Aaron suggests—then why would they allow me to fly to Switzerland on holiday? Someone must surely be watching us."

There was another rumble in the belly of the plane, the sensation of dropping altitude, of slipping into the clouds. Outside the window, the turbojet engine whirred and churned, a tiny red navigation light blinking on the wing tip. Beyond that, utter darkness.

Miriam tensed. "I hope they serviced this jet before we took off."

"We'll make it!"

"Floy Belmont thinks flying puts you closer to heaven. All I can think about is terra firma."

Robyn leaned closer. "Mom, what made you so afraid of flying?"

"Your father," she said unexpectedly. "Actually, on our first date, he took me up in a small Cessna. I'm still not sure if the butterflies in my stomach were from being so close to your father or so far from the ground." Her voice was light, her gaze far away. "Every time I had to say good-bye to him at the airport, that same sinking feeling engulfed me. Sometimes I'd stand there clutching your hand—so afraid his plane would crash and he'd never come back."

Gently, Robyn said, "And then he went away for good. Now you don't have to worry about him crashing."

Miriam wiped her eyes as though she were trying to blot out a painful memory. "I sent him away, Robyn."

"You asked him to leave?"

"Yes, or to get a job and settle down at home. He couldn't do it. He always had the stars and stripes tattooed on his heart. Patriot. The government has been his whole life. Did you know he joined the Army when he was fifteen—almost sixteen? His mother lied and signed for him. They did that back then."

"Why would Gramma do something so stupid?"

"Your dad didn't get along with his stepfather. I guess your gramma thought it best for everyone to let him go into the Army."

Miriam folded her hands in her lap. "Promise me, Robyn, that you won't look for your father in Europe."

"Don't ask me to promise you that. Maybe he could help us. He's working at the embassy in London right now."

"Who told you that?"

"The Prescotts. Andrea and Sherm."

"That young couple who visited our gallery? They have it all wrong, Robyn. He works for—" She stopped herself. "He's always worked for the government, but not the embassy."

"The Prescotts know him, Mother. They're friends."

Her mother visibly withdrew. "Friends of your father! So that's why they came to the gallery. To check us out. Aaron is right after all. Your father may be involved in this whole mess. Oh, Robyn, making friends with the Prescotts. How could you?"

"Andrea used to work in Beverly Hills. They were browsing when they saw your name—"

"You believe that? The gallery has been under surveillance for months. We have no idea who this Sherman Prescott really is."

"He works for a worldwide investment company."

"He would—knowing your father. Everything your father ever did was worldwide, government stamped all over it. Thank goodness, the

Prescotts didn't linger in the shop."

But we lingered over a meal, Robyn thought bitterly. *And I bared my soul to them.*

Miriam was adamant. "Don't do anything foolish, not where your father is concerned. I don't want you hurt again."

Miriam faced the window and stared out at the pitch blackness, dreading, Robyn was certain, the dawn that was only an hour away.

"Mother, let's not let my father come between us."

Miriam reached back blindly and patted Robyn's hand. "We won't. We'll never do that. Now get some sleep."

Robyn turned out the reading light and closed her eyes, fighting tears. He was already a wedge between them. Surely Miriam was wrong. Or was someone on board watching them? Had she walked blindly into a trap? A fax was on the way to the Prescotts, asking them to contact her father—a betrayal her mother might never forgive.

Seven

Sigmund felt the ski cable sway as it took the slow, squeaky climb toward the craggy mountaintop. The pristine beauty of Switzerland with its snow-frosted Alps surrounded him. Far below the deep snowfields, the lower valley was still engulfed in the early signs of autumn. Sigmund's attention riveted on the lone occupant in the chairlift ahead—a man sixty or more with his gloved hands taut on his upright ski poles. He felt confident that this was Ingrid von Tonner's dining companion, the stranger from the Schweizerhof.

As his own chair swung in the brisk air, he wondered about Smith's wife. Was Monique Dupree living in the Smiths' apartment in Paris, playing the role of the grieving widow? Or was she waiting expectantly for Harland's return?

Surely Smith knew—he could read the news clippings—that his wife had not gone home to the farm at Isigny. The social column of a popular woman's magazine described the lovely Monique Dupree Smith attending the opera, stunning in one of the latest fashions, her first outing since the tragic death of her husband. The article described her glittering diamond brooch and elegant gown. When the camera flashed, it had caught her soft, restrained smile. A false image, Sigmund wondered, or a true expression of grief?

As he had looked at the accompanying photograph, he wasn't certain which was the most magnificent—the neo-Baroque opera house or the glamorous Mrs. Smith. Nor which was more dazzling—the lavish ornate interior of the building or the charming widow making her way up the wide stairs on the arm of an attentive escort under the hand-painted Marc Chagall ceiling. *Why,* Sigmund asked himself, *would a woman of such beauty marry a man twice her age?*

As the chairlift reached the top, Harland Smith stepped off—tall, proud, comfortable in his surroundings and unhurried as he surveyed the slopes. Strands of silver hair whipped against his ear muffs. He gripped both poles, his skis gliding back and forth in position over a patch of frozen snow.

Sigmund swung from the lift and felt the crisp mountain air chafe his cheeks. Sun glinted off the summit, drenching the slopes with its brilliance. Dozens of skiers formed a rainbow of colors as they sped toward the bottom. Watching them, Sigmund savored his solitary moment, the exhilaration of looking down from the mountain heights.

As he edged closer to Smith, Harland pushed off—an agile, powerful skier carving a graceful pattern down the hill. His Volkl skis sent splintery flurries of snow in every direction. The silver runners caught the reflection of the sun, momentarily blinding Sigmund. Seconds later, he adjusted his own goggles. He crouched into his tuck and pointed his skis downhill—traversing the slope with his upper torso in a chest-to-knee position that cut the wind resistance. His speed was breathtaking as his new pair of Authiers cut fresh tracks down the mountain behind the older man.

At the bottom of the run, he slid to a stop beside Smith, who stood resting for a moment, his Volkl upright in his hand. "Good job, Mr. Smith," he said. "You ski well."

The man's coal-black eyes restricted. "I believe you've made a mistake. My name is not Smith—"

"No mistake, sir. I know who you are."

"And you are—?"

"My name's Sigmund Valdemar. Are you going back up the hill?"

Smith shaded his eyes with his gloved hands and looked toward the cliffs. He was a big man—his face ruddy from the frosty wind, his goatee so stiff that it looked like unsoaked paintbrushes. He stomped clumps of snow from his boots, his self-composure returning slowly as he stared back at Sigmund.

"No more runs today," he said. "The snow's getting too wet. I'll go up early in the morning when the powder is fresh."

"So you like to make the first tracks down?"

Smith glanced at the younger skiers around them. "Yes, before these kids take over. It's my mountain then."

"I understand the feeling, sir." Once more, they riveted their gaze on the majestic peak, each possessing it in his own way. An early afternoon sun splashed a glimmering pink across the snowfields making it look like a mountain on fire.

"I've been an Alpiner all my life, Mr. Smith. I guess I cut my teeth on the slopes. Chamonix. Albertville. Grenoble. Zermatt. St. Moritz. Innsbruck." He checked them off with pride. "I've tried them all. And you, sir?"

Smith answered in French, his words hinting at his Brooklyn heritage. "I learned to ski in upstate New York. I was a rowdy kid in need of something to challenge me, something bigger than myself."

"It paid off. You handle yourself well."

"Yes," he agreed. "I spent a lot of time at Lake Placid and Calgary. When I moved to Europe, mastering the Alps became my first concern—before I met my wife, that is."

He made a move toward leaving and then said, "So you're Sigmund Valdemar. You must be that friend of Baroness von Tonner's?"

"You might say that."

"The Rembrandt forger, I hear! She speaks well of you."

"Not to my face. I am an art copyist, not a thief, sir. I simply emulate the work of Rembrandt. I've studied him for years."

The black eyes lit with interest. "An artist then? Did Mrs. von Tonner send you to me, Mr. Valdemar?"

"No," Sigmund answered honestly. "Quite the opposite. I came to offer you the von Tonner art collection."

He laughed heartily. "Hardly at her invitation?"

"No, but for a price."

"It seems unlikely that Frau von Tonner is selling, not with the baron still alive."

"That's what I wanted to discuss with you."

"Then we'll find ourselves a place in the lodge and talk."

"That will be crowded with every seat occupied."

"All the better," Smith assured him. "We'll merge with the crowd. That will draw less attention. I'm registered here as Smythe Williams. Do me the courtesy of remembering that."

Shouldering his skis, he led the way to the lodge. Inside, he dumped his parka and gloves by a chair and eased down, totally untroubled. He adjusted the neck of his knit sweater, stretched his booted feet toward the fireplace, and closed his eyes. When he opened them again, he smiled at Sigmund. "So you have a plan, Mr. Valdemar? A scheme perhaps?"

"A proposition, sir. Advantageous to both of us."

Harland formed a teepee with his hands, his fingertips touching, his cold black eyes fixed on Sigmund. Sigmund's gaze strayed briefly to Smith's crooked left thumb.

"Tell me about yourself, young man. I'm curious. Why didn't you pursue your own artistry? Why copy the old masters? The world has had ample Mona Lisa reproductions. Perhaps too many Rembrandts as well. Why waste so many hours when laser reproductions are quicker and more accurate—their fakery so difficult to detect?"

Sigmund found himself intrigued by Smith's directness. "I don't have access to that equipment. Besides, I'm a painter. In my younger days I did art restorations for museums. Actually my mother was a gifted artist, so I learned from her."

"But why did you choose Rembrandt?"

"Why not? The von Tonner collection specializes in the Dutch masters. I studied Rembrandt's style under my mother's tutelage and learned to make copies of his work just to perfect my own skills."

"Ah! The art of the forger from boyhood. So you became a modern day Henri Van Meegeren?"

Sigmund resented the comparison to the Vermeer copyist. He controlled his irritation, his thoughts on the Vermeer painting in the studio—the one he would copy with great skill. "Van Meegeren was a mad man. He had difficulty distinguishing between admiration for the artist's work and identifying with him. I know the difference between Rembrandt and myself."

"Several centuries," Harland mocked.

"Time, yes, but even Rembrandt imitated the works of others and painted for a meal ticket. Scholars credit him with hundreds of paintings and drawings. He's an easy one to discover again."

"So he's easy to copy?"

"His field was wide open—he did everything from landscapes to portraits, from nudes to religiously inspired works. He kept few records about his art. Yes, he's a safe man to emulate. Safe to discover again," he repeated.

"And Renoir?"

"I've done some French Impressionist paintings, too, but I consider myself a Rembrandt specialist. So far, they've paid better."

"So you're the son of an artist,. but what about your father?"

At the thought of his father, Sigmund hesitated, then said, "My father was a hotelier. When I was a boy, we moved from one great hotel to another. It offered a marvelous opportunity to meet artists. My father's position allowed us to have a more cosmopolitan life than most Communists. We spent our vacations in Eastern Germany. I never questioned why we went freely through the Brandenburg Gate or crossed the Glienicke Bridge without being stopped."

"So you grew up as one of the privileged few?"

He heard resentment in Smith's voice. "Yes, until I was fifteen. Then we moved back to the east side of the barbed wire, where my father was welcomed back as a hero."

"An unusual honor for a hotelier."

"My father was an unusual man."

Sigmund glanced at the sunburned skier beside them. Scuff marks blotched the young man's face from a head-on encounter with the slopes. He was taking his teasing good-naturedly, toasting the runs of the day, hardly interested in the men beside him.

Smith interrupted his thought. "Mr. Valdemar, you wanted to sell me something—the fake von Tonner collection or the original?"

Sigmund leaned closer. "Both. Frau von Tonner sold fake paintings through galleries in several countries. If she ends up with a prison sentence, the genuine collection would be confiscated."

"Isn't it safely hidden in her underground bunker? Or did the baron lower it into some Austrian lake?"

"It's in a vault. I've seen the collection, sir, and it is vast. On the open market, it will bring an outrageous price."

"In deutsche marks or dollars? Or just the best price?" Harland reconstructed his fingertip teepee, his deformed thumb more evident this time "Are you suggesting that I buy a collection that's about to be confiscated by several governments? What kind of a fool do you take me for, Valdemar?"

"You're a smart businessman, Mr. Smith. You have worldwide contacts. Possibly you are still trading arms for money."

Harland remained stoic, but the ebony blackness of his eyes changed—brightening one moment, overshadowing with anger the next. "My business is in Paris," he said.

"*Was* in Paris. You've been shut down there. The Plastec Corporation no longer exists on the Champs-Elysees. Surely you know that. Your assembly line is dead—there are no more medical parts or computer chips or any other supplies for that matter."

"What else do you know about Paris?"

He considered answering, *"Your wife is beautiful and far too young for you."* Instead he said, "Your wife and children are there, your oldest boy in a private school. Their lifestyle is unchanged with no expenses curtailed in your absence. They are doing very well without you, sir."

There was a flicker of sadness in Harland's face. "You're right, Mr. Valdemar. My wife's finances are quite intact—and will be for years to come. She promised if anything ever happened, she would wait for me at least a full year."

Veiled in black, Sigmund wondered. *Out of respect or love?* "But she won't wait forever for a dead man to return."

"I think not. That's why I cannot risk dabbling in art treasures at this time. I have another matter to tend to first."

"Couldn't you do both? Dealing in art would be much safer than the sale of weapons. We could sell the von Tonner paintings immediately to buyers in Japan or Australia, They'd pay well."

"Is it money you want from me, Mr. Valdemar?"

"I figure your assets might be tied up in the banking system—since your plane crashed. If so, we both need money."

Smith sat in pensive contemplation. The Alpiner with the scuffed nose stole a glance Smith's way. His sudden interest silenced Sigmund. Then the young man's ski mentality took over again, and he resumed talking about powder and slopes, speed and Olympic heroes. He lined himself up with the "down-hillers" of the past: Jean-Claude Killy and

Pirmin Zurbriggen, boasting of himself as one worthy of the gold. His companions snatched away his Alpine dreams with uproarious laughter.

Valdemar touched Smith's arm. "Are you listening, sir? The sale of any of those paintings means ready cash for both of us. My friends and I could take the collection out of the mansion in the next few days while Ingrid is in Zurich and hide it elsewhere. In your private chalet perhaps?"

"Robbery," Smith mused. "Have you considered the risks?"

"Yes. We'd have to leave the caretakers in the vault."

"Dead, I presume? And what do you and your friends expect in exchange for my marketing expertise?"

"A million or two for myself. And weapons for my friends."

"Weapons? Give me time to think about it."

"We're short of time. Once Miriam Gregory arrives, Ingrid's world will fall apart. We need to get the paintings out of the mansion before that. And sell them."

"You're too reckless, Valdemar. Too impatient. The baroness is in trouble. We both know that several countries want that collection. Yet you propose walking right in and stealing the von Tonner art treasures. Do you think you would go in and out of the mansion unnoticed?"

"Time is still against us."

"Then I will work it out without you, Mr. Valdemar."

"Time is against your trying to do it by yourself. The Klees would die before they'd let you take anything from the mansion."

"Then let them die as you suggested. What other obstacles exist?"

"Concrete and a three-ton steel door. Try blowing that up, and you'd have the whole community there with the first blast…besides destroying the paintings."

Smith stroked his goatee. "So we need each other to break into the underground system? Who authorized its construction?"

"Felix von Tonner, as far as I know. Possibly as early as the 1930s or toward the end of World War II. Maybe long before."

Smith thought a moment. "Valdemar, if the entry to the bunker is through the mansion, then there must be an exit somewhere else. They'd never build a blind coffer."

Sigmund hesitated. "There's a trap door through the stables."

"That's too close to the property. The tunnel systems are usually more detailed. They are built with escape in mind. An exit exists beyond that trap door, perhaps in the wooded area beyond the mansion." He lapsed into deep thought and then smiled. "What was the name of that village in East Germany where Erich Koch's art loot was buried?"

Sigmund knew, but he didn't say.

"The systems may be similar. You have an eye to valuable collections, Valdemar, but the wrong approach. We must take the collection without going through the mansion, without arousing suspicion. If things do not go well for Frau von Tonner, we can seal off the inside entry with a concrete or stone facing."

"We'd have to seal off the trap door in the stables, too."

"Yes, with a concrete flooring. In time—when we locate the other exit—I could use that whole bunker system to store weapons. But it's too soon," Smith decided. "I have other priorities."

Sigmund controlled his disappointment. "You're not worrying about Zurich? Drew Gregory will never show up. He's not interested in his ex-wife."

"He won't stand back and let something happen to his daughter."

Sigmund sensed a new urgency. "If I went to Paris and brought your family safely to Zurich, would you reconsider my plan?"

"About selling the von Tonner treasures?"

"Yes, there's no profit in destroying the Gregorys."

"But there will be great satisfaction for me."

"More than in seeing your family again? Why make your wife wait any longer for a dead man to return?"

"My wife is no doubt being monitored constantly."

"Let me worry about that."

The chairs around them were empty now, the Olympic dreamer and his friends off for an early dinner and a night of dancing. Smith stood and stretched his bulky frame, smiling unexpectedly. "Tell me, Valdemar, has Ingrid catalogued all the paintings?"

"I doubt it. There are several concrete containers not even opened yet. I tell you, the collection is vast."

"For now, we'll work with Mrs. von Tonner as long as she is useful to us. We need her to coax Miss Gregory to the mansion."

"What for?"

"Fraulein Gregory has studied art history. She will know which paintings to sell first. And she will be more than willing to help us sell the paintings to protect her parents."

"Even the father she barely knows?"

"He's still her father. She'd protect him."

"Ingrid will never help you kidnap her. But I have friends who can be persuaded to get Miss Gregory to the mansion."

"Good." Smith smiled again. "When we leave the Klees in the vault, we can leave Fraulein Gregory and her father there with them."

"Dead, I presume?" Sigmund asked, mocking him. "Should I remove some of the paintings to your chalet just to be safe?"

"Only a few of the choice selections."

"But auctioning them through Sotheby's or Christie's is out."

"Just leave that to me. There's a newer auction house, very reputable. Altman and Pierson work out of London with a small branch office in Zurich. One of the junior partners was an art dealer in the past with fine contacts, a man very anxious to maintain his new role. We may be able to work through him."

"And if that fails?" Sigmund asked.

"Then I will reconsider your proposition, Mr. Valdemar."

"It may be too late then."

"I'll think of a way."

To exclude me, Sigmund decided.

Eight

Pierre Courtland strolled down the Bahnhofstrasse in Zurich at a relaxed pace, cheerfully whistling "Lili Marlene." He had switched over easily to the unhurried timetable reserved for holiday living, gladly dropping the feverish, maddening schedule of his workaday world in Geneva.

As he ambled along, the scent of linden trees still filled the air. He admired this city steeped in history and banking, yet he loved the picturesque setting best—plaza squares with fountains and bronzed statues, window boxes with red and white geraniums. Distant snow-capped mountains and the River Limmat, wending its way toward the lake, added to Zurich's natural beauty.

Off the main street, winding alleys fanned out in spidery patterns that led to quiet cafés or trendy clubs. The clubs, overrun with carefree youth, reminded Pierre of himself a few years ago. And there were steps, plenty of steps. His legs ached from the climbs, but in a day or two he'd be in good shape again, the charley horses gone.

He delighted in unwinding from the long year's grind. After ten years at the surgical supply company, he still considered it a splendid job with an enviable salary. Working his way up from selling precision instruments to a permanent spot on executive row added to his satisfaction. At thirty-two, he'd made the move to the top in good time, even with that year off for a study program at Schaffhausen.

Since leaving Geneva yesterday, each time business thoughts surfaced, he had pushed them from his mind, determined to stay totally absorbed in vacationing. But seedling concerns for Felix von Tonner prodded him again, refusing to be squelched.

The baron was his friend, an old family loyalty that dated back three generations. Pierre's grandfather Hans grew up with Felix. As adults, they solved the world's problems from cushioned armchairs—

the baron with a pipe in his mouth and Hans lecturing on the evils of smoking. In later years, when Pierre's own father died, the baron stood by him, a tough assignment at best after losing a man as great as Johann Courtland. Under Felix's strong influence, Pierre moved to Switzerland and took the job in Geneva.

Then Ingrid von Tonner came into the baron's life, putting a wedge between the two men. Pierre's utter dislike for the woman hadn't helped. By the time he slid back into Felix's good graces, Ingrid had raked in a hefty portion of all the baron owned. But there was one guardianship account that Pierre still managed.

Pierre took a left at the Rennweg, leaving the bustling Bahnhofstrasse for the quieter quayside of the River Limmat. The Grossmunster Cathedral and St. Peters-Kirche dominated the city, perfect landmarks no matter where Pierre stood. They loomed above the timeworn buildings on either side of the Limmatquai.

When he reached the lake, Pierre rested on a bench, soaking up the sun. Swooping birds and screaming kids bade for his attention. He ignored them, indulging himself in the solitary pleasure of watching the boats cut through the water.

The tiny undulating motions on the surface of the lake sent a rippling effect across his mood. Zurich was not his first choice of a vacation spot. Usually he drove to Madrid or Seville or caught a few weeks on the Italian Riviera. Last year he flew to Norway to visit friends he'd met at the United Nations in Geneva. The political, multilateral diplomacy carried on at the Palais des Nations bored him, but it offered a striking view of the city and Mont Blanc. The pretty young woman standing near him that day hadn't hurt the scenery either, but her charm died somewhere between Geneva and Norway.

The older he got—thirty-two was a perfect age for marriage he reassured himself—the more he disliked taking his meals alone and waking up each morning to an empty room. He wanted a girl he could pamper and appreciate on a permanent basis. Someone to dream dreams and set goals with, a person who would believe in him. Someone to love—the word almost scared him. Pierre needed strokes—a wife to laugh at his humor, share his faith, enjoy music, and the out-of-doors the way he did. Maybe even bear his children. He ran from these ideas at thirty-one, but now he hated the thought of ending up like the baron with no one glad that he existed.

Pierre rested his eyes from the glare of sun against water. His mental meanderings turned to a tiny bird that had swooped down onto the bench beside him. It perched on its clawed toes and cocked its sharp beak toward Pierre.

"I was here first," Pierre said.

The round, beady eyes stared back.

"Sorry," Pierre said amiably. "I've no food for you."

Its blue-gray wings fluttered. The bird took flight, like the baron would do soon, never to come back. It curved a pattern over the water's edge, veering dangerously close to the snowy-white feathers of a swan preening herself there.

The swan glided away, its slender neck held high as she skimmed across the lake—proud and graceful like Ingrid von Tonner glissading through life, touching others with her beauty. Why, then, did he despise the baroness so? Had coming here to challenge Ingrid's schemes been a mistake? Even if he salvaged the rest of the von Tonner collection, what good would it do Felix?

Sometimes, he felt convinced that he was the baron's only friend. But nothing jogged the baron's memory anymore, not even Pierre's visits or the wheelchair rides around the clinic grounds. Twice a month, Pierre flew there. Twice a month he came away, chiding himself for being too involved in the old man's life.

When he heard rumors that the von Tonner collection had resurfaced, Pierre remembered the tunnels of his boyhood, the room with ancient paintings and the baron forbidding him to go there again. Felix's prattlings stirred new questions. Had Pierre stumbled on the art collection of the century? Had Felix really hidden the paintings out of fear—not even trusting Hans or Johann Courtland with his secret? Pierre had scoured art catalogues and exhibits, browsed at auction houses and in museums to study the Dutch masters circulating there. None bore the von Tonner label. He searched through library archives looking for a listing of the von Tonner collection. None existed.

Finally, he had called on Kurt Brinkmeirer, his uncle at Interpol. Kurt, a man in his late fifties, admitted that paintings credited to the baron's collection had made it to the marketplace with record-breaking returns. Some originals. Some forgeries.

Kurt had taken the unlit cigarette from the corner of his mouth and had tossed it in the waste container. "Nasty habit," he muttered.

"Your smoking or the frauds, Kurt?"

"The frauds. Copies of the von Tonner paintings—ones supposedly lost—are still being marketed worldwide. That netted Interpol's renewed interest. Baroness von Tonner may be in over her head this time."

"Well, if Interpol doesn't stop her, I will. I won't let her sell any more of the baron's property."

His uncle arched one straggly brow, his square face stern. "Leave that to Interpol, Pierre. You stick to your precision instruments. Otherwise, you'll both be under surveillance."

Reluctantly, Pierre agreed. Then on his last visit with the baron, he changed his mind. He found Felix slumped in a wheelchair, rumpled and smelling of urine. He was banging his hands wildly on the arms of the chair.

Pierre touched the old man's shoulder. "Hi, friend," he said. "What are you doing?"

The glint in Felix's eyes startled Pierre. The fingers kept thumping. "I'm pounding the nails in my coffin. I have to. The Sûreté are looking for my paintings," he mumbled. "Hide them for me. Keep them from the baroness." One frail, flawed hand gripped Pierre's. "Rescue one of the paintings for me, boy."

The French police? Here at the clinic? Or the Germans? Pierre wondered. In spite of his confusion, the old man seemed convinced that Ingrid was selling his whole collection— piece by piece to a greedy art world that would lap them up and cry for more.

He sat beside the baron, patting the old man's thin hand. The whole concept was ludicrous. Unreasonable. Some demented, cockamamie story for the Sûreté to pursue. Words kept bombarding Pierre: *moronic, unthinkable.* Felix's hand trembled beneath his.

"Felix, didn't your family lose those paintings in the war?"

The hoary head turned slowly side to side.

"Did Goering steal them back in the forties?"

A single tear tracked its way down the whiskery cheek. Pierre brushed it away, pained at the baron's ancient wrinkled face—the sagging skin; the watery, red-rimmed eyelids; the dry purplish lips starved for oxygen. Pierre's denial of old age and art fraud sought escape in a prayer. He always prayed before leaving Felix, meaningless words to the baron, but a mustard-seed effort for himself. This time he prayed silently, *Dear God, help Felix. Dear God...*

Mid-prayer, he paused, totally shocked. *Dear God, the old man's telling me the truth. The collection is still in the tunnels.*

"Are you saying the art collection was never lost, Felix?"

Another solo tear brimmed at the eyelid, another tremulous nod of the head. Pierre tightened his grip on the baron's hand to keep it from shaking. He would not ask—feared asking—which side of the war Felix had served on. It no longer mattered. But he did whisper, "Why did you hide the paintings? Why Felix?"

The eyes blinked, the reason trapped in his memory. "Stop Ingrid," he pleaded. "She must be stopped."

The conniving, catlike baroness? She'd already wrung the baron dry. For the sake of an old family friend on a steady course downhill, Pierre determined to block the sales, at least until the baron died. "I'll do my best, Felix," he promised. "But you have to tell me where the paintings are hidden."

"In Goering's tunnel," Felix mumbled. "Or Bormann's—"

Felix had lived with the rumors so long that he was repeating them now, his words and his mind both wandering. Pierre squeezed his hand again. "Never mind, Baron. I already know. Rest now."

The hoary head bobbed. Within seconds, the hand went limp beneath Pierre's as the old man dozed. Pierre slipped out of the room, stopping for a moment at the nurse's station. "I'll be on vacation for the next several weeks," he said. "I'll call back with my holiday numbers in case of an emergency."

"You're so good to your friend," she said. "He'll miss you while you're gone. Baron von Tonner is not doing well. The police were here, insisting he knew where some famous paintings were hidden. The poor baron, in his condition— being harassed like that."

Pierre glanced toward the baron's room. "Perhaps a doctor's order would prevent them from disturbing him again?"

"Oh, I hope so. I'll ask the doctor. I'll tell him you requested it, Mr. Courtland."

"Tell him I demanded it."

"I'll do that. Will you holiday in Spain again this year?"

"No in Zurich—at the Schweizerhof."

A breeze cut in across the lake, bringing a chill with it. Pierre got up from the bench, cast a glance at the dock at St. Peter's, and headed back to the Hotel Schweizerhof. On arrival, the concierge at the reception desk smiled warmly. "I've located Frau von Tonner for you," he said. "She's booked at the Alpenhof."

"Good. Can you get me a room there?"

The smile faded. "That's most unusual, Herr Courtland. You're settled here. Your accommodations, they're not—"

"Excellent. But I'll need to transfer to the Alpenhof."

"But Herr Courtland—"

"My room here looks out on one of the busiest squares in Zurich. I need peace on this vacation—not trolleys whizzing by."

The manager scanned his registry. "We can change rooms."

"No, I must change hotels." He thrust a substantial tip across the counter.

The concierge cupped the money in his hand and slipped it into his pocket. He made the necessary adjustments and politely offered to hold Pierre's luggage until his room at the Alpenhof was ready.

"That won't be necessary. I'll just take it with me."

By the time he came back to the desk with his suitcase packed, the manager had already rented his room and was in good spirits. He even remembered to give Pierre a message from Kurt. Pierre tore it open and laughed. Uncle Kurt would fly in from Paris to join him in a few days.

Stay away from the baroness, the message warned.

Pierre jotted an answer and left it with the concierge. The man nodded, smiling more now. He snapped his fingers for a bellhop, amiably sending Pierre on his way to the smaller hotel. A flood of Swiss

German—"Come back someday when you can stay with us"—and Pierre was gone.

He reached the Alpenhof by taxi just as Ingrid stepped through the wide carved doors, two uniformed bellmen gushing over her. Pierre hopped out of the cab and held the door open.

"*Guten Morgen,* Baroness," he said, cheerfully lifting her hand and brushing it with a kiss.

"What are you doing here, Pierre?" she snapped. "I'm on holiday."

"You never come to Zurich for holiday."

"I did this time. And you always stay at the Schweizerhof."

"In other cities, yes."

He glanced at the hotel. The Alpenhof offered an unhindered view of the lake that was within walking distance from the hotel. It was an attractive chalet-styled building with red-shuttered windows. A wide porch ran down both sides of the hotel and cut across the back of the building. Flowers were everywhere. A bright striped canopy snapped above the entryway, its colors blending with the Swiss flag beside it. "You've made a fine choice," he said.

"A friend booked me here."

"So you're not alone."

"I'm rarely alone, Pierre."

"I wish I could say as much for Felix."

The taxi driver thumped his fingers against the steering wheel to the beat of the song on his radio. As the music crescendoed, he flagged the meter.

"So you're still visiting Felix?" Her dark eyes flashed as she slipped into the back seat. "When do you find time?"

"Someone has to."

"I'm in a hurry, Pierre. I'm meeting friends at the airport."

"You're not leaving?" The surprise was his this time.

She leaned across and patted his face. "Don't worry, darling. I'll be back. And you be prepared to tell me how you found me. Now be a good boy and let me be on my way. The meter is running."

He nodded, stepped back, and slammed the door.

Well, Baron, we surprised her this time. She wasn't expecting me. The thought delighted Pierre.

As the taxi disappeared, he picked up his luggage. He entered the Alpenhof whistling "Lili Marlene" again, the German lyric the baron had taught him as a boy, a song that Ingrid hated.

~

Miriam and Robyn deplaned at the end of a straggly line of weary travelers. They came through the, gate, weighed down with cosmetic cases and raincoats, their steps more brisk than Ingrid expected as they headed toward the custom's checkpoint.

She watched them from a glassed-in walkway. Except for the dark crescents beneath her eyes, Miriam looked self-controlled and disarming, much as she had looked that first day at Radcliffe.

Ingrid felt a touch of remorse. For only a moment, she allowed herself to admit the betrayal of a friendship. A costly betrayal. They'd been friends so long—too many years to count. And now too many problems to think about. She feared predicting what might happen once Harland Smith arrived in Zurich.

Robyn looked plain and whitewashed beside her mother; yet she was pretty in her own way. Her bright auburn hair was casual and windblown, her complexion soft and delicate like Miriam's.

As they neared the baggage turnstile, the luggage clunked around in dizzying monotony. Ingrid recognized the passenger with the scruffy beard standing beside them. So he had caught the same plane after all! He cut in front of the Gregorys and hoisted his luggage on the counter for inspection. He glanced back at Miriam, scowling irritably at her. Then he looked up at Ingrid, half-smiling.

I told you to make yourself inconspicuous, she thought angrily. *Your job is over. I'll be watching them now.* He would be calling soon enough, wanting money for his efforts.

The Gregorys took no notice of her; they made no effort to look up and wave. Their seeming disinterest in her presence worried Ingrid. Whenever they met—and they had done so many times since Radcliffe days—it was always an exuberant meeting. Ingrid, bubbling and gushing. Miriam reserved, eyes sparkling. But Robyn sulking and distrustful of Ingrid's intrusion into their lives. Or was she embarrassed by Ingrid's flutter and flurry, her royal entry bedecked with jewels and Dior finery?

Forty minutes later, Ingrid faced Miriam. "My dear friend," she said, hugging Miriam and glancing over her shoulder toward Robyn. "You were practically the last ones off the plane. I was getting worried, wondering whether you were on board."

Robyn's gaze seemed to say, *"I bet."* She tolerated Ingrid's brief embrace. Ingrid made no attempt to brush that smooth cheek with a kiss. One went cautiously with Robyn. "Come, my dears, you must be exhausted."

"We are tired," Miriam said. "Thanks to that irritable little man. He just spent the last thirty minutes arguing with the customs' official, to say nothing of annoying us on the plane."

He was dragging down the corridor just ahead of them, his suitcases banging against his bulging hips. He stood a stocky five-nine, a tiny ring of gray hair fringing his baldness, his striped suit a wrinkled, rumpled mess.

"So what did he do?" Ingrid asked. "Talk the whole flight?"

"Not exactly. He snored all the way in a static rumble."

"He did nothing but sleep?" she asked.

"I don't trust him. He boarded the plane at the last minute."

"Oh, Miriam, someone had to board last."

"And sit behind us? They shuffled passengers so he could do so. When I asked for different seats, they refused."

"Mother," Robyn said calmly, "switching around kept one family together. Mr. Chubby was traveling alone. If he was there to watch us, he slept on the job. Once we both get a good eight hours of sleep, we'll feel better, too."

"On the plane to watch you? What on earth for?" Ingrid asked.

"I intend to find out!"

Ingrid cast a frank glance Miriam's way., The expression was controlled, her lips parted in that detached half-smile so characteristic of her; but Miriam's tone had been icy.

"Relax, Miriam," she advised. "You said you were coming for holiday. Remember? We've planned this for years."

"Not this trip. This is strictly business. I'm fighting to salvage my gallery, and nothing, absolutely nothing, will stop me."

Worriedly Ingrid said, "Our hotel is near the lake. You'll love it. Once you've checked into your rooms, you can rest."

"No, first you and I need to talk."

"We have your whole holiday to talk, my dear."

"Right now, Ingrid, I'm more concerned about the paintings."

"We have plenty of time to talk about the paintings. I have some marvelous ones to send your way. And in a day or two we can fly over to Vienna. I have a lead on some really quality works that will please your customers."

"Ingrid, surely Aaron told you what's going on. It's the three paintings that didn't please my customers that worries me. Three forgeries that you mailed to me!"

"Impossible. There's no way I could have sent you frauds. Every painting was documented. You know that, Miriam."

Miriam pulled free. "Perhaps they were easy to forge."

"You're tired, Miriam. Wait here with the luggage. I'll get the car and meet you out front in ten minutes."

When she tried hugging Miriam again, it was like putting her arms around a bronzed statue. The rebuff was infuriating, but she managed a calm, "I'll be out front in ten minutes."

As she walked away, she reconsidered. Perhaps the safest thing for her to do was flee. She made her way to the nearest phone and placed a call to Aaron Gregory at the hotel.

He answered on the fourth ring. "Did they arrive?"

"I walked right into Miriam's fury. Her anger is more than lost sleep. What's going on, Aaron? How much does she know?"

"Enough to be careful," he said. "If we can persuade her that Drew is behind all of this, it may work out."

"With that sly daughter of hers on hand?"

"That hardly describes Robbie. She's a special person. Don't forget, Ingrid, I'm fond-of both of them."

"Fond enough to go to jail for them?"

"If it comes to that, I'll consider an alternate plan."

"And do you have one in mind, Aaron?"

"Certainly. Don't you?"

"Why should I? I'm a baroness, Aaron. I have friends in high places. I don't intend to give up my name or my possessions."

He chortled. "Legally, you have nothing. A title from marriage only And an art collection that doesn't belong to you as long as the baron is alive. Think seriously about that, Baroness. Your life may depend on it."

Nine

Drew saw distrust in the old man's eyes as he opened the door. "Herr Klee? Albert Klee?" Drew asked.

He nodded politely, disdain in his expression. "I'm Klee."

His canny gaze went from Drew to Vic and back again. He seemed old to Drew, timeworn. A straight shock of thinning gray hair drooped across his temple. The skin flabs of his neck hung loose; the weather-beaten face was set in wrinkles. Something in the way he squared his shoulders, a proud stance with fire in those hawk eyes, discounted age; his bearing declared itself in defense of the mansion and perhaps of the baroness herself.

"This is the von Tonner residence, isn't it?" Drew asked.

"The baroness is not here. Nor is Herr Valdemar."

Valdemar, Drew thought. *Who in the world is Valdemar?*

Klee stepped back to shut the door.

"Wait," Vic told him, using his size ten as a doorstop. "We've driven all this way. We're friends of Baron von Tonner."

At the mention of the baron, a fragile smile repositioned the wrinkles. As quickly, it faded. "I know the baron's friends."

"We came from seeing him—two days ago," Vic insisted. "He's in a medical clinic in Cannes, south of Nice."

"You've really seen the baron?" A tremor shook Klee's voice. "How is he? Are they caring for him?"

"He seemed comfortable," Drew said. "But he—"

Vic nudged Drew. "The baron wanted us to talk to you about his art collection, Herr Klee."

Blandness returned to Albert's face. He started to push the massive double doors shut.

Vic's shoe-stop worked again. "The baron doesn't want anything to happen to his paintings."

From behind Albert, his wife, Hedwig, came to his side, her uniform stiff and starched. A high-strung, pudgy woman with pale, troubled eyes, she twisted the ends of her apron. In a waspish voice she said, "Albert, tell them we know nothing of any paintings."

"Frau Klee, we just came from Cannes—"

Hedwig glared at Vic. "Then you know that the baron is doing poorly, not eating, and barely aware of his surroundings."

"Apparently you never go to see him, Herr Klee, yet the baron asked for you. Clearly. As clearly as I am speaking now."

"He remembers me?"

Vic nodded. "I think he did. We're the same size, Herr Klee. Both thin and fair. At first the baron thought I was you. You really should visit him—and soon."

"What good does it do to tell Albert that?" Hedwig asked. "The baroness has forbidden that we visit him."

"Would she even know?" Vic asked. "She never visits him. According to the staff, he just has one regular guest."

"Sigmund Valdemar?" she asked.

"That wasn't his name. What was it, Drew? Court something."

"Courtland. Pierre Courtland."

The Klees exchanged glances. "He still visits the baron?" "Frequently, Herr Klee," Drew said. "It seems that this Courtland is the baron's only friend."

"Yes, his only friend. Now go, please. Both of you. Hedwig and I have work to do. Guests are coming."

As the large oak doors slammed behind them, Vic grinned. He ran his finger over the von Tonner coat of arms carved in the door, a crescent shield with crossed swords above it. "Impressive," he said, "but so much for seeing inside the mansion."

Drew eyed the electronic gate that lay between the house and their borrowed car. Far below the winding road, the Rhine River surged toward the sea. Here on the bluff the baron's property—all five hundred acres of it—stood like an island, an isolated fortress built to withstand any assault.

The mansion, an imposing edifice of grayish-white stone, rose three stories to the round turrets on its slate-blue roof. It offered a commanding view of the German countryside, yet maintained its privacy. Drew detected not a shadow at the windows, nor a rustle of the drapes, but the Klees were surely watching them. He felt the captivity of the place, his own obscurity, the power and greed that must go with its ownership. Vainly, he tried to disassociate Miriam and Robyn from the baroness, but the building overshadowed his fears.

Shade trees and neatly trimmed hedges hugged the high brick wall. Garden flowers brightened the grounds with clusters of reds and yellows, pinks and delicate lavender. A well-worn bridle path led along the back wall to the stables at the far end of the grounds. Beautiful things and power had always impressed Miriam. In spite of its peaceful solitude, Drew wondered if the mansion and the baroness held the secret to his family's safety.

He struck out across the open courtyard toward the gate. "Come on, Vic. We're wasting time."

"Wait. How did your wife's buyer afford a place like this?"

"She married into it."

"Then why was Porter Deven so interested?"

Drew whirled around. "In the von Tonner mansion? Or the missing art pieces? Neither one is Company business, Vic."

"That's what I told Porter. Let's look around before we leave."

"On Porter's orders?"

"My own curiosity."

"Let's not trespass. Let's just get through that gate and into the car before Albert challenges us with a rifle. That's one thing the baron seemed clear about. Old Klee is a good marksman."

Vic was not to be discouraged. He skirted the mansion on the double, raced past a man-made pond with a family of ducks skimming the surface and ran to the shelter of the trees. Drew followed reluctantly, skidding across the well-kept velvety lawn in his leather shoes and coming to an abrupt stop at the tree line.

"Good," Vic said. "Come on."

They kept in the shadow of the evergreens all the way to the elaborate stables with their well-spaced stalls and tiled roof. Outside, the upper partition of each solid wooden door was hooked back, and a gelding and a mare watched them approach. The stable yard consisted of a large fenced-in grazing area and bridle paths going out in several directions toward the woods. Vic crept around the stables and went inside the airy, well-lit building, Drew close on his heels. A magnificent chestnut stallion with a gold mane snorted as they entered. He stomped his back hoof and sniffed the air, his nostrils flaring. Vic approached cautiously. "Whoa, fellow. Easy now."

Drew went the length of the middle aisle, noting the long row of stalls on either side, five of them occupied. He walked past the feed room with the loft above it and peered into each empty stall with its automatic drinking fountain and feed bucket. In the tack room at the far end of the stables, fancy saddles were flung over the wooden horses, and expensive bridles hung from hooks on the wall, two riding crops beside them. And in the corner stood a sulky with its spiked wheels in a state of disrepair.

From here Drew had a clear view of the house, a straight line, an open view for Albert Klee to be watching them. The stallion grew agitated; his persistent whinnying stirred a restless chorus from the other horses.

Drew walked back toward the chestnut stallion, pondering the importance that Vic and Porter placed on the von Tonner property. For Miriam's sake, his curiosity sifted through the possibilities. He could come up with no answers. Art had never captivated him. It did so now only because Miriam was in trouble. If the baron had hidden an art collection somewhere here on this estate, what did it matter? Perhaps it mattered a great deal, he decided. His own growing agitation was evident when he said, "Vic, let's get out of here before this commotion brings Klee on the run. It won't help Miriam's case if we're caught here."

"It's to your wife's advantage if we can locate the von Tonner collection before Porter or Langley do."

"That's not Company business."

Vic kept his eyes on the stallion. "You're a beauty," he said. "If we could just get inside that mansion—"

"Count me out, Vic. I'll wait for you by the car."

"How do you plan on getting through the gate?"

"The same way we came in—when a delivery truck arrives."

"That could be awhile." Vic turned. "Drew, it's hard for me to believe the von Tonner collection was stolen by Goering or Bormann. Most of the art loot came out of Holland or France or from the Jewish collectors in this country. The von Tonner collection was one of the top ones, a source of German pride."

"All the more reason for Goering to want it, Vic."

"All the more reason for the baron to hide it, right here on his own property. Discovering it would advance Porter's career. Instant favor with the art world. Maybe money in his pocket."

"And not in yours."

"That's my luck. Look, Drew, I judge Klee to be seventy or seventy-five. If Albert were a Nazi, a German officer back then, maybe the baron hid the paintings from Klee all along."

"What do you want me to do? Knock on the door and ask Klee?"

As they slipped out of the stable into the shelter of the trees, Drew said, "Vic, I worked with one of those art commissions after Germany surrendered. Instead of rotating home, I volunteered to drive one of the Jewish art experts around. The major loved art as intensely as he hated the Germans. He was obsessed—dedicated to tracking the plundered art."

"Was it a successful hunt, Drew?"

"It was a fascinating one, much of it classified as top secret. Whatever was found was appraised and identified, but all too many of the rightful owners were dead. Even now, there's no telling how much of the art is still hidden in sandstone quarries or buried in labyrinthine vaults beneath the ground."

"After all these years?" Vic shaded his eyes and scanned the property. "Where do you think the baron hid his paintings?"

"I'd be more interested in *why.*"

They ran a straight course toward the tangled braided vines that spread across the back of the mansion. Vic tested his weight on one, scrambled up to the second floor, swung himself over the balcony railing, and disappeared through an open window.

The minutes dragged until Vic reappeared, gripped the vine, and descended more hastily than expected. "Whew! I made it."

"Is that the way you call on those young maidens in England."

"Some of them."

"I don't think it's good for your health."

"The climbing or the girls?"

"Both. You look terrible."

"I shouldn't. I just flopped down on the biggest bed you've ever seen. That has to be the baroness's boudoir. I'd hate that crystal chandelier dangling over my bed at night and waking up to those fancy pink tapestries. I checked the drawers and closets. I can't decide if she's growing rich selling frauds or just fell heir to all this luxury."

"Now let's climb over the fence and get out of here."

Drew led the way around the newer wing, the part of the house that started out low to the ground like a lean-to shed. It rose with the slope of the hill—clerestory windows along one side and a picture window in the front. Drew grabbed a limb, swung his body up, and peered inside the window.

A sofa lay open, the bed unmade, giving the room an untidy, lived-in appearance. He took another appraisal, his gaze settling on an easel. A cover hid the painting, but it was definitely an art easel with a palette and brushes on the ledge beside it.

"This is living quarters for someone," he called down to Vic.

"Klee and his wife?"

"Did they impress you as artists?"

"Not really. The old man's hands are too gnarled to grip a paintbrush, Frau Klee too nervous."

"Then someone else lives in the mansion."

Vic didn't answer as Drew swung free from the limb and dropped to the ground, getting splinters in his hand in the process. As he caught his balance, he saw Vic lying on the lawn, out cold, and still. Drew looked up and found himself staring into the barrel of a gun.

"Have you seen enough?" the old man asked.

Drew made a move to help Vic.

"No further," Albert said. "Hedwig will take care of him."

Klee stood tall, his back rigid, a rifle gripped in his knobby hands. "I warned you to leave."

Ten

In Paris Sigmund Valdemar scaled the honey-colored stone wall and dropped with a thud onto the freshly turned earth. Across the enclosed yard, Monique Dupree knelt in the flower bed, radio music playing beside her as she weeded. Sigmund stood, unnoticed, studying her with an artist's eye, a mental palette in his hand.

His image of the glamorous socialite attending the opera in a St. Laurent gown vanished. Monique wore denim shorts and a floral halter, her midriff and slender, bare arms suntanned. Loose sandals flapped at her narrow heels, and garden gloves covered her hands. A cocky garden hat tilted capriciously at the back of her head with locks of black hair curling around its brim. The hat shaded Monique's eyes, but not her delicate profile.

She seemed at home with the soil, working among rows of raspberries and crimson red peonies. Other flowers grew closer to the wall—some with spiked petals in stark purple and a cluster of yellow perennials standing on their wiry stems, glowing like lanterns.

The garden had an artist's touch—foliage with puckered leaves, moss growing in the rockery, a shrub-tree with corkscrew branches silhouetted in the afternoon sun. Tiny sparrows splashed in the bird bath beside the twisted tree. For a moment, Sigmund wanted to paint it all—especially Monique Dupree, as enchanting as the garden in which she toiled.

He snapped a twig and then broke a second one.

She turned and gasped, her mouth open to scream.

"Don't," he warned. "Your husband sent me."

"How did you get in here?"

He nodded toward the six-foot wall.

Her brimmed hat fell as she scrambled to her feet; the shiny dark hair fell loose. "Harland?" she whispered.

Sigmund nodded. "Yes, Mr. Smith sent me."

"Harland," she repeated.

The word *Harland* caught in her throat as though she had half expected to hear from him again, half feared it. She whipped the gloves from her hands—lovely hands—and dropped them on the ground beside the trowel and hoe. "So he is alive?"

"Yes—very much so."

Her enormous brown eyes widened. A ripple of a smile danced at the corners of her mouth. "And you expect me to believe that?"

He nodded again. "I'm Sigmund Valdemar. Perhaps this will be proof enough." Slowly he removed a jeweled watch from his right wrist and handed it to her. "This belongs to—"

She put her finger to her lips—well-shaped, sensual lips—and beckoned him to follow her to the back of the garden.

"We can speak here," she said as she faced him.

Clutching the watch in the palm of her hand, she glanced back toward the apartment. "How do I know you didn't take this from my husband?"

"You don't," he said. "Do you have company?"

"My maid and my younger son, Giles. He's not well."

"I'm sorry."

She smiled disarmingly. "It's just a head cold, but even that is hard on Giles, especially in Harland's absence."

"And your maid?"

"Felice? She's trustworthy. But the possibility of laser microphones exists. Inside, we speak of Harland in the past tense. It is easier on the boys. And better if someone is monitoring our words." Her eyes sharpened. "So my husband sent you?"

"Yes."

"Then I must go to him."

He had not expected it to be so easy. "He wants you to come."

"Is he well?"

"Lonely, mostly. Will it be safe for you to go?"

Her face clouded. "Why did he wait so long to send for me?"

He considered shielding her from the truth. Harland's own safety took priority Sigmund had come to take her to him, a man who didn't deserve her. "Your husband needed time to establish a new life, to make certain that his 'death' was accepted."

She responded with a rapid flow of French, most of it lost on Sigmund. "Don't tell me that," she said. "He was always prepared for a new identity. A villa in Spain. A chalet in Switzerland. A home in Norway. With no forwarding addresses and no thought of what would happen to the boys or me."

"He expected you to wait for him in Isigny."

"On my parents' farm? My parents ask too many questions about him. I have unanswered questions myself." That fragile smile touched her lips again. "I've come to love living in the city. Anzel, my older son, would not be happy on the farm. Here in Paris he has a new school, new friends." She looked away. "Giles would be happy in Isigny, but not Anzel."

"The boys will have to come with us," he said. "Will you tell them that their father is alive?"

She considered. "Not yet. Not until I see him myself."

He risked another suggestion. "It is safer if you travel as Monique Dupree, not as the wife or widow of Harland Smith."

Again that tiny smile played at the corners of her mouth. "I grew weary of being a widow—of not knowing whether Harland was living or dead. I've been using my family name for months now."

"Yes, you were difficult to find."

She puzzled him. Her beauty tantalized his whole being, yet he sensed her anger. He wanted to reach out and comfort her. Perhaps she should remain in Paris. But the risk for Sigmund was too costly. He had bartered—Monique in exchange for Smith's help in marketing the von Tonner collection.

"These months have been lonely for you, too," he said.

"I have my garden and my boys. After Harland's jet crashed under mysterious circumstances, I determined to stay in Paris and fight the nasty rumors about him. Lies, all of them. We were once welcomed in high places. Now, for the most part, I'm shunned, exiled like my husband—his business dealings in question."

"Surely, you knew about his work, *Monique.*" He said the word with care, intrigued by the sound.

"He kept our lives separate from his livelihood. Does he know that the Plastec Corporation has been confiscated? That was the final shame for Anzel, to have his father's integrity questioned. Giles is too young to be troubled, but Anzel is so sensitive, so pained by his father's reputation. Even more by his absence."

She plucked a flower from the garden and smoothed its petals, an unexpected sadness sending ribbons of worry across her brow. "He and Harland never got along. They rarely did anything together."

"Perhaps your husband was too busy or too old to relate to your son."

She flushed, her dark eyes tearing. "I would have expressed it more kindly, Mr. Valdemar. Harland did try. It's just—Anzel could never please him, especially in skiing. Harland is at home on the slopes, Anzel terrified of them."

"And the boy—what does he like to do?"

"He's a marvelous student. And a violinist," she said shyly. "I—I hate to pull him from his studies and music. I want him to study at the conservatory someday. Mr. Valdemar, when will we come back to Paris? Did Harland say?"

"It's unlikely your husband can ever return here."

"Never?" She glanced pensively around her garden. "I'll keep the apartment. The boys and I may come back to it."

Without Harland? he wondered. "When you pack, make it look like you'll be back soon. Harland wants you to travel light. He'll buy you new wardrobes when you arrive."

"I'm very fond of some of my old clothes. When are we leaving?"

"Today."

"No. I'll need a day or two. I'll make arrangements for Felice to stay on in the apartment. She'll need funds."

"Harland authorized me to set up an account for her."

"He did?" There was both surprise and pleasure in her expression. "He remembered how fond I am of Felice."

"Perhaps he did it because he is fond of you."

"Yes, he's in love with me."

"I'll be back for you tomorrow afternoon. Be ready then."

"No. Meet us at the train station. Felice is used to us going to

Normandy. I don't want Giles to face saying good-bye to her. We can leave from there. For Spain perhaps?" she asked.

No, not Spain, he thought. *But you'll know soon enough.* "I'll meet you at the train station," he agreed.

"Will you travel separately?"

"Yes, but you'll recognize me. Travel toward Rouen. We'll change trains several times. I'll handle the ticketing and transfers. When I leave the train, keep behind me. Once we leave France, we'll travel together."

"I'm not certain what this will do to the boys—finding out that Harland is alive. Anzel may never forgive him."

Sigmund studied her again, surprised at her candor, charmed by her natural beauty. "Once you're settled in, perhaps I could help Anzel. I ski well myself. I could teach him—"

"So it's Norway or Switzerland," she said. "And not Spain. I've wondered all these months."

"They have ski schools in both countries, an excellent one at Zermatt. Would Anzel like my help?"

"As a friend of his father's? No."

"As your friend then, Monique."

Color crept into her cheeks. She turned, dismissing him. "Please leave the way you came. I don't want to wake Giles."

He followed a few steps behind her around the rows of peonies toward the apartment. Her sandals slapped against her feet as she walked. She stopped so abruptly that his foot caught on her shoe, twisting it from her foot. As she stumbled, she fell back against him.

Embarrassed, she pushed him away and pointed toward the sliding glass door.

Two boys stood framed in the doorway, listening. Watching. Thick dark hair. Dark eyes. The older boy, lean and handsome, draped an arm protectively around his brother.

Giles sneezed, broke free, and ran to Monique. His features were almost identical to her own.

She crushed him against her. As she rocked him, one hand ruffling his hair, she called across to her older son, "Anzel, this is Sigmund Valdemar, a friend of your father's."

Anzel glared back, his face twisted with anger. "I won't go," he said. "I won't go with you."

※

Ingrid von Tonner stood by the hotel window and watched the Gregorys walk along the lake. She had argued with Miriam into the wee hours, fending off accusations— neither of them bending. Ingrid had not bargained on the mature Robyn interfering—the child she had once ignored, the expert art historian she had become. Robyn stood between them—a buffer for her mother, a barricade to Ingrid.

Now they were more united than ever—mother and daughter— arms linked, heads close together, walking, talking. *Talking about me,* Ingrid decided.

She kept her eyes on the Gregorys even when Harland Smith stepped up to the window beside her. "I don't have to ask," he said. "You've been watching the Gregorys. Attractive, both of them."

"Both of them? A man's opinion. Miriam is a beautiful woman. Always has been. Engaging and intelligent."

"Perhaps she would say the same of you, my dear." He stroked his goatee. "You do not favor the daughter, do you? She has confidence. I see it in the way she carries herself."

"Not always. She's spent a lifetime feeling inferior to her mother. But this trip they both seem strong-willed."

"All the more challenging for me," he said. "We shall see."

His tone was threatening. She glanced at him, hating him, yet admitting that he was a commanding personality. He was controlling them all with his own hatred, deception, and vengeance. All directed against one man.

Harland's eyes turned cold. "I suppose I owe you my gratitude for bringing them so quickly. When did they get here?"

"Yesterday. Two days ago. I don't remember."

He gripped her arm, his fingers selective as they pressed against a nerve. She winced as he said, "Come, Mrs. von Tonner. When did they reach Zurich?"

"Yesterday."

"And you didn't call me."

"I wanted time to talk with them."

"To warn them about me?"

She shoved his hand away with a violence that irritated him. "I'm not a fool, Mr. Smith. I never mentioned you. I've done what you asked. I want out now."

"No. Your responsibility doesn't end until Drew Gregory arrives in Zurich. Let's sit down and work this out together." As they turned toward the hotel conference desk, she gasped, startled at the sight of Aaron Gregory sitting there. "I thought we were meeting with Sigmund Valdemar."

"The clever copyist? Valdemar won't be coming. I invited your friend Aaron instead."

"Harland, where is Sigmund?"

"In Paris on business."

"Not on some fool's errand?"

"My wife is not a fool."

"She is if she travels with him. He likes attractive women."

"My sons will be with them."

Ingrid frowned. Sigmund going to Paris had been *their* plan, not Smith's. "You've been in touch with Sigmund without asking me?"

"You have it wrong, my dear. Valdemar got in touch with me."

"How dare he."

"He's a very intelligent young man."

"Gifted," she admitted. "And useful."

"To both of us, as it turns out."

"He's a double-minded man, Harland."

"Then we will get on well. He offered me the von Tonner art collection, for a price, of course."

"It belongs to me."

"No, my dear. To your husband, Felix."

Her fury erupted. "He is a senile old man."

"But still alive. That's the problem as Sigmund sees it." Harland grinned, enjoying her discomfort. He offered her the chair across from Aaron, saying, "Legally the art collection belongs to the baron. That's why I invited Miriam's brother-in-law to join us. We need a criminal lawyer—one with a criminal mind."

Aaron didn't even look up when Ingrid sat down. His hands were folded on the tabletop, his knuckles chalk white, his silk striped tie askew, marring his usual immaculate appearance.

Smith drew a chair close to Ingrid, their elbows touching. She pulled away from him, despising him.

"I took the liberty of having Aaron study the provisions of your divorce settlement. You own the mansion, but not the stables, nor the ground on which they sit."

Ingrid's fist thumped the table. "Aaron had no right—he knows nothing about European law."

"Enough to know that you were extremely clever, but not clever enough. The art collection is not in your agreement. It's not mentioned, not spelled out at all. We've looked over the baron's will, too. It's possible that you can make claims to the art treasures in the event of the baron's death."

"He *will* die," she said angrily.

"The human spirit..." Smith shrugged. "It offers surprising longevity, my dear."

She glared at the bowed head across from her. "You betrayed me, Aaron. What right did you have to discuss my private papers with this—this man?"

Gregory lifted his head and looked at her. His gaze seemed hollow, his skin blanched. The leanness of his face and his slack jaw made him appear weaker. "What choice did I have? This man—as you call him—has made threats against all of us, even my brother, Drew. Survival, Ingrid. It's important to all of us, especially to me."

"I should never have trusted you."

"I didn't know you ever did. I cared about you, Ingrid."

"Like you cared for your sister-in-law? You're the one who wanted to cheat Miriam."

"Wrong. I wanted to use her gallery to destroy my brother."

Smith's smile was insidious. "Then we have something in common, Mr. Gregory. A problem with the same man."

Aaron rubbed his eyes with his slender, bony hand. "Yes, Smith, but my problem with Drew is strictly financial. He took the bulk of our family inheritance."

"And poured much of it back into his family."

"I'm part of that family. I never saw a dime of it."

"You handled the business affairs for Mrs. Gregory at a heavy stipend. A wise decision. I can help you accomplish what we both want."

"I want no part of harming my brother."

"But you wanted to destroy him."

"To ruin his reputation. Not kill him."

"I can help you salvage your own reputation. You and Mrs. von Tonner will need money to fight any charges of fraudulent sales through Mrs. Gregory's gallery."

"They'll never hold," Aaron said. "I'll make certain of that."

"The best way to assure that is to remove the von Tonner art collection from the property. Without evidence, the charges against you won't hold. My dear Baroness, Sigmund suggested that we steal the collection from you and sell it on the black market."

"I'll throw him out when he gets back from Paris."

"Not so hasty, my dear. We need Sigmund, particularly his artistic talent. We'll continue to sell his Rembrandt copies until we can safely dispose of the von Tonner collection."

"You'll never steal my property."

"It is not yours, Ingrid, not until the baron is gone. As I see it, we can wait for the baron to die from natural causes, although I deplore waiting. Or, as Sigmund suggests, we can remove the baron's property from the mansion and market it while he's still alive. I, for one, need money now."

"You're crazy, Smith," Aaron said. "Do you think you can fool the world? The Americans, the French, the Germans, Interpol, the Sûreté, the CIA—they've all been alerted. They all have a vested interest in finding the von Tonner collection; it's worth millions."

Smith's smile turned cynical. "Then we must prevent all of them from finding it. Apparently, they know nothing about the underground tunnels—not yet."

The wild glint in Aaron's dark eyes brightened. "I thought the collection was hidden inside the mansion. Well, Ingrid, is Smith guessing, or do we have access to tunnels?"

Ingrid sucked in her lower lip, recoiling at sharing the treasures of a century with these men.

"Is it true? Ah, Ingrid, your face says that it is."

"Yes," Smith told him. "We must move swiftly and seal off the entry to the tunnels. The art collection must not be traced back to the von Tonner property. In time, my wife, Monique, and I will present ourselves as the owners of the collection. Family heirlooms that passed into our family possession back in World War II. Sold to us by the von Tonners during financial straits."

"That's ridiculous, Harland. No one will believe you."

"It won't matter, Ingrid. The collection was never fully catalogued. That gives us some leeway for immediate sales."

Smith smoothed his silver hair back with one broad hand. "With the entry to the tunnels sealed off, we can remove a few major pieces at a time—through the exit and there surely must be one—and market them immediately in Japan or South America."

"What about Australia?" Aaron suggested. "There are bona-fide collectors there who would bid without question on originals, no matter who owned them."

Ingrid wanted to clamp her ears shut and flee. As she pushed back her chair, Harland studied her with renewed interest. Rising gracefully, she managed a natural smile for him. He rose beside her—this Janus-faced man. He was frightening, evil but powerless without the blueprints to the tunnel. A chestnut stallion guarded one exit, and no one knew about the far exit through a wine cellar in the village parish. Sensing an amazing calm, she offered him her jeweled hand, still smiling. Smith pushed his thick-rimmed glasses higher on his nose, the act slow and deliberate as he focused on her.

"I must go. I have a luncheon engagement with Miriam."

"Keep it, by all means," he said.

She knew by the look in his black, penetrating eyes that he was in control. He would destroy all of the Gregorys, Aaron and Drew included. But he would work with her and use her as long as she cooperated—until the tunnel exits were located. As he let her hand go, he said, "Prod Mrs. Gregory. Find out when Drew is coming."

"I've told you. She isn't in touch with him."

Aaron stood. "Smith, how does my brother fit into this?"

"As the CIA scapegoat," Smith said coldly. "We will leave a trail that will ruin him and embarrass American Intelligence in front of the rest of the world."

Smith's cord was twisting tighter around all of them. But, no matter what he had said in this room about building an art empire, it was merely a clever distraction, she decided. Yes, Smith wanted the money, but he had a single purpose in mind—the destruction of Drew Gregory.

☙❧

Aaron followed Ingrid out of the conference room. "What are we going to do about Smith?" he asked.

"Nothing. I won't help him. Miriam and I have been friends for years. When we quarreled last night, I realized how much I will miss that friendship. I may have lost her as a friend, but I will not destroy her."

"Circumstances will do it for you. Go with Miriam and Drew, if you wish. And go down with them. Smith will pull it off with us or without us."

"I'll think of someone to help us."

"Sigmund Valdemar is out. He's already betrayed us."

"Smith wants us to believe that. But right now Sigmund may still be useful to us. Leave it to me, Aaron."

"I've already made that mistake. You have me up to my neck in international art fraud."

"No one twisted your arm, Aaron."

"We're going to need money to fight this."

"I don't have a cash flow for both of us."

"What about one of the paintings at the mansion, Ingrid?"

"What about it?" she asked.

"Let's sell one—the one on the landing between the first and second floors. The Rembrandt. It's beautiful. It would bring a good price at auction. We need funds, and we need them in a hurry."

"Aaron, all you can think about is money. Don't you care what happens to your family?"

"Miriam and Robyn? Of course. But I have nothing to do with the problem between Smith and my brother."

"You're not even going to warn Drew?"

"I tried to call him at his London flat. No answer."

"Then call him at work."

"He always cautioned against that."

Aaron disgusted her. "I'm late for lunch."

"I'll go with you," he offered.

"You weren't invited."

He reached up and straightened his tie. "Thanks. I flew over here as Miriam's lawyer. And yours. You need me."

"Not if you don't get better control of yourself."

He flinched at her condemnation. "Ingrid, I understand that a friend of the baron's is staying here at the Alpenhof."

"Pierre Courtland? He's an old family friend."

"Did you arrange for him to be here?"

"No. He's here on holiday."

"Really? Isn't he determined to protect the baron's art? Admit it, Ingrid. Courtland wants only one thing—access to the baron's art treasures."

"Apparently, everyone does."

"Then eliminate him."

The very thought made Ingrid ill. "You've gone mad, Aaron. Pierre is harmless. He wants to befriend the baron. That's all."

For the first time in months, she saw Pierre as a potential ally. The Klees and Pierre would help her, not for herself, but for the baron. "Pierre can be useful to us," she said. "I will ask him to keep Robyn busy until I convince Miriam that the shipments to her gallery were all legitimate."

Aaron chortled. "And you perfectly innocent?"

"I never meant to harm anyone."

Ingrid walked hurriedly away, surprised at the angry emotions Aaron had stirred within her. She would struggle to regain that friendship with Miriam—anything to prevent Harland Smith from stealing her treasures.

As she reached the concierge's desk, he waved frantically. "There's a message for you, Baroness, about your house guests," he said. "From a Herr Klee. He seemed upset when I couldn't disturb you."

"Albert?"

"Yes. He wants you to call him right away."

"I will, right after lunch."

She smiled, half to herself. Whatever was rattling Albert and Hedwig must wait.

Eleven

Albert Klee sat in the chair, the Mauser rifle cradled in his arms, his wary eyes straying to the phone and then back to Drew Gregory's face. Each calculated motion set Drew on edge. Hours ago the old man had kicked off his muddy boots at the front door and padded in his stocking feet across the shiny marble floors of the mansion to the kitchen. Klee never missed a step as he nudged Drew to the table, the barrel of the rifle hard against Drew's kidney.

Drew didn't know where they were holding Vic Wilson or how badly he was injured. Hedwig, a surprisingly strong woman, had dragged Vic into the mansion, hauling his limp body over the threshold and down a long corridor. She had reappeared moments later to boil a pan of water and was gone again for an hour.

Now the old man looked sleepy, his grip loosening on the rifle. Drew could topple the table and take him, but would he have time to put in an emergency call before he felt the power of a "spitzer" bullet slamming into him? Even if he succeeded, what excuse would he give? They had trespassed on the von Tonner property. As he mulled over his plan, Hedwig came into the kitchen once more, the door closing silently behind her.

Albert watched sleepily as she moved through the damp, half-modernized room. She communicated to him with a shrug, eyeing Drew contemptuously. She seemed as cold and indifferent as this centuries-old room with its stone wall—a room holding some surprisingly up-to-date equipment, including a modern stainless steel sink. The rest of the kitchen had touches of the past—tiled countertops, antiques ornamenting the walls. Old and new blended—a sparkling electric stove and a drafty rock fireplace. A full phone panel hung on the wall with outside lines and a row of intercom buttons that surely reached throughout the mansion.

Drew eyed the heavy carved door, bolted to the outside world, and allowed his gaze to stray to the quaint oriel window cut into the stone wall above Hedwig's sink. He saw it as a possible escape route, depending on the drop beneath it. He wondered how long the Klees had worked for Ingrid von Tonner. They worked as a team, ready to defend and protect her. Possibly even to die for her.

Ingrid had done well for herself. He remembered her as attractive, gushy, impressing Miriam with her charm and shrewdness, and boring Drew straight out of his mind. He had argued endlessly with Miriam against Ingrid's conniving enterprises—her risky ventures that gambled on profit.

He had never liked her, never trusted her. She had too much influence on Miriam. Then suddenly, after a whirlwind courtship with a French count, Ingrid moved back to Europe permanently. Drew was relieved. Years after Drew's own divorce, Aaron had informed him that Ingrid had married again—this time to a German baron with plenty of property and another title to add to her collection. Countess. Baroness. And, no doubt, the title to this mansion as well.

He chewed over the word *baroness,* knowing how hard she worked to keep up a good impression. The upkeep of the mansion would be costly, too. *Costly enough for her to turn to art fraud?* If so, Ingrid was in deep trouble. She had to be, with Porter Deven and Langley interested. But if Ingrid was in so deep, where did Miriam stand in this pitiful charade?

Hedwig was in constant motion, an ample-sized woman whose steps were muffled by a pair of fleece slippers pulled snugly over her laced shoes. She scowled at the scuff marks left on the marble tiles where Drew had dragged his feet back and forth. He remembered how much Miriam hated scouring floors—remembered, oddly enough, leaving his own slippers by the front door. Hedwig glared down at him, her face cold and marbled like the shiny floor, her hair combed back in a Victorian topsytail that lent a sharpness to her coarse features.

"How's my friend?" he asked her in English. He didn't reveal his fluent German, hoping that the Klees might speak to each other in that language.

"Well, Hedwig," Albert asked, "how is the man?"

"Awake." She turned abruptly and went back to her sink.

"Is he talking?" Klee asked.

"Explosively."

Angry *as a bull,* Drew could imagine. It still didn't tell him where Vic was held in the mansion or whether he could move on the double if given the chance. Hedwig kept watchful, without allowing her eyes to settle back on Drew. She stood at the cutting board now, butcher knife in hand, expertly chopping raw vegetables and dropping them into a soup pot. But she was listening, her senses alert like some animal on the hunt.

Klee stood and stretched, the rifle wobbly in his gnarled hands. He made his way to the stove. Drew stirred.

"Don't," the old man warned without looking back "I am an accurate marksman."

"So the baron tells me."

He came back with a mug of steaming coffee for Drew and a hot rum for himself. He shoved the coffee toward Drew. It spilled over the sides, spreading a rivulet across the table. Hedwig came at once, scooping up the spill with a hand towel, her obsession with tidiness amusing Drew.

Albert sat across the table from him again, the phone to his back. He slurped his drink and dunked a hard roll in cheese sauce. Drew could tell he was growing weary, impatient with waiting for the baroness to return his call.

Drew swallowed the coffee. He was hungry, and he worried about the long delay in getting to Zurich. He rehearsed his options, limited at best. He was here without diplomatic immunity, without authorization, a man on suspension from his job. Klee not only had a rifle in his hand, but the deck stacked in his favor. He knew every inch of this mansion. But the urge to reach Miriam and his daughter goaded Drew. In his own quiet way, he was a patient man. But sitting here waiting for the baroness to return Albert's call was getting on his nerves.

"When are you going to let us go, Herr Klee?" he asked.

The watchful eyes narrowed. "When I have the order to do so."

"I've told you, Klee, my wife and the baroness are friends. They won't be happy to hear you've held us."

Hedwig snorted. "Your friend won't be able to travel."

The harshness in her eyes had slackened as though she opposed their captivity. Had Vic picked up on this? Or was his sponged brain too numb to reason?

Come on, Vic, Drew thought. *Get that impulsive brain of yours working. I'm depending on you.*

As Drew took more of the bitter coffee, Hedwig picked up a tray and made her way toward the door.

"Frau Klee," Drew said, "if that's for my friend, he needs food. He hasn't eaten since early morning."

Neither one of us has, he thought.

She hesitated, looking back at her soup pot. "Later. Hot coffee now. It will help his headache."

She was right, of course. With that wallop on the back of Vic's skull, Drew hoped it wasn't worse than a headache. Vic didn't need another concussion in the line of duty.

Drew listened, trying to determine if Hedwig took the stairs or remained on the main floor. Not a sound reached him. Inwardly, he cursed her padded shoes. Three floors. This place had to have thirty rooms or more, but even as strong as she was, Hedwig would not have taken the time to drag Vic up the stairs. Somewhere on the main level, behind one of those closed doors, Vic sat drinking that miserable black coffee—waiting for Drew to find him.

With barely a flick of his wrist, he checked his watch. Noon straight up, give or take a few minutes.

"12:05," the old man said. "My wife will be right back." He predicted her return without interest, like some timepiece that would go on ticking whether he waited for her or not. "You drove onto the grounds five hours ago."

Klee's Mauser lay flat on the table now, his trigger finger moving affectionately over it. Drew pictured it as Klee's close companion, a camaraderie more congenial than his isolated life here with Hedwig. The gun appeared old but well-serviced.

Drew calculated the arm's length to the rifle, the longer distance to the kitchen window. Klee's eyes closed, time forgotten. Drew slipped his hands on the table, fingers stretched out, ready to grasp the gun.

Across the room the phone panel lit up, a single red button blinking. Drew pulled his hands back into his lap and tensed for the ring. Nothing. Somewhere in the mansion Hedwig had placed a call. Another call to Ingrid?

Klee's drooping eyelids opened.

From the corner of his own eye, Drew watched the steady flashing light. Behind him, Hedwig entered and went directly to the stove to stir her soup, her back to both of them.

"Well?" Albert asked her.

"The man says he needs a doctor."

Someone was still on the phone, placing an outside call. It had to be Vic. Drew's chance for the rifle and the window were gone. Now escape depended on Vic Wilson, a man with a soft spot in the back of his skull and an exceptional love for daring.

Drew shoved his empty cup toward Klee. "Please."

Albert cocked the rifle and shouldered it. He snatched up the mug in his empty hand and walked toward the stove.

Drew fixed his eyes on the phone panel, on the flickering red button. The pit of his gut churned. He had warned Vic against reporting their whereabouts to Porter Deven in Paris. And Vic had promised: *"You'll never catch me calling."*

༺༻

In Paris Porter Deven took his emery board from his shirt pocket and drew imaginary lines around the latest list from Langley. Eight more von Tonner art frauds on the market in less than a year. Three in Beverly Hills. One in Edinburgh. One in Tokyo. Two in Australia. One in Sao Paulo, Brazil. Five of them Rembrandts. Three Renoir. All copies of the von Tonner originals.

Not part of Company business, he reminded himself again.

Porter had deliberately marked the file classified—top secret. He looked up and faced Kurt Brinkmeirer, an old friend from Interpol—an old friend from Vietnam. "This is out of our league. You know that, Kurt. We can help you with some of the information, but art fraud is not our responsibility."

"I know the count already. And the locations. It has the touch of amateurs, yet it may be the tip of the iceberg."

Porter nodded. "Some buyers may not want to admit they've been taken. Some may not even know it. Not yet. That's why it was so puzzling to have three of them show up in the Gregory gallery in Beverly Hills."

"Isn't that the ex-wife of one of your officers?"

"Kurt, isn't that why you're here? Don't look at me that way. You know Gregory. He's become a burden to me lately."

"Why don't you let him go? He's old enough for retirement."

"Past retirement, if you ask me. But I don't need some disgruntled officer out there writing a book that exposes the Company or smears me in some way."

"You've had it in for him for a long time."

Porter sat back, feeling smug. "With good reason now. He may be linked to this art fraud mess along with his wife and von Tonner. The two women are old friends."

"If I didn't know better, I'd say you are pleased about the possibility."

"Who wouldn't be? If Gregory goes down in a scandal, he won't risk writing a scandalous book about the Company."

"He wouldn't anyway. He's not that kind of man."

Porter matched silence with Kurt. In the last two decades, Kurt, a quick-witted six-footer, had gone from a handsome Marine with thick blond hair to a mature man with gray overtones in his wavy hair. His broad forehead had taken on wrinkles, the square jaw more stubbornness, the nose a hook from a severe break. But Kurt's clear green eyes shone as directly and sympathetically as ever. An unlit Marlboro always dangled from his wide lips. That hadn't changed from their days in Vietnam. Kurt and his unlit Marlboro—waiting to go out on patrol, coming back from a mission, standing alone after a comrade's death. That unbroken habit—an unlit cigarette.

"How's the wife?" Porter asked, breaking their silence.

"Ina? Much the same. She's the one who made me leave Kansas and move back to Europe. My sister and I liked it in America while we were there, but our roots here brought us back." Kurt tapped his pack of

Marlboros. "What about it, Porter? Am I to believe those rumors that Drew is involved?"

Porter sucked in his breath. He himself had allowed the rumor to seep through to Langley. The weight of Porter's hangdog moustache drew his mouth tighter. "That's crazy, Kurt."

"How crazy? I have a nephew in Zurich, walking in blind. Pierre's a good man. He knows just enough to get him into trouble."

"What do you want, Kurt?"

"Answers before I go to Zurich and meet Pierre. Interpol's international list of criminals on this art fraud reads like an invitation list to the Queen's coronation. A German baroness. A New York lawyer. A gallery owner. A senile old baron. And a CIA agent. None of them with a previous record. I don't want anyone adding my nephew's name."

"Why would they?"

"Our family has been lifelong friends with the von Tonners. I drifted away from them, but not Pierre. His loyalty to the baron is indestructible."

"Tell him to get out."

"I can't, Porter. My nephew is a visionary, a godly young man. He can't separate his friendships and his religious commitment. I won't ask him to. Come on, Porter. Go to Zurich with me."

"Sorry, we're not officially in on this. Besides, I'm the Station Chief here, not the errand boy."

Kurt glanced around the office. "So you like the security of this granite and steel refuge here at Neuilly?"

Porter sank deeper into his worn leather chair. "I have a good man on it. Vic Wilson was assigned to Zurich."

"Should I get in touch with him when I arrive?"

"I haven't heard from him. He was scheduled to check in every twenty-four hours. But he seems to be lost somewhere between Kaiserslautern and Dusseldorf."

"That's not the direct route to Zurich."

"Wilson never plays by the books."

"Then why do you keep him on?"

"He's a new breed. No ties to Vietnam. No ties to anyone but himself." He didn't express his worst fear—Vic's friendship with Drew. "Vic doesn't usually quibble about assignments."

"What's that mean?"

"He dragged his shoelaces on this one—kept reminding me that this wasn't in Langley's league."

"What about Gregory? Will he be there?"

"If he does what we think he'll do, he'll be there."

"So he's a threat to my nephew's safety?"

"Kurt, I can't discuss Gregory's involvement," Porter lied. "Until now he's had a good record. He's still a Company man."

Kurt pocketed his Marlboros and shifted. For a moment Porter thought he would stand and leave. Instead Kurt said, "Do you think about Vietnam much, Porter?"

After twenty years, Porter still thought about it, his waking hours often haunted by the memories. "After all these years? A few nightmares. That's all."

"What about that recent Saigon delegation?"

"What about it?"

"I hear you were one of the chief interpreters. Were they open to more answers on the MIA/POWs?"

"The usual skimming of truth. It's too late now. We should let it alone. I don't believe there's another survivor. God help him if there is."

"That doesn't sound like you, Porter. Twenty years ago it was your personal battle. I thought you were crazy. All I could think about was getting out of there."

"Well, we did."

"But you went back for another two years. When I heard that, I couldn't believe it. I still can't. Four years in Indochina—you're lucky you came out with your hide."

Porter was sweating, his shirt collar ringing wet. The blurred memory of Luke Breckenridge flashed before him, the hellish nightmare about the man he had left there to die. "God help any survivors left behind," he repeated.

"Four years. You were a glutton for punishment."

"I've spent more years than that in Paris."

"That's different. Everybody has an ongoing love affair with Paris. My wife and I do."

Sweat kept forming on Porter's brow. He reached for his antacid bottle and swallowed some pills without water. He felt his neck bulging over his collar and thought once again of going on a diet. "I've put Vietnam on the back burner, Kurt. And turned off the pilot light. You should do the same."

"You look like you can't. Anything wrong?"

"You sound like Drew Gregory now. Forget it. I did my duty with that recent Saigon delegation and never again."

"You have a good hold on the language, Porter. You speak like a native. No wonder they use you."

"They used me all right," he said bitterly.

"Look, man, I'm sorry. I didn't mean to upset you. I just get to thinking about it now and then."

"Don't," Porter said. "It's not worth it."

"But I left friends behind there."

"We all did."

"One of my nephews—Pierre's older brother, Baylen—didn't get out, either. That's one of the reasons I take such a personal interest in Pierre. He came along twelve years after Baylen, squeezing through life between wars." Much to Porter's relief, Kurt stood. "I'm flying to Zurich in a few days to join my nephew. We should get together again, Porter, when I get back. Maybe we can talk this out. Your memories can't all be that bad."

Bad enough, Porter thought, *for me to be constantly trying to ruin Drew Gregory so he won't know the truth.* He extended his hand to Kurt and felt it go limp as they shook hands.

Kurt gripped harder, trying to reassure him. "Do you still have that floppy-eared basset hound of yours?"

"Old Jedburgh? I sure do, Kurt. He's the best thing that ever happened to me since this job in Paris."

As the phone rang, Kurt gave a quick salute and was gone.

Porter leaned forward and answered, "Deven speaking."

"It's Vic. Vic Wilson," said a voice on the other end of the wire. "We've got to talk, Porter."

Twelve

As Sigmund drove the Fiat up the winding road toward the von Tonner mansion, he glanced at Monique. She sat stiffly on the passenger side, her hands clenched in her lap. He sensed her distrust since leaving the train station and her deep concern for the boys on the back seat—Giles coughing and fretful, Anzel close beside him, brooding.

"I'm sorry, Monique. It's been a hard trip for you."

"Why did you pass by every turnoff to Switzerland?"

"We must wait here for Harland's instructions."

"Giles's cold is getting worse."

He turned and smiled at her. "The boy's cold isn't fatal. He just needs rest and juice. The Klees will take care of him."

Her eyes stayed fixed on the winding road. "Do you have a family, Mr. Valdemar? Or do you just hand out your advice freely?"

He wondered with her whether there might be a child in his world, somewhere, a child of his own making. Being a father had never mattered to him—until he held Giles on his lap during the train ride. Now he vaguely understood Monique's concern.

"Well," she asked again, "do you have a family?"

"No."

"Not even a wife?"

"Not even a wife."

"Were you too busy or too selfish?"

Sigmund's mouth clamped so tight that it sent a pain along the nerve, immobilizing his jaw. Monique half-turned in her seat to face him. *Yes,* he wanted to say, *I loved someone once, an officer's daughter. Sada, blond and voluptuous, her eyes as blue and clear as the Mediterranean Sea where we met.* So sweet and innocent—Sigmund had robbed her of both, and in the end, he made a cold, calculated choice: her betrayal and imprisonment for the favor of his own promotion.

"So there was someone? Why didn't you marry her, Sigmund?"

"Our political views differed."

"So strongly that it kept you apart? Wasn't she a Communist?"

"No, not even openly. Sada worked in the bakery in the town where I lived. She spoke out too freely against the government and encouraged small factions to meet together. I warned her."

"Wasn't she afraid of the secret police, the old hardliners?"

His mouth tightened again, his inner core still hard and running strong and loyal for the Stasi. "Sada told me there would never be freedom for anyone if we didn't speak out. Even when I told her that the Stasi had infiltrated every factory and school in town, she refused to suppress her opinions." He thumped his chest. "She told me they hadn't infiltrated her heart. They never did."

"She must have been brave."

"She was a fool."

"And you loved her, but you were afraid of the Stasi?"

"No," he said coldly. "I was one of them."

This time their eyes met. She challenged him, saying, "Everything has changed since then. The Wall is down. Germany is unified. Can't you and Sada get together now?"

"She died before the Wall came down."

As he drove through the gate of the mansion, he felt as though Sada were bleeding again. Sada, the officer's daughter, taking a job in the bakery out of pure defiance. He still remembered the day the state security police led her away.

He hadn't even pled for her release. The trial was so brief and condemning that he shuddered remembering it.

His commanding officer assigned him to the firing squad. Sada stood barefoot and blindfolded, her back to the stone wall. Sigmund lifted his rifle, fixed her in his sights and felt that, in spite of the blindfold, she was staring at him.

And then, with an indiscernible move, he aimed above her, his sights on the barren wall. Shots screamed through the stillness. Sada was blown off the ground and hurled against the wall. She slid to the ground in slow motion, her long blond hair sprawling freely, her shapely body still.

Sigmund had turned on command and marched away with the rest of the firing squad. The next day he had his promotion, but something of himself still lay bleeding with Sada.

He parked the Fiat in front of the mansion. The burning in his jaw felt like fire as he stepped from the car and tried to smile at Monique. "Wait here for me."

"Of course. You're my link with Harland."

He let himself in with a key and stopped short in the entry hall. A stranger stood near the stairs brandishing a pistol and swaying unsteadily on his stark white Rockports.

"I assume that's loaded," Sigmund said.

The man nodded weakly. "Yes, and I know how to use it."

Sigmund offered no argument. He sized him up: thirtyish, thick straight hair, and a wary, pinched face, the thin mouth drawn down at the corners. He couldn't decide whether the man was troubled or ill as he rocked on his feet. His clothes looked rumpled, a red stain on his shirt collar. His eyes were hazy, but it wasn't a tipsy gaze. Weak as the stranger appeared, he remained threatening as he waved his pistol.

"Who are you? What are you doing here?"

"Name's Vic Wilson. I'm trying to find my way out."

"The door's behind me."

"I'd like to go, but I can't leave without my friend."

"The baroness?" Sigmund asked.

"No, she's not here." His words slurred. "It's the woman in the apron. She left my room unlocked."

It had to be Hedwig.

The stranger swayed again and steadied himself by gripping the handrail. Sigmund took a step, trying to narrow the gap between them. In a sluggish gesture Wilson felt the back of his head, his befuddled expression increasing. "Old Klee whacked me with his rifle."

"He's the unfriendly type," Sigmund agreed.

Vic nodded toward the kitchen. "Klee's in there with Drew."

Sigmund reached the kitchen door first and kicked it open. "Put that rifle away, Klee. We have company."

The old man glared at Vic and Drew, then back at Sigmund.

"These men are meddling strangers, not company,"

"Not them, you old fool. I've brought a friend and her sons. I don't want the boys to see, that gun."

Sigmund turned to Drew. "What's going on?"

Drew stood cautiously. "I'm Drew Gregory. Mrs. Gregory and the baroness are good friends."

Sigmund wanted to laugh, thinking, *Everyone is expecting you in Zurich. Let's make it easy for you to get there and keep Smith calm.* "I believe the baroness is with your wife in Zurich right now—at the Alpenhof."

He turned on Albert. "Go on, Herr Klee, put that away."

Klee's rage smoldered. He picked up the Mauser and left.

"Where's he going?" Drew asked.

"He keeps his gun collection in the library. Old Klee does a good job of guarding this place. I suggest that you gentlemen leave for Zurich immediately. I'll see you out."

Sigmund turned to Hedwig. "Our guests are waiting outside. The little boy isn't feeling well."

Hedwig swooped out the front door ahead of them, her apron flying. When they joined her, she was bending over Giles as he cowered against his mother. "Don't be afraid of old Hedwig," she said, her harsh smile easing. "I'll get lunch ready for you, and then we're going out to the stables to see the horses. You'd like that, wouldn't you?"

Giles nodded, his head still pressed against Monique.

She ushered them into the kitchen and settled them around her wooden table, humming as she placed bowls of soup in front of them. Outside, shots rang out as Gregory's car squealed off.

Giles tumbled out of his chair into his mother's lap. His brother remained stony-faced, his dark eyes wide and alert as he looked at Monique.

"What was that, Sigmund?" she asked.

He smiled to reassure her. "Don't worry. Albert is just cooling down with a little target practice. Now have something to eat. Hedwig is a marvelous cook."

Hedwig was beaming at Sigmund's compliment when the phone rang. Her smile faded. "It's the baroness," she said.

He snatched the phone from her. "Good afternoon, Baroness."

"Sigmund, I thought you were in Paris."

"I was. I'm back."

"But I have a message here from Albert about house guests."

"Yes, we have three of them here."

"Friends of yours, Sigmund?"

"I hope so. Monique Smith and her sons."

He heard Ingrid gasp. "You took them there to the mansion?"

"Until we know what Smith's plans really are."

"Clever," she said at last. "But get the Smiths to Zurich in the morning. To the Alpenhof. Make certain the Klees take good care of them tonight. Give them comfortable rooms."

"Hedwig has the little boy slurping homemade soup right now She'll keep him happy. But, Ingrid, you had two other guests—Albert gave them an unfriendly welcome with the Mauser."

"Who?"

"Drew Gregory and his friend. They're headed your way—straight to Zurich."

The phone slammed in his ear. He held it for a moment, amused. He could picture Ingrid with a flick of her jeweled wrist already making her way to Harland, saying with her usual cunning, "Mr. Smith, I think we should talk."

☙❧

Drew Gregory roared down the autobahn, his speed surpassing the German drivers. Wilson sat beside him, trying to focus his blurred eyes on the roadmap on his lap. "I can't see it, Drew."

"Look again. I want the shortest route to Zurich."

"I have a splitting headache. This tiny print is just—"

"Give me the fastest route. Not the Rhine River cruise."

When they turned east out of Bonn, Vic slouched in the seat. "You act like that whole fiasco back there was my fault."

"The credit does go your way."

"Look, I got the biggest problems out of it. A borrowed car with bullet holes and a shattered back window. And a head the size of an elephant." He brooded for a moment. "What am I going to tell Nicole when I take her car back to her? How do I explain bullet holes?"

"Tell her you almost got us killed."

"You don't care about the damage to her car?"

"I have other things on my mind, Vic. Like who was that man back there? Do you think it was Valdema?. They mentioned a name like that. Sigmund. Sigmund Valdemar."

"I don't care what his name is. But the woman! Nice."

"I have the feeling she's taken."

"Valdemar's girl?"

"Or somebody's wife," Drew said. "Get her and two kids go with her. One cute and one surly."

"I didn't think about that."

"You haven't done much thinking since old Klee dented your skull. But that oldest boy didn't want to be there."

"Really?" Vic's words were slurring again.

"Keep awake, Vic. If you've got a concussion, I don't want you passing out on me."

"So you've got heart after all."

"I ought to let you go, period. I warned you about calling Porter Deven."

Vic stretched his legs. "I didn't notice any phone booth."

"The phone panel at the mansion lit up. No rings, so it was an outgoing call. The Klees were present and accounted for when the panel light went on, and Valdemar hadn't arrived yet."

"I had to call Brianna and let her know I was okay."

Drew slammed the steering wheel. "I was being held at gunpoint, not daring to risk an escape without knowing where you were, and you placed a social call to your cousin?"

Silence gave them both time to recoup, a last-ditch effort to keep their friendship from fragmenting completely. Drew spent the miles planning and replanning, interspersing his thoughts with questions on Langley and Porter. He let Vic rest, knowing that when the man complained, the pain had to be unbearable.

The map slipped to the floor. Drew didn't care. He had already cut across on the E50 past Heilbronn. He planned to turn south on the 81 and head straight on through Schaffhausen to Zurich, with petrol breaks only.

Vic sat upright unexpectedly. "Pull off this road; I'm ill."

A glance was all Drew needed. Vic was the color of dust. "I'm taking you to the nearest hospital."

"No. Just keep driving. I'll stick with you."

"Porter's orders?"

"Does it matter?" Vic's neck was hard against the back seat again, his mouth open, sucking in air. "Old Klee really gave it to me. Like Porter did to you. Porter set you up, Drew."

"Did he? Well, I'm not changing my plans. Tell him I intend to make it to Zurich and find out what's going on."

Vic's eyes closed, a mixed moan and wheeze slipping from his lips. "I'm really sick, Drew." He sat bolt upright. Rolling down the window, he leaned out and did a 120-kilometer upchuck.

Drew took the first exit he came to and pulled into a petrol station, a combined restaurant and gas stop.

He dragged Vic inside. *"Bitte.* Get this man some broth and tea," he told the waitress. "And some ice for the goose egg on the back of his head." He tilted Vic's head forward, exposing the dry matted hair and the three-inch open wound.

The waitress cocked a curious eye at Vic's head. "If you ask me, he needs stitches," she said.

"I didn't ask. What I need is ice."

She nodded. As she walked away, Vic said, "Drew, I can't let you go into Zurich alone. There are those who don't plan on you getting out of there alive."

"Do you plan to take a bullet for me?"

Vic's cocky grin hit Drew at the gut level. "Maybe I will, just for old time's sake."

"You need a doctor more than you need a bullet."

"And you need a friend, Drew."

The waitress came back with a pan of water. Ignoring the curious tourists at other tables, she deftly washed the wound herself, her hands gentle and efficient. "I gather you don't want a doctor," she said.

Vic groaned. "Not yet. We're driving through to Zurich."

In English Drew said, "Thanks for telling her our plans. We'd better grab that bowl of ice and get out of here before our sympathetic waitress takes to calling the police."

Once they were back in the car, he let Vic sleep. He needed time to plot a course. Driving in the evening cleared his mind. Until this moment he had gone in blindly, impulsively seeking to protect his family—gone in with anything but a clear head.

He was wanted in Zurich. But not by Miriam and Robyn.

If they had needed him, Aaron would have called him. Aaron's professionalism overrode sibling rivalry. He kept Drew informed on business matters: late alimony checks, Robyn's childhood diseases, her emergency appendectomy in high school, her broken wrist on a skiing trip. Aaron even told him about Miriam's serious bout with pneumonia. No, if Miriam or Robyn faced serious trouble, Aaron would have notified him through the usual channels. And he'd be specific, very specific, about the amount of money needed.

Yes, Aaron contacted him on serious matters, but what about fraud? Would the logical Aaron become illogical then? He harbored protective feelings toward Miriam, seeing himself as the brother she should have married. *Ah, Aaron, did you think me ignorant of that? Is that why you gobbled up the opportunity to handle my business affairs? And if you gave short-sighted advice in running the gallery, what then? Would you notify me of a problem?*

No, Drew concluded, Aaron never admitted failure.

He considered Ingrid's financial ventures and immediately rolled down the window for more air. He raced across the path of the driver who had cut him off moments before, the risk pumping his blood and clearing his thoughts even more. *Zurich. Wanted in Zurich.* There was no logical reason so the answer, like Aaron and Ingrid, was illogical. *Okay, I'm coming,* he thought, *but who benefits the most by my arrival? A vengeful half-brother? An ex-wife? The baroness, or Porter Deven?*

He felt betrayed by the man beside him. Information, as scattered as it was, had slipped into Drew's hands too easily. No matter which angle he considered, someone wanted him in Zurich, but it kept narrowing down to Vic and Porter. To the Company.

They had set him up.

He glanced at Vic's ashen face and listened to his uneven breathing. How did this old friend fit into the Zurich game plan? Drew couldn't turn the car around and forget the safety of his family. He had worked all his life by a code of honor.

Wilson stirred. "Do you want me to take the wheel, Drew?"

"No need. We just hit Schaffhausen. I can handle it."

"What's the plan?"

"We'll stay at a friend's *zimmer frei* just outside of Zurich. He belonged to Swiss Intelligence a few years back."

"A good man then? He can help us find Harland Smith."

"Forget Smith, Vic. He'll help me keep an eye on you."

"But Smith might be in Zurich to get rid of you, Drew."

"Then we'll need firearms."

"We're going in shooting, eh?"

"We're going in protected, Vic."

"You've always been a straight-shooter."

"I wish I could say the same for you. I'm going to stick with you because I need you. We won't let anything happen to my family. And if Smith is the one who wants me in Zurich, I'll be ready. It's a point of honor with me."

Thirteen

In Brussels Sherman Prescott turned the key to his hotel suite and thrust the door open with his foot. Andrea came running across the room, radiant in a white batiste dress trimmed in delicate violet lace, the fragrance of her St. Laurent perfume growing stronger as she reached him.

He tossed his briefcase aside, caught her in his arms, and swung her around, his lips already touching hers. He stepped back, holding her hands and gazing fondly at her again. "Do you realize how much it means to come home to you?" he asked.

"I think so. I spent hours getting ready just for you. Look. I even had my shoes dyed."

"Purple?"

"No, silly. Violet to match the trim in my dress. So hurry, Sherm, we have a dinner reservation for eight."

"Oh, Andrea, I don't want to face another dish of mussels, no matter what kind of sauce they pour on them."

"But that's the Belgian specialty, honey. Now go get your shower. I have your clothes all laid out."

He started for the bathroom, then turned back "Would you consider having dinner here in the room? Just the two of us?"

Andrea looked away, trying to hide her disappointment. "I've been cooped up all day, Sherm. I was really looking forward to going out this evening—what's left of it." But with a fading smile, she was already at the phone.

"What are you doing, Andrea?"

"I'm calling the maitre d' to cancel our reservation. Then I'll dial room service and order a couple of sandwiches, some fruit, and coffee. Will that be enough?"

"Plenty. You don't mind?"

She did, and he knew it. Her lonely day must have dragged on. He tried to explain his own long day, saying, "It's been a rough eleven hours at the office, sweetheart."

"I can tell."

"I'm expected to iron out the problems here in Brussels and report back to my boss, Buzz Kippen."

"It's okay, Sherm. We'll have other evenings." She had already slipped out of her clothes and into a lounging gown, the strawberry birthmark clearly visible across her breast.

"What are you going to do now?" he asked.

"I'm going to curl up on the bed with my sketchbook and pretend you're not home yet."

It was borderline sulk.

"I'd like to curl up there with you."

Normally she would have said, "Then do."

He watched her, intrigued, as she shook both of their pillows and made herself a feathery backrest. She sank into it, her legs crossed, the manicured toes wiggling freely. Andrea managed a smile, not even a hint of her frustration showing.

"I'm sorry. Honestly, sweetheart."

Her bright blue eyes met his. "I promised you I wouldn't interfere with your job. I'd rather be here for you than back home worrying about you."

"I expected to have more free time, Andrea. I'm sorry, but the manager at the office hasn't turned out to be the help I expected. Dirk just isn't the person for the job."

"I thought you liked him."

"I do. He's a good man, but not for leadership."

"Wasn't he your choice?"

"No, Buzz Kippen owed him a favor, but Dirk is not an organizer. He'll go right on losing money for the company. I need to call Buzz about it this evening. Our Brussels' office will fold if we don't get a new man in there."

"Buzz won't like it."

"He'll like losing money less."

"Are you working a long day again tomorrow—on Saturday?"

"I'm afraid so. I've got to work out a way for Dirk to stay with the company in a less demanding role. Sales maybe."

"Will he agree to that change?"

"Not at first." Sherm tried to catch her eye. "Andrea, I don't want you left alone in this hotel room any more than necessary. We have a dinner engagement with Dirk and his wife early next week, but what about a trip to Zurich after that?"

"Do you think you can get away?"

"Not until next weekend. But you can go on ahead. A friend of yours is there."

He was teasing now as he swung his Hartmann on the foot of the bed. He flipped it open, took out an unmarked folder, and dropped it beside her. "See what you think of this."

She scanned the fax. "This is from Robyn Gregory."

"Yes."

"But you got this last week."

"Dirk got it last week. He just passed it on to me."

"Sherm, we talked Robyn into coming to Europe after all."

"I don't think so. Calm down and read the rest of the fax. Robyn and her mother are here at Ingrid von Tonner's invitation."

Andrea read it again. "They arrived last Friday. And Robyn wants to see her father. It says so right here." Her finger hit the middle of the fax. "We've got to call Drew."

"Go slowly, Andrea. Robyn was adamant about not wanting to see him again. And now this."

"You didn't really believe her, did you?"

"I take people at their word."

"Yes, and you don't read between the lines. So call Drew."

"I did."

The lilt left her voice. "What did he say?"

"I don't know. I wasn't able to reach him."

"Then call again."

"It's not that simple, Andrea. Three weeks ago in London, I had no trouble at all reaching Drew. I called the embassy. They put me right through." Sherm sat on the edge of the bed and pushed his briefcase aside. "This time they kept transferring me from one department to another. Everyone hedged. First he was away from his desk. Then he was unavailable. Then it changed from unavailable to out of town."

"Maybe he's on a special assignment with the Agency. They wouldn't tell you that."

"I've got this gut feeling that it's something different."

"Did you try his friend Vic Wilson?"

"They said Wilson was on the Riviera, holidaying for a couple of weeks. I even called Porter Deven in Paris. He didn't exactly throw out the welcome mat."

"He never does."

"I thought he could at least be civil."

She laced her fingers with his, concern in her eyes. "Did Porter say anything at all?"

"That Drew was out of touch, indefinitely. Finally, I told Porter that Drew's daughter was in Europe and that I wanted to get them together. And Porter said, 'I should have known Drew would pull a trick like that.' But he kind of chortled, as though that's exactly what he wanted."

"That doesn't make sense, Sherm."

"Porter has a knack for that. I don't know what he means any more than I know what Robyn meant in her fax when she said there was a business problem at the gallery. One thing is certain: Porter doesn't want us involved in a Gregory reunion."

The sketchbook slipped from Andrea's lap. "Robyn's mother was upset about a lawsuit when we were there. Remember?"

"Yes, she said it would ruin her."

"That wouldn't have anything to do with Drew Gregory?"

"It might. I'll try to reach him again tomorrow while you make arrangements for Zurich, but somehow I don't expect the answers will be any different."

"Sherm, should I tell Robyn that her father is missing?"

"We don't know that, Andrea."

"We apparently don't know anything."

Picking up the fax, he put it back in his briefcase. "It sounds as though Robyn is counting on her father's help. Honey, you go to Zurich and be there with her."

"What am I going to tell her about Drew?"

"The truth—that we haven't reached him yet. I'll keep trying. If I bug Porter enough, he might tell me. He wanted to know where the Gregorys are staying. I didn't tell him." He stroked her cheek. "I don't like sending you on to Zurich without me. But Robyn may need a friend with her."

"Will you miss me?"

"Dreadfully." He knuckled her chin, tilted it up, and kissed her. "I can join you in Zurich next weekend, maybe. That's the. best I can do. Will that be all right?"

The sparkle in her eyes hid her disappointment. "Come sooner if you can."

"Yes. I don't want Robyn leaving Europe until she sees Drew."

"Is it that important to you, Sherm?"

"I keep hoping that she'll get to climb Heidi's Alps with her dad after all these years. It's a rough spot to be in—facing past hurts and having no real faith to sustain them. Robyn may be more like Drew than she realizes. Drew is convinced that his lifestyle and belief in God are incompatible."

Sherm stood abruptly, still smiling down at Andrea. He locked the briefcase, set it on the floor, and toed it under the chair. Then he closed Andrea's sketchbook.

"What are you doing, Sherm?"

"You don't have to finish that design tonight, do you?"

"Did you change your mind about dinner?"

He slackened his tie and removed it. "No, I have something better in mind."

"That shower?"

"Later," he told her, tossing his shirt on the chair.

"The phone call to Buzz Kippen?"

"Later."

"But you brought home a briefcase full of work."

His shoes hit the floor, the thud muffled by the thick carpet. "I'm calling it a day. The problems will seem smaller in the morning."

"Oh, Sherm," she said, laughing, as he pulled back the sheet. "Room service is bringing up some sandwiches."

"Are you hungry?"

"Not really," she whispered as he eased down beside her.

"Then they can leave the tray outside the room."

Fourteen

Robyn sat by the window watching the dawn light the lake with pink hues. She breathed in the fresh air, fragrant from the flowers that surrounded the hotel.

Switzerland! Heidi's storybook land. Heidi's Alps. She longed for a footpath to the summit, a Peterli goat herder of her own, an Alm-Uncle's hut on a high cliff with fir trees that whistled, and winds that sang. And a father to climb the mountain with her.

Across the room beside Robyn's empty bed, Miriam tossed and turned—one soft cheek buried in a feather pillow, her slender hand curled into a fist as though, even in sleep, she struggled to shut Robyn out. As their days in Zurich had lengthened, Miriam spent more time alone with Ingrid going over the records and shipping invoices. They talked for hours as they had always done, but heatedly now, their friendship stretching to the breaking point.

Robyn turned from the window and hurriedly dressed. Picking up her running shoes, she tiptoed to the door and unchained it.

"Will you be gone long?" Miriam asked sleepily.

"I'm going jogging for an hour. Mom, come and go with me."

"Not this morning. I'm meeting with Ingrid."

"At this hour?"

"For breakfast. Will you be back in time to eat with us?"

"I don't need any more von Tonner indigestion."

"Robyn, I wish you didn't dislike her so."

"There's a difference between dislike and distrust." When Miriam frowned, Robyn said, "Rest until I get back. We'll take a quick swim in the cold lake; then I'll go to the meeting with you."

Miriam flicked her half-smile. "You'd be bored, darling."

"Angry, perhaps. Is anything getting accomplished?"

"Aaron thinks so. He's going over all of Ingrid's records."

"Let *me* check them out. I'm tired of spending my time browsing in museums and bookstores or strolling around Zurich. We're in this business together, Mother. Why am I being shut out?"

"Aaron thought it best."

"Aaron? He's your financial adviser, Mother. He knows nothing about art or running the shop. I do."

"I need his help. He agrees with Ingrid that the problem started at the warehouse with mishandling in the shipments."

"Roj Stapleton oversaw some of those orders."

"We've discussed that. I'm more interested in the missing records and two or three misplaced art pieces."

"Misplaced in a small warehouse? Come on, Mother."

"Stolen then. Outside tampering, Robyn. Not one of us." She hesitated. "Your father perhaps."

Rage flushed Robyn's face. "I told you that's ridiculous. He doesn't even know we own an art gallery, let alone care."

"Someone is trying to destroy us. Deliberately. Aaron is convinced that Drew is behind it."

"And you believe that?"

"I don't know what to believe anymore. Your father set up a Swiss account for us—for you mainly—a long time ago. It was being reserved for you when you turned thirty."

"You never told me about that."

"Haven't I? But then, you aren't thirty yet either. Ingrid and I went to the Schwzizerische Kredit Bank yesterday. The account was closed."

"You closed it?"

"Someone did. Only your father and I knew about it."

"Not Aaron and Ingrid?"

"Well, of course they had access to it. Ingrid used it to buy some of the paintings."

"So what happened—a bank robbery?"

"Sweetheart, this isn't Los Angeles with four bank robberies a week. Here, they're shocked if they have one every ten years."

"Maybe you went to the wrong bank."

Miriam's pillow muffled her sigh. "It was the right bank. You know I don't like borrowing money or taking out long-term loans.

When I wanted to expand the gallery, Aaron encouraged me to use the Swiss account for our European transactions. He set it up for me—with plans to pay it back before you turned thirty. I've trusted Aaron on business matters."

"It seems you've trusted everyone except my father and me."

"You're not listening to me, Robyn. Your father is the only person who could have closed the account. Ten days ago a Mr. Gregory closed everything out."

"Which Mr. Gregory, Mother?"

As Robyn cracked the door open, Miriam sat up on the side of the bed, hand-combing her hair. *You're still beautiful,* Robyn thought, in *spite of the sleep-starved circles beneath your eyes.*

"I need more money to salvage the gallery. How can I if my account here in Switzerland has been emptied?"

"I thought it was my account."

"I should have remembered that from the beginning. Go on. Enjoy your time in Zurich. Let me worry about the problems."

"Mother, I'm worried about you. But I think I'd better fly home early and get out of your way."

Miriam put her hands to her cheeks and rocked, her bare legs swinging back and forth, her voice hopeless as she said, "Don't leave. I want you to go with me to Ingrid's warehouse."

"In Germany? Ingrid's idea?"

"No, mine. Roj and Julia may be there. Floy took them to Los Angeles International yesterday for a Lufthansa flight direct to Frankfurt. They'd transfer from there to Dusseldorf."

"That's not far from Ingrid's home. Did she send for them?"

"They told Floy that I asked them to come."

"You didn't, did you?"

"No, but someone did."

Robyn was still mulling over Roj and Julia's departure for Europe when she saw Ingrid and Aaron sunning themselves on the porch. Aaron stood as she reached them and kissed her on the cheek. "We're not seeing much of you," he said.

"Your choice, Uncle Aaron."

"You're on vacation, Robbie. Enjoy it."

"Alone? I'm sick of doing Zurich alone."

"Not for long," Ingrid said lazily. "Your friend from Belgium is coming for a visit."

"Andrea Prescott? How do you know?"

"The concierge told me. Andrea's husband made a reservation for her. I asked the concierge to put her in the connecting room next to yours. Doesn't her visit please you?"

"Not now. Not with Mother fighting to salvage the gallery."

"The whole thing is just a misunderstanding. You'll see."

"Then prove it, Ingrid." She touched her uncle's hand. "Aaron, include me in your meetings. I need to know what's going on."

"Robbie, we're discussing some serious problems and mergers."

"Then I should be included, Aaron. If anything happens to Mom, I'll be the owner then."

Ingrid lifted her sunglasses. "Not quite, dear. If anything happens to Miriam, you and I may be in business together."

"Never."

"My 25 percent says that I am. Close your mouth, Robyn dear. It doesn't become you. For a certain percentage, I agreed to help Miriam out of her present difficulty. I've been doing the legwork here in Europe for three years, supplying your mother with the choicest of paintings. Her profits have tripled since I've been helping. My own benefits have not."

"You're tying a noose around Mother's neck."

"Lower your voice, dear. We must not upset the hotel guests."

"Is all of this true, Uncle Aaron?"

"I helped draw up the papers, Robbie."

"Satisfied, dear? I do have the money. For starters, I'd sell the baron's favorite Rembrandt. That would net me at least seven figures—enough to bail Miriam out. Or I'll get rid of the baron's portrait. Some fool collector would find his face charming." Ingrid waved her ringed hand, inspecting the well-manicured nails. "My only problem would be barren spots on the walls at the mansion." She leveled an intense gaze at Robyn. "If something happens to Miriam, we *will be* partners."

Robyn did a quick mental calculation. Three years ago she was in Europe finishing her art studies when the gallery sales skyrocketed—

shortly after Ingrid became her mother's European buyer. But it didn't sound like Miriam's business aplomb to be partners with Ingrid. "Did mother sign those papers?" she asked.

Aaron hedged. "Does she have a choice, Robbie? She needs cash to fight the lawsuits—to salvage her shop and reputation. Partnership with Ingrid is a small price to pay."

"Uncle Aaron, my father would help us."

Ingrid's dark eyes flashed. More calmly, she said, "Perhaps I should withdraw my offer, Aaron. Let Robyn solve her mother's problems. After all, it is her father who is destroying the gallery."

"Is he? I'll ask him when I see him."

"Aaron, stop her from such foolishness."

"Ingrid, Robbie makes her own choices."

"Are you hoping I won't find him, Uncle Aaron?"

"If Drew wants to be found, you'll find him."

❧❦

After jogging, Robyn sat in a chaise lounge on the porch and watched the swan fan gracefully around the wading pool. Dreams for a career of her own—away from the gallery—kept slipping away.

Her inner turmoil deepened as two boys ran in front of her, yelling—the older boy tall and lean, the younger overweight and defiant.

"Come, Giles," the older boy urged angrily. "We're going to the lake."

Giles held back, his chubby legs braced, his wide brown eyes watchful. He had to be five or six, as handsome as his brother.

"Then stay here," the older boy commanded. "Don't go anywhere; I'll be right back."

The tall boy was near the steps, but he swung lithely over the railing and headed toward the lake, his hands thrust deep in his pocket, his head bent down, a boy with the weight of Zurich on his shoulders.

Giles skipped over to the pool and crouched on his well-padded knees, his elbows propped on the scalloped ledge. His eyes grew bigger as the swan glided by him.

When Robyn looked up again, the child was gone. She leaned forward, her feet on the porch, searching. Her heart did a fractional standstill. The boy lay submerged in the water, his facial features distorted as he floated limply to the top, his thin shirt ballooning around him.

Robyn kicked her shoes free. In four quick strides she was in the pool, making a shallow dive beneath him. She grabbed the child and thrust him upward. He sputtered and cried, his lungs bursting for air as his face broke the surface of the water.

"You're all right," she said, tossing the wet strands of hair from her face. "You're safe."

She fought against his flailing arms, subdued him, and spoke softly to him, her language conflicting with his own. When he caught sight of the swan fluttering in circles at the far end of the pool, its upraised wings threatening, its loud hissing call scolding their intrusion into its peaceful world, the boy's massive brown eyes widened in terror.

Robyn cradled him against her, heard him regurgitate, felt him spewing his breakfast over her new outfit. Still she held on, supporting his face, comforting him.

From across the porch a striking couple came running toward them. "Giles," the woman screamed.

Giles held out his arms to her.

Robyn waded through the pool and lifted the child to her.

"I didn't realize he had fallen in until—" Robyn began.

"Until he almost drowned." A flow of French words caressed the child. His dark hair had turned to tiny ringlets, pond water still dripping down his chin. The woman kissed him on both cheeks and hugged him again.

Giles stared up at the tall, broad man with stern eyes.

"What were you doing, Giles?" the man asked.

The boy shrank back against his mother, drenching her sheer sun dress and forming an ugly wet outline against her body. She kept rocking him, unconcerned about her appearance.

Robyn smiled at her, her own clothes a soggy mess.

In a rapid onslaught of French and English, the woman said, "I owe you so much."

"No," Robyn told her. "Your son was just frightened."

They had stirred quite a crowd now, and this infuriated the man further. "Where's Anzel?" he demanded.

Robyn guessed he meant the older boy and pointed toward the lake. Anzel was coming on the run. "Giles, what happened? I told you to sit still."

The enormous brown eyes looked reproachful. "The swan," Giles said. "He wanted me to play with him."

As the man gripped Anzel's rail-thin arm, the boy winced. "Your *maman* asked you to watch Giles, did she not?"

Anzel nodded, wordless.

"I asked you a question."

"Yes. I wanted Giles to go with me."

The pressure of the curious crowd eyeing them embarrassed the man. He released the boy's arm. "Go with your brother. Take Giles up and change him." He was giving the older boy a man's command, his order directed at Anzel, the responsibility placed on those narrow shoulders, not his mother's. "Go on, Anzel. They've taken your luggage to the room. I'll be there in a moment."

The boy obeyed him without flinching.

To his wife he said, "Let Giles walk."

She put him down, her face still radiant as she smiled at her younger son. His hand stayed clenched in hers as they walked away, Anzel close behind them. Glowering at Robyn, the man extended his broad hand and helped her step from the pool. He reached for his wallet, saying, "Thank you."

"No, don't. It was nothing. The boy was just afraid from swallowing some of the pond water."

He looked scathingly at her wet clothes, smelling now of the boy's vomit. "You'll need new clothes."

"I'll wash these."

He glanced around, angry at the rest of the hotel guests still crowding them. "A whole porch full of people and you're the only one who saw the boy struggling."

"The first one perhaps."

He studied her intently. "Tell me your name," he demanded.

"I'm Robyn Gregory. I'm a guest at the hotel."

"Robyn Gregory?" He seemed to recoil. "I'm indebted to you." He spun on his heels and stalked off toward the hotel lobby.

☙❧

Harland lay in the wide bed beside Monique, listening to her soft breathing. She had been asleep for hours, drifting quickly away from him. He watched the moon play games with the clouds, listened to the night sounds, felt the cool breeze from the open window across his bare chest. Sleep refused to come. He turned toward her. "Monique," he said.

Silence.

"Monique."

She stirred this time.

"I didn't mean to upset you."

"It's all right," she said, her words sleep-filled.

"We can't let Anzel come between us."

"Time came between us, Harland, not our son."

"Are you upset with me about Giles?"

"He's only a little boy. You're his papa. You should have comforted him, held him—not yelled at him."

"He didn't want to come to me."

"I know," she said softly. "Falling in the water like that won't help his cold. I should take him to the clinic in the morning."

"I can't go with you."

"To the doctor's? You've never gone with us."

For a minute, he thought she had fallen asleep again. He searched for the right words to bring her back to him. "Monique, I'll make it up to you. We'll be happy wherever we go. You'll see."

She propped herself up on the pillow and faced him. "Happy? After all these months when we thought you were dead?"

"You knew better. I always told you to give me time to get back to you if something happened. I couldn't send for you right away. You know that."

"What was I supposed to tell the boys?"

"I thought they'd understand."

"Your sons didn't. We were alone in Paris. Your old friends wanted nothing to do with us."

"We'll make new friends."

"Will we? You wouldn't even let me stay and talk to the woman who rescued Giles." Her voice softened. "Giles's accident frightened me, Harland. I want to go back to Paris with the boys."

He gripped her wrist. "I need you here with me. Someday we'll go back." *When Drew Gregory is dead,* he thought. "But not yet. I promise you, we'll go back."

"But I miss my garden and Felice."

"You can have another garden wherever we go. In time, we'll send for Felice. That will please Giles. And you."

"She won't come."

"She will for you."

"No, she'll never leave Paris." She crawled across the bed and sat beside him. "After your...after I thought you were dead, Harland, I tried to call some of our old friends, particularly the ones who sent flowers. But no one would talk to me."

"I'm sorry."

"You're sorry? That's all? I even called your CIA friend."

"Not Porter Deven?"

"Yes. He refused my calls, so I went to his apartment—where we used to visit him. He never even offered me a chair. He made me stand by the door like some servant. His old basset hound growled the whole time I was there."

"Monique, why did you go to him?"

"I tried everyone else first. The President. Our friends from the embassy dinners. No one wanted anything to do with me."

He groaned inwardly. "But why Porter?"

"I thought he would understand. He was always so friendly to me. When you were busy at the official dinners, he would dance with me or just sit and talk about the children. I thought he'd know what happened. Did you know they closed your offices?"

"Yes, the reports filtered back to me."

"Harland, the government wouldn't even let me take your personal effects, not even your picture." She sucked in her breath. "It was as though I were being punished for your dying. The DGSE and the Sûreté asked me such horrible questions about your foreign negotiations. I didn't understand, Harland."

He tried to take her hand. She pulled away.

"Why didn't you go home to your parents?" he asked.

"To Isigny? They didn't want me either. They asked so many questions. They never wanted us to marry—you know that."

"After all I did for them?"

"Money doesn't buy their trust. They offered to take Giles—but not Anzel. Anzel was so unhappy there."

"He's unhappy wherever he is."

Her body went rigid. "Harland, don't say that. Anzel suffered in your absence—suffered deep humiliation and shame at all the nasty rumors about you."

He wanted to defend himself, but he had no defense.

"Harland, I'm not the young girl you first saw in the fields of Normandy leading a stray cow back to the farm. I'm not barefoot and unsophisticated now. I'm a grown woman. I'm your wife, but I'm a mother. What happens to my sons is more important to me than anything."

"More important than me—than us?"

Gently, she ran her fingers over the back of his hand. "Yes. I can't go on not knowing who you are or what you are."

He thought he would snap under the strain of the rage boiling inside him. "I don't want to lose you."

She considered that in silence.

"Did you hear me, Monique?" he asked, his voice turning harsh. "I don't want to lose you."

"You already have."

"I'll stop you if you try to leave."

"Not if you love me." He knew she was watching him intently in the darkness of their room. Her voice was almost a whisper when she said, "That's the one honest thing about you, Harland. You have always adored me, always loved me."

He felt his shoulders caving in, the load of who he really was weighing heavily on him. His voice was taut with emotion as he answered, "I used to ask you, 'Why do you stay with me, Monique? I am an old man.' Do you remember how you answered?"

She sighed, perhaps for the memory. "It's still the same answer. 'You are young in my eyes. You are handsome. You adore me.' I know these things, but I can no longer stay with you."

"Will you stay a few days?"

"Perhaps. But I must get the boys back to Paris. Anzel misses his friends."

He wanted to threaten her, to tell her that he would cut off her finances, but he couldn't. She had been everything to him. He thought of his mother—defeated by the hard life she knew in Brooklyn. He would not let this happen to Monique. His anger at Drew Gregory mounted in violent waves. *You are the cause of all of this,* he thought.

"I won't give you a divorce," he said.

"I won't ask for one." She leaned over and placed her cheek softly against his. "I can't divorce a dead man."

She stood then and walked to the window. The moon drifted in and out of the clouds, brightening the room one moment, darkening it the next. He caught fleeting glimpses of Monique silhouetted there—her white gown molded to her body, her shimmering dark hair blowing in the breeze. Except for their breathing, the room seemed deathly still. Finally, she made her way back to bed. "I'll stay until the end of next week, Harland."

"We'll take the boys to the mountain chalet. They'll love it."

"But we're not taking them skiing on the higher slopes," she warned. "No matter how deep the snow is up there. You know skiing terrifies Anzel—and I won't have him embarrassed in front of Giles. Let these last days with your sons be pleasant ones." Monique pillowed her head again, her back to him. "I'm so tired, Harland, and homesick."

Harland leaned over and kissed her as she drifted off to sleep. Unless he could stop her, what he had feared since the day he had met her in Normandy would happen—she would leave him. He swung to the side of the bed and stared out at the overcast sky, an inner darkness engulfing him. He would risk everything for Monique—even a return to Paris or the farm at Isigny—if only Drew Gregory were dead.

Fifteen

Pierre Courtland awakened with the noon sun pouring into his hotel room and muffled voices beneath his balcony. In spite of the lake breeze coming in through his open window, the spacious room felt stuffy. Overheated. He tossed back the top sheet, swung himself upright, and padded barefoot to the window.

Down below, he saw a flower-shaped pool in the center of the portico, its scalloped edges like rose petals, its waters as blue as the Zurichsee. Four marbled steps lay submerged in the water, but the pool, though deep enough for swimming, was only for the pleasure of the swans that glided there. The fence and rough-hewn pillars had been painted white, offering a soft romantic effect with the lake in the background. Hotel guests relaxed in the lounge chairs, but the lone hammock on the far end of the porch was empty.

Pierre watched Ingrid von Tonner make her way to the pool, a sketchpad in her hands. She kicked off her fancy slippers, sat on the edge, and dangled her toes in the water. One swan eyed her curiously, as Pierre was doing.

"Good morning, Baroness," he called.

She looked up and waved, her whimsical "Hello there—come on down" rippling through Pierre's open window. He turned and headed for a shower and a shave He reached Ingrid fifteen minutes later, carefree in his khaki shorts and hunter-green shirt, a magazine tucked under his arm. Dropping into the chair closest to her, he quipped, "When did you take up painting, Baroness?"

She acknowledged him with her enchanting smile. "You remember Sigmund Valdemar. He gave me some pointers."

Not enough, Pierre thought. But the drawing had Ingrid's special flare. "Ingrid, you've been avoiding me all week."

"Have I? Well, darling, how did you find me here at the

Alpenhof?" she asked.

"I called Albert and told him the baron needed you."

"You're so clever. So what's wrong with the baron this time?"

"Felix is lonely," Pierre said. "He needs company."

"He has you."

"It's not the same. I'm only there every other weekend."

"You should be out with the girls—dancing at the cabaret or sailing on Lake Geneva. How can Felix survive with you on vacation?"

"He counts on my visits, but he can't count weeks."

"It's a marvel that he even remembers you."

"By name? He doesn't. He simply knows that I'm an old friend. He's a frail old man, Ingrid. Surely you can spare him a visit?"

"Why? He'd just want an accounting of his possessions."

"They don't mean anything to him anymore. His life has been reduced to pureed foods and bed restraints."

"You can't blame me for that."

"You put him there."

"It's the best clinic available. And the most expensive, I might add. What do you expect of me, Pierre?"

"A chance for Felix to see the Alps and breathe fresh air again."

"You've both grown soft on me."

"Felix has grown old, Ingrid. But he asks for you often."

"And when I get there, he doesn't even know my name. The last time I went, Felix threw a flower vase at me."

"I thought you threw it at him."

"What difference does it make? I went as you suggested and took flowers. We quarreled. So I dropped the vase on the floor."

"Just as he reached out to take the flowers from you?"

"Don't be a cad, darling. You weren't there. You know that Felix is not very steady. He just couldn't hold onto them."

Pierre lowered his voice. "When I saw him the next day, he still had one of those wilted flowers in his bathrobe pocket."

"A sentimental fool. Did he save the shattered vase, too?"

"You've changed, Ingrid. When I first met you, you were dancing with the baron, whirling across the ballroom in his arms."

"Times change." For a second she brightened. "He was such a

marvelous dancer. We did make a magnificent impression on people."

"You seemed so happy then."

"Of course. I was on the verge of possessing everything he owned."

"Not quite everything."

"Meaning?"

"The lost pieces of the von Tonner art collection."

"The baron convinced me they were stolen by the Nazi regime."

He leaned forward. "Then you must have been surprised when you discovered them in the tunnels beneath the house."

Her long dark lashes flickered. "What tunnels?"

"I played in them when I was a boy."

"Impossible. The baron said no one—"

"I discovered them quite by accident."

"Next you'll be telling me they're hidden in cement vaults."

"They are. Felix thinks you sent him away so you can steal those paintings."

"That's nothing but the ramblings of an old man. Tell him his mansion walls are filled with paintings, even his favorite Rembrandt."

"Take him home again, Ingrid. The Klees would help you."

"Felix is too sick for me to take care of him. The von Tonner mansion just isn't big enough for both of us."

Pierre didn't know what troubled him most—the state of the old man's soul or the physical debilitation that he suffered. If the old man could once again feel the wind to his face, look at the mountains that he loved, sense the freedom of his youth, could he then better understand that God cared about him? "Ingrid, is it asking too much of you to go and see Felix again? Don't those years as his wife count for something?"

"Very long years," she reminded him.

"He doesn't have much time left."

"Felix plans to live forever."

"There's only one way for him to do that."

She lifted one tapered finger and shook it in his face. "Don't pull that lecture on me. You may believe in living forever and ever. But I don't. This is it." Her hand swept the portico, her gaze turning toward the lake and the view of the Alps in the distance. "This is all there is until life plays out. Afterwards, kaput. You're finished. Extinction.

Nothingness. I'm telling you, Pierre, enjoy life while you can. I intend to."

"You're wrong, Ingrid."

"Am I?" He heard the unexpected catch in her voice, saw her lips quiver. "The baron is not a man prepared for heaven," she said, her lips white, her rage building.

"He can be."

"How? He doesn't believe in heaven or God any more than I do."

He pitied her but felt no compassion; this troubled him. "I grew up believing that God was way out there beyond the Alps, until—"

The puckered brows arched. "Spare me. The baron often spoke of your religious fervor—your turnaround for Jesus. I'm not interested."

He wanted to say, *Someday, every knee will bow, every tongue confess....* The words caught in his throat. He tried to imagine her bowing to anyone or making a statement of faith in a confessional. To him, that process for Ingrid seemed totally alien; yet he knew that one day every knee would bow, including Ingrid's.

"Ingrid, my turnaround was genuine."

"So was mine, dear. I went to the cathedral when I was a child. I knew the Stations of the Cross—even took confirmation classes. But they were a waste of my time." Mockingly, she added, "Pierre dear, as I grew up, I *put away childish things.*"

He scowled, angered by her ridicule. She had a shrewd way of short-circuiting his thoughts, of disqualifying his words about God. Before he could retaliate, she said softly, "Perhaps I will visit the baron soon and say good-bye. Will that satisfy you?"

Pierre doubted Ingrid. He leveled his gaze on her, trying to understand the attraction that had so captivated the baron. He did a mental rundown, struck again with her outward beauty and seeing what Felix must have seen—her oval face with its high chiseled cheekbones and well-formed mouth, the flawless skin, the slender neck, the slim figure—enhanced now by elegant clothes and jewelry.

She was still beguiling with gleaming silver hair and lovely eyes—those pools of directness, sparkling with amusement as he looked down at her. One brown eye was a fraction smaller than the other, as though she were squinting at him. But beyond the sparkle, he sensed the emptiness. The baron had doubtlessly loved this woman for her beauty as intensely as Pierre disliked her for her cunning deception. For the baron's sake, he decided not to antagonize her further. He smiled, thinking, *For now, heaven can wait.*

"You're such an idealist, darling," she said again.

He stood, hovering above her, and listened to the soft magnetic pitch in her voice, the persuasive quick wit that blinded people to her deception. "Ingrid, perhaps we could have dinner together tonight?"

"I have guests."

"Then some other evening while I'm here?" He turned to leave.

"Wait, Pierre. I need your help."

His guard shot up. "Mine? That's quite unusual."

"I have a friend visiting. We have business matters to settle. Do me a favor, Pierre. Keep her daughter busy for the next few days."

"Get yourself another babysitter, Baroness. I won't spend my vacation keeping some girl entertained. Besides, my uncle is flying in today."

"Kurt Brinkmeirer?" She blotched her sketchpad. "On business?"

"Don't worry. It's nothing official with Interpol. You know we spend a couple of days holidaying together each year."

He walked away, deliberately whistling "Lili Marlene."

Pierre made his way along the veranda toward the hammock on the east portico. Down the sloping hill from the porch, the lake lapped gently at the shore, the old buildings of Zurich pink reflections in its waters. He felt a genuine affection for Felix, but even more, he worried about the baron dying and having no hope beyond the grave. Once or twice, he had broached the subject of eternity with him. The gaunt face had lifted, the gaze vacant, as though Pierre were speaking a foreign language. It wasn't just his confusion—the whole topic of God and life beyond the grave was unfamiliar to the baron. But Pierre wouldn't give up, not as long as Felix stayed alive.

Pierre paused as he ambled along and took another look at the lake—calm, sapphire-blue, inviting. He nodded absently to a guest or two. Then his gaze drifted from them toward the hammock on the far end of the veranda.

Occupied now! *Unfair,* he decided. He had counted on its privacy to sunbathe. He considered walking over and tipping the hammock or blaring a radio.

From where Pierre stood, he saw the shapely legs and the polished toenails. The lady was engrossed in a book, and he heard her laugh out loud at something she had read—a quick easy ripple so light and so cheering it invited a response. He sauntered over, still wishing for a way to take over the hammock. She wore raw silk shorts and a bright blue halter with a plunging neckline; her skin was a lobster-pink from too much sun.

He rested against the stark white railing, watching the sun filter down on her auburn hair. The lake breeze caught wisps of it and blew them across her cheek. Large, squared sunglasses clung precariously to the narrow bridge of her upturned nose. Pierre guessed that behind those dark glasses lay a pretty face to match the lovely wind-blown hair and the bubbly laughter.

She lowered her book. "Do you always watch strangers so intently?"

"Not always," he said, spellbound.

The dark lenses hid the color of her eyes. He had the strange urge to take them off and tilt her chin up.

"Is something wrong?" the girl asked.

"You're sunburned, for one."

She inspected her arm as Pierre added, "Your glasses hide your face. I can't tell how pretty you are." He stepped over at once and gently lifted them off. "There," he said at her startled gaze. "That's better."

He tucked them in his shirt pocket and scrutinized her more closely. Saucer sea-blue eyes peered up at him. *Perfect. Beautiful.*

"Do you always go around pulling off people's sunglasses?"

"Always." He smiled approvingly.

She sat motionless, doubt in her expression, surprise playing at the corner of her well-shaped mouth. Then she smiled in return. He nudged the hammock with his knee and made her sway, his gaze settling once more on her eyes.

For a moment, he had the ridiculous notion that love at first sight was possible. A rather bold, unpredictable notion for a man who prided himself in sensible, precise, businesslike decisions. *Take it easy,* he told himself. *You're not looking for a bride.* But he was on holiday—and after his frustrating encounter with Ingrid, it would be pleasant to talk and laugh with this stranger. He could tell she wasn't very tall, and he wondered whether she would come up to his chin or only to his shoulders if she stood. At five-eleven, he might well tower above her, a protective advantage.

He was aware now she needed another type of protection. Two blanched circles framed those lovely eyes, making the sunburned face glow more brightly. He reached for the lotion in his hip pocket and handed it to her. "It's a bit late," he said, "but it might take some of the sting out of the burn."

She sniffed the wild thyme fragrance and then bathed her arms and face with it. He swung the hammock again. "Are you on holiday?"

"You could call it that. I came to Europe with my mother. She's here on business."

"From?"

"California."

He smiled. "I've been there."

She matched his smile. "It's so crowded, I think everyone has."

"If you're here on vacation, then are you free?"

"I am right now." Her voice lost its lilt. "Actually, I'm looking for someone."

"Me, perhaps?" he suggested.

"Could be," she said, unable to stop another chuckle. His own laughter, deep and base, rippled with it.

Pierre glanced at his watch. He'd invite her to dinner and convince her that he was the one she sought. When Uncle Kurt arrived, he'd have to cancel their evening together—cancel tomorrow's boat ride—cancel everything to be with this girl.

"Will you have dinner with me this evening?" he asked.

"Sorry. I'll be having dinner with Mother."

"But you have it with her all the time, don't you?"

"Yes, I guess I do."

"Then have dinner with me tonight."

"I guess Mother wouldn't mind," she teased.

"Then it's settled. I'll meet you at the reception desk at seven. And—we'd better have names. Mine's Pierre. Pierre Courtland. And I'm on holiday. For as long as you're here."

"And mine is Robyn. Robyn Gregory."

"I like it," he said. "By the way, how tall are you?"

Lightness came back to her words. "Five-four. Five-seven with my dressy heels. Will that be tall enough?"

"Perfect," he said. "Except—" He touched the tip of her nose. "You'd better get out of this sun. Your nose shines like Rudolph, your American reindeer."

She swung from the hammock and slipped into her flat sandals. "I'll be sure to powder my nose before we meet this evening."

"I like it the way it is." He squared his shoulders, towering above her as he thought he would. He whisked back a lock of his wind-tossed hair, suddenly conscious of the tiny mole on his left cheek. He hoped that this girl with the auburn hair and sunburnt nose wouldn't notice. He felt his grin spread from ear to ear.

Robyn snapped her book shut and reached up and rescued her sunshades from his pocket. She slipped them on, hiding her eyes once again. "See you, Pierre," she said. "At seven."

"You're leaving?" he asked, eyeing the empty hammock.

She gave it a swing. "Yes. That's what you wanted, wasn't it?"

She left, sashaying away, without waiting for his answer. He flopped into the hammock and smothered a yodel. In spite of Ingrid von Tonner, this was going to be some holiday after all. It was a good thing he had refused to babysit her friend's daughter. That wasn't his bag anyway. This girl was more to his liking—a delightful young woman with time on her hands. Pierre was anxiously willing to share it.

❧

Pierre went on brushing his hair. "Look, Kurt, I'm sorry about dinner tonight, but I've met this lovely lady."

"Smitten again? Your aunt and I can't keep count."

Pierre laughed good-naturedly. "Maybe I'm serious this time, Kurt.

That's what Aunt Ina wants to hear, isn't it? She's been trying to marry me off for years."

"I suppose this one is rich and ravishing or a smashing beauty with a great body?"

Pierre grinned as he put the hairbrush down. "Not smashing, but very attractive." His first glimpse of her in the hammock flashed into his mind: pink polished toenails and slender, shapely legs. Laughing, he said, "She has a fresh open smile and flaming auburn hair. The sun set it on fire. Give me time, Kurt. I could easily be smitten." More seriously, he said, "The girl seems worried about something. She didn't say much, but there's a sadness about her. I think she needs a friend."

Kurt jammed a Marlboro between his lips. "Is she religious enough for you, Pierre?"

His words set Pierre back on his heels. "This isn't some long-term relationship. We're just having dinner together. But, yes, when I marry, I would want a woman who shares my faith. That will be top priority—far above good looks and intelligence."

"So priorities are only important if you marry the girl? Anything goes for a date?"

Pierre's mental priority list was out again to prerequisite number two—or did he have them in reverse? How could he convince Kurt that the girl would have to be chaste, unsullied? His list sounded egotistical, even to himself, given his past way of life. He wouldn't have said this ten years ago—not even five. Beauty was the big thing then.

Back then, a skiing accident had placed him in a church camp—a whole group of people banded together over a single Book. Intellectuals—chemists, philosophers, artists, doctors, and graduate students—each with the conviction that this man called Jesus was more than theology. With his injured leg elevated, Pierre had fought his mountaintop encounter, fought the Book, fought those who defended it, but in the end, he came to terms with what life was all about.

"Kurt, this evening really is just a date."

His uncle shrugged and tossed his suitcase on the bed. "Go ahead. I'll catch supper alone. And I'll call your aunt and tell her what you're up to—so I'd better have a name. You know Ina."

"The girl's name is Robyn Gregory."

Kurt stood stock still. "Drew Gregory's daughter?"

"I don't know."

"Find out. Stay away from her if she is."

"Hey, Kurt, who's Drew Gregory?"

"A government agent here in Zurich. And we need to know why he's here. The girl's mother—does she own an art gallery?"

"I'm interested in the girl, not her mother."

Kurt slapped his shirts into the drawer. "Pierre, it's not too late for us to get out of Zurich."

"I can't do that. I'm here to keep an eye on Ingrid."

"And while you do that, men from several other countries are going to have their eyes on you. Especially if they see you with Ingrid or Gregory's daughter." Kurt's bushy eyebrows furrowed. "I hope she's not related to Gregory."

"I'll ask her, but it won't matter to me. We're just having dinner together. And maybe I'll take her to the Jungfrau."

"Make certain she doesn't toss you over the cliff."

Pierre's irritation mounted. "I'm sorry about dinner. I'll try and work both of you into my schedule tomorrow." He slipped into his blazer and ran his comb through his hair once more.

"You pass inspection," Kurt said wearily. "Except for your tie. Just come in quietly tonight. I'll be asleep."

Pierre faced his uncle again. "What's with this Drew Gregory?"

"He's on suspension from the CIA."

"For killing someone? Intelligence agents are good at that."

"You don't respect them any more than you do Interpol."

He heard hurt in his uncle's voice. He crossed the room in quick strides and knuckled his forearm. "I'm sorry, Kurt. You know I respect you. I'll find out what I can. But I'm not here to spy out the father, no matter what he's done in the dark world of intrigue. I see enough deception in Ingrid. I'll be careful."

"Moonlight and a pretty girl don't add up to caution."

"I'll put my blinders on."

"That's what I'm afraid of. Now go. I'm going to call Ina."

"And your old CIA friend in Paris?"

"Porter?" Kurt toyed with the idea. "Yes, I'll see whether he has anything new on Gregory—or Ingrid."

Pierre straightened his tie again.

"It's still crooked," Kurt said. "Here, let me help you." He redid the knot and then put his hands firmly on Pierre's shoulders. "I wish you'd get out of Zurich."

"Don't worry about me. I'm not doing anything wrong, Kurt."

A shock of unruly gray hair slipped across Kurt's forehead. He swiped it back. "There are people gathering here in Zurich who won't know that. Ina would never forgive me if anything happened to you. You're all we have since—"

Pierre took the unlit Marlboro from his uncle's mouth and tossed it into the ashtray. "Since my brother died twenty years ago."

"Baylen was special to us. I talked him into joining the Marines."

"You didn't talk him into Vietnam." At the door Pierre turned again. "I can't fill Baylen's shoes. I've tried."

"You're your own man, Pierre. That's the way we like you. We want to keep you alive, so don't play with fire."

Pierre winked. "Just with the moonlight."

Sixteen

They sat across from each other, smiling. Robyn tried to study his face, but each time she looked squarely at Pierre, he charmed her with another smile. He had sun-bronzed good looks, a wide forehead, a strong, pleasant face. The cut of his Italian tweed jacket fit nicely over his broad shoulders, the shades in his wild-life tie blending perfectly. His manner seemed polite as he ordered, his tastes nutritional, his cologne clearly masculine.

As the waiter left with their order, Pierre said, "Where is this lovely mother of yours?"

"She's spending the evening with her European buyer."

"Was she afraid to meet me?"

"She *is* worried about me having dinner with a foreigner."

He laughed. "Tell her I lived in America. I did, you know. My father's job took him back to Washington after I was born."

"You're serious?"

"Yes, we came back to Europe when I was three. But my older brother, who held dual citizenship, stayed in America to finish high school at a military academy." For only a second, the sparkle in his dark eyes dimmed. "After Baylen was killed in Vietnam, my dad wanted me to go back to America to the same military school. I did, and I hated it."

"You're so—so European."

"Am I? I should be. My roots are here."

"In a way, mine are too. My father lives in London."

"Will you be seeing him this trip?"

"No, we'll fly home once Mother settles her business affairs."

"Without seeing Switzerland with me? Pack a suitcase and we'll—"

"Do what?"

He laughed again, a replay of that wonderful chuckle she first heard on the veranda. "A gentleman's honor. Two rooms everywhere we go. Have you been to Basel? Lucerne? Bern?"

"I mostly know their museums. I lived in Europe several months while studying art."

"And I never saw you?"

"Do you like art?"

"Enough to know whether I like a picture hanging on a wall. I make a better tour guide. What about Schaffhausen? Let's go there. It's a wonderful, quaint city on the Rhine. I studied there for a year."

"Can we take in Heidi's mountains?"

"Heidi?"

"Yes, a storybook character. I read *Heidi* over and over."

"Weren't there any other books in town?"

"*The Secret Garden, Treasure Island—I* read them all."

He ran a finger across the back of her hand, gently over her wrist. "What was so special about *Heidi?*"

She repressed her father's promise. "Heidi had a wonderful grandfather and goats and a goat herder for friends."

"A goat herder named Pierre?"

"No—Peterli."

"And when you were a little girl, was there a grandfather too?"

"No—a father."

"I have nothing but good memories about my dad." Pierre's face glowed, animated by the memory.

"The few I have were good, too, except when Dad left us."

He didn't pry further. "Then we will look for Heidi's mountain soon. And if we can't find it, then I'll take you to the Jungfrau—we'll overnight in Grindelwald."

She started to protest.

"Separate rooms, remember? They have a cable train up the mountains. You'll love it. What about Monday next week for the Jungfrau?"

"I can't. We're flying to Vienna that day."

"Not for good? I'll kidnap you, if necessary."

"That won't be necessary. I'll only be gone a few days. We may bid on some works offered at auction there for resale at my mother's art gallery in Los Angeles."

"We could drive over," he offered. "I know Vienna. I'll rent a car, and we'll take the long way back, past the Jungfrau."

On impulse she said, "I'd like that."

He propped his chin in one hand, his long fingers almost covering the small brown mole on his left cheek. "Yes, tomorrow we'll go to Schaffhausen. My uncle won't be happy about it, but I'll pick you up at eight in the morning. We'll be gone all day."

"If tomorrow's wrong for you—"

"Tomorrow's just right. My uncle will survive without me."

Early evening had fallen, leaving the dining room dimly lit with candles. The dancing light shaded Pierre's face in deep bronze tones as the waiter put the steaming plates of food in front of them. *"Danke,"* Pierre said.

Robyn was ready to bite into a succulent scallop when she realized that Pierre had bowed his head, praying. She heard the mumbled conversation at the tables around them exploding like a roaring waterfall in her ears. She put the fork down and folded her hands around her napkin, her lips taut. After what seemed like forever, her cheeks reached the boiling point.

Then they faced each other again, the gentle pressure of his hand on hers, an irresistible grin cutting across his face. "I didn't mean to embarrass you, Robyn."

The warmth that had flooded her cheeks cooled as they started their meal. "I know. Now and then I sit on the church lawn on Sundays and listen to the hymns, if that counts."

"It counts. Someday I'll tell you about my rowdy search for God. God is at the top of my list, Robyn. And since this afternoon when I took a pair of dark glasses off to see the color of your eyes, you've been second."

His voice was full of humor, as though he had kissed the Blarney Stone before dinner, but his words were weighty, truthful.

She frowned, thinking about her Irish Gramma Gregory, comforted in the end by thoughts of God. Robyn hesitated, not certain what anyone else in her family really believed. She stared at the ring that had passed down from the Gregorys. It was difficult to picture Gramma Gregory now, to recall the way she looked, the lilt in her voice, their times together. They had little in common except Robyn's father, an enigma to both of them.

"Is something wrong?" Pierre asked.

"I was thinking about my family. We're not exactly churchgoers. Mother considers most religion poppycock, a balm for fools."

"That bad?"

"It does sound bad, doesn't it? She was grounded on the front pew of a church throughout her childhood and vowed she wouldn't force that on me." She wondered if she dared tell him that her mother's gallery was on the line? Instead, she hinted to it. "Right now—with everything that's happening—Mother might find comfort in knowing how to pray."

"Why don't you introduce me to her?"

"I wouldn't dare. Mom is never impressed with the men in my life. Not even Gino," she teased.

"And your father?"

"I don't know much about him."

Gently, Pierre eased the conversation to his job in Geneva, to his friendship with the baron, and his deep sense of pain at the loss of his dad. "Are you certain, Robyn, that you won't have time to fly to London to see your own father?"

"I'd like to see him, but he may not want to see me. I'll know when my friend gets here this weekend."

He registered immediate displeasure. "Gino?"

"No, a friend from Belgium."

"But I was planning to spend every day with you."

"What about your uncle?"

"What about him?"

"I thought he came to Zurich to be with you."

"I hadn't planned on meeting you." He leaned forward. "Your friend from Belgium—is it serious?"

She smothered a chuckle. "We've only met recently."

"Do I have a chance?"

"With Andrea? I think not. She's already married."

"Your friend is a girl? Marvelous. As you Americans would say, I can ditch my uncle; can you ditch your friend?"

"I could. But I won't. She's contacting my father for me."

"Is he so difficult to contact?"

She bit her lip. "I haven't tried."

Politely, he changed the subject. "I hope you don't have any boyfriends coming to Zurich. Not while I'm here."

"None that I'm expecting." *The jet set outpaces me. The baby-boomer professionals are too old for me. I'm in a stopgap, Herr Courtland,* she thought. *Eligible and that's all.*

She said lightly, "I'm between boyfriends. Gino just keeps me in Apothecary roses—from Mother's rosebushes, I might add."

He could tell by the look in her eyes that Gino was no competition. "Good, Robyn. I've cleared my slate recently, too. I'm glad you haven't settled down yet."

"No way. I won't risk someone running out on me, Pierre."

His hand slid across the table, encircling her fingers. "Robyn, why would anyone run out on you? I know we just met. I know you will be heading home as soon as your holiday is over—but loyalty to my friends and business associates is important to me. More so since God took over my life." He hesitated. "I'd like to think I'm the kind of friend who would never run out on you."

"My father ran out on me—just before Christmas and the first snowfall."

"That's a long time ago."

"Like yesterday. He left Mother to fend for herself."

"You told me she's self-sufficient, businesslike."

"It's the face she wears. She's quite vulnerable right now. She may lose the art gallery, and that's her whole life."

"And is it yours?"

Reflectively, she said, "I love the paintings that make up Mother's world, but I don't want to spend the rest of my life there selling them. It's hard to explain and more difficult to explain to Mother. Her world is plush and exclusive."

"And you want more than high-class clientele?"

"I trained as an art historian, Pierre. Someday I'd like to be a museum curator or work in a museum library. Mother did once, but our business is so profitable now—at least it was. She wants me to stay where the revenue is."

"Follow your heart, Robyn."

"I want to. Once when I was little I said, 'I thought we were poor, Mommy.' She gave me that precise half-smile of hers and said, 'We are poor, darling. But your father isn't. Someday we'll have more than we need.' That's Mother, but it's not me."

He seemed pleased. "So she's the financial wizard?"

"My dad called her that shortly before he ran out on us. He told her she didn't need him; she could take the world without him."

"And quite successfully."

"Very successfully."

From the corner of her eye, she caught sight of Monique entering the dining room—charming in a dark, narrow-waisted evening dress with swirls of *soutache* embroidery on its sleek black bodice. Her husband walked proudly beside her. The older boy lagged behind them. Robyn smiled as Giles ran ahead and skidded to a stop in front of her, his enormous brown eyes on Pierre. "This is Giles, Pierre," she said.

Pierre stood, bent eye level with the boy, and soberly shook hands. He switched from German to French; the child's eyes widened with pleasure as he did so. When Pierre straightened, he smiled at the boy's mother. She glanced anxiously at her husband and then walked away, Giles's hand clutched in her own.

"The boy likes you," Pierre said, taking his chair again.

"When he fell in the pond yesterday, I went fishing for him."

"I heard about that. I didn't know it was you."

"His father was more than displeased."

"With the child toppling in?"

"Yes, but Mr. Williams was angry with my interference, too."

"Could Giles have made it safely from the pool by himself?"

"We'll never know. They're on holiday from Paris."

"Williams. Odd name for a Frenchman. I'll check on him."

"Don't, Pierre. I'm not apt to run into him again, not if Smythe Williams has his way. But I really don't understand why he's so angry with me."

"Maybe he was just embarrassed at the attention."

"And maybe I jumped in too soon. But I couldn't let Giles flounder in the water. He was terrified."

Pierre's gaze drifted toward Smythe Williams' table. "Robyn, I really should check on that man. He's sitting there, not taking his eyes off of you." The merry crinkles in his face tightened. "And it's not a very warm appraisal."

"He has no reason to dislike me. I'll just avoid him."

"That won't be a problem tomorrow. We'll have breakfast on the way to Schaffhausen. And no excuses. We're going to do as much as we can before your friend Andrea gets here."

Pierre kept his voice expectant, but as he glanced once more toward Mr. Williams, the worry lines deepened around his eyes.

❧

"Why, Harland?" Monique asked. "Why are you being so rude to that young woman?"

"I offered her money."

"Money for saving Giles?" She crooked her fingers around her emerald necklace. "Is everything to be bought? Even kindness?"

"Monique, I will not be obligated to her."

"You don't have a choice. She saved your son's life."

The ebony of his eyes darkened. "If Anzel had obeyed me, there would have been no need to rescue Giles."

Little bumps prickled her skin. She turned and smiled at Anzel. "Darling, what is it? You seem so unhappy this evening."

"He's always unhappy."

Like you, Harland, Monique thought. *So frighteningly like* you. She reached out and touched her son's hand. "What is it, Anzel? What worries you?"

"I want to go home to Paris, Maman. Back to my music."

She nodded. "We will soon. We're staying with your papa a few more days. And then—" she struggled to sound cheerful—"and then, my darlings, we are going home. But first a trip to your father's chalet. You'll like that, won't you?"

Giles jumped from his chair, spilling his water glass as he stood. A waiter was there at once mopping up the spillage. "Can we go today?"

Giles asked. "I want to ski."

"You'll have to learn first, little one. Let's wait until tomorrow or the next day."

"In a few days," Harland corrected.

"I don't want to go," Anzel said. "Ever."

She was still patting his hand. "We're not skiing, Anzel. Your father just wants us to see—where he'll be living."

She felt Harland's cold gaze on her, but she avoided his eyes. "It's beautiful up in the mountains, Anzel. Your papa and I went there many times when we were first married. We'll take a camera. You can take pictures to show your friends. You'd like that, wouldn't you?"

"We won't have time for cameras," Harland exploded.

Anzel pulled his hand free, the hurt in his eyes intense. Monique's growing fear turned to fury. A *few more days, Harland,* she thought. *No more. I'm losing Anzel.*

She turned defiantly to Harland, ready to argue with him even here in public, but the look on his face silenced her. He stared beyond her, an intense hateful gleam in his eyes that she'd never noticed before. He had always been a secretive, moody man, but with her he had been caring, his emotions controlled. Now for these fleeting moments, she saw what she had always feared—another side to Harland, an aloofness that excluded her. His rage roiled on the surface, his face shadowed in darkness that seemed as bleak and black as his dark eyes.

Monique didn't dare turn around. She knew he was staring at Robyn Gregory.

❧

"Uncle Kurt, I'm sorry," Pierre said. "I meant to spend more time with you, but I promised to show Robyn around Switzerland."

"You're getting in too deep."

"It's just another date, Kurt. Nothing more."

"A date with the wrong girl."

"You don't even know her."

"Neither do you. I've warned you, you're playing with fire."

Pierre slung his sweater over his shoulder. "I'll make it a point to be back in time for a late dinner with you. And tomorrow we'll spend time together."

Kurt continued to stare out the window, his back to Pierre. "And Thursday we'll go to that auction you want to attend, and you'll really be in over your head."

I'm already in over my head. "I want Robyn to see Schaffhausen. I thought we'd drive out to the school."

"Is she that important to you? What do you expect her to do when she finds out you were holed up in a theology school for a year? Will that persuade her to your own zany beliefs?"

"I want her to meet Saundra Breckenridge. Robyn will like her."

"The war widow? What woman ever liked competition?"

"Sauni's a friend, Kurt. I promised to go back and visit her."

"Even after she got that letter about the Vietnam Memorial?"

"It was rough when she didn't find Luke's name on the Wall."

"It doesn't accommodate traitors, Pierre."

Pierre stiffened. "Is dinner on, Kurt, or not?"

"It's on."

Pierre walked over to the window and put his hand firmly on Kurt's shoulder. "I've never crossed you before, not really. But you're wrong about the women in my life. You asked me to find out what I could about Robyn Gregory's father."

For a moment, they stood side by side, Kurt three inches taller than Pierre. Those three inches had always intimidated Pierre, but now his uncle's shoulders slumped, the square jaw tightened. "Kurt, Robyn hasn't said much about her father."

"And you haven't asked?"

"She insists her father's a diplomat; he works out of the American embassy in London."

"That's the clue, Pierre. He works out of there. Period. It's a government cover."

"I've never been interested in politics."

"You've always been opinionated about them. Sometimes I think you needed a war—so you'd take sides."

"It was after Baylen's war that I swore I'd never take sides. I was old enough to know I hated war, hated politics. My big brother promised to come home. I didn't figure it included a pine box." Kurt remained distant as Pierre continued, "I've done everything this family wanted, including going to Baylen's military school. And I hated every minute of it." He let his hand drop and walked back to the door. "I don't like this rift between us."

"I don't either, Pierre."

"Are you the one opposed to my date with Robyn Gregory? Or does it go higher up?"

"Both. I know her father well enough to shake his hand. I've already told you, he's CIA, Pierre, not a diplomat."

Pierre walked out, leaving his uncle standing at the window. Kurt never lied to him. But had Drew Gregory lied to his daughter?

Robyn was waiting in the hotel lobby and broke into a smile when she saw him. As he held out his hand, she took it.

"It looks like a great day for our trip," he said. He hoped that she hadn't heard the gloom in his voice.

Seventeen

The hour's drive to Schaffhausen mellowed Pierre's anger. By the time he parked the car and they began wandering down the quaint bricked walkways, his mood matched hers. Robyn's smile was contagious, and he found it refreshing to see the town through her lovely blue eyes. She seemed to be introducing him to Schaffhausen—one moment rushing him to an enchanting square filled with fountains and flowers; the next holding him back—her slender hand in his—as she stared with an artist's eye at the magnificent timbered Haus zum Ritter with its massive painted exterior. Robyn's eyes danced at the *confiserie,* and in the end he bought her a sack full of candy, one of every kind.

At noon, instead of climbing to the sixteenth-century fortress on the hilltop, she insisted on going to his favorite tearoom for lunch. He rushed her by the display counter with its tempting pastries and up the winding stairs to the second floor to a window table overlooking the street.

One hour. Two hours. They laughed and held hands between sips of spicy soup and bites of ham sandwiches and danish.

And then, unexpectedly, she asked, "Pierre, what worried you as we left the Alpenhof?"

"My uncle and I weren't seeing things eye to eye."

"Me?" she asked pointedly.

He glanced out the window, not wanting to admit the truth. Across the street a young man lit one cigarette after the other and then tossed them away after only a puff or two.

"Do you know him?" Robyn asked.

"No, but he's waiting for someone."

"He stopped there when we came into the café."

"You noticed him before?"

"Didn't you?"

"No, you had my attention." He looked around. "A friend and I spent hours here drinking coffee and rehashing Vietnam. Her husband died there. My brother died there. But that was all we had in common—except a love of languages and French literature."

"Was she important to you?"

He felt amused at her concern, eager to tease Robyn about Saundra Breckenridge. "She's the older woman in my life. Ten years older. When I was a student, I didn't think it mattered."

"And she did?"

"She didn't even know I had heart palpitations. To her I was just one of her students. I went to Busingen to study—fresh from not believing anything to suddenly wanting to know everything I could about God. Professor Breckenridge had been on both sides of the fence. Robyn, you'll like her."

Would she? He saw the question in her eyes and felt her hand slip from his. Back outside, they browsed silently along the street. They had only gone a few yards when he stopped abruptly and balanced one foot on the base of a lamppost to tie his shoelace.

"Pierre, you've tied your shoe three times already."

"Sorry, I'm watching that man across the street."

"So was I. And I think he knows we're watching him. Come on." She held out her hand, and he took it. "Forget him, and let's go meet your friend and see whether she's still important to you."

"Risky, isn't it?" he teased.

"I'll know after I meet her."

Ten minutes later, when they reached the Schweizerhof patio café, the same dark-haired young man sat under a bright red umbrella. When he saw them, he shoved back his unfinished sandwich and grated his chair against the sidewalk as he stood. Blatantly, he followed them across the bridge toward the campus on the German side. Midway he tossed his cigarette in the Rhine and turned back.

"Pierre, I thought we lost him in the crowd. What does he want?"

"To pick our pockets! But he's gone now. Everything is fine."

They followed the footpath for another two miles—the river rippling beside them—and finally came to the school. Robyn stared at the seminary sign. "Pierre, did you study for the ministry?"

"Most of my classmates did."

"Then why did you come here?"

He grinned rakishly. "To meet Professor Breckenridge."

He realized now that they were walking hand-in-hand toward the administration building. He held the door open, and a secretary recognized him. "Pierre Courtland," she exclaimed.

"*Guten Tag*, Marcella. *Wo ist* Dr. Breckenridge?"

"She's gone to America."

His mouth went dry. "For good?"

"We hope not. She'll be sorry she missed you."

As they left the building, Pierre was shaken. He wanted to joke and say, *Your Gino. My Saundra. So much for your gardener. So much for my older woman.*

Robyn squeezed his arm. "You're worried about her."

"Yes," he admitted. "I hope there's nothing more on Luke."

"I thought her husband was dead."

"He was killed in an intelligence mix-up twenty years ago. His parents won't let it rest, and the government keeps fighting back. Saundra is caught in the middle. That's one reason she moved to Europe—to put it all behind her."

He heard the resentment in his own voice and regretted it. For Saundra Breckenridge it would always be *No body. No joyful memories. No hope of Luke's name ever being on the Memorial Wall.* He wondered now as he walked Robyn around the campus if he hadn't come to despise the intelligence community when he learned about Luke Breckenridge's death. His smoldering anger was his weapon, a way of hitting back at Baylen's dying, too. His uncle's words surfaced in his mind again: *Drew Gregory is CIA, Pierre, not a diplomat.*

☙❧

Late in the day, they stood by the thunderous Rheinfall and watched the water's three-tier plunge to the bottom. As the sun shimmered through the foamy white spray, Pierre had to ask her, "Robyn, isn't your father in intelligence work?"

She turned, the wind whipping strands of her flaming hair across her cheek. She brushed them back. "I told you, Pierre, my father works in the embassy in London."

"Then why is it so difficult to reach him?"

"It's a long story."

"Sixteen years old?"

"Pierre, Mother's problems are serious. She's accused of selling art forgeries and thinks my father is involved."

He slipped his arm around her. "And what do you think?"

"I don't know. Help me find him, Pierre. Then I'll ask him."

He stared down at her upturned face, wanting to protect her from her father. He kept his voice lighthearted. "Robyn, I'm interested in you, not in missing fathers or art forgeries. What do you say we just enjoy the rest of our time together?"

She whisked her hair from her face again, catching a tear with it. "It's been a long day, Pierre. Why don't we start back to Zurich?"

She pulled free and walked rapidly toward the car. He glanced around, wondering whether the man who had followed them was aware that they were leaving Schaffhausen—leaving the Rheinfall.

                        ❧❦

Heinrich Mueller looked carefree behind the counter at his *zimmer frei*, not the sharp, guarded man that Drew remembered. Unexpected mirth sparkled in the pale green eyes. *If his eyes are a door to this man's soul,* Drew thought, *he's finally at peace with himself.*

On the shelf behind Mueller sat the photo of his wife. His life had changed drastically since his wife took a bullet meant for him. Ursula's sudden death had taken him from an intelligence officer, par excellence, to four years of compulsive drinking before he became the owner of a *zimmer frei* that could overnight twenty guests and feed a local clientele of fifty or more.

As he faced Drew, he stood tall on thick-soled shoes, his dark knit sweater stretching over a broad chest, the name *Heinz* boldly emblazoned on the pocket. He gave an extra polish to the glass in his hand and smiled. "Did you sleep well, Gregory?"

"Soundly. You've got a splendid place here, Heinz."

"I like it. Where's your friend?"

"Vic? He's still flat out. Every time he moves, he complains that his head feels like a roaring waterfall. But the doc says he's improving."

Heinrich put the glass down and stirred the simmering soup on the stove. Then he slapped a bowl on the counter and began pouring in ingredients. "I'll send breakfast up," he offered.

Drew sipped his coffee and studied Mueller; he wondered whether he'd be as content in his own retirement. Mueller moved behind the counter with ease and efficiency in the same way he had once handled a gun and a detail of men in the line of duty.

Mueller's face still shone a ruddy red from too many Octoberfests of his own, the ruddiness spreading in pink blotches over his bald forehead. Crinkle lines formed around his eyes, revealing some of the merriment that filled his life now. His hair was more sparse than Drew remembered, the beard shorter and scraggly, the gray moustache like straight up-and-down clippings across his lip.

Heinz stirred in some eggs and smiled, his broad grin making his ears look like sails at the sides of his head. "How long are you staying?"

"A few more days. Longer maybe."

"I welcome you as my guest—as a friend. But don't bring your problems here. I've built a good reputation. I don't need the old life. If you're in trouble, do me a favor and move on."

Heinrich cracked one more egg and then poured the contents of his mixing bowl into a pan on the stove. As it bubbled and glowed a golden brown, he flipped it. He turned back and put a plate of steaming omelet in front of Drew. "Don't use me." The smile faded. "I won't tolerate it."

Drew pushed his cup for a refill. "I need your help, Heinz."

"My friends have the answers you wanted, but no more. I won't pursue your exploits further. That all ended with Ursula."

"You still have contacts? Put me in touch with them."

Interest lit in the pale eyes. "Not wise."

"I need their help, but I'd settle for yours." Drew glanced around at Mueller's guests. "Can we talk here?"

"Safer here than in my quarters. My guests are accustomed to my presence." He interspersed his words with a cheery *Guten Morgen* to each new arrival and then leveled his gaze on Drew again. "Owning a *zimmer frei* was Ursula's dream." He wiped his hands on his half apron. "I promised it to her. I won't spoil it for her now."

Drew ate in silence, savoring the taste of onions, peppers, and hot spices. On the last bite, he said, "Heinrich, you've turned into an excellent cook. Thanks. Now—what answers do you have for me?"

Heinrich scooped up the dirty plate. "I've located the waiter Garret at one of the Schweizerhofs. He remembered Smythe Williams."

"And did he remember the baroness?"

"Men always remember the baroness. If you want Garret loaned to the Alpenhof dining room, my friends can arrange it. He's quick and observant, an expert rifleman. We served together once—"

"Another disgruntled intelligence officer? Does Garret's transfer come with a price?"

"Yes. Keep my friends informed about your activities."

"What else did you learn about the baroness?"

"She's registered at the Alpenhof, along with the Gregorys."

Drew felt a sudden erratic heartbeat. He sucked in his breath, overcome for a moment at the expectation of seeing them again. "Heinz, is Swiss Intelligence involved in my wife's arrival?"

"Porter Devin requested their help, citing the threat of international art fraud. Miriam's association with Ingrid is not good. And interest doubled when intelligence learned that an American agent was sent to Zurich to keep an eye on von Tonner."

"Me?"

"They know you're here. They know your family's here. But my bet is on Wilson—unless you've had an agent in place all along."

Drew's heartbeat went wild again, anger gripping him. Porter Deven? Had Porter already sent another agent here—someone Drew would not recognize?

Heinrich was back to polishing glasses, his hands in constant motion. "Art fraud isn't CIA business. That alerted my friends. So they're digging into the archives for information on the von Tonner collection—trying to find the real link. Don't forget, Drew, I'm uneasy about you being here."

Drew deliberately glanced at Ursula's photograph again. "Your wife would have trusted me."

The pale green eyes darkened. "She trusted too many people. That's why she's dead."

"And that's why you're stuck here in this *zimmer*."

Drew regretted the words immediately. In the old days, Heinz would have landed a fist to his jaw, leaving him immobilized for days. Instead, he went on chopping vegetables for the noon meal, whatever rage he felt coming out in diced carrots and celery.

Drew folded his hands on the counter and studied his friend, marveling at the new image. A good five minutes ticked away in silence except for the muffled sounds at the tables behind them. Finally, Heinrich stopped his culinary endeavors long enough to take an ad from his hip pocket. "My friends sent this along. One of the auction houses here in Zurich is selling a von Tonner painting. Did you know that?"

Drew flattened the ad and frowned. "A Rembrandt original?"

Mueller's eyes were sharp now, the merriment gone. "You'll have to check it out."

Warily, Drew asked, "Do you want me to attend?"

"Someone does."

"Is Porter Deven behind this? He has close friends in Swiss Intelligence—maybe you, Mueller."

"Not me." Heinrich waved the butcher knife in the air. "This is my life now. Remember?" He hesitated. "They'll be covering the auction, particularly those who bid on the Rembrandt painting. So if you go in, you go in forewarned. They'll have a photo of you."

"What are they looking for?"

"Whatever the American agent is looking for." Heinrich was sparring with him, some of the old quest for excitement burning in his eyes. "They wouldn't be looking for you, would they, Drew?"

"That depends on Porter Deven in Paris."

"What happened between you and Porter? His promotion? Did you want that spot?"

"I wouldn't have turned it down. I guess I felt entitled to Station Chief after all my years with the Company."

Heinrich shrugged. "You seemed more qualified for the job."

"Porter's a capable man. But our friendship toppled before his promotion. My time in Croatia didn't help."

"You were in on that, eh? My wife's family came from there." Mueller spoke rapidly in German to a waiter. The young man picked up Vic's breakfast tray and headed for the stairs. As he disappeared, Heinz shoved a clean cup toward Drew and poured fresh expresso for him.

"I value old friendships, Drew. Yours included. But rumor has you involved in your wife's escapades."

"Porter's rumors maybe."

Mueller nodded toward his wife's photo. "My wife always believed in you. That's the only reason I rented a room to you. I'm caught between two sides. You never really answered me. Are they looking for you?"

"Maybe they're looking for Harland Smith. I am."

"Isn't Smith dead?"

"You don't believe that any more than I do. I think Smith and the man who calls himself Smythe Williams are one and the same. Smith was linked with terrorism in Paris, yet he traveled in embassy circles. When his true identity became known, the humiliation went right to the top brass. It hit Porter Deven personally."

"And did it hit you?"

"It did when Smith faked that plane crash."

"You're a hard man to convince, Gregory."

"If he's alive—and I believe he is in spite of Porter Deven—he'll find a way to be back in business selling weapons."

"Pretty crafty."

"Machiavellian all right. Someone's got to stop him."

"Noble, Drew. So how does that link up with art fraud?"

"Smith may be using my family to get me in Zurich."

Heinrich's brows lifted. "Don't push too far. The men I've been talking with know we're old friends. Let them handle it. Switzerland is not your territory, Drew. Unless, of course, you're the agent sent to Zurich."

"I'm here on my own."

Drew swallowed his last sip of coffee, picked up the auction house ad, and made his way up the narrow wooden stairs to his room on the second floor. Every step squeaked like a warning alarm for Heinrich Mueller, a way to keep track of any unwanted guests.

Vic sat on the window ledge in their rented room, one foot against the sill, his arm around his knee. He stared down on the street below, his expression glum.

"You're up! How's the head, Vic?"

"Throbbing."

"Then lie down again."

"Can't. I'm bored. What a lousy vacation this turned out to be. I'd like a little action."

"The action so far has almost killed you. But what about a nice quiet auction sale at Altman and Pierson's?"

Vic almost fell from the ledge. "That sounds about as exciting as another visit to the clinic in Cannes."

Drew spread the auction ad on the desk and met Vic's gaze. "I'm serious. They're selling one of the von Tonner paintings."

"Are we going to bid on it?"

"Yes, on Thursday. In the meantime, I want to check out the Alpenhof and make certain my wife and daughter are really registered there."

Vic held his head and staggered back to his bunk in slow motion. "Porter told me you were crazy enough to do that. What's with you, Drew? You're walking right into his game plan. Let me check out the Alpenhof for you. I have nothing to lose."

"We both do. Our lives."

❧

Pierre and Kurt sat in their hotel room talking until long past midnight.

"Pierre, what happened to the young Gregory woman? You haven't called her all day."

"You told me not to get in too deeply."

"Were you?"

"She's a very special person, Kurt, but we're heading in different directions. I won't hurt her."

"How do I interpret that? She's not religious enough for you?"

"She's searching—trying to sort out what she believes about God." *That's more than you're doing,* he thought gloomily. "Besides, I'm attending that auction on Thursday—and I need your help. Uncle Kurt, I'm going to buy back that Rembrandt painting for the baron."

"You're mad."

"I'm serious. I promised him."

"Pierre, he's old and confused."

"Is that why you and Ina never visit him anymore?"

Kurt heaved a sigh. "We were never as close as you and Felix. You know that."

"What I know is the old man is lonely. Ingrid has taken him for almost everything he owns."

"You're still guarding one of his accounts."

"His," Pierre repeated. "And he wants one of his paintings."

"Are you going to empty the account just to keep the old man happy? What good will it do? He won't have time to enjoy it. Once Ingrid gets wind of it, she'll search for the painting."

"Why? She's obviously putting it up for sale."

"But if you buy it, she'll want it back. To say nothing of every intelligence agent in Zurich being interested in anyone who bids on that painting. They're looking for the whole collection."

Pierre stalked to the window and stared down on the lake. "I think they're right. The whole collection has resurfaced."

"Not just a few pieces?"

"No, all of it."

"And you think you know where it is?"

Pierre hesitated. Kurt was Interpol. "Yes, I think I do."

"Does Ingrid have access to all of it?"

"If she does, she won't risk waiting until the baron dies. She'll sell black market, if necessary. Anything to prevent the baron from claiming what is rightfully his. I don't know any way to stop her from selling the whole collection. I've got to rescue this one." He choked with emotion. "This one used to hang at the mansion—it was the baron's favorite. I'm doing this for him."

"You're obsessed. You never did like the baroness."

He spun around and faced his uncle again. "Baroness!" He spat the word. "She's as fake as that title."

Kurt put an unlit Marlboro in his mouth. He twirled it like a toothpick. "She was the baron's choice," he said from the corner of his mouth. "A foolish one, my wife says, but Felix's choice nonetheless. Keep in mind that Ingrid takes good care of him."

"She dumped him."

"It's the most exclusive clinic in the area. It must cost her a pretty shilling."

"It's the baron's money."

"*Was* his."

"Are you going to help me, Kurt, or not?"

Kurt took the Marlboro out of his mouth and shoved it back again. "Ina can hardly wait for me to give up this nasty habit."

"It looks like you have. You never light them anymore."

"I'm afraid of cancer."

"You? I've never known you to be afraid of anything."

"I was the day that telegram came."

Pierre frowned, but he knew what his uncle meant. He'd lived with it for twenty years, always knowing that his brother's death had left its impact on his uncle.

"I thought we buried Baylen," he said.

Kurt nodded, his face pensive. "You'll know what I mean the day you bury the baron. You never quite forget."

"I knew when we buried my father, and I was sick when Baylen got killed. But I didn't know him that well. He was twelve years older—remember? Off to military school in the States while I was still learning to read. Then the Marines and Vietnam, leaping in your footsteps. Baylen and Kurt: Two of the Marines' *good men.*"

Pierre backed off, allowing the fragile air to cool. He'd spent the last twenty years wanting to say, *Forget Baylen. I'm still alive. Think about me.* The pain of never quite measuring up to Baylen had diminished over the years. But once in awhile, like now, it raised its serpent head, reminding him that his old nature was still kicking around inside. That was another wall between Kurt and him. Discussions on Christianity remained taboo in the Brinkmeier house, except now and then in Ina's kitchen when his aunt would ask Pierre to "hum a hymn or whisper a little prayer for your uncle and me."

"What about it, Uncle Kurt? Are you going to help me?"

"I'm here on Interpol's behalf."

"I thought you were here to vacation with me."

"Both."

"I'm only asking you to drive a car."

"You're crazy, Pierre—risking the baroness's anger and blowing the baron's account."

Pierre went on, "The sale at Altman and Pierson's will be legitimate, but there's no guarantee I'll win the bid."

"How far are you willing to go?"

"I'll zero out the account if I have to."

"What's your rough estimate?"

"Into seven or eight figures."

Kurt whistled, the Marlboro spewing to the floor.

"Look, I just want you to park behind the auction house. Then I can whisk the painting right on out of there."

"Don't bring it back to the hotel," Kurt warned.

"I won't. I'll hide it elsewhere. That's where Ina comes in."

Kurt's broad palm shot up like a stop sign. "Absolutely not. Leave your aunt out of your foolish schemes."

"Too late." Pierre leaned forward and grinned. "This is the way we planned it—Ina's already en route to Zurich."

Kurt pounded the wall with both fists. "You're crazy, Pierre."

"I must be. That's the third time you told me."

                              ☙❧

Vic Wilson walked boldly into the Alpenhof and made a straight line for the bar. If anyone knew the guests at the hotel, the bartender would. As long as Vic didn't turn his head, he could keep on even keel, but old Albert Klee's blow to the head had left him more dizzy than he cared to admit.

He straddled a stool and propped his elbows on the bar for support. He managed a weak grin for the bartender. "Make it something light and easy," he said. "I already have a splitting skull."

The man poured a mineral water. "Are you new at the hotel?"

"I'm just here looking for some old friends."

The bartender's mouth twitched. "Someone in particular?"

"Young woman—late twenties, reddish hair, about so high." Vic drew the height with his hand, making Robyn Gregory shorter than she was. "She and her mother are in from the States."

"Many Americans vacation here." He nodded to a customer sipping his drink. "Maybe this gentleman can help you."

Vic turned, the very act almost spinning him off the bar stool. "Name's Vic Wilson," he said, extending his hand.

The stranger gave an unfriendly nod. "Aaron Gregory."

"He's looking for a young woman," the bartender offered.

"Aren't we all?" Gregory stood and picked up his drink.

Vic kept his head fixed in one position and watched through the mirror as Gregory walked into the dining room and sat down at a table with four women. He groaned as Gregory pointed his way. Four women zeroed in on him, Andrea Prescott staring blankly his way. He took his drink with one long gulp.

Gregory and the women were ordering their meals now. Vic tipped the bartender and walked away as steadily as his spongy legs permitted—up the steps to Miriam Gregory's room.

He had picked many a lock long before in his training days at Langley. The years had perfected his skill, but this evening he had no stomach for the job. He blundered on three tries; finally, the old lock clicked, and the knob yielded to his turning it.

He looked around the spacious room. Feminine garments lay strewn across the double beds; the bathroom light was still on; the connecting door to the next room stood ajar. The air still held the heady blend of two perfumes. He made his way to the first bed, picked up the invoice ledgers lying there, and thumbed through them. The number sequence was out of order.

He tried the desk and flipped through Miriam Gregory's fancy briefcase. More invoices on art purchases and records of shipment with precise penciled notations in the margins. Beside several paintings, she had underlined a single word: *Where?* He checked the invoices on the bed again—and noted the same precise marginal notations. The invoice dates covered only the last few months. Drew bragged that Miriam was systematic. *Why then,* Vic asked himself, *were her invoices numbered out of sequence? No,* he decided, *they were not out of sequence; there were missing vouchers.*

Something was wrong with the gallery records, and Miriam Gregory was in Zurich to find out why. Porter Deven had said she was in Zurich to spread her fraudulent sales internationally. Why would he lie?

Vic heard voices in the hallway and the turning of a key in the lock. He slipped hurriedly through the connecting door into the next room and came face to face with the maid. "Excuse me," he said. "I must be in the wrong room."

Eighteen

After forty-eight hours, Robyn stopped listening for Pierre's firm tap on her door. She still saw him, but only at a distance—walking toward the lake with his uncle, in the lobby teasing young Giles, or sprawled comfortably in the hammock at the end of the veranda. But it was seeing him in the dining room talking privately with Ingrid von Tonner that hurt her most. She felt betrayed by both of them. Only Andrea Prescott's arrival at the Alpenhof had softened Robyn's disappointment. She still missed Pierre intensely, but she no longer ran when the room phone rang. Now the ring was always for Andrea, a lonely Sherm Prescott on the other end calling from Belgium—not once, but four times already.

This was Andrea's first full day in Zurich. They were up early, too early for Andrea, but as they jogged along the woodland route toward the sun-filled quayside, they chatted amiably like old friends. "Do you catch a sunrise like that every day?"

"Almost every day since I've been here. And those two days it rained. Another fifteen minutes and we'll be back at the Alpenhof."

She glanced at Andrea, admiring her natural beauty, picture-perfect except for the tip of the ugly birthmark showing against one breast. A sweatband held the sun-golden hair from her eyes.

"I'm glad you came, Andrea."

"You just wanted someone to jog with you."

"What I wanted was a friend who believed in my father." She smiled, trying to camouflage the deep emotion that swept over her.

"I can only stay a few days, Robyn, unless Sherm joins me."

"You're certain?"

"Sherm said to stay longer, but I miss him already. I just wish we had better news for you about your father."

"If—if he doesn't want to see me, it's okay."

"Robyn, we haven't been able to reach him."

She felt frown lines cut across her sweaty brow. "You tried?"

"Sherm left several messages at the embassy."

She made an effort to keep the hurt out of her voice. "Maybe it's best this way. As long as Dad doesn't know I'm here, I can pretend he still wants to see me."

Andrea reached over and gripped her arm. "Don't second-guess your father. Why would half a dozen people act as though they'd never heard of him? Frankly, we're worried. We think something may have happened to Drew."

"Mother always says he can take care of himself."

They were running along the quay now, close to where the river flowed into the lake. They ran in silence. As the sun brightened, a tiny wash of freckles spread across the bridge of Andrea's nose. She brushed her hand across her forehead, her cameo ring glinting in the sun.

"That's a lovely ring."

"Sherm designed it for me for a wedding present. He wanted it to match my grandmother's cameo necklace." Robyn heard the catch in Andrea's voice as she spoke of her grandmother. "He knew how much Katrina meant to me."

Andrea seemed to muster up some speed to keep abreast of Robyn. "Your dad spent some time with Katrina. He was so kind to her."

"You mentioned that the day we met. Dad never made it home for his own mother's death."

"Maybe that's why he was so gentle at Katrina's bedside. Perhaps she reminded him of his own mom."

Robyn's emotions were mixed—anger and tenderness, jealousy and pity. She remembered Gramma Gregory longing for Drew to come. For Robyn to come. She fought the blurred image of her father sitting at someone else's bedside. Though the muscles in her legs ached, she sprinted the last few yards to the Alpenhof and sank into the nearest chair on the wide veranda.

Andrea dropped beside her, breathing heavily; she picked up the *Zurich News* lying by the chair and shielded her eyes. They sat there, cooling down from the run, sharing' their common love of the art world—Andrea talking about fashion, Robyn about her love for famous paintings. "Andrea, I'm going to take you to some of the museums while you're here."

In her mind, she brought the old Dutch masters front and center, stripping away the centuries that separated them. She sighed unexpectedly. "Art stood like a wedge between my parents."

Andrea cocked her head, those lake-blue eyes frankly. curious. "I thought your parents met at the Metropolitan Museum of Art."

"They did, but Daddy hated dusty museums almost as intensely as he loved Mother. I think that's one reason Ingrid von Tonner and Mother became so friendly. They talked art for hours, but Dad never trusted Ingrid. He fought Ingrid's money schemes for years."

The newspaper slipped to Andrea's lap. She caught it before the breeze blew it away. "You don't seem to like Ingrid either."

"I don't." Robyn considered telling Andrea about the frauds at the gallery. Instead she said, "After Ingrid married Felix, she boasted about his art collection. Mother seethed with jealousy until she found out that most of the collection had been lost for fifty years."

"Lost?" Andrea asked.

"Well, off the market at least. When Ingrid suggested selling some of her paintings through the gallery, I opposed it. Little good that did. Dad would never have let it happen."

"Why did you come to Zurich, Robyn? Back at the gallery, you were adamant about not coming. Then, suddenly you are here."

"It was sudden, wasn't it? It was Mother's idea. There were problems at the shop, best solved on this end."

"Can Sherm and I help?"

Quietly she said, "Mother is facing lawsuits."

"Here in Europe?"

"Back home. For selling frauds that Ingrid shipped to us."

Her eyes drifted to the child running across the porch, his chubby legs carrying him toward the pond and the swan peacefully swimming there. "Look, there's Giles, the boy I told you about."

"Giles," the boy's father thundered. "Come back here."

His father spoke so sharply that Andrea glared at him. At once she sank deeper into the chair and tented her face with the *Zurich News*. "Oh, no," she whispered. "Not him. Pretend you don't know me."

"Giles," the father roared again.

The boy turned, but he saw Robyn and cried out excitedly in French. He dragged his mother to her, then held back shyly.

"Mademoiselle Gregory, I'm Monique Dupree—Mrs. Smythe Williams. Giles and I are so grateful. How can we ever thank you enough? Perhaps we could have dinner together?" Her wistful invitation came out slowly, like the boy's smile.

Giles's father stood by the stairs, scowling impatiently. The *Zurich News* rustled beside her. Nervously, Robyn touched the child's face. "Perhaps we could take time for pastries with the boys tomorrow?"

"That would be nice. I don't think Harland will join us, but bring the young man you had dinner with the other evening." With an anxious glance toward her husband, she said, "I must go."

Monique took the child's hand and left, swaying gracefully like a model going down the runway. Her husband's stern features eased as she reached him and linked her arm in his.

"Come up for air, Andrea. They're gone now."

"I met that man in a cemetery. He's Harland Smith."

"No, he's *Smythe Williams.*"

"Didn't she just call him Harland?"

"I guess she did, but he gives his name as Smythe Williams."

"Yes, I heard her. Just stay away from them until I can talk to Sherm. Monique's friendship can only be short-lived. Just to be safe, let's leave the hotel for a while."

Scanning the newspaper, she rolled off the entertainment possibilities nonstop—the castle at Rapperswill, the ninety-nine steps to the Old Town, the Brahms symphony. "If that doesn't interest you, the zither music will."

"Why not shop on the Bahnhofstrasse?" Robyn asked.

"Can't. The last thing Sherm told me was not to go on a wild spending spree, but here's something that'll interest you. The Altman and Pierson Auction House is featuring a Rembrandt."

"Do you have a million to spare, Andrea? Believe me, the Gregory art gallery is not up to buying any more Rembrandts."

"It's an original—it says so right here. Altman and Pierson is offering a von Tonner painting at eleven on Thursday as part of their fall season. Lot number 1030. Let's go and bid on it."

Robyn grabbed the paper. "Baron von Tonner's Rembrandt? It can't be. They rarely announce the collector's name." She chewed her lip. "Then Ingrid is determined to buy into partnership with Mother. We're going to call Altman's today and ask for a private appointment. I must check the catalogue description and preview the painting—to see if it's authentic, if it really belongs to Felix von Tonner."

"Who cares if it belongs to Felix or not? Just look at this presale estimate. I want to watch people bid into the millions."

Robyn faced Andrea. "I care. Felix is Ingrid's husband. What if the painting is another one of Ingrid's schemes or frauds?"

"That's crazy"

"I told you what's going on at Mother's gallery."

She summarized it again slowly, her voice trembling. Andrea's sympathetic gaze comforted her as they talked. "But why would she attempt to sell one of the paintings while Mother is here in Zurich?"

"Maybe Mrs. von Tonner needs money."

"I'm so afraid for Mother. So afraid for both of us."

"Robyn, I was joking about bidding at the auction. But we'd better go and find out what's going on. Now let's get out of here before that Smythe Williams family comes back."

They linked arms as they walked toward the lobby, Andrea's eyes turning suddenly merry. "Robyn, who was the friend you had dinner with the other evening—before I arrived?"

"Pierre Courtland. He's one of the hotel guests."

"Am I keeping you from seeing him?"

"He was with another woman at breakfast."

"And you're disappointed?"

"I'm angry. He was with Ingrid von Tonner again."

"Maybe he had something serious on his mind."

"It certainly wasn't me."

❧

Hedged in by trees, Altman and Pierson's Auction House stood in a park that overlooked the Zurichsee. The large square-shaped building with its stark white pillars had once been a private residence, converted now into a thriving enterprise. A high iron gate surrounded the property and a uniformed doorman kept a watchful eye at the carved entry.

Unlike the cold, sterile auction houses of the past, the inside reception hall was plush, the ceilings vaulted, the floors covered with thick beige carpets. Robyn and Andrea stood by a marble fountain and gazed up at three floors of open-air balconies, the walls filled with spectacular paintings. Staffers stood at intervals along the rails. As Robyn caught the eye of the tall young man on the second floor, he looked away, and then mingled unobtrusively with the visitors.

"That man was watching us, Andrea."

"He's paid to observe. Now stop fretting."

"We should never have come back here today."

"Why not? Yesterday you said you thought this Rembrandt was authentic. I could barely drag you away."

"But Mrs. Altman got a good look at us."

"And we got a good look at her. Stop worrying. We represent Miriam's Art Gallery in Beverly Hills, don't we?"

"But it's Altman's job to know that her clientele is prepared to bid on works like the Rembrandt."

"She'd find out your mother's shop is doing well."

"Ingrid represents Mother at several auction houses, so Altman may know about Mother's connection to Ingrid."

Andrea studied the international clientele milling through the reception hall, their voices mellowed as they moved into the main salesroom. "We can't mistrust everyone, Robyn."

"Some of our first shipments came from sales like this one. Mother authorized Ingrid to purchase them, then resold them at a real markup. Our clients depend on Mother's expertise. They won't handle the purchase themselves. They trust Mother to act as their agent. Still, I'm uneasy about all of this."

"And I'm ready to watch the price go soaring."

Andrea urged Robyn toward the registry desk where they took their numbered paddles in exchange for a name, address, and bank number. "Sherm would have fits if he could see me now. And be in total collapse if he thought I would bid on the Rembrandt."

"You won't want to at the prices that flow this evening. And don't wave that paddle around, whatever you do, Andrea. The winning bid is irrevocable."

They found their cushioned seats in the warm, crowded room, a steady hum of excitement building as they waited for the auction to begin. Robyn's grip tightened on the bidding paddle, an unsettled stirring in the pit of her stomach. "Why did you persuade me to come here?"

"So we could find some answers," Andrea reminded her. "So let's enjoy ourselves. Look—that's us a hundred years from now," she whispered as she pointed to a wall painting, Curran's *Lotus Lilies.* It pictured two young women at the turn of the century, their rowboat gliding through water lilies afloat in a pond.

"That's us a hundred years *ago,"* Robyn corrected, but the thought of a long friendship with Andrea appealed to her.

The countdown was on, the crowd more restless. Inside, Robyn grew more apprehensive. Ingrid was up to something, allowing one of the baron's paintings to go on sale. She always hinted that she had ample money, but now this. Or was this the loan that would tie her mother to partnership? She glanced at the people around her, half expecting Ingrid to be among the sea of faces—some animated, some bland, others solemn, many expectant. But none were as beautiful as Ingrid von Tonner. Robyn took another sweeping glance of the audience and gasped. Pierre Courtland sat across the room from her.

"What's wrong?" Andrea asked. "You're pale."

"Nothing," she said as her fears magnified. Pierre had shown little interest in art when they talked. Why then was he here, a bidding paddle in his hand? Why else? He knew Ingrid. Had she sent him to represent her, to raise the bidding price? Tears formed in Robyn's eyes. Their betrayal stung.

She allowed herself to look his way again as he signaled to Mrs. Altman and she bent down to speak to him. Altman was well-dressed, well-jeweled, her skin age-worn around the eyes and mouth, her dark eyes curious as she looked up and met Robyn's gaze.

Within minutes, she passed Pierre's note down the aisle to Robyn.

Coffee afterwards? it asked. *Dinner tonight? Tomorrow? And all the tomorrows after that? My uncle leaves this afternoon.*

She crumpled the note and dropped it in her purse.

"Your friend?" Andrea asked softly.

"Yes," she said as Mr. Altman, the day's auctioneer, walked onto the platform in a tuxedo and black bow tie, a handkerchief in his breast pocket. Staffers stood like sentinels in front of him, waiting to pinpoint the bidders. Television monitors flicked on, connecting the salesroom to the overflow crowd in the anterooms. A row of phones lit up; shy bidders in the lobby and the worldwide collectors waited on those lines.

Altman smiled as he pinned the microphone to his coat lapel, and stepped confidently to the podium. He was a mild-appearing man with a full face and silver-rimmed glasses. In a strong, booming voice he said, "I'm Jacob Altman."

He pointed to the international monetary exchange on the board, the Swiss franc at the top of the list. Then, focusing on the first item on the block, he said, "Ladies and gentlemen, this evening we offer for your competition this Ming dynasty dish."

A hush fell over the room as Altman set the bidding price. Bidding rose at once, narrowing quickly to a Brazilian agent in the audience and an American collector on the telephone. The seven minutes seemed like an eternity to Robyn. She did a mental calculation. The person on the telephone had taken the winning bid for $45,000.

She stole glances at Pierre. He had made no effort to bid on the blue and white dish. Nor did he show interest in the Chippendale wing armchair that came next or in the ugly bronzed figurine offered after the chair.

Robyn's own interest mounted as the Impressionist paintings and pastel drawings went at spectacular prices. And at last lot number 1030 was placed on the auction block. *The Rembrandt.*

Altman announced the arrival of the painting and his partner in the same breath—the Rembrandt in the hands of Saul Pierson, a stodgy little man with sagging jowls, a fringe of gray hair circling his baldness. Robyn tensed as the man placed the painting on the display easel. Even today, as well dressed as he appeared, his suit pants sagged at the knees.

And if he snored, as he had done on their flight to Zurich, it was sure to be the loudest noise in the room.

"That's Mr. Chubby," she whispered to Andrea.

"Mr. Chubby?"

"Hush," said the hard-nosed investor beside them.

"Andrea, that man followed us to Zurich."

"Hush," the investor demanded again.

As Pierson adjusted the lighting on the picture and stepped back, Robyn sensed the electricity charging through the audience. Mr. Altman smiled as his ringed hand lifted toward the painting. "Ladies and gentlemen…Rembrandt."

He said the word with the same air of mystery seen in Rembrandt's painting. This one was beautiful, the lighting striking, the painting itself more mellow than Rembrandt's earlier portraits. Altman captivated the audience, saying, "This is one of his lesser-known works, perhaps one of his last great paintings." His voice was soothing, dramatic, as he quickly summarized the skills of Rembrandt as an artist—his contrasts of color, the subtle mystery of his work.

With a fixed, sad smile, Altman explained that the von Tonner collection had been lost in the war—that much of it had never been recovered. "This adds to the value of the remaining pictures still in possession of the von Tonner family. Baron von Tonner is elderly and ill and anxious to share some of these great works in his own lifetime."

Robyn lifted a Kleenex to blow her nose and was immediately mistaken as the opening bidder. Color drained from her face as Altman said, "I have $500,000 against the young woman in the center."

Mrs. Altman put her fingers to her lips, surprise on her face. Andrea Prescott couldn't speak.

To Robyn's relief, spirited bidding followed. The second bid came from the back of the auditorium. Robyn craned her neck to see the man; he was hidden from view. Bids increased in rapid increments. A Japanese man held a pen to his chin, his interpreter beside him. A white-haired gentleman in a tweed suit with a distinctive British accent cast his bid with a touch to his lapel. Pierre was more vocal, his voice strong and determined.

Altman incited them all to a frenzy of bidding.

180

"I have three million on the phone. Will you say three point five?" he challenged, his eyes on Pierre.

The bidder in the rear took the challenge. And Pierre, with a flick of his paddle, kept on bidding.

Nineteen

Drew Gregory noticed the auctioneer on the sidelines, a shifty-eyed, portly man, whose attention seemed riveted on the women taking their seats toward the front of the auditorium. They sat down, their backs to Drew—two redheads, one a flaming auburn.

"Vic, do you have an I.D. on that man up there?"

"That hefty one? He's the Pierson part of the auction house."

"What's his interest in those two young women?"

"What's any man's interest in pretty women?"

"Vic, I like you better when a bump on the head slows you down. Can you find out who those girls are?"

He was back moments later. "You won't like what I found out."

"Try me."

"One of them registered as Andrea Prescott."

"Sherm Prescott's bride?"

"You've got it. But are you ready for this? The one with the darker hair may be your daughter."

Involuntary flutters churned in Drew's gut. He struggled to keep the emotion out of his voice. "You knew my daughter was coming, didn't you? Is that why we're here?"

"I'm here to keep a check on you, Drew."

"And I'm here to bid on the Rembrandt. Is that the plan? If I hadn't been willing to come, you would have dragged me here."

"I'm just doing my job, Drew."

"And I'm doing mine." Drew noted the time as the Rembrandt went on the block. He lifted his paddle and placed the second bid on Lot 1030. In a wild gambling charade, Drew stayed with the rival bidders, pushing them to the limit.

Six minutes. Seven. Ten.

Vic perspired as Drew kept pace with his competitors— the art collector on the phone line; the Britisher in tweed; Sigmund Valdemar on the right, sullen and angry; and the young man on the left, calmly out-bidding them all.

Thirteen minutes straight up. Altman paused, looked around, waited, then declared, "Six million, point two then."

He gaveled down. "Sold," he trumpeted.

Applause broke out. Media crowded in. When the commotion died, the winning bidder had already been ushered from the salesroom. The fat little man called Pierson was gone as well.

"Neat," Drew said. "Well-orchestrated. Either that young man is a big fool, or he's headed for serious trouble."

"What about you, Drew? You're crazy, bidding like that."

"It's a famous painting. Besides, when I registered, I guaranteed *Company* funds to cover the sale."

Vic turned a battleship gray, sweating profusely like a man too late for 9-1-1. "Drew, you are insane," he hissed.

"Someone in the Company wants me for a scapegoat. So the Company can pick up the tab."

"Yeah, and the auctioneer almost brought the gavel down on you. What would you have done if no one else had outbid you?"

"I counted on that young man. He wasn't bidding for himself."

"For whom then?"

"Ingrid von Tonner. Harland Smith. The Company? Who knows?"

"What would Smith do with a handsome piece of art like that?"

"Hang it in his flat like I would have done. But not if it's a fraud. What about the young man? Can you get me a name on him?"

"They keep the winning bidder anonymous. Auction-house policy."

"Let's make our way out of here."

"You don't want to wait and meet your daughter?"

"I don't want to disturb her in this crowd. Right now, I want to get to the back exit and be there when the buyer leaves. Someone may be planning to meet him—someone he's not expecting."

"You're in the same room with Robyn, and you're walking out?"

Drew tried to cover the concern in his voice. "Does it foul up your plans, Vic? My daughter is safer not knowing I'm here."

"And Andrea Prescott?"

"If she recognized us, she's keeping silent about it." He glanced at the middle aisle, overwhelmed at just seeing the back of Robyn's head. *I'm sorry, Princess. I'm running out on you again.*

At the risk of losing her forever, he turned brusquely and left.

※

In the back room, in a well-equipped office, it was not going well for Pierre Courtland. He had planned to get the painting out of the building immediately. Kurt was in the car waiting. "Where is the Rembrandt?" Pierre asked quietly. "I saw one of your men carry it out of the showroom."

Mrs. Altman looked visibly shaken. "It's in our temperature-controlled vault. Very safe. We'll keep it there until Monday."

"Get it, please. I'd like to take it with me."

"We must wait until your check clears the bank."

"Since it's Baron von Tonner's check, I doubt there will be a problem! Pick up the phone. Call the bank. They'll confirm."

She hesitated. "But this is most unusual. We always arrange for insurance, packing, and safe delivery. As soon as my husband finishes in the salesroom—"

Saul Pierson fidgeted. Sweat covered his fat face. He fingered the check and tapped it against the desk.

"Get the painting for me, Pierson."

"I'm a junior partner," he whined. "Altman makes the decisions."

"That bidding was too low," Mrs. Altman said angrily.

"Much higher than the catalogue estimate," Pierre countered.

"Mr. Courtland, it should have hit the ten million mark."

Pierre was fighting against time. "I have a driver waiting."

Ready to whisk the painting to safety, he thought. Befuddled as the baron had become, Pierre had done what the old man asked: "Rescue one of the paintings for me, boy."

Pierre could only hope that he had figured correctly and had the money to cover it. He was adding in the taxes and auction-house commissions when he sensed someone behind him.

Fear clouded Saul Pierson's eyes. "You can't come in here," he stammered. "This is a private office."

Before Pierre could turn around, he felt the blow crashing into his skull, felt himself spinning, slipping into darkness.

❧☙

"Don't move."

Saul Pierson froze. Mrs. Altman clasped her hands to her mouth. She spread her fingers. "You've killed Mr. Courtland. What do you want?" she cried.

"The Rembrandt."

From his dazed condition on the floor, Pierre heard the words, sensed the commotion all around him. He tried to open his eyes. The effort exhausted him. He tried again. A tall, muscular assailant glared down at him, his features blurred by a stocking mask. He held a metal crate in one hand, a revolver in the other.

Pierre moaned as the man kicked him.

"No more," Mrs. Altman begged. "We can't have someone dying in this room. My husband—"

"Get me the painting," he ordered in a high, unnatural voice.

Pierre moaned again and tried to stir. It was useless.

"Now," the man ordered.

When she still didn't move, he nudged her with his revolver. "Open the vault," he demanded. He glanced at Pierson. "If you so much as move a finger, I'll kill her."

Pierre slipped in and out of consciousness, his thoughts hazy, yet clear enough to despise Saul Pierson. The frightened little man was more concerned about himself than Mrs. Altman. They were both unable to help her.

Pierre kept forcing his eyes open; except for height he could never identify the man. As Mrs. Altman reached the vault, there was more commotion, a more violent scuffle. Pierre rolled over, but it was impossible to push himself to a sitting position.

"Get him," someone shouted.

"The thief is getting away," Mrs. Altman screamed.

"Let him go," another man said.

Pierre felt strong hands lifting him to his feet. Two men gripped his arms. They half dragged him from the room. When they hit the outdoors, he felt a cold breeze on his face and then sudden, overwhelming nausea.

He heard his uncle say, "What's going on? What happened to Pierre? Just a minute—not you. What are you doing here, Drew?"

"I was just going to ask you the same thing."

Pierre focused on the man now. Older than his Uncle Kurt. Strong. Tall. In control. Unsmiling. His eyes kind. The man's hand stayed steady on Pierre's arm until he was safely in the back seat of Kurt's rental car.

"Take this, too," the stranger said. "It's worth six million. The young man here paid for it. Fair and square. But someone else was willing to kill to get it."

Pierre felt a cold metal case shoved in beside him.

"Now get out of here, Kurt, before I wish I hadn't seen you again. Before I wish we hadn't made that little art exchange inside the auction house. Come on, Vic," the man said. "Let's go. Our Rembrandt thief will be on our heels any minute."

Pierre doubled his legs as the car door slammed shut. He reached out and put his hand limply over the thin, metal box.

As Kurt lurched forward into the traffic, he muttered angrily, "Goodness, lad, you didn't pay six million for that, did you?"

Pierre fought more nausea. Then he felt himself spinning, slipping into darkness again.

ல‍ே

Sigmund Valdemar waited near the children's bookstore on Grossmunsterplatz, hands in his pockets, his appearance casual, his anger smoldering as he waited for Harland. The Smiths rounded the corner and came toward him. Giles walked between his parents, his hands securely in theirs. *The perfect family image,* Sigmund thought, except for Anzel lagging sullenly behind them.

Sigmund's gaze strayed back to Monique; he was pleased to see her again. He hoped that her beauty wasn't wasted on Harland.

"Harland, why didn't you tell me Mr. Valdemar was meeting us?"

"He's just meeting with me. You don't mind, do you, Monique?"

Sigmund couldn't tear his eyes from her.

"Another time, perhaps," she said looking up at him. "Soon."

"Take the children inside the bookstore," Smith said. "Buy them whatever they want." He glanced at his watch. "I won't be long."

He leaned down and kissed her. As his family disappeared into the store, Smith nodded toward an empty table at an outdoor cafe. As they sat down, he said, "You find my wife attractive?"

"Don't most men?"

"I suppose they do."

They ordered and waited in silence until their drinks arrived. Smith stirred his coffee, his mood churlish as the spoon clanked against the cup. "Did you see Miss Gregory at the auction?"

"Yes."

"And her father?"

He hesitated. "Drew Gregory? He was there?"

"In the back of the salesroom. You were bidding against him."

Sigmund couldn't smother his surprise. "I had several rivals, but my attention was on the new owner of the von Tonner painting."

"You play-act well, Valdemar. Wasn't that one of your works of art on the auction block?"

"One of my copies? *That* was a genuine Rembrandt. I wanted that painting." *I wanted them both,* he thought—*the original and the forgery that was to replace* it.

Smith frowned. "Weren't you and von Tonner in this together?"

"No, sir," he lied. "I thought you and Ingrid arranged the sale. I was there because you told me to bid on the painting for you. I thought you were double-crossing her." *Like I've been doing.*

Smith dropped his spoon, splattering coffee on the table. "It seems we've both been duped."

Sigmund wiped his hands on his trousers. "By Ingrid?"

"By someone."

"Then why did you ask me to bid for you, sir?"

"To confuse you and Ingrid." He plucked at his goatee with his crooked thumb. "We have another problem, Mr. Valdemar. It seems that someone has taken the Rembrandt."

Sigmund licked his lower lip. "Stolen?"

"From Mr. Pierson's office. Bold, wouldn't you say?" Sigmund couldn't say anything. His lips felt dry. He had fled, his stocking mask intact, both paintings left behind—the baron's Rembrandt and the forgery he had made himself.

"And now the time has arrived for you to steal it back."

"Steal?" *Steal it back. Which one?* he thought. *I was forced to leave them both behind.*

"I believe this was your idea in the beginning, Sigmund. Our profitable little enterprise at the baroness's expense. Would it be any worse than copying the great Dutch masters?"

Sigmund protested. "Mine is a form of art."

"Really? I need the names of anyone who bid on that Rembrandt."

"That's all confidential, Harland."

"Saul Pierson can get you the answers."

And Pierson might be able to identify me. Aloud, Sigmund said, "Some of the competition dropped out right away."

"Then get the names of anyone who stayed with the bidding beyond seven minutes. What about Aaron Gregory? Was he there?"

"I didn't see him."

"You didn't see Drew either, so he slipped away from me again."

Sigmund glowered. "You sent me to buy a painting, not to look for the Gregory brothers. Aaron wouldn't have the stomach for bidding. He's a weasel. He doesn't dirty his hands. He stays within the fringe of the law."

"That doesn't give him a very big playing field." He fluffed his goatee. "Your field is narrowing, too, Mr. Valdemar. We spoke before about Miss Gregory. I want her out of Zurich and taken to the von Tonner tunnels as quickly as possible."

"Kidnap Gregory's daughter? I told you, count me out."

"Then use some of your old Stasi friends. But get her there."

☙❧

Ingrid pulled her car to the curb and urged Saul Pierson to get inside. She said nothing, her lips tight with fury, as they sped toward the outskirts of Zurich. Reaching an isolated wooded area, she swerved onto a narrow road and slammed on her brakes. The jolt bounced Saul's forehead against the dashboard.

He stared up at her, his face dotted with perspiration.

"You broke your promise to me, Saul. Why?" she demanded. "You were to handle the sale—you were to replace my original with Valdemar's forgery."

"I'm sorry, Baroness. Sigmund didn't arrive with his reproduction in time. And I didn't handle the auction. At the last minute, Jacob Altman insisted on taking it himself."

"He suspected?"

The beady eyes regressed, then refocused, and narrowed even more. "His wife was behind it, I'm sure."

"Then why didn't you pull the Rembrandt from the day's sales? You were to pull the painting if the bidding got out of hand."

"I would have stopped the proceedings at eight million, not at six. But Jacob insisted on selling it."

"At six point two? It's worth ten million in the art world."

He twisted the seat belt. "It's not worth anything now."

"What does that mean?"

"It's gone, Baroness."

"Gone where? Did the buyer take it?"

"Someone took it. We have Valdemar's fake in the vault now. Jacob is enraged. We're going through with the sale, as is. Once it's out of our hands—"

"Saul, where is my painting?"

"There was a scuffle after the sale. Two or three men. We don't know who they were, but the buyer was injured—"

"I want my original back. That was our agreement. The forgery is worthless to me."

"We didn't plan on someone stealing the original." Saul's words were fluttery like his hands. "Mrs. Altman was left in the vault with the forgery. Your Rembrandt was taken."

Sigmund doing a turnaround? "And where were you, Saul?" she snapped. "Under the desk?"

She had wounded him. The thought surprised her. More calmly, she said, "It amazes me that the Altmans took you into partnership."

"I was an art dealer. I knew the art world."

"Yes, I'm certain you did. Every crooked inch of it. I want my painting back. I don't care how you do that, but get it for me."

"But, Baroness, it's gone."

"And surely you know exactly where it is."

He wrung his hands. "I don't know, Baroness. Believe me."

"For your sake, I hope you locate it. And soon." She turned the key in the engine. "I have a mind to leave you out here in the *wald,* but I won't. Now fasten your seat belt, Saul."

❦

Ingrid was still fuming when she reached her hotel room and found Aaron Gregory stretched out on her bed, his hands propped behind his head. "What are you doing in my room?"

"Waiting for you—waiting for an explanation. We planned the sale of the Rembrandt together. Remember?"

She worked her gloves off her hands and tossed them beside her purse. "How did you get in here?"

"The maid let me in. She didn't question me." He smiled sardonically. "She's accustomed to seeing me here."

She went deliberately to her dresser, selected clean clothes, and then headed toward the bathroom. "Get out. Be gone by the time I shower and change."

"Will perfumed soap wash away your sins?"

She turned and lunged at him. "Get out, Aaron."

He swung to a sitting position, his hand twisting her wrist until she sat down, limp and frightened, beside him. His Safari tickled her nose. "What happened at the auction house, Ingrid?"

"How would I know? I wasn't there." She winced in pain and anger as his grip tightened.

"Something went wrong." With his free hand, he picked up the pad by her telephone and shoved it in her face. "I talked to the switchboard operator, Ingrid. You had three incoming calls, one from the auction house. And two outgoing calls—one to Smith's room, one to Saul Pierson."

"I'll have that operator fired."

"She's young and foolish, easily pleased with money and promises. She's also the daughter of the hotel manager. It's most unlikely that he will fire her." Without easing his grip, he asked, "What happened to the Rembrandt? Did the sale go through?"

"Yes—no." Tears brimmed in her eyes, the pain in her wrist unbearable. With unexpected fury, she kicked him with her spiked heel and pulled free. "There were problems."

"Was there a buyer?"

"Yes. And he was attacked when he tried to leave with the painting." She had put distance between them now, her injured wrist cradled in her hand.

"Ingrid, you called Saul Pierson after the auction. Why?"

She wondered as she looked at Aaron why she had ever thought him attractive. His face was much too narrow, his nose too wide, his expression bland. He twirled his signet ring on his narrow finger. A colorless face. A colorless man.

"I'm waiting, Ingrid," he said. "For answers. For money."

"The sale didn't go through, Aaron." She began taking off her jewelry and dropping it piece by piece on the dresser. "Let me correct that. The painting sold all right—to the highest bidder. But when he tried to claim the painting, one of his opponents thought differently. The Rembrandt was stolen in broad daylight."

"You can't be serious?"

"Oh, yes, and if the baron could walk, I'd accuse him. But in his babbling state, he wouldn't be able to hold the painting, let alone steal it."

Aaron ran both hands through his dark hair, anger remolding the bland face to an animated fury. "I need money, Ingrid."

"What's wrong with your law practice?"

"Nothing. I've just invested poorly."

She laughed at him, the laughter rising to hysteria. "Do you mean me? Or is that what you call your trips to Atlantic City and Monaco?

How delightful. You'll have investors lined up at your door for years to come. And if they link you with the frauds at Miriam's gallery, you will be running the rest of your life."

"And you?"

"I'll find a way out. Count on it."

"I was counting on the sale of that Rembrandt. And Robbie and Miriam are depending on me to bail them out."

"From what, Aaron? They are simply victims of our art capers. Now do get out. Wash your sorrows somewhere else. In fact, go home, Aaron. Go back to your courtroom— the place where you shine."

He stood and adjusted his tie and brushed the wrinkles from his navy blazer. He was as always the immaculate Aaron Gregory. The weak, whimpering Aaron Gregory. "Ingrid, I need your help."

"I owe you nothing, not even the courtesy of a reply. Now get out and leave me alone. I'm expecting Smith any minute." *And I can only deal with you one at a time.*

He stared in disbelief. "You're meeting with him alone."

"Stay if you wish. I had nothing to do with the loss of that Rembrandt. I don't expect him to believe me either. He may well know where the Rembrandt is hidden. But frankly I think he's more interested in your brother. That's where the deutsche marks and franken are right now. If you want money, Aaron, find your brother and deliver him to Smith. The price on Drew's head keeps rising. You might as well cash in. Smith is going to find Drew one way or another."

❧❦

The knock on Robyn's door was familiar. A firm, distinct tap—louder this time. *Pierre?* She thought of the crumpled note at the bottom of her purse: *Coffee afterwards? Dinner tonight? Tomorrow? And all the tomorrows after that?*

"It won't be Sherm," Andrea said gently. "So why don't you answer it? It might be your friend."

The knock was more determined this time. A tiny smile spread across Andrea's face. She closed her Bible. "Go on, Robyn. We'll read more later. I'll slip into the bathroom. Go on. Open it."

Robyn swung the door open and then drew back, startled. The man standing there was big—square-shouldered, square-jawed. His bright green eyes watched her intently. "Miss Gregory? I'm Kurt Brinkmeirer."

"Pierre's uncle? I thought you were leaving town."

"I am. But I need someone to look in on Pierre."

The wrinkles cutting across Kurt's wide forehead worried her. "What's wrong, Mr. Brinkmeirer?"

Something in Kurt's eyes was warning enough. She followed him down the hall and into Pierre's room. Pierre sat slumped in an easy chair, holding an ice pack to his head. He groaned. "What did you forget this time, Kurt? Please just leave. You and Ina and Rembrandt."

Pierre opened his eyes and saw Robyn standing in front of Kurt. She went to him at once.

"I'm sorry about coffee, Robyn."

"I'm sorry I didn't meet you. What happened?"

"There was a scuffle in the back office at Altman's."

"You were hurt for a painting?"

The door closed behind Kurt, leaving them alone. Pierre tried to smile; his pain thwarted the effort. "The painting is safe, and I'll be all right—now that you're here. Don't look so worried, Robyn. I know you have questions—about me. The Rembrandt. Ingrid. Please, for now don't ask them. Believe in me."

She fought the runnel of doubt that flowed inside her.

"I missed you, Robyn."

"Did you?" she asked. "Then why didn't you call me?"

"Your line's been busy."

She knelt down by his chair and touched his hand. *Tomorrow? And all the tomorrows after that?* "I'm to look after you, Pierre."

"Kurt said that?"

She nodded. "Why did he leave when you needed him?"

Pierre closed his eyes again. "He had an important errand to run. But he left me in good hands."

⁂

Late Friday afternoon Kurt and Ina Brinkmeirer smiled down at the baron as he sat in the wheelchair, his worn face uplifted. The watery eyes stared up at the painting on the wall.

"That's mine," he said.

"Yes," Kurt answered. "Pierre sent it."

He reached out his vein-riddled hands. "Let me hold it."

His hands shook as Kurt laid the painting in them. Slowly, Felix ran his gnarled fingers over the picture. "Goering didn't take this one."

Kurt and Ina exchanged glances. She knelt beside him and patted his hand. "Goering didn't take any of them, Felix. You hid them, remember? From all of us."

The deep ridges on the old man's face furrowed even more. The watery eyes went back to the painting. He lifted it with shaky hands, his eyes squinting as he studied the strokes. "It's genuine," he said, smiling. "A Rembrandt original."

"Yes," Kurt answered.

"Is it safe here, Pierre?"

"I'm *Kurt*. And it's safer here in your room, Baron, than anywhere else." Kurt hung the Rembrandt back on the wall and stepped back to scrutinize it.

"It's hanging evenly," Ina said.

"There, Baron. How do you like it?"

Felix rocked now—back and forth in his wheelchair, his gaunt face content. "It was the first one in the von Tonner collection. It was always my favorite."

Kurt sighed. "Felix, where did you hide the rest of them?"

"Don't get involved, Kurt," Ina warned.

"But Interpol—"

"Forget Interpol. This was a family matter, a favor for Pierre."

"Baylen wouldn't have asked me to do it," he said gruffly.

"Baylen is dead. Pierre is all we have now—except for Felix."

"You never even acknowledged Felix before."

"Until now—" She brushed hastily against her tears.

The baron's eyes stayed fixed on the painting for several minutes. Then his head drooped and he slept.

"Kurt, let's get out of here. I'm worried enough about Pierre getting into trouble. We must not be caught here."

"It was a legitimate sale, Ina."

"What about that ruckus in the back office at Altman's?"

"I was surprised to see Drew Gregory, but for some reason, he wanted Pierre to have the painting. No questions asked."

Ina leaned down and kissed the baron on the top of his head. Then she slipped her hand into Kurt's as they left him. "Is it really the original?" she asked.

Kurt lingered at the door and glanced at the painting. "Yes. And my nephew was right. It belongs to the old man."

Twenty

Pierre shaded his eyes and stared out at the well-dressed man on the water's edge. Three days in a row, the same gentleman had watched Robyn swim. *Her father?* Pierre wondered. *Not her father!* He grabbed his sunglasses and headed toward the lake on the double. He stopped when he reached the stranger, a serious, pleasant-faced man with a cowlick in his grayish hair.

"What are you doing here?" Pierre asked quietly.

"Sunning myself."

"To me, it looked more like you were staring at my friend. I don't like strangers watching Robyn so intently."

"I'm no stranger. I'm her father."

"Then you are Drew Gregory!"

"And you?"

"Pierre Courtland."

Their gaze locked. Drew's alert, appraising eyes seemed familiar to Pierre. "For some reason, sir—"

A crooked grin stretched the crinkle lines around Drew's eyes. "We met at Altman's auction, Courtland."

Pierre's anger eased. "You and your friend helped me out of there. I never got to thank you."

"You weren't in any condition to do so."

"Someone wanted to get away with the Rembrandt."

"Someone did." Gregory turned back to the lake, his eyes on his daughter. "The water looks chilly this morning."

"Robyn is the hardy type. Really into exercise."

"She's lovely. Like her mother. I remember her auburn hair. I used to wonder what she'd look like when she grew up."

"Don't you want to speak to her?"

"What I want doesn't really matter. It's best for Robyn if she doesn't know I'm here."

She was within shouting distance, swimming toward them now—using a powerful butterfly stroke, her face bobbing in and out of the water in a rhythmic beat, her hair flowing freely.

Drew turned to leave.

"Wait. Don't walk out on her. She asked me to help locate you."

Drew whirled around. "And what have you done to find me?"

"Nothing, sir," Pierre admitted. "I didn't want to get into a family feud looking for some CIA agent."

"But I'm with the American embassy in London."

Robyn was almost to the water's edge. "That's what she said, but when her friends called, the embassy had never heard of you."

"Really?" He turned on his heels and left.

As Robyn stepped from the water, Pierre threw a bath towel around her. She tilted her head and tapped one ear gently. Then the other. "Who was that with you?" she asked.

"Just someone interested in the lake."

"Was he rude? You look angry."

He slipped his arm around her shoulders. "I'm just angry that I didn't get up in time to swim with you."

"You're crazy, Pierre."

"About you. Now hurry. We're going to Lucerne for fondu and sausage at the Stadtkeller and a cogwheel ride to Mount Pilatus. Tell your mother we'll be back for dinner. Bring Andrea, if you like."

"Not this time. She's expecting her husband any minute."

❧❦

In the early evening Pierre held Robyn's hand as they stood on the porch at the Alpenhof and watched the fading sunset. For breathtaking moments the final ambers of daylight spread shadowy pink patterns across the lake. Then night fell gently over Zurich, turning Heidi's mountains into dark silhouettes against the sky.

"I still want to climb those mountains," she said.

"Without your father?"

"We haven't found him yet, Pierre."

"I have."

For a minute, he thought she would collapse against him.

"You what?" she whispered.

"He's here in Zurich, Robyn."

"My father? Why didn't you tell me?"

"I'm telling you now, but I didn't know for certain until this morning. There's something else—he was at the auction sale."

"At Altman and Pierson's? The day you bought that painting?"

"Yes. He's one of the men who helped me when I was attacked. What's worse, he bid against me."

"Impossible. My father couldn't afford a painting like that."

Pierre smiled in the darkness. "I couldn't either," he admitted. "Apparently your father had other reasons for bidding. He told me he knows about the forgeries at your mother's gallery."

"Please, Pierre. Don't lie to me."

He brushed a tear from her cheek. "I wouldn't do that."

"Does he know I'm here?" she asked.

"Yes. But for your safety, he's keeping his distance."

"My safety? Did he tell you that?"

"Yes, and my Uncle Kurt confirmed it; Kurt says there are men in Zurich who want to get rid of your father. His presence here threatens them. Kurt thinks it's all mixed up with art fraud."

She trembled, but he risked alienating her. "I don't care about your father. I dislike the CIA and Interpol and the whole intelligence charade. And God knows, I have little interest in art—"

"Then why did you buy that Rembrandt?"

"For a friend." He surprised himself with the intense emotion in his voice. "Robyn, I don't like broken family ties and dads who run out on their kids, but I care about what happens to you."

Tears still glistened in her eyes. "I thought you didn't want anything from me except that old hammock on the veranda."

"It doesn't interest me, not since you vacated it." He rubbed the back of her hand. "I don't believe in what your father represents, but he may be in town because of you and your mother—maybe risking his own safety to clear the Gregory name."

"And not just *his* name?"

"It's your mother who is facing some serious charges."

She pushed Pierre away and ran toward the hammock. He overtook her and drew her to him. Her sobs turned into uncontrollable hiccoughs that choked off her words. "I—I just want Dad to be the man I remembered."

"You've changed. We all change," he said kindly. "I wanted nothing to do with helping you find your father. I wanted to spend my holiday with you, not get involved in your problems. But this morning when I saw him standing by the lake, I had to confront him."

"Not the man you were talking to when I was swimming? He didn't even wait to say hello to me."

"I know. But when you went up to change your clothes, I followed him into the lounge. He told me he loved you."

"He has a funny way of showing it."

Pierre tilted her chin up. "Your dad promised to come back for dinner this evening. Why don't you go inside and find him?"

"He made promises before."

"Then give him a chance to make this one good."

She gasped. "Pierre, I was supposed to be back in time to have dinner with Mother and Ingrid. What if Mother saw Daddy?"

He squeezed her hands. "Would that be so bad? I'm going down and walk along the lake for a while. *Alone.* It'll give you time to decide what you want to do."

"Pierre, it's been sixteen years. I'm scared."

"So is your father."

༄༅

Miriam Gregory tried to keep her attention focused on her dinner companions, but she was worried about Robyn. She glanced toward the doorway as she had been doing all evening.

"Stop worrying, Miriam," Ingrid said. "Pierre Courtland is a nice young man."

"He's too attentive."

"Isn't that good for Robyn?" she asked.

"Forget about Robbie for now, Miriam," Aaron suggested. "We

need to tend to business. All we have to do is call the Central Intelligence Agency in Langley."

Miriam glared impatiently. "And tell them what?"

"Tell them what we suspect. They'd pick Drew up in a minute."

"What *you* and Ingrid suspect. Robyn and I will go over Ingrid's ledgers again this evening." She looked at her old friend. "Except for the missing ones. We'll get to the bottom of this."

"I thought we agreed to leave Robyn out of this."

"Your decision, Aaron, not Robyn's. You've made accusations against her father. Your own brother, I might add."

"Are you afraid to admit that Drew is involved in art fraud?"

"Aaron, Drew wouldn't recognize a Rembrandt or a Renoir if he stumbled over them. So he'd hardly be in the business of stealing paintings or selling frauds. And he'd never use the CIA to launder such earnings. Thank goodness, Robyn has helped me see things more clearly. You have two more days to find those missing ledgers, or I'm going to the Swiss authorities and ask for their help."

"We can solve it without them," Aaron warned.

"That might cost me the gallery—and my reputation." Miriam's voice lowered. "And probably the respect of my daughter. Show me the missing ledgers and stop dropping innuendoes about Drew making a profit on his own investment." She sighed unhappily. "I've been such a fool listening to you, Ingrid. And trusting you, Aaron, with my legal matters. What have you two done to me? Poor Drew doesn't even know we used his money to help purchase the gallery."

"Doesn't he?" Aaron chortled. "I send him annual reports. Don't you think I've told him all of that?"

"And did you tell Roj Stapleton and Julia Lewan to come here?"

Miriam watched the color deepen around his shirt collar as he said, "We need Roj to help with the purchases in Vienna and to clear out the warehouse."

"Forget the trip to Vienna for now. I need Roj back at the gallery. Apparently, it didn't occur to you what I needed!"

Aaron glanced at Ingrid. She refused to look at him. "We thought—I thought—"

"Lately, I've been wondering if you ever do think, Aaron."

Miriam stood and tucked her clutch purse under her arm. She didn't have the courage to accuse them of fraud, of deceiving her—not yet. The truth seemed too painful. She looked at her old friend and said sadly, "Oh, Ingrid. Oh, Ingrid—why?" She wet her lips. "I'll leave you two alone. I'm too tired to continue this argument."

She walked slowly, her legs feeling unsteady. She hadn't even reached the maitre d's desk when a tall gentleman stepped in front of her. "Hello, Miriam," he said.

"Drew!" Her shock mellowed the word. "What are you doing here in Zurich? Aaron said you were in London."

"I'm on suspension," he said quietly. "The Company thinks I've been working with you, selling fraudulent paintings."

He reached out to steady her.

She nodded toward the dining room, her voice tremulous as she said, "Your brother and Ingrid are in there."

"I know. I've been watching all three of you. Please, let's sit down, Miriam. I want to talk about our daughter." He looked around. "How about the lounge?"

She recoiled. "I don't drink; you know that."

"Nor do I. But we can avoid Aaron this way. Please."

He touched her elbow and led her across the room to the bar stools. As they faced each other, she said, "Well, say it, Drew. Go ahead and say it: 'You've grown old, my dear.'"

"No, you've grown more lovely, more elegant."

"You look the same, Drew. You always were a handsome rogue." She smiled, the familiar half-smile. She kept her voice light. "You're the same—except for a few wrinkles and graying hair."

The bartender leaned across the counter. "Drinks, sir?"

"No thanks, Garret." Drew looked at Miriam. "Orange juice perhaps? Or coffee?"

She smiled at the bartender. "Coffee sounds good to me."

They were alone again. Drew watched her intently, his eyes tender as she returned his gaze.

"Drew, did Aaron tell you we were in Zurich?"

"No. An old friend of mine in Paris tricked me into coming."

She frowned. "Are you in trouble?"

"Are you, Miriam?"

His long fingers rested on her hand. She fought the memory, the old excitement.

"Miriam, I wish we had kept in touch for Robyn's sake."

"It's too late to think of that."

"You're the one who sent me away."

She hated the reminder. "And I'm the one who stayed behind and watched our daughter cry her heart out. For years she had nightmares about you leaving."

"Let me see her while I'm here. Let me tell her I'm sorry. I promise. I won't say anything to hurt her."

With a bone-weary shrug, she said, "You made promises before."

"Miriam, I promised you funds and you've had them."

"Not lately."

"Our financial agreement was until Robyn was twenty-one. I went well beyond that."

"She'll inherit the gallery when I'm gone. I want to make it larger and better for her. Can't you help me do that for Robyn?"

"Is that what Robyn wants?"

Miriam's anger rose. "I'm strapped for funds, Drew. The gallery may go under if I don't—"

"I know about the problems there, Miriam. That's why I'm on suspension. The Company—my old friend Porter in particular—is just waiting for me to sink some money into the shop. For some reason they want to tie me in with the frauds being sold."

She gasped at his bluntness. "You don't mean that?"

"I do. And I'm pressed for time. I came to Zurich looking for you and Robyn. To help you. Tell me—what's she like?"

Softly, she said, "Like you. Your chin and eyes. Your father's flaming auburn hair. You'd recognize her. No question about it."

"I saw her swimming this morning."

"You what? Did she see you?"

"We didn't speak."

Miriam swallowed the last of her coffee and cleared her throat. "She's very special, Drew. Honest and fair. Artistic. But I have no intention of sharing her with you."

"Does she know anything about me?"

"A little. But you walked out on her. On both of us."

"Wasn't that what you wanted?"

"Yes, but there's no need to remind her of you now She's had Aaron. He's been good to her."

"I can well imagine." He looked around. "Where is she?"

"Out with a young man."

"Courtland? We've locked horns already. May I see Robyn tomorrow?"

"She may not want to see you, Drew."

"Then at least let me look at her once more."

Miriam hesitated. "She runs every morning over a woodland route and then down by the lake. Then she swims. And after that, we have Pierre Courtland on our doorstep."

"Is it serious?"

"I hope not. We'll be going back home soon. Nothing can come of it except Pierre walking out on her—like you did."

ಶಿಶಿ

For each halting step she took toward the hotel, Robyn seemed to slip back two giant steps. She turned to call Pierre, but he was walking rapidly toward the lake.

She went into the Alpenhof, blinking against the bright lights in the lobby and adapting again to the dimness in the crowded dining room. She saw Ingrid and Aaron, but not Miriam.

And her father? Would she recognize him? Robyn allowed her gaze to move slowly around the room, pausing at tables of one. She waved off the maitre d', not certain where to wait. Then she turned toward the adjoining lounge, shocked when she spotted her parents sitting together, facing each other. They made a handsome couple, Miriam stunning in a silk chiffon off-the-shoulder evening dress, her father regal in his black tuxedo and blue cummerbund.

Robyn collapsed in the nearest empty chair and fought off tears as she watched their double image reflected in the mirror. Miriam's face seemed etched in sadness in the dim light of the lounge. Her father leaned forward, his fingertips touching her mother's, his expression gentle as he looked at her. He was most attractive, except for deep frown wrinkles and an unruly tuft of hair that fell limply across his forehead. Sixteen years had made a difference, stealing her childhood memory of him.

She looked away, allowing her eyes to shift the length of the counter to the angry face of a young man staring intently at her parents. As he ran his hand through his murky brown hair, Robyn remembered seeing him before— and always with Ingrid.

She ducked behind the menu, peeking over the top cautiously as her father slid off the stool and offered his hand to Miriam. Miriam ignored it, standing without his help. He towered above her, his posture straight as they headed toward the exit. Immediately, the young man at the other end of the bar dropped some money on the counter and followed them.

Robyn caught the faint scent of musk as her parents walked by, her dad's eyes barely slits as he studied Miriam. Their shoes echoed against the tiled lounge—her mother's going clickety-clack, her father's a sturdy, solid footstep. They' stopped just beyond her table, the stranger walking slowly by them.

"What time does Robyn run?" her father asked.

"Between five and six—right around then."

He smiled down at Miriam, a kindly gaze. His dark brows arched. "You've had Robyn all these years," he said, his voice deep and emotional. "Can't I have her for a few moments?"

"Whether you have time with Robyn is up to her. She runs the woodland route and then down along the lake quays every day. But don't upset her, Drew. Don't open old wounds for her."

"Robyn's old wounds? Or yours?" He leaned down and kissed Miriam on the cheek and was gone.

෴

Garret politely mixed two drinks, set them on the counter, then turned, and stowed his apron on the shelf. "Cover for me, Pablo," he told a nearby waiter. "I need to make a phone call."

Heinrich Mueller answered on the first ring.

"Mr. Mueller," Garret said, "the Gregorys just made contact. They left the Alpenhof bar together. Should I call the others and report in?"

"No," Heinz said huskily. "I'll take care of it."

Robyn was up earlier than usual, dressed in jogging shorts and a bright turquoise knit top so her father wouldn't miss her. She ran slowly, searching for him along the route. Disappointment mounted. She rested, then began to jog again. But as she came down to the quayside by the lake, she saw him sitting on a low stone wall—one leg drawn up, one flat on the ground, his arms drawn casually around his knee. She could barely catch her breath as she approached him. He was casually dressed in an open-neck blue shirt, gray slacks, and a dark cardigan. His thick brows shaded his eyes—blue eyes like her own. She tried to catch his attention with a smile, but there wasn't a flicker of recognition.

She ran by him, stumbling more than jogging—her heart breaking all over again and thumping wildly inside her chest. She staggered against a tree, unable to run away from him. She turned and cried out, "Daddy. Daddy."

He was already on his feet, staring after her. At her pathetic cry, he took purposeful strides to her and crushed her against him. "Princess. My Princess," he said, lips pressed against her hair.

They stepped back to look at each other. Tears zigzagged down his cheeks, splattering against her upturned face. Moments passed while they studied each other—as they examined each line, each crease. Finally, Robyn touched his cheek with her fingers. It was such a noble face—discerning and decent. She saw firmness in his jaw, strength in his face, kindness in his eyes.

They tried to smile and hugged instead.

"Robyn, I promised your mother I wouldn't—"

"It's okay, Daddy. I overheard you talking last night. I wanted to see you and have these moments together."

He smiled at last. "I named you. Did you know that?" he asked, leading her to a bench.

Robyn grinned, a tear-washed smile. "Did you?"

"When you were born, the first thing I saw was that little fluff of flaming red hair. And then you started kicking those legs of yours—as though you were already taking off for a race through life. I insisted that we call you Robin." He laughed. "Your mother agreed, as long as we changed the spelling."

"I've always liked my name."

"Honey, for years I've wanted to see you again, and now I'm tongue-tied, struggling for the right words."

"And I always wanted you to come back and bring me presents for my birthday and Christmas. I cried when they didn't come."

"But, Robyn, I sent gifts every holiday for several years. I remember one gift—three figurines that I bought here in Europe. A little girl on a swing. One on a ski run. One climbing a mountain."

"Uncle Aaron gave me a gift like that once."

Her father's frown deepened. "All I ever had from Aaron was an annual report and a few snapshots. Sometimes he'd add a little note like: *Robyn is growing fast. She graduated with honors. Robbie is twenty-one now. Robyn broke her wrist skiing.*"

"That's all you knew about me?"

He reached for his wallet. "I always had this picture."

"Daddy, I was ten then, the year you went away."

"I never wanted to go away."

"You never even said good-bye to me."

"I couldn't."

Robyn stared out on the quiet Zurichsee, gathering her courage to face her father again. "Did you know we had an early snowstorm the day after you went away? I've always dreaded the coming of winter since then."

"Me, too," he said quietly.

"We were always going to come here together and climb Heidi's Alps."

"I didn't forget my promise, Princess." He wiped her tears and then held her tenderly against him again. "Don't cry. We can still climb that mountain someday."

☙❧

Drew waited anxiously in a small café not far from the Alpenhof. Heinrich Mueller had warned him against meeting with Robyn again, saying, "Drew, they're on to your every move."

Back at the *zimmer frei* Heinz had slapped surveillance photos on the counter: Drew in the Alpenhof lounge with Miriam, a blow-up of him standing by the lake with Courtland, another of his reunion with Robyn. There was a picture of Courtland and Ingrid von Tonner and several photos of Pierre and Robyn together—at the Rheinfall outside of Schaffhausen, on the cogwheel at Lucerne, and the two of them window shopping at Grieder, Bally Capitol, and the candy store along the Bahnhofstrasse. Courtland was good looking. Well-dressed. Intelligent, with strong features. But it was the look in Robyn's eyes as she gazed at Pierre that bothered Drew. He shuffled the photos, glaring angrily at each one, and tossed them back at Mueller. "Did Vic Wilson take these?"

Heinz's ruddy face blotched a deeper red, his bulky frame filling the doorway. "I warned you, Drew, if you were in trouble to move on. Why didn't you?"

"I thought we were friends."

"We were."

"I'll move out today."

"It's too late. You're safer here now."

Drew swallowed, not certain whether to trust Mueller or not. "How much time is Robyn spending with Courtland?"

"Enough. Too much maybe."

"Who is he? One of yours?"

"No. He has a good position with a surgical supply house in Geneva. If anything, he's anti-political, anti-intelligence."

"What's his connection with von Tonner?"

"We're looking into that."

Drew eyed the photos. "Well, are they Vic's pictures?"

"Swiss Intelligence took them."

"Porter's influence again?"

"Does it matter?"

"It does if something happens to my family."

Slowly, Heinz massaged the back of his neck, his expression

creeping from annoyance to pity. "They know every move you're making, Drew. I lost my wife because I took risks. I figured I could handle the problems alone. I've relived Ursula's last day a thousand times. Don't do what I did. Get out while you can."

In his deep urge to see Robyn again, it hadn't mattered.

Drew turned his back on Heinrich's warning and slipped out of the *zimmer frei* while Vic was showering. Now he waited just inside the café door, pacing. He checked his watch again. Finally, he saw Robyn coming alone. He fought disappointment and stepped forward to meet her.

She kissed him on the cheek. "You look so far away," she said.

"Just reminiscing. Your mother isn't coming?"

"No. She said we should have tea without her."

"I hoped she would join us."

"I know. But let's not be sad. There's so much I want to know about you."

He nodded, thinking, *And so little I can tell.* Aloud he said, "I'm not very interesting."

"Mother must have thought so. She married you."

He smiled, remembering how quickly the romance had grown. As they took their seats and ordered tea, he regretted that Robyn had not favored her mother more. She looked like a Gregory. But on Robyn, it looked good. He sat wide-eyed, grinning, as she filled in the missing years.

She was nibbling her second pastry with her third cup of tea half-empty when she said, "Dad, what do you do for a living?"

"This and that. Some research. A lot of paperwork."

"Be serious. What is your job? Whom do you work for?"

"The government."

"That could mean anything from a postal clerk to the President."

He smiled. She was quick-witted like Miriam, but not abrasive. Robyn was direct, amusing, shy like himself.

"I'm waiting," she said.

"The diplomatic service. How's that?"

"That's a broad field. Then you're not CIA, like Pierre thinks?"

"Do I look like a cloak-and-dagger man?"

"I don't know how they look. I just know that Mother said you move from country to country." She paused. "I remember her talking about your Army days. Then college and officers' training. Then the military again—and then several years in Washington doing who knows what."

"Are you doing my biography?"

"No, just putting two and two together. Once when Uncle Aaron said you were Army intelligence, Mother was furious." Her gaze was intense. "Dad, you still haven't answered me. Are you CIA or not? I've got to tell Pierre something."

"What does it matter to Pierre?"

"He wants to know everything about you."

"Why, Robyn?"

She blushed. "He teases me about you being his father-in-law."

"Robyn, you can't be that serious. You just met him."

"Wasn't it that way with you and Mom? Quick and romantic?"

He thought about the surveillance photos, the unanswered questions. "You don't know anything about Pierre Courtland."

"Mother didn't know anything about you either."

"I loved your mother."

"You barely knew her," she challenged.

He leaned back and laughed. "I met her at the Metropolitan Museum and tried to persuade her to run away with me that same day."

"And you were married six weeks later."

"Did you know we honeymooned in Europe?" he asked.

"Paris, wasn't it?"

"Yes, I'll take you there someday, Robyn."

"Like you promised to take me to Heidi's Alps?"

"I told you. Someday I'll keep that promise."

"If you can fit it into your schedule with the CIA?"

She was persistent like Miriam. "Honey, I told you. I'm with the diplomatic corps." He hated himself for lying, for deceiving her. "I want you to trust me."

She lifted her teacup. "Mother told me you'd say that."

Drew could see Pierre Courtland cutting across the tearoom toward them. "My time's up. Your young man is heading this way."

Robyn followed his gaze and broke into a smile. "I wonder how he knew I was here?"

Miriam, he thought. Drew was grateful for the interruption. He stood. "I'll leave you two together, Robyn." *But not for long. I'll make it a point to find out who he really is and what he's up to.*

Robyn grabbed Drew's hand. "We'll talk again, Dad, won't we?"

He considered Mueller's warning. "Yes, of course."

"I don't want you dead in some dark alley for no reason at all."

He was touched by the depth of feeling in her voice. He leaned down and kissed her. "I love you, Robyn."

"I love you, too," she murmured. "Stay safe."

He grabbed the bill. "Is it that important to you?"

"I've just found you. I don't want to lose you again."

He nodded as Courtland brushed past him and Robyn tumbled willingly into his arms, her eyes bright with pleasure, her face animated. It was like a video replay—he remembered Miriam looking that way when they first courted. But, like Miriam, was Robyn falling in love with the wrong man?

Twenty-one

The next morning Drew was waiting by the quayside when Robyn approached. She smiled and sat down beside him.

"I didn't think I'd ever see you again," she said.

He told her the truth. "I could hardly wait for morning. I even considered camping here all night so I wouldn't miss you."

"Where are you staying, Dad? In Zurich somewhere?"

"It's best if I don't tell you."

"I won't tell Mother."

He looked around, alert to the growing number of joggers, more people than he wanted near them. "I'm worried about you, Robyn. How many are on to your morning routine?"

"Does it really matter?"

"Your safety matters."

Casually she said, "Mother knows."

"Anyone else?"

"Ingrid. The concierge. A couple of joggers I meet on the way. A young Italian on vacation." Shyly she added, "And Pierre Courtland—and Monique and Smythe Williams, guests at the hotel."

"Monique and Smythe Williams?" He turned the words over slowly: *Smythe. Smith. Harland.* Good ol' Harland had tracked his family to the hotel before Drew even knew they were registered. "Are you and Monique Williams friends, Robyn?"

"She doesn't run with me, if that's what you're worried about."

"Are the Williamses Parisians?" he asked calmly.

"Yes. The wife is. Do you know them?"

"The Prescotts mentioned them."

"Oh, Dad, I forgot the Prescotts. They know my morning routine. Andrea ran with me several days—until Sherm arrived."

"So they told me last night. It was good to see them."

"They speak highly of you, Dad."

"Perhaps they can speak to your mother about me then."

"They're not on the best of terms with Mother."

He sighed. "Neither am I. Promise me, Robyn, that you'll change your routine. Don't run the same route each day."

"I'll think about it. But let's not talk about that anymore. I want to know more about you. Gramma Gregory never said much."

"She wouldn't. She was a pretty tight-lipped old girl."

"Especially where you were concerned. You could do no wrong…at least that's what Uncle Aaron always says."

"He's been pretty good to you, hasn't he?"

"Always until this trip. He hasn't been very happy with me being here in Zurich with Mother. He's done his best to keep me out of their business meetings with Ingrid von Tonner."

Drew's frown lengthened. "So Aaron is here in Zurich with your mother? I don't like that."

"He's staying at the Alpenhof, but he's with Ingrid mostly. You won't have to see him."

He smiled at her concern. "Negotiating art sales?"

She flicked a strand of hair behind her ear. "I wish I knew. Dad, tell me about your family. Were they religious?"

"What brought that on?"

"Pierre asked me."

Drew ran his knuckle across her cheek. "Is that another prerequisite for a future father-in-law? If so, tell him my father was Protestant in name only, Mom an Irish Catholic. 'A cradle Catholic,' she called herself. It never went beyond that."

"How sad," she mused.

"Mother was not a sad person, but she broke a lot of church rules when she divorced Dad and married David Levine."

"The flamboyant actor who swept Gramma off her feet?"

"She got fallen arches soon enough. When Aaron was thirteen, Mother divorced David. They'd never been happy. Eventually she remarried my dad and moved back to the farm in upstate New York."

"I used to visit her there in the summertime. She fascinated me, but in a way I was a little afraid of her. Now and then when she hadn't heard from you for a long time, we'd go into town to the cathedral. She had me wait on the top step, and then she'd go inside and sit on the back pew. All alone."

He winced. "Faith was a private matter with Mother. Maybe she was rehearsing the Stations of the Cross."

Robyn squeezed his arm. "Maybe she was praying for your safety. But she never went to Mass regularly, nor to confession. She called herself an outcast. Is that why you have no time for church either?"

"I've never thought about it," he admitted. "Maybe I'll be like Mother and make my confession at the end of my journey."

"That may be too late," Robyn said softly.

"It wasn't for Mother. According to Aaron, she seemed to make her peace with God in the last few weeks of her life."

"Pierre doesn't want me to wait that long."

To Drew it sounded like the way of the Prescotts—and Pierre was another Christ-follower. *The way of the cross.* Was this what Robyn wanted? If so, how would Miriam handle it? He dreaded it himself, feared that it would distance him from his daughter. She misread his silence, saying, "Your mother had cancer in the end."

"I know. I've always regretted never getting back to see her, but I was on—" He didn't finish. It seemed like an empty excuse that the work of the Agency had taken priority.

"I wasn't there either, Dad. I was in Europe studying art, but strangers—people from a little country church—came to the rescue with meals and sang hymns. They talked to her about Heaven."

He shifted. "Apparently it helped. She died peacefully."

"Toward the end, Aaron was there sometimes."

"He would be—just in case Mother wanted to change her will."

"DAD! That's unkind."

"It's true. Aaron took, took, took. He never gave." He saw the question in her eyes, and remorse gripped him. "I guess I wasn't any better. I just didn't think she'd die so quickly."

"She loved it when you wrote and called." Robyn held out her hand and spread her fingers. "My ring belonged to your mother."

"I thought so."

"I treasure it, but you won't like the way I got it."

213

"In a battle to the finish with my brother, no doubt."

"No. Mother took it from Gramma's finger at the funeral."

"Miriam was there?"

"She went because I couldn't get back in time. Do you mind my having the ring?"

He grinned. "It wouldn't look good on my hand, but it's a miracle Aaron didn't argue against your possessing it."

"He did, but not to me. Dad, why did he take on the family name?"

"To please Mother. She didn't want any reminders of David Levine. But that was crazy. Aaron looks just like him. I always thought Aaron changed his name so he could share equally in the family inheritance." He shrugged. "He should have. But it didn't work out that way. Mom left me the bulk of the estate."

"Uncle Aaron has never forgiven you for that."

Somberly, Robyn watched her father shade his eyes and stare out on the lake. It struck her again that he was an attractive man with a strong, well-chiseled profile; a serious, unsmiling face—such a solitary, self-contained man. Would she ever know him…really know him? He seemed so guarded: distant one moment, cautious and alert the next. And his eyes—bright with kindness when he spoke of his mother; wounded when he mentioned Miriam; harsh when he spoke of Aaron. Did he know that Aaron had once cared deeply about her mother? Was it more than sibling rivalry? Or had jealousy split her parents long ago?

She made no attempt to break their silence. *When I get home and tell Floy Beaumont about my father, what will I say? Handsome. Stoic. Aloof. My father—my friend. My father—the stranger.* She didn't even risk glancing at her watch; she was certain she was late for her date with Pierre. She wanted to think that he would understand, but would he? Sometimes Pierre acted as though he would do anything to keep her from her father.

Without warning, two piercing shots rang out, thundering into the silence and shattering her thoughts. Drew reeled around and slammed Robyn to the ground, hovering protectively over her. He swore at the screams around them—at the early morning joggers fleeing in every direction.

Lifting her smudged face an inch from the ground, she stared at the revolver in his hand. "Dad, what happened?" she whispered.

"Gunfire. Swiss marksmen doing a little target practice."

There was no humor in his gaze. As he eased his hold on her, she rolled over and sat up, rubbing her skinned knees, her thoughts on Pierre and his Swiss friends. "They don't use tourists for targets." She touched his face, her hand shaking uncontrollably. "Were they shooting at us?"

"At me." With a fierceness that frightened her, he said, "Now maybe you'll believe me. I don't want you running here."

"My figure depends on running."

"Your life depends on picking a different route."

Her' father's strong hand gripped hers, lifting her to her feet. "I love you. I never meant to put you in danger."

"I won't be frightened off," she said.

He slipped his gun back into his shoulder holster, his eyes as cold as the revolver.

"Do you have a permit for that?"

"For the Luger? No. And neither did the person who loaned it to me." He smoothed his thick sweater in place. His slate-blue eyes remained watchful as he searched the area again. "We're sitting ducks, honey. Let's get out of here."

He was troubled, yet controlled; not even his eyes hinted at his full fury.

"Who are you?" she asked.

She expected a stony response. He said simply, "Your father."

"I don't mean that. Who is hunting you down like an animal?"

"If I knew, Robyn, I would have found him first."

The chill was not in his tone. That was calm and monotone. She licked her lips, wondering whether he would kill any man who stood in his way. She stared at the sudden emptiness in his face and the barrenness of their surroundings. The crowd had dispersed. They were alone—the trees in one direction, the isolated quayside in the other. The rippling lake looked black and threatening, the trees like hideaways for marksmen.

You're a stranger, she thought. *Who are you? Who is hunting you down?*

A frangible smile cut at the corners of his mouth. He took her elbow and began walking rapidly toward the river. She tried to slow their pace. "Dad, the Alpenhof Hotel is back the other way."

"I'll send you by taxi."

"By a different route?"

"It may be the only route I can get you there alive."

Something inside clicked. *I'm like this man. Stubborn and cautious in the face of danger. I haven't seen him for sixteen years, yet we think alike. We challenge each other. Miriam would have defied him with her half-smile and then retreated on the direct route back to the Alpenhof, maybe with bullets flying all around her.*

"What are you thinking, Robyn?"

"I'm like you."

"It doesn't pay to be stubborn."

"It does when you want answers. What have you done wrong?"

He chuckled unexpectedly. "I've been wondering the same about you and your mother."

As they passed the Teuscher candy store on the wide, tree-lined Bahnhofstrasse, she said, "Don't parade me down the main street dressed like this."

He slowed his long strides, allowing her time to window-gaze in front of the exclusive dress shops as he looked back over the route they had come. "We'll get you something to wear.'

"I have clothes back at the hotel."

"Clothes your mother bought?"

"Well, yes—some of them."

A sad smile played at the corner of his mouth again. "Then it's my turn to get you something. Let's slip in here, Robyn."

"Headband and shorts? No way."

He dragged her, urgency in a sly maneuver that placed them in a glamorous dress shop. He guided her quickly toward the back of the room, far from the display window.

A clerk approached, frowning. Her frown turned suddenly into a smile. "Mr. Gregory," she exclaimed. "You haven't visited us for a long time. Herr Steinman is in his office. He'll be delighted to see you." She glanced at Robyn. "Now how can we help you?"

He rummaged through the display models—scowling at the rose slacks, long-sleeved blouses, and the lavender dresses. "These aren't your colors, Robyn."

"Dad, this is ridiculous. I have clothes back at the—"

Drew cut off the hotel name. The clerk held up a pale blue.

"No," he said. "I want something for a princess. A classy summer outfit in a royal blue or an emerald green if you have it."

She shook her head. "This is our fall display."

"Something elegant," he persisted.

She returned with a stunning forest-green sarong and a cream silk blouse like the one in the window display. He fingered the material clumsily. "This is more like it. Yes, I like this one." He smiled at Robyn. "You'll look lovely in this. What size are you?"

"A small," she answered. She'd never worn forest-green before, but she saw approval in her father's eyes as he held it against her. "It's too expensive," she warned him.

"We don't know that. There's no tag."

"There wouldn't be in a big-money store like this. I can't let you spend that much."

"Would your mother worry about that?"

"No, she always wants me to have the latest styles."

He choked on his response. "Then just this once, let me dress you like a princess."

She looked down at her running shoes and her shorts. "I'm more comfortable dressed in these."

"You'll be more beautiful in this. It's the way I want to remember you."

"Don't! Don't say that."

"Go on, Princess. Try it on."

The clerk nodded approvingly as she led Robyn to the fitting room. Robyn was back moments later, dazzling in colors that high-lighted her eyes and skin. She twirled in front of Drew, her bruised knees sending quick messages of pain.

"You'll need a second blouse to go with it," he told her.

The woman held three more selections in her hands.

"Try them on, Princess."

She chose the print one and hurried off to the dressing room. She returned, eager to please her father, but he had stepped from sight. She looked around, growing anxious at his absence.

"Your friend is gone," the woman said. She glanced down at Robyn's running shoes. "Herr Gregory paid cash for everything. He asked me to give you the change for shoes and the taxi home."

"Gone? Without me? I'll walk home," she cried.

"He was anxious that you not do that."

Robyn glanced past the shoppers toward the street.

"He didn't go that way. He went to see the manager of our store. Herr Steinman and Herr Gregory are old friends." She held out the Swiss francs. "I believe your friend left by the back of the building. He will call you later."

Perhaps—in sixteen years. Robyn smoothed the silk sarong against her slender hips. "I'll just wear it," she said, placing her shorts and knit top on the counter.

The woman nodded to the clerk behind Robyn. "Your friend— your father," she corrected, "asked my assistant Helmut to take you down the street to Bally Capitol or to Grieder's. We don't offer shoes here."

"And put me in a taxi afterwards?"

"Your friend—"

"My father."

A dignified shrug again denied the parentage. "Yes, your father made arrangements with the manager. You do look lovely."

"I should at this price," Robyn mumbled. "Except for my running shoes." *Lovely. But what price will it cost my father to see me again?* She refused to cry. "You've been most kind."

"It's a pleasure to serve Mr. Gregory. He has such fine taste in women's clothes."

Twenty-two

Harland C. Smith sat on a bench facing the River Limmat, his lanky legs stretched in front of him, his head bare, his goatee trimmed. He tossed some croissant crumbs to the birds and watched them squabble and peck at the dirt for the meager offering. In his despair, he wished evil on Monique—the same miserable, hard life his mother had known in Brooklyn.

Vividly he remembered the neighborhood of his boyhood—the loud call of neighbor to neighbor as they hung their sheets on the lines that stretched across the alley from one tenement to another. Even then he had despised that way of life as a human pecking for crumbs, all of them trying to eke out a living at the tail end of the depression. So often he had hidden with a gnawing empty gut and watched his father drink up the food allowance, leaving Harland's mother wrinkled too early, old too soon, defeated before she ever reached fifty. He saw her again in his mind's eye, mumbling in broken Hungarian, "Be a good boy, Cornelius. No drinking. No fighting. Be good, son. Be good."

He hated his middle name, but he'd always say, "Sure, Ma," as she tugged the shawl tighter around her thin shoulders and tucked the loose strands of hair beneath a scarf. She would smile and bravely turn back to the kitchen and to the demands of a boorish, drunken husband. Now and then she would look out the window and wave to Harland—exposing her soapy, rough hands, the fingernails chipped and brittle.

Harland had given Monique everything that his mother never had—wealth and abundance. He was ensnared with her beauty. As he thought of how much he loved her—how consumed he was with longing for her—he knew he would never let Monique go. She was the strength of his life. He would give her another opportunity—at the mountain chalet. They would stand together on the ledge, where they had stood in those early days of their marriage; he would ask her again to remain with him, not to leave him. If she refused...

Harland looked up as Sigmund Valdemar took the far end of the bench and stared blankly across the river.

"You're late, Sigmund. Several days late. What's happening?"

"Courtland and Robyn left for Basel this morning."

"And you didn't follow them?"

"I'm not your errand boy, Smith. We're partners."

Smith felt utter contempt for Sigmund. The man's arrogance annoyed him; he represented money to Harland, nothing more. In a few weeks at most, Harland would be in possession of the von Tonner tunnels. In his wildest imagination, he had never conceived a more brilliant hideaway— a cache from which he could once again deal in weapon sales to Third World countries. With a thorough study of the tunnels, he might find it possible to produce bullets and bombs there— far from the eyes of the nearest neighbor. The famous von Tonner art collection would be an added bonus; he would sell it piece by piece. More money for arms. And the mansion! He would give the mansion to Monique for an anniversary present. They would send the boys away to private schools. Paris was the city he loved, but he could be content in a mansion overlooking the Rhine as long as Monique stayed by his side.

He must rid himself of the Gregorys, the baroness, and the housekeepers at the mansion. Valdemar was still useful to him, but he was on the expendable list. His thoughts turned to the missing painting. "Courtland and Miss Gregory may be transferring the painting somewhere in Basel today," he said.

He had meant to keep the contempt from his voice, but it was there, grating on his own nerves and angering Valdemar as well.

Sigmund met sarcasm for sarcasm. "They don't have the Rembrandt with them."

"How would you know? You allowed them to go off without you."

"They carried no luggage." Valdemar grinned wickedly. "But they took your sons with them, so check it out with Anzel when he gets back."

Rage ripped through Harland. "What was Monique thinking of?"

"The boys. She wants them to have a good time while they're here. You never take time for them, so Courtland volunteered to take them on a day's outing."

Harland considered strangling Sigmund. Blindly, he tossed more crumbs away. "Then they know my true identity?'

"If they knew, they would have turned you in days ago."

"I told you we must get rid of that woman."

"Miss Gregory? That won't be necessary. The Klees are expecting Ingrid and her guests at the von Tonner mansion any day. They plan to go in separate cars—Ingrid, Aaron, and Miriam in one, the couple in the other. My friends will intercept them before they reach Ingrid's place. It's all arranged."

Harland tapped his fingers. "Valdemar, what happened to the Gregorys' trip to Vienna, or was that Ingrid's lie?"

"It's been delayed. Mrs. Gregory refuses to purchase any more pictures for the gallery until her missing ledgers are found."

He thought again of the auction at Altman's. Courtland had bought the Rembrandt, but who left there with it? Courtland or the thief? He studied the young man sitting beside him: the dark unkempt hair; the cold, merciless profile, the clay-hard eyes.

Harland prided himself in never having killed a man—not since Normandy. Now others killed for him. But this man, power-hungry to see East Germany rise again, would kill for the Stasi without hesitation. He felt a dry, humorless chuckle rise in his throat. *He* was undoubtedly on Sigmund's expendable list, too. How much playing time did Harland have left with this man— how many days to outwit him and possess the art collection of a century?

"Are you certain Courtland and Gregory didn't take that painting to Schaffhausen and hide it there? I waited here for you that day, Valdemar. Why didn't you come back and report to me?"

"All they did was wander around the city."

"You stayed with them every minute?"

"Until they crossed the bridge to the German side. The area was too small. I couldn't risk being picked up."

"And where did Courtland and Miss Gregory go?"

"Three miles upstream to Busingen."

"How do you know?"

"I paid a schoolboy a couple of rappen to follow them. But

Courtland and Robyn weren't carrying a thing. They were too busy holding hands."

Holding hands in Busingen, Harland thought. *Holding hands like Monique and I did in the early days at the mountaintop.* Rage ran its course again, flushing his neck and earlobes.

"Courtland attended school in Busingen," Sigmund said. "I thought he went to universities in Basel and Germany."

"He did. But Busingen was some kind of religious outfit."

Harland tossed the last of the croissant roll. "Endowment plans! Maybe Courtland is giving the painting to one of the schools or placing it there on loan. Maybe even this out-of-the-way religious school. Check it out, Valdemar."

"Check it out yourself. I won't drive back there. If you want to play games on the German side, go ahead. I have other work to do." Sigmund risked a glance at Harland. "Roj Stapleton and I took several of the masterpieces up to your chalet. We'll take another load this weekend."

Harland's tone remained unfeeling. "Are they your paintings, Valdemar, or part of the von Tonner collection?"

"Both."

"And how will I know the difference?"

"You won't, Smith. You can pass them all as originals."

"Your method is so slow and tedious. You should learn the laser process. It gives a perfect image."

"I have painted all my life. It is neither tedious nor boring."

"Then why don't you create your own works of art?"

"One needs recognition in his lifetime, Mr. Smith. I cannot wait to be recognized. I *must* mimic the great masters."

"As you wish. This Roj Stapleton—is he trustworthy?"

"He's Ingrid's boy. Always has been. She planted him at Miriam's gallery. He thinks we're transferring the paintings to your place to keep them safe. For the baroness, of course."

"And when he finds out?"

"There's a steep precipice near your chalet."

Harland sat musing. Yes, he had already considered that deep drop-off for Monique or Valdemar. Or anyone who tried to thwart his plans. "What about the outside entry to the von Tonner tunnels? Have you mapped that out for me yet?"

"I wouldn't risk giving you a map, not until I have my money—"

"I'm running out of time, Valdemar, and patience. I want Gregory's daughter kidnapped and taken somewhere today or tomorrow before my son Giles becomes any more attached to her."

Without even turning, he knew that Sigmund was wiping the sweat from the palm of his hands against his trouser legs.

"Today is out, sir. When Robyn and Pierre leave Basel, they plan to swing down to Bern and show Anzel the music conservatory before coming back. They won't get in until late."

"Tomorrow then."

"If we intercept her as she's leaving Zurich, we could take her to the chalet on the pretense of evaluating the paintings."

"The chalet is out. My wife and children will be there this weekend. I don't even want to know where you take Miss Gregory. I want her father. Once I deal with him, you will have your money. All of it. You and your Stasi boys can wreak havoc anywhere you want—"

"There's an easier way to deal with Gregory. Why harm the girl?"

"A hired assassin? No, I want to watch him crawl to me to protect his daughter. And then I want to watch him die. He has ruined everything for me. For fifty years I've hated that man."

Harland stood abruptly and walked toward the river's edge. He lingered there, tall and stately, staring at the water for several minutes. When he turned again, Valdemar was gone.

❧

Across the river on the other side of the Limmat, a cluster of guildhouses nestled among the age-old buildings of Zurich. Heinrich Mueller sat at a window table, an untouched glass of beer in front of him. He lifted the binoculars and surveyed the distant lake—yachts with wide, white sails and two old-fashioned steamers crisscrossed the Zurichsee. With a steady hand he swept back along the opposite shoreline, his eyes settling once more on the two men on the bench across the river.

"You're certain the older man is Smith?"

"We're old friends," Porter answered bitterly. "I'd know him anywhere. He can't hide behind a goatee."

"Does Drew know Smith's in town? Is that why he's here?"

"Drew has a way of knowing everything." Porter reached across the table, took Heinrich's beer, lifted it to his lips, and drained the glass. "Drew knew Smith was still alive. I really didn't want to believe him." He wiped his mouth dry. "Drew will want to escort Smith back to Paris."

"And you won't like that, Porter. I don't like the way things are going. I'll ask Gregory to clear out of my *zimmer frei* today."

"Don't do that. I want you to keep an eye on him for me."

Heinrich slid the binoculars across the table to Porter. "Do your own birdwatching from here on out. Or use Vic Wilson."

"I'm doing that. But Swiss Intelligence promised that you would cooperate with me."

"They no longer have power over me." Mueller ran his fingers over his eyes. "And I won't betray a friend."

"I'm telling you, Mueller, Drew's involved with his wife in international art fraud. Is that the kind of friend you want? He's a disgrace to the Agency."

"Doesn't Drew deserve some credit for leading you to Smith?"

"I'd be better off still believing Smith died in a plane crash. You want to give Drew credit for tracking Smith, and I'd just as soon they were both dead. I've been making excuses for Drew ever since Croatia."

"It wasn't Drew who betrayed his country back in Normandy."

"No, Smith did. But that was fifty years ago, Mueller."

"And time makes a difference—time says it doesn't matter?"

"*Now* is important to me." Porter wiped his moustache again. "Sometimes good men are sacrificed in our business."

"Porter, art fraud isn't CIA business."

"Smith is. The way I see it, Smith and von Tonner and Gregory's ex-wife are partners. The minute Drew knew they were gathering in Zurich, he came straight away. They're working this art thing together, whether you want to admit it or not. Do you think I like seeing a good officer bite the dust?"

"Drew may not come out of this alive, not if Smith gets to him first. Is that what you want?"

"What I want is to keep the record clear at the Agency. We can't risk any scandal. I'm too near retirement myself."

"Porter, what if you're betraying an innocent man? Why don't you confront Gregory? Make certain."

"I'll leave that up to Vic Wilson. Vic and I are in touch."

As Mueller stood to leave, Porter beckoned for a refill.

"You're not coming?" Mueller asked.

Porter glanced at his timepiece. "No, I'll wait here awhile."

ॐ

As Drew and Vic entered the Alpenhof, Drew said, "I'll stop at the desk and check on Miriam's room number. And you?"

"I'll take a look inside your brother's room. You may not like what I find, but it's got to be done."

When Drew climbed the steps to the second floor, he met Vic coming off the lift pushing a linen cart, his jacket stowed among the towels. "Where's the maid, Vic?"

"Up on the third floor looking for her cart. I borrowed it—her keys too." He grinned, twirled the keys on his fingers. "Easier than picking locks. Won't even matter if the rooms are occupied. I'll get in and look around. See you back at the *zimmer frei.*"

"Are you going anywhere else first?"

"Might hit one of the guildhouses on my way back to Mueller's."

Drew had reached Miriam's door and knocked. "Don't forget to leave ample towels for the guests, Vic," he said as he knocked again.

When Miriam opened the door, Drew grinned. The tape recorder in his hand played softly, "Could I have this dance for the rest of my life?"

Miriam looked unhappy, dark half-moons beneath her eyes. "Drew, what do you want?"

"To come in and talk with you."

She tugged at her black pearl earring, the set he had given her so many years ago. "I'm tired."

"So am I—of you avoiding me."

She held the door wider. "Robyn is out with Pierre again."

"I didn't come to see Robyn this time."

He put the tape recorder on the table and turned up the volume. She sat down beside him, listening. He sang the words in his rich tenor, trying to coax a smile from her. He could tell by her melancholy that she remembered the song—that she remembered him asking her to be his partner for the rest of his life. But she had lost that old sponaneity that had first drawn him to her. Her smile looked fractional, her eyes sad.

"Where did you get that, Drew?"

"The song? I bought it a long time ago. It reminds me of you."

"You played it on our tenth anniversary."

"And we danced to it. It was the last time we were really happy."

"The dance has been over for a long time, Drew."

He studied her, trying to see behind the mask that she wore, trying hard to remember something that would make her smile or laugh. But the memories that haunted him were easily shattered. The song ended. She reached over and played it again.

"Would you like to dance, Miriam?"

"No, not really."

"Or not really with me?"

"I don't remember you liking music that well, Drew. You were always into politics and football."

"It's British history and soccer now."

"Since when?"

"Since Croatia."

Her mask lifted for a moment, revealing her contempt and intense disappointment. "The same old game. You were one of those involved in that tragic civil war?"

"We went there to gather intelligence data, Miriam."

"Did you? That's not what the media said about the U.S. intervention. Why didn't you just stay at your desk in London?"

"London came after Croatia. My demotion."

He played the song again, and it reminded him of those magic moments when he had held her close. The song was wasting him emotionally. He tried to catch her eye and each time he did, she looked away. Had she really forgotten how often they had danced together or how much they had enjoyed listening to records? Football and politics. Did she only remember the things she disliked about him?

"I want to help you, Miriam, if you'll let me."

"What did Robyn tell you about the gallery?"

"Enough to know you're in trouble. But I still believe in you."

She brushed her hand hastily against her cheek, wiping away a tear before he had time to do it for her. "Why don't you say it, Drew? 'I warned you about Ingrid von Tonner.'"

"*Liebling,* I couldn't have warned you about art fraud."

She glanced at him sharply, and he realized that he had used his old term of endearment. He decided against apologizing, saying instead, "Miriam, I still don't know the difference between the works of Julia Leyster or van Gogh."

She did smile now. "*Judith* Leyster," she corrected.

"Is my brother Aaron involved in the fraud?"

"I don't know," she whispered, and this time she couldn't hide her tears. "He and Ingrid may both be involved, but I'm afraid to confront them."

Drew clasped his own hands so he wouldn't grasp hers. "You have to—sooner or later."

"You haven't asked me yet, Drew—" She hesitated.

"Whether you're involved? I know differently. How can I help?"

"I don't know. There are missing ledgers and a damaged Italian painting. Three or four frauds have passed through my gallery. I don't know where to turn. I know I'm being watched all the time."

For a moment, he feared paranoia had set in. But he thought of Smith—here at the Alpenhof—so close to Miriam and Robyn. "Miriam, have you met a man named Smith or Smythe Williams?"

"The family from Paris? Robyn knows them. I don't."

"Does Ingrid know them? But of course. She would know everyone."

He had dropped the name. It was enough for now. If Miriam remembered the old days, his subtle warnings, she would be cautious. "Miriam, take Robyn and go home. Forget the missing ledgers. Go back to your gallery. I'll see what I can do at this end for you."

"Go home—when Robyn is so thrilled about seeing you again?"

"It's for her safety, Miriam. And yours."

"We can't go yet. Ingrid has invited us to her place in Germany."

He thought of the Klees. "That's not a good idea."

"I didn't ask your opinion. Robbie is determined to travel there with Pierre. We'll meet at the mansion."

Drew didn't like it. There were too many kilometers between Zurich and Dusseldorf and too many people still wanting the missing Rembrandt. He wasn't keen on Robyn traveling alone with any stranger, particularly with a man that he didn't even trust.

"I'd rather Robyn travel with you," he said.

"So would I. So we agree on one thing."

They talked on for minutes, tossing out ideas—plans that excluded Pierre. Drew worried, lest Robyn never reach the mansion. "If you won't go home, then you and Robyn come with me. I'll be gone a few days, Miriam."

"You said that once before. You never came back."

"You *told* me not to come back."

She avoided his gaze again. "Yes, I suppose I did."

For a moment he forgot Robyn and the mansion. "For old time's sake, Miriam, go with me to Paris for a few days. Paris is still a beautiful city. Your kind of city. I'll show you everything."

"Like you did once before?" She studied him, her smile faint. "Like the song says, I was young, Drew, the last time I saw Paris."

"I remember. Our honeymoon."

"Yes, I was foolish enough to think you wanted to take me to some romantic paradise, but you were on a CIA assignment."

"I was just closing out a case. There were reports to do."

"I married the Agency when I married you, Drew."

"But I gave up the Agency for a while."

"Yes, you went back to politicking in Washington, and you were miserable with your nine-to-five job."

"You won't go with me, then?"

"It's too late. Besides, you're not really going to Paris."

"No," he admitted reluctantly. "Not this time. But soon." He leaned over and cupped her chin. "I've never stopped loving you."

"I've always wondered why you never married again."

"You were the only woman for me. There was never anyone else."

"No quick romances?" Her voice turned brittle. "No one-night stands?"

"I wasn't talking about my morals, Miriam."

"Aren't they the same?"

He picked up his jacket. *"Liebling,* things could have been so different between us. Tell Robyn I'll be back in a few days."

"In time to climb the Alps with her before winter comes?"

"I promised her, didn't I?"

"You've made promises before, Drew. Don't disappoint her."

☙❧

When Heinrich Mueller reached his *zimmer frei,* he marched up the narrow steps, entered Drew's room with a passkey, and began emptying the drawers and tossing everything on the beds. Staring at the havoc he had created, he spied Drew's briefcase. He debated only long enough to throw the contents on top of the clutter: copies of Miriam Gregory's business papers, photographs of Smith with Miriam's partner, other pictures of Smith and Porter Deven.

"Mueller, what are you doing?"

Heinz froze, his hands still holding Drew's paperwork "I'm looking for a reason to throw you out of my *zimmer frei.* And do you know what I found? You're being framed by your own Company."

"It looks that way—by one or two men only. The Agency has been my life. I'd hate to think they've all turned against me."

"Drew, Porter may be sacrificing you for Harland Smith."

"They were friends. If the Smith scandal hits the headlines, it could ruin Porter's career. He could have been rid of me long ago, but he blocked my retirement." Drew stared at the mess on the bed. "I'll leave, Heinz, but I need a place to stow my gear. I'm going back to the von Tonner mansion."

"Not without me," Vic said, strolling through the open door. "If you're going back for the von Tonner art collection, I'm going with you. I'm on assignment to protect you."

"You're back from the guildhouse sooner than I expected."

"The guildhouse!" Mueller exploded. *"You met with Porter?"* He turned apologetically to Drew. "I think Porter is counting on Smith to kill you and using Vic here to make sure it happens."

Drew touched the Luger that Mueller had loaned him. "Smith won't kill me, not if I see him first. I'll take him alive if I can."

"Don't," Vic warned. "Porter won't like it."

❧❦

Robyn stood in the Prescotts' room, whispering to Andrea as Sherm slept on the bed. "I just hate to see you go, Andrea."

"You still have Pierre, but we'll keep in touch."

She glanced at her husband. "Sherm needs to get back to Brussels. But if you need us for any reason, you'll call? Promise?" Andrea gave Robyn a quick hug and placed a Bible in her hands. "I want you to have this. It has the answers you're wanting, Robyn."

"But it's yours."

She hugged her again. "I'll get another one."

Andrea barely had time to put the chain in place when Sherm swung his bronze legs to the side of the bed and planted his feet firmly on the plush carpet. Running his hands through sleep-tangled hair, he glared groggily at Andrea. "Honey, don't even think about apologizing for waking me up! I know you will miss Robyn, but you'll see her again at daybreak when she's out on her morning run. We're to meet her and Pierre in front of the Antique Collector on the Bahnhofstrasse. They're not coming back to the hotel for their car."

"We're taking them to Brussels with us?"

"Just part of the way." Sherm looked worry-worn like her father often looked. A taut smile lifted the corners of his mouth. "Pierre is concerned for Robyn's safety—after that shooting down by the lake. He wants us to detour to the von Tonner mansion and leave them there before Drew arrives. He insists it may be the only way to get Robyn safely out of Zurich."

Twenty-three

Nostalgic memories engulfed Pierre as he swung open the double doors and surveyed the familiar landscape, his riding stick clasped in one hand. He loved this old mansion and the terraced courtyard, but always before he had stood here with the baron's arm on his shoulder listening to Felix say, "This land will be yours someday, Pierre."

Ingrid owned it now. It would never be Pierre's, but for this moment in time, he wished that he could give it all to Robyn. The seventeenth-century stone house formed an H—with two wings on either side of the main entry—its walls moat-gray in color, its roof and turrets a slate-blue, the numerous narrow windows all shuttered. Well-kept gardens and Hedwig's abundant pink flowers created an artistic scene of beauty that enchanted Robyn.

In the valley below, the Rhine River flowed northward. Far to the south, the baron was living out his days in the clinic at Cannes—never again to see the neatly trimmed shrubs that edged the brick wall. Never again to enjoy the acres of flat velvety lawn that stretched east of the property to the stables and the wide bubbling brook. Across that mountain-fed stream, the lower wooded slopes of beech and oak gave way to silver firs and Norway spruce that completely hid the riding trails where the baron and Pierre had spent many happy hours. And now it would all belong to Ingrid.

Pierre's gaze settled on Albert Klee trudging across the grounds toward him, his steps speeding up when he spotted Pierre. Klee's face was smudged with dirt; streaks of dry blood smeared his jacket. "Are you all right, Albert?" Pierre asked.

Klee brushed against the bloodstains. "Just a problem in the stables." Fondness lit the old man's face as he grasped Pierre's hand. "Boy, it's so good to have you back. Hedwig and I have missed you. Tell me, how is the baron?"

"Not well, Albert. Why haven't you gone to see him?"

"The baroness forbids it. She says he wouldn't know me."

Pierre tapped Albert's shoulder with his riding crop. "Felix would know an old friend. I'll take you with me the next time I go."

Albert nodded; his brief smile turned to a frown. "You're going horseback riding, Pierre? Now?"

"As soon as Robyn comes down for breakfast. I'm to ride the stallion with Ingrid's blessing. She says Monarch needs a workout. I rather imagine she hopes I'll break my fool neck."

The gruff hand nudged Pierre. "Monarch likes you almost as much as he likes the baroness, but he's wild today. Even peppermints won't calm him. Don't take *your fraulein* riding now Wait," he urged. "The stable boy is cleaning up down there. There's been a—a most unfortunate accident."

Pierre ran his finger over the bloodstains on Albert's jacket. "No one was hurt, I trust?"

"Klaus cut himself pitching straw."

You're pitching me a lie, Pierre thought. *I've got to get down there.* "I promised Robyn an early ride through the woods."

The old man shook his head. "We'll have breakfast first."

From where they stood, the smell of Hedwig's cooking reached them—a blend of potatoes frying, sausage sizzling, gingerbread baking, and black coffee brewing. Klee kicked off his shoes and left them by the door. He stepped back politely and allowed Pierre to enter.

Pierre's eyes were drawn to Robyn as she came down the spiral stairs, the brilliant light from the windows framing her face. She paused on the landing to smile down at him.

"Hurry up," he said.

She ran down the steps past the vacant spot on the wall where the Rembrandt once hung.

"The baroness sold that painting, boy."

Pierre winked. "You'll see it again when we visit Felix."

The old eyes brightened. "Does the baroness know?"

"I've told no one—until now." He turned and took Robyn's hands. "Albert, this is my young *fraulein.*"

"So you're Herr Klee? I'm so glad we didn't wake you last night. Our stopover in Heidelberg delayed our arrival." She smiled. "You do take such good care of the mansion!"

"I keep hoping the baron will come back someday."

Pierre caressed the old man's shoulders. "Someday, my friend. For now, we'll have breakfast with Hedwig before we go riding. And, Albert, we're expecting Robyn's father. Keep an eye out for him, *bitte.*"

Albert's gaze went automatically to the front door. "The baroness mentioned no other guests. She just brought the woman."

"My mother," Robyn offered. "But didn't my Uncle Aaron come?"

"No, he stayed back at the Alpenhof." The weather-beaten face brightened. "They arrived in the baroness's usual flurry. But Frau Gregory is gracious. Even Hedwig is taken by her beauty."

"What about Valdemar, Ingrid's artist friend?" Pierre asked. "I heard someone prowling around in the studio last night."

The old man's voice filled with contempt. "He's here again. Stealing the baron's possessions, if you can believe Hedwig."

Pierre frowned. "Does the baroness know Sigmund's here?"

Albert shrugged, his eyes narrowing even more. "She hasn't inquired about him this trip. But he was up early—off walking in the woods Hedwig says. She keeps her eye on him."

"Good," Pierre said. *Perfect,* he thought. *We won't run into Valdemar in the tunnels....*

Later as they walked into the stables arm in arm, a bunch of Hedwig's pink flowers in Robyn's hand, an uneasiness settled over Pierre. Something was wrong. An eerie stillness replaced the familiar prancing and neighing.

He left Robyn and ran to Monarch's stall. *Empty.* In a way, it looked too perfect. Walls were washed down. The room had been mucked out, and a thick, even layer of fresh sawdust chips covered the floor. No hoof marks. No feed bucket. The automatic drinking fountain was dry. There was no evidence of Monarch ever occupying the stall. Pierre ran a zigzag pattern down the well-lit aisle, checking each enclosure. Empty. Empty.

The stallion's frantic neighing began as Pierre raced toward the far end of the stables. "Monarch," he yelled. "Where are you?"

He glanced in the tack room, then rushed on to the unused foaling stall, cluttered now with things in storage. The chestnut stallion pranced back and forth in the compact chamber. A mixture of straw and sawdust chips had been kicked back in spots, and Monarch slid over the cement in his frantic pacing. From wall to wall he ran, stumbling against the bales of straw and upturned shovels.

"Whoa, boy. It's Pierre."

Robyn had reached his side. "What's wrong?" she whispered.

"He's trapped. The space is too small. I've got to get him out of there before he breaks a leg."

"Don't you dare go in there."

"I have to."

The cellar door into the tunnel stood ajar. Albert or Klaus had left it that way. Pierre glanced toward the tack room. "Klaus?" he called. "I know you're here somewhere."

The muscular stable boy came creeping from the tack room, a pitchfork in his hand. "Oh, Pierre, it's you," he said, relieved.

"Get the stallion out of this room and back in his stall."

Klaus shook his head. "Can't, Pierre. Albert's orders."

"I don't care. Put him in his own stall."

"He'll go wild again, no matter how clean I got it."

Pierre looked at him sharply. "What happened in there?"

Klaus tightened his hold on the pitchfork. "A woman died in there. Someone mistook her for Baroness von Tonner's young guest." He nodded pathetically toward Robyn.

Pierre forced himself to keep his gaze away from her. He could only pray that she had misunderstood Klaus.

"The girl insisted on riding the stallion. She went in—"

"Or was she thrown in there, Klaus?"

Klaus looked miserable. "Somebody forced her in with Monarch—and the stallion went wild—"

"Did Monarch stomp her to death?"

"Herr Klee thinks so, but he's not sure. He carried her down into the tunnels—until he can talk to the baroness."

"And someone is down there with her now? Speak up, Klaus. I want to know. Now."

"Someone is down there. An older man for one. And maybe Valdemar and his friends. I don't know. That's why we've got to keep Monarch in the foaling block. They won't try to come back up this way with the stallion thrashing there."

"There are other exits," Pierre reminded him.

Monarch kept at his frenzied pacing, nostrils flaring, eyes wide and wild. He skidded on the cement, his buttocks crashing against the wall. Pierre unlatched the half-door and stepped inside. "Come on, fella. It's Pierre."

Klaus grabbed a halter and followed Pierre. Reining the stallion in, he panted, "What now, Pierre?"

"Take him out to grass. Tether him if you have to. I'm going down into the tunnels—"

Robyn finally spoke. "I'm going with you, Pierre—"

"No, Robyn, go back to the house and get Albert."

"I won't let you go alone," she whispered, but she shrank back as Klaus pulled Monarch from the stall.

Pierre threw back the trap door, grabbed a sledge hammer and a lantern, and started the descent into the cold, chilling darkness.

Robyn's plea followed him, "Let me go with you."

"Robyn, go get Albert."

Down the creaky steps and deeper into the dank subterranean passage he went, picking at boyhood memories. He still felt the fear of that first entry as a boy, when the yawning emptiness of the cave engulfed him. Courage had come with each new venture into the tunnels, until he knew every labyrinthine twist and turn—to his left, the winding passages beneath the mansion; to his right, the path that cut beneath the woods and up through the wine cellar of the parish. It had been his hideaway, his haunt, until the baron discovered him holding a painting and forbid him ever to enter the tunnels again.

Pierre had forgotten the light switch at the bottom of the steps, but he refused to turn back. His eyes grew accustomed to the darkness and to the dimness of the lantern he had chosen. At the fork in the cavern, he heard distant sounds to the right. People? Running water? He knew the vaults were to the left, that marvelous discovery of his boyhood: room after room and the main one with its steel-lined vault where he had found the musty painting.

He kept to the left, trying each door—some too rusty to open, others with broken padlocks. *No one.*

He moved cautiously to the main room and slipped through the unlocked door, almost falling over the body of a young brunette lying on the floor, her thin arms stretched out in death, a torn quilt draped over her legs. From behind him, Drew Gregory said, "She's dead."

Pierre lifted the sledge hammer. "You killed her?"

Gregory made a quick exodus from the room, rolling a metal vase across Pierre's path. He tripped, regained his footing, and started after Gregory empty-handed., They cut to the right and stumbled down the dark cavern, Drew's sturdy flashlight like a flickering candle casting shadows on the damp walls.

Pierre was aware now that there were others in the tunnel running far in front of Gregory. He saw flashes of light as they wound around the twisting passages, light enough to recognize the muscular form of Sigmund Valdemar—not walking in the woods, but racing through the von Tonner underground.

The back office of the auction house came flashing back, almost blinding Pierre. An anxious Mrs. Altman. A fat, sweating auctioneer. A man with a stocking mask. The painful whack on his head. The muffled voice threatening and demanding. He felt it again as though it were just happening. The muscles. in his neck twitched. The flashback was there again even as he followed Drew. The masked man at the auction house. The man who wanted the Rembrandt. *Valdemar? Yes, Sigmund Valdemar.*

Gregory turned and slammed Pierre against the wall. "It isn't the way you think. We can't work against each other, Courtland. I need you."

"I'm turning you over to the *polizei.*"

"And let Valdemar and his friends get away?"

"I don't trust you. You were standing over that girl's body back there."

"But you trust my daughter."

"I plan to marry her."

"She won't agree to that if you turn me into the *polizei.*"

"I dislike you, Gregory. You made a lousy father."

"An inexcusable one, but I didn't kill that girl."

Altman's again—voices, strong arms lifting him. Drew and his friend? "Did you really help me out of Altman's? Somebody else—"

"Somebody else hit you. And he won't stop at one Rembrandt. He plans to take the whole collection and hide them at Smith's chalet."

The sound of footsteps down the passageway had died away. "Courtland, is there an exit up there for Valdemar to use?"

"What does it matter?"

"To you? Considerably. I believe Valdemar is the man who tried to kill you back at Altman's. Will I find an exit this way?"

Slowly, Pierre said, "It's a good half-mile or so—and then up through a wine cellar in the village."

"Without this edge on Smith, I don't have a prayer."

"That's all you have."

"Save the sermons for men like the baron, son. Either help me, or I'm going to turn around and walk out on you. If I don't leave, my daughter's life is in danger. So is yours."

"I don't buy that."

"Like you didn't buy the painting from Altman's. I don't know your game, Courtland, but as long as someone is looking for that Rembrandt, my daughter isn't safe traveling with you."

"Then why did you give me that painting?"

"You paid for it, didn't you?"

"And you bid on it. I was hurt. You could have escaped with it. Instead you helped me and gave me back the painting."

"I didn't know your game plan, Courtland, or who financed the purchase of it. Besides, at that moment, it was safer with you." His hold on Pierre's arm loosened. "Right now we're among the few who know that painting really isn't missing. But once Valdemar finds out…."

Sigmund Valdemar. "I'll show you the way," Pierre said.

❧

Fifteen minutes later they were out through the wine cellar and safely behind the church cemetery. The lush green countryside stretched out around them. Drew looked back toward the mansion and sized up the height of a wide row of virgin timber. "Forty or fifty years of growth, not much more. They cleared this land in the baron's lifetime—when they put in the tunnel system and planted fresh forest."

"Looks that way. Can you make it from here, Gregory?"

"I'll catch a ride with one of the farmers. I'm heading back to Switzerland and then on to Smith's chalet. And you?"

"I need your flashlight. I'll go back through the tunnels. Robyn is waiting for me." He glanced at his watch. "You don't have much time, sir, not if Albert Klee called the police."

"I've been running against time all my life."

"I never thought I'd be helping a CIA agent," Pierre said.

"A *case officer,* Courtland. There's a difference." His grin was marginal. "For Robyn's sake, I'm a diplomatic attaché."

"That's still short for under government cover."

"Do you want my embassy number so you can check me out?"

"Back in London? Don't bother," Pierre scoffed. "I know about those Pentagon and London exchanges. I'd be put through to your CIA operator, and she'd tell me they never heard of you."

"They usually don't remember renegades."

"I still don't trust you, Gregory. None of this art fraud business has anything to do with gathering intelligence."

"There's a connection. To Smith and Valdemar, the von Tonner art collection is secondary. A tunnel system like this one could hide a lot of arms to be used against us. Your country and mine."

"I'll write to you at Langley and tell you how it comes out."

"It would only be returned. My address is London." Drew shook Pierre's hand. "Take good care of my daughter, Courtland."

Pierre was almost back to the steps that led up through the stables when he realized that a narrow row of forty-watt bulbs brightened the tunnels. Robyn sat on the bottom step crying, Hedwig vainly trying to comfort her. He knelt down and took Robyn's hands.

"Julia is dead," she cried. "I saw her."

"I know. I'm sorry, Robyn. The *polizei* should be here soon."

"No." She nodded to Albert. "He won't call them until we leave. He wants us to take Mother and go at once."

"It's best that way, boy. Klaus and I will board up the tunnel exit. No need to involve the village in this."

As Robyn and Pierre made their way up the narrow steps to the foaling stall, Albert and Klaus shouldered the heavy planks and disappeared down the winding passage.

※

Ingrid and Miriam had been sitting in the drawing room most of the morning in old brocade chairs with the eight-foot portrait of the baron glaring down on them. Miriam's expression tensed as she said, "I haven't wanted to face it, Ingrid, but you deliberately shipped me fraudulent paintings."

"You didn't complain when your profits tripled and quadrupled."

"I didn't know they were frauds."

"Who will believe you, Miriam? You've spent your life studying art and working in museums. Didn't you even suspect?"

"No." The word was barely whispered. "They looked so real. I'll talk to Aaron about this. Surely he can—"

"Run you through the legal system with a clean slate? That precious lawyer of yours helped plan this whole mess."

Miriam's impeccable mask crumbled. She stood and paced the room, her rich complexion washed-out in her anger. At last she faced Ingrid, her arms clasped around her chest as though the embrace would support her breathing. "You've ruined me."

"I'll work it out, Miriam. Leave it to me."

"Leave it to you? You were my friend, Ingrid. I trusted you. Robyn tried to warn me, but she reminds me of Drew. She is so like him and so unlike me. When she made caustic remarks about the paintings you were sending, it was like listening to Drew all over again."

"What a pity you didn't trust her judgment; it's wasted on you. Why don't you cut those apron strings and let her go, Miriam? You tried to change Drew's career to accommodate your lifestyle. Now you're doing the same thing to Robbie."

Miriam's neck vein pulsated so rapidly that Ingrid feared she would have a stroke in front of her—like the baron had once done.

"I loved Drew. You know that."

"I think you still do, but he couldn't live up to your expectations as a nine-to-five man with a briefcase. Neither can your daughter."

Miriam was crying, but Ingrid was certain she was unaware of her own tears. "They're so much alike," she repeated. "That's why I didn't listen when Robyn questioned the authenticity of those paintings." She tried her familiar half-smile and failed. "Until now I've always had Drew's brother to advise me."

For a moment, Ingrid pitied her. "Aaron was the last person you should have trusted. He's been under my control for months." She fluffed her silver hair. "Brief illicit moments together and he was mine. Don't look so shocked, Miriam. You didn't want him."

"That, too? You sicken me, Ingrid. Was that the only way you could control the gallery? You here in Europe, Aaron there in New York—working together to destroy me? Why?"

"It was Aaron's way of getting back at his brother."

"Did he really hate Drew that much?"

"What he hated was the uneven Gregory inheritance. He saw that as his punishment for being the son of David Levine and not Wallace Gregory."

"And chose me for the scapegoat? But why the art frauds? You have hundreds of original paintings in your husband's collection."

"Those precious old paintings won't be mine until he's dead."

"You told me you owned everything."

"Oh, yes. Felix signed over his possessions to me. I agreed to the settlement: the mansion is mine, the cars, most of the money, the furnishings listed, item by item. Monarch is mine, but the stables and the grounds behind the mansion and east of the mansion are held in the baron's name. What lies beneath the grounds still belongs to Felix—that means most of the von Tonner art collection."

She chortled. "But all of that will be mine when he's gone. He kept me in his will. He knows I will be good to his possessions. Pierre Courtland is my only competition. He champions the baron's cause; he might be the one behind that legalese in my divorce papers. Yes, Pierre is my only worry."

"Pierre? He's not even interested in art."

"Oh, he's well-versed in the von Tonner collection. And he doesn't intend for me to dispose of it. He'll try to claim it himself. Who knows what the baron has promised him?"

"In the beginning you cared about the baron."

Ingrid puckered her brows. "I cared about his money."

Miriam sat down and closed her eyes. She looked physically drained, her neck still pulsating. More tears stained her cheeks. The confident, self-assured Miriam Gregory was crying.

"You've used everyone who ever loved you, Ingrid. But why did you involve Robyn in all of this and tell her that foolish business about being in partnership with me?"

"My offer still stands. If you don't accept it soon, Aaron and I will make certain that you and Robyn both go down with the gallery. What will Robyn think when she finds her mother's a fraud?"

Ingrid glanced up as the door opened and Robyn entered, looking even more blanched than her mother. She ran over and hugged Miriam. "Mother, I have dreadful news."

Miriam's fingers dug into Robyn's arm. "Not Drew?"

"No, Mother, not Dad." She kept one hand on her mother's arm. "Julia Lewan is dead."

"No, no, no," Miriam cried out.

"She was thrown into Monarch's stall. The stallion went wild."

Ingrid covered her lips. "You're lying."

"Like you lied about the paintings and the missing ledgers? Julia is dead. I saw her. We found her body in the tunnels."

Miriam's voice was a hoarse whisper. "The horse killed her?"

"We're not certain, Mother. Someone may have pushed her in."

"Murder?" Ingrid exclaimed. "Here at the mansion?"

"The *polizei* will determine that. Albert is calling them."

"Without asking me? How dare he!"

"You have other problems, Ingrid. Roj Stapleton is outside with Pierre. Roj admits that he was ordered to empty the warehouse and dispose of the baron's paintings in the vault." Robyn let the words hang in the air and then said, "Roj is already admitting everything at the top of his lungs."

Ingrid twisted her largest diamond. "That has nothing to do with me. If Roj has stolen from the mansion or cheated at the warehouse or in the inventory vouchers—"

"Ingrid, Ingrid. You've always had a fall guy. Uncle Aaron. Roj. Your husbands. Mother. But you never quite won with Pierre. Roj told us you destroyed some of the business records before Mother and I arrived in Zurich."

Miriam groaned. "Oh, Ingrid—"

"Quit blubbering, Miriam. Roj wasn't even here then."

"No, but Uncle Aaron was. You're the one, Ingrid, who persuaded mother to hire Roj and retain Uncle Aaron for the gallery projects. That's in the records."

"You'd make a good lawyer, Robbie."

"You may need one."

"I have Aaron." Ingrid picked up her gloves and worked them deftly over her fingers. "Yes, I have Aaron."

"Yes, poor Uncle Aaron. You definitely will need a lawyer." Robyn leaned down and placed her cheek against Miriam's. "Mother, Pierre is waiting for us. We're to pack and leave at once."

Ingrid picked up her purse and tucked it under her arm. She felt an overwhelming chill and stiffness in her body as she moved mechanically toward the door. She kept her head high as she walked away. Surely, the Klees would help her reach the car safely.

Roj Stapleton. Sigmund Valdemar. Harland C. Smith. They had all betrayed her. Fear chilled her even more. There was only one place for Smith to hide out—his chalet in the mountains. She turned for a final glance at Miriam, trying vaguely to remember their happier days at Radcliffe.

Softly, she said, "Miriam, I am sorry."

Miriam's tears kept falling. "So am I. Sorry that we ever met."

Their gaze held briefly.

"I'm leaving. Is that what you want?" Ingrid asked.

"What I want is to forget I ever trusted you."

As Ingrid reached the massive hallway, Albert stepped back and let her pass swiftly from the mansion. Roj Stapleton stood by her car, dangling her car keys in her face, his expression harried.

"You! Did you come back to steal the rest of my paintings?"

"I'm looking for Julia, Baroness. She's not in the stables. She was going to ride Monarch when I saw her last. Mrs. von Tonner, I've got to search the house for her. Please, let me go in. We want to get out of here."

"Don't bother searching, Roj. Julia is dead."

Twenty-four

From the foot of the mountain, Smith's chalet was hidden from view, the property nestled in a forest of evergreens with a private trail leading to it. Beyond the house, the trees thinned out and the mountains rose in sheer cliffs, the top peak shining with snow. Harland often approached his place from another town on a more defined, well-traveled path, closer to the ski runs. But in those early days, he and Monique rode horseback to reach their house. Taking refuge here after the plane crash, he purposely allowed tangled underbrush and weeds to cover the once well-marked path, discouraging even the best of hikers.

The villagers on this lower side came to accept him as a retired general. Didn't he have the carriage of a general? Wasn't he wise about weapons and warfare? An American, they concluded, who isolated himself in order to write his memoirs. He did nothing to keep these rumors from spreading.

Harland loved climbing. He moved agilely up and down the steep slopes, skiing down in the winter to buy his supplies. The people had often cautioned him against staying alone in the winter and warned, "You risk an avalanche burying you."

He'd always responded that the sturdily built chalet could withstand the wind and cold. But one night during that first month of refuge, distant thundering slides of snow and rocks plummeted down the cliffs. He skied down the following morning to wait out the bitter cold of February and March in the village. He made friends slowly, cautious as he was with strangers.

But for the sake of acceptance, Harland trained himself to charm the women and say kind words to the children. To silence wagging tongues, he told them that his wife's health did not fare well in the mountains. Only one guest came periodically: Mandel Reynard, an older English gentleman with snow-white hair. Reynard would be waiting for them today when they reached the chalet, admiring the von Tonner paintings with a practiced eye and planning ways to market them.

As Smith and his family started up the mountain, Monique frowned. "Harland, I don't remember the village. It seemed more like a town before. No one seemed to recognize me."

That was as it should be. She had started up the trail with him as a stranger. The villagers would be buzzing about her now, asking questions among themselves, perhaps saying, "This must be the wife. Remember, he spoke kindly to the children. No wonder. He has sons of his own."

These isolated villagers would sympathize with him if something tragic happened to his family. The men in the village were accustomed to rescuing stranded hikers or injured skiers. They would pity him if Monique slipped over the edge of the mountain.

Harland and his family were forty minutes away from the village, climbing the mountain toward the chalet, when Giles began to whimper. "Maman, carry me."

Harland glared back at the tired, fretful boy, his knees already skinned from falls. "She can't carry you, Giles. Walk."

Giles flung himself at Monique and wailed louder. She held him to her. "Unless you carry this child, we're going back."

"Monique, he's old enough to walk."

"He's too little to make it all the way."

She turned, the boy's hand in hers, Anzel right behind her.

"Monique," he said sharply. "Anzel goes with me."

"Never," she said.

He saw terror in her face as she turned back and faced him. She was afraid of him, afraid for Anzel.

The boys were taking her away from him, the boys he never wanted.

"I'm taking the boys, Harland. We'll wait in the village."

He knew she was lying. She must go to the mountaintop with him. It was all planned out. "We'll walk more slowly," he said.

She wasn't budging. Down at the base of the trail, he saw two men

245

beginning to climb. Strangers never came this way. "Hurry, Monique," he urged.

"I'd forgotten how far away the chalet was. Go on without us, Harland. I promise, we'll wait for you."

He gripped Anzel's shoulder. "Go back," he said, his eyes on the men below. "And take that whimpering child with you. But Anzel goes with me."

"No. Please don't hurt him."

Infuriated, he slapped her. She reeled backwards, stunned.

Anzel stepped between them, his narrow shoulders squared as he faced Harland. "Let her alone. I'll go with you, Papa."

He noticed his son now as Anzel gave his mother a faint smile. It was a sensitive face. Thick black brows made his eyes seem even darker. His hair was black and full, fitting over a finely shaped head. Little wisps of hair were visible on his upper lip—a fragile-looking boy, leaving childhood behind. Overcome with his sudden emotion toward Anzel, he shoved the boy in front of him. Then, with one more glance at the men on the trail far below them, he said, "We've wasted time. Let's move quickly."

The boy he scorned for his cowardice and fear of skiing walked stoutly, swiftly in front of him. Harland turned his back to Monique and followed his son up the tangled, winding trail.

❧

Ingrid von Tonner reached the town side of the mountain early that morning, her Mercedes Benz dusty from the long, hard drive. She went from house to house, seeking direction to Smith's chalet, but met with tight-lipped resistance from the villagers. They stared at her fancy clothes and jewelry. She stared back—vexed at the colorful simplicity of their clothing, the sensible shoes and laced aprons, the mothers calling their children to them. Finally, misunderstanding her request, one woman led her to the local priest. Her annoyance at spiritual counsel was immediate. The priest shrugged and nodded to his guest in tweed, a man sipping tea by an unlit fireplace.

Exasperated, Ingrid said, "I'm looking for Harland Smith." She pointed to the mountains. "He's up there somewhere."

The man, closing in on eighty with thick white hair and bright, alert eyes, leaned back and picked up his pipe. "There's no one up there by that name," he said in his clipped British accent.

"What about Smythe Williams?"

"Ah, yes, the art dealer," he said guardedly.

"The art thief. He's stolen my Rembrandts—and who knows how many more of my paintings."

He watched her with renewed interest. "It seems that others have laid claim to those paintings today, too." He drew at his pipe, his thin lips smacking with the effort. "Why all this sudden interest in Rembrandt?"

She ignored him. "How far is it to his place?"

"An hour or two straight up. We run into snow at the higher elevation, especially near the chalet."

"Is the trail good?"

"Not in those shoes," he told her. "No paintings are worth climbing a mountain for in Italian pumps."

Ingrid wanted to laugh in his face. "Part of the von Tonner art collection is up there. That's worth millions. I'm going up if I have to crawl."

"It would be easier to ride."

She barely noticed his quick appraisal of her. His interest waned and turned back to the Dutch masters at Smith's chalet. He took out his tobacco pouch, relit his pipe, and puffed contentedly. "I'm Mandel Reynard," he said. "We seem to have a mutual interest in the Dutch masters. I bid on one recently and lost."

On the baron's painting? she wondered.

He smiled pleasantly. "I'm here to discuss marketing possibilities with Mr. Williams. I have a client who would find great delight in owning one of the von Tonner collection."

"Even if it were stolen?"

"I would hardly tell my client that, my dear. Would you care to ride up the mountain with me?"

"By car?"

Amused he said, "By horseback. You do ride, don't you?"

Better than you do, she thought. "Do you know Smith well?"

"We go back five decades. We met in an English pub during the war years. He was young and foolish even then."

"He's no longer young. Was he stealing art then too?"

Reynard considered that, his amusement growing. "No, he was selling invasion plans back then. Your Mr. Smith was not exactly schooled in the arts."

"No, he was educated on the streets of New York."

"Is that a fact? I find him a shrewd businessman."

"And a thief!"

"Perhaps. Perhaps not. Come, we shall pay him a visit and see whether you can lay claim to the treasures at the chalet."

☙❧

Heinrich Mueller and Drew Gregory stepped aside and allowed the distraught woman and whimpering child to pass them in silence. Then the men went on, walking steadily up the mountain trail at a fast clip, pausing now and then to check Harland's position. "I think he saw us," Mueller said.

"Yes, and he'll be ready for us when we arrive."

"But, Drew, he's alone except for the boy."

"Is he? He may have reinforcements coming in from the other trail. We do. Vic Wilson and Garret will be there long before we arrive. Others from Swiss Intelligence won't be far behind. Isn't that what Porter promised you, Heinz?"

"He said the name Smith persuaded them."

Drew took several steps in silence as they passed more patches of snow. "Heinz, you've helped me more than I had a right to ask. It sounds like we'll have ample help at the top. Why don't you head back to Zurich? Garret can take charge for you until the others arrive."

"There's no turning back now. Your arrival at my *zimmer frei* ruined all of that."

☙❧

Robyn held the village phone away from her ear as Pierre demanded, "Where are you?"

"I'm at the foot of the mountain. I'm on my way up to Smythe Williams' chalet. *Smith,* as my father calls him."

"Robyn, you can't do that. You don't know the mountains. Wait there for me. Julia Lewan wasn't killed intentionally. She was mistaken for you."

"I know," she whispered. "But Dad is up there. I'm going to him."

"Robyn, I'm begging you."

"Pierre, I asked you to climb Heidi's mountain with me, and you wouldn't do it. I asked my father, and he hasn't yet."

"That's not Heidi's mountain."

"It'll do, Pierre. Will you bring help?"

She could hear him suck in his breath. "What kind of help?"

"Does your uncle have any friends in Zurich?"

"This isn't his jurisdiction. I'll bring the *polizei.*"

"No, please, Pierre. Not until I know if my father—" She stifled her sobs, but her voice gave her away. "Monique is here in the village with Giles. I just talked with her. She's frightened. She thinks her husband might kill Anzel or anyone who stands in his way."

"Where's Anzel?"

"Harland forced him to go with him. There's trouble up there, Pierre. Monique says we may need some medical help."

"I'm coming. Walk slowly, Robyn. Or just wait with Monique. Hon," he said, "be careful. I love you."

Did he? Or was he trying to stop her from climbing the mountain? Was he one of Harland's boys? Or Ingrid's? Was he out to destroy her father, too? "Pierre, have you seen Ingrid? Or Aaron? Are they there in Zurich with Mother?"

"Your mother is here at the Alpenhof—looking for your uncle."

"Is Ingrid with her?"

"No. According to the concierge, Ingrid is heading for the mountains. Smith's chalet would be my guess. She may already be up there. "

249

Harland was waiting for her when she opened the door. "What are you doing here, Baroness?"

"I've come for my paintings."

"The baron's paintings," he corrected. "Sigmund Valdemar won't like it if you take them back. It took Sigmund and Roj Stapleton several trips to bring them up here."

Her hopes faded. So they had all sold out to Smith and double-crossed her. Without Valdemar's help and scheming she risked losing everything to Smith—the mansion, the house on the Riviera, the cars, along with acceptance into the best homes in Europe. And what would be left?

Betrayal! Fear wedged itself into her mind. Suddenly her knees felt weak; her boldness was gone. She had been a fool to come here—with only a stranger with her.

Smith smiled as he always did at her discomfort. "So you've met Mandel? Where is he? I watched you come up the trail. You ride well, Baroness."

"Mandel is tethering the horses."

"I thought you were in Germany."

"I left before the *polizei* arrived."

"And you came alone except for Mandel?"

She kept up her brave facade. "Of course, the paintings are mine."

"The *polizei?*" he repeated as Mandel joined them. "Were they looking for the von Tonner paintings, too?"

Reynard tapped his pipe against the palm of his hand. "The baroness tells me there's been a murder at her mansion."

Harland caught the back of a chair. "Not Robyn Gregory?"

"Was that the plan, Harland? If so, they made a mistake. Julia Lewan was an employee of Miriam's. Stapleton's girlfriend."

"Murdered, you say? What about Gregory's daughter?"

"I didn't stick around to find out what happened to her. I came here for my paintings." She looked around. "Where are they?"

Some were stacked by the fireplace only feet from where Anzel stood. In her fury, she hadn't even noticed the boy or the paintings.

"The rest of the pictures are in the storage shed behind the chalet," Harland said. "Would you care to see them, my dear?"

Fear nudged her again. Time was against them both. Harland was running a wild obstacle course, fighting for his own survival. She was fighting for her possessions.

"Mandel, perhaps you could show Anzel my gun collection. The baroness and I have business matters to discuss."

Alone with her, he said, "We could work together, Baroness. I have worldwide contacts—places to market the collection."

"That would be an unsavory and unscrupulous alliance."

"Ah, but a profitable one," he said.

"I told you before, no deal. I can manage without you."

"You are such a foolish woman." He took her elbow and led her brusquely out the door and to the porch. With her thoughts on outwitting him, she heard only half of his soothing words as they stood there. She understood why he loved this mountain and the isolated chalet. It offered a spectacular view of the snow-covered Alps, the kind that never ceased to thrill her. She'd almost forgotten her anger with him as he pointed to the cliffs above them. Then vaguely again she heard him mention partnership in the sale of the von Tonner collection.

"No. Never. I told you I won't share it with anyone. Least of all you."

"Then you'll have no joy in it," he threatened. "Come," he said fiercely. "The shed is in back." He gripped her elbow again, almost dragging her around the side of the chalet, her Italian pumps slipping and sliding in the snow. The shed lay just ahead of them, tipping precariously on the mountain ledge.

She tried to pull free, but before she realized what was happening, he tore her purse from her and tossed it over the cliff. Ingrid's spine stiffened, fear bracing it like a metal support. The pressure winded her. She blew tiny puffs of air through her mouth, trying to ease the pain as Smith said, "It's a pity that no one will miss you, Baroness."

She looked up in time to see the loathing hostility in his face and knew in that futile, fleeting moment—before she felt the power of his hands—that she would never sell the von Tonner collection.

She opened her mouth to scream, the sound empty and hollow against the wind, as her feet slipped over the edge. She clawed at him and then at the ground, her long fingernails tracking lines in the snow as she slipped from his iron grip and spiraled down into the cavernous valley below.

Twenty-five

Drew crouched low and ran. He halted at the crack of gunshots and glanced back in time to see Heinrich Mueller grab his leg and fall. As Mueller inched along toward the chalet, leaving patches of red on the ground, Drew started back. Mueller waved him on. "Go on, Gregory."

Sprinting to the back of the chalet, Drew boosted himself through a window and dropped with a thud onto the log floor. As he straightened, he faced a startled, white-haired gentleman who held a painting in his hands, a pipe in his mouth. The man peered over the picture frame, his glasses riding the tip of his nose. "What an ungallant entry. Do you always come in uninvited?"

"No one was at the front door," Drew told him.

With meticulous care, the man leaned the painting against the wall and offered a patronizing smile. He nodded toward the commotion outside—horses neighing, men running. "I'm not armed. I'm a nonviolent person. When they stop killing one another, I'll go, but what a shame to leave this lovely art collection behind."

To Drew, the man sounded dangerously out of touch, but the way he had scrutinized the painting showed innate intellect. As he puffed on his pipe, he looked like a pleasant, upperclass gentleman, one of the brilliants from Cambridge, the British accent evident. His hands were smooth, the nails clipped. Tweed-clad and precise, he did not look like a man ready for battle nor desirous of it.

Drew took a chance. "I have a friend wounded out there."

"Sorry. Things are a bit wild around here, but this gun room—library if you wish—is the safest place in the old chalet."

"Where's Harland Smith?"

The weak mouth turned down. "So many of you inquiring about Smith today. I assume you mean Herr Williams. He's been busy with unwanted guests. Whom shall I say is calling?"

"Drew Gregory. And you?"

"Mandel Reynard."

"I've heard the name."

"I daresay in London. I seem to have crashed a most important party just trying to obtain these paintings for Her Majesty."

"Mandel Reynard? You're the Queen's art historian."

"Not quite that high a position. But I've been lucky." He smiled his pleasure. "I sometimes advise Her Majesty on paintings for the palace and Windsor Castle. Unfortunately, a few of those were damaged in a fire. We're looking for replacements."

"Reynard. Reynard the photographer. World War II."

The man relit his pipe. "The Blitz mostly."

Drew kept his eye on the door, expecting Smith to burst through.

"I wouldn't walk through that door if I were you, Gregory. Smith will come along soon—looking for Anzel, if nothing else."

Mandel nodded toward a young lad sitting mutely in a winged chair, tenderly fondling a pistol, a gun rack on the wall behind him. Anzel seemed chiseled in stone, his thick black hair framing a boyish face. He was slim and studious looking, barely into his teens.

Twelve, thirteen. Fourteen at the most, Drew decided.

"Is that thing loaded?" Drew asked.

The Englishman shrugged. "I trust not."

Wounded dark eyes lifted toward Drew. "You're after my father?"

Drew had known about the boys and their mother, about their rich lifestyle in Paris. They had been names, faceless people to him. Drew's only goal was to take Smith in. He had not counted on the soul of a young boy being destroyed in the process. "I just want to take him back down for questioning, son."

"He won't let you." Anzel's words came out toneless as he ran his fingers over the barrel of the gun again.

"Your dad has hurt people, son. Done bad things."

"Mr. Reynard says my father's a good man."

"Perhaps Mr. Reynard doesn't really know him."

"Fifty years of friendship says that I do, Mr. Gregory. Smith and I met in a London pub during the war. Before we could finish our drinks, we had to run for an air-raid shelter. While the bombs exploded outside, I told him how we could end the war."

Drew eased past the boy, mute again, and made his way along the wall to the door, listening.

Reynard interrupted the silence, asking, "Didn't you ever want to end the war, Mr. Gregory?"

Drew eyed the doorknob, waiting for the slightest motion.

"Smith was a courier for the American general. Did you know that, Gregory? I told him that if we blocked the invasion plans, England would have to surrender to Germany, and the war would be over."

"You make me sick. You both betrayed your countrymen. Harland certainly did. Where is he, Mandel?"

"Find him if you want him."

Drew yanked the door open and stepped into the empty sitting room. He moved cautiously to the next door and kicked it open, his Luger ready.

A startled Vic Wilson stared up at him. "Don't ever do that to me again, Drew."

Vic was kneeling by a chair, tying Sigmund Valdemar's hands behind him. Stapleton lay unconscious on the floor, his wrists secure. As Valdemar looked up at Drew, his eyes blazed with anger.

"When I get free," he said, "I'll kill you both."

Vic jerked the rope tighter. A crack resounded as the bone in Valdemar's right wrist broke the skin. He cried out in pain and sputtered obscenities. "You clumsy oaf! You fool…now look what you've done. I won't be able to paint with that hand."

"It's a stroke of luck for us. It'll keep you off the art market." Vic taped Sigmund's mouth and glared in disgust at Drew. "Where are those reinforcements that Porter promised Mueller?"

Drew kept his voice to a whisper. "Caught in a tangle of Swiss bureaucracy. Maybe they're not coming." He knuckled Valdemar's head. "Are there any others like this one?"

Vic's smirk downgraded to a scowl. "A couple of foolhardy villagers came up here to protect Smith. *Their friend,* they call him. They came when they saw some woman fall off the cliff."

Drew's strangled words came out high-pitched. "Not Miriam?" He clenched his fist. "Where did she go over? I've got—"

"Hang in there, Drew, until we know for certain. The men from the village sent out a mountain yodel, calling up a rescue party They'll do everything they can."

Vic nodded toward the window. "I'm going out that way to scout around. I'll check on Mueller and Garret."

Drew's temple pulsated as he stormed back into the sitting room. As he charged in, a bullet tore through his right shoulder, sending his revolver crashing to the floor. He fought to stay on his feet and almost stumbled over the stack of Dutch masters.

"Don't move," Harland told him. "Now, kick your gun over here."

The weapon slid toward Smith; he toed it further away. "It's been a long time, Gregory."

Drew staunched the blood flow with his bare hand; it seeped through his fingers—bright red droplets splashing over a van Ruisdael painting. "My wife—where is she?"

Smith shrugged, his black eyes savage, dark slits. As Drew lunged at him, Harland fired again, deliberately missing.

Drew steadied himself. "If you killed her, Smith—"

"Someone fell over the cliff; I didn't ask for an I.D.!"

Reynard slipped quietly into the room from the adjoining library. "Your guest is bleeding, Harland. I do hate bloodshed." He tore off his ascot and pressed the scarf against Drew's shoulder.

"Let him bleed. I want to watch him die slowly."

"Yes, Smith, let me die the way you let Captain York die."

"That was fifty years ago."

"Right now, Corporal Smith, I remember it like it was yesterday."

Drew felt himself growing weaker as Mandel eased him into a chair; he slumped there gratefully. "Smith, you're a turncoat. I've never understood how you got an honorable discharge."

"A medical discharge from the Army, *thanks to* you."

"You didn't even deserve that." Drew nodded toward Mandel. "And you sold military secrets to this man."

Except for the revolver in his hand and the intense hatred in his dark eyes, Smith was a commanding presence. He stood tall, his expression controlled. His watch and ring and even the cut of his sport clothes held the mark of quality. A tiny twitch began at the corner of his mouth, but his voice was even. "I thought we were going to lose that war, Gregory. Hitler already owned half of Europe. It was only a matter of time."

"Time was in our favor, Smith. We did win."

Mandel bit back. "We were watching the clock, too. It didn't take a military genius to know the Allies would start a second front. We wanted to know when and where you would strike."

"I gave him the facts," Smith said calmly. "Photographs of our remote training beaches: the Mulberries and Gooseberries."

"Nothing but artificial harbors and breakwaters," Mandel scoffed. "And you were sometimes inaccurate about the number of troop trains or the number of camps in Cornwall—"

Smith grew agitated. "But you liked the Neptune Plan with every convoy and minesweeper mapped and plotted out for you. And for what?"

"Come now, old chap. We were heroes in our own way," Mandel assured him. "But I hated losing that bloody war."

Drew fought to stay alert. "It's too bad you didn't hate selling out to the Germans."

Mandel's eyes narrowed. "No way, old boy. I was schooled at Cambridge in the thirties after Burgess and Philby. They tried to recruit me for the Russians, but I had a heart for the Germans, views my German-born mother instilled in me."

Drew fought nausea as Mandel said, "I could sip tea with the best of the English and curse Hitler and his madman approach to world conquest, but inside I wanted to be a part of it. Everything went quite well until this general's orderly sailed off to the Normandy Invasion. Alas, when Germany lost the war, I was still in merry old England, and Smith here was home with a facial injury."

Drew sucked in his breath remembering how Smith had lunged at him in a foxhole and how he fought back with the butt of his rifle. He had puzzled over that attack for years until the microfilm was found in Captain York's watch. But it went back even further than that—to their landing craft hitting the beaches at Normandy and. Corporal Smith firing his government-issued rifle directly at the captain. Drew had skidded through the blood-splattered sand in time to see Smith trying to steal a watch from the dying man.

At seventeen Drew had been afraid, but the man he faced now no longer frightened him. A weary fifty-year-old sigh escaped him. "Smith, you killed Captain York, didn't you, all for a watch?"

"Not for a watch," Smith scoffed. "For microfilm."

Mandel shook his head in disgust "So you did hold out on another secret document, Harland, ol' boy? Why didn't you follow the usual channels or make arrangements to meet me in the pub?"

"Shut up, Reynard."

The Englishman stood taller. "What good is all of this now? Isn't it too late for a court martial? And," he said smiling, "Gregory here is in no condition to share it with anyone."

Drew's words slurred. "I'll make it. I'm taking Smith in on charges of terrorism in Paris."

Smith's gun clicked. He leveled it at Gregory's temple. From the doorway Anzel cried out, "Papa, did you kill someone?"

Drew's head spun as he turned to look at the boy standing there, the shiny pistol still clutched in his hand. His dark eyes darted back and forth between his father and Drew. "Is it true, Papa?"

"People get killed in war, son."

For a moment, the boy's gaze lingered, transfixed, on the art pieces streaked with Drew's blood. "Is this war, too?"

"Get out, Smith," Drew said. "Get out of the boy's sight, and then I'm coming after you." He dragged himself to a sitting position. "It's okay, Anzel. Let him go."

"I don't want to let him go. He's my father. I-I love him."

Harland gave Anzel one final gaze—half love, half scorn— before he turned his back on his son and stepped into the crisp mountain air. Sun goggles balanced on top of his thick silver hair. Slowly, he zipped his jacket as he sized up the trail to the village, the bridle path to town, the sheer precipice beside-the chalet. An empty, hopeless expression seemed embedded on his face as he untethered the horses and sent them riderless toward the bottom.

"Fool," the Englishman said. "That was my ride off the mountain."

Anzel watched intently as Harland shielded his eyes and scanned the peaks. Then Anzel walked in a straight line to the door, his eyes on his father as Harland lined up his skis on the ground. Drew staggered unsteadily to his feet and followed the boy. Outside Harland faced them, a mocking smile filling his swarthy face.

He's going for the mountain, Drew thought. *Up and over.*

Drew squinted. A hazy mist cut the tips of the mountains from view, but he knew that Harland was going up to find a way of escape through the crevices. "You won't make it, Smith. The snow isn't deep enough for skiing," he warned. *Except on the higher levels.*

Harland bent down to adjust his skis, his gaze fixed on his son. As Drew rested against the door casing, the cruel ridges around Harland's mouth deepened; rage filled his face. He took his revolver from his pocket and, for the second time, leveled it at Drew.

"Get out of the way, Anzel," Harland shouted.

Drew attempted to shove the boy aside, but Anzel gripped the shiny pistol with both hands and aimed it at his father.

Harland laughed. "Put that away, Anzel."

Smith kicked off one ski and stood up. As he straightened, a shot rang out, echoing hollowly across the Alps. His face twisted in pain and disbelief. He stretched his hand toward his son and fell.

"The boy jolly well shot him," Mandel said in surprise.

Anzel looked up at Drew. "He was going to kill you, Mr. Gregory."

Drew nodded. "He knew I was going to take him in, son."

The boy turned and walked blindly into the chalet, his papa's pistol still in his hand. Drew staggered outside and, reached Harland in time to see Smith's body convulse violently and go limp.

ॐ

Drew and Anzel began the slow, tortuous descent down the mountain, boy and man leaning hard against each other.

"You're wounded, Drew. I could go for you in half the time," Vic called.

Drew felt Anzel stiffen. He had to get him down the mountain, away from the still body of his father.

"I need you and Garret to stay here and watch the Englishman and

Valdemar."

"We've got them well secured."

"I know, but I wouldn't be much help if more Stasi boys came over the other trail. No, Anzel and I will go it alone."

"You're still bleeding some, Drew. You may not make it."

I have to try, he thought. He slipped his hand in his jacket and felt the soggy shirt. He wavered, his thoughts on the woman who had gone over the cliff. Miriam? His knees almost buckled. If something really had happened to her, he had to be there for his daughter. He wiped his sticky hand on his trousers. "It's just seeping a little now."

"Smith has a good radio set here," Vic said. "I could call for help."

"No, not until this boy is safely with his mother. And you won't call Porter, will you? I want to confront him myself."

"No, Heinrich Mueller set me straight. I didn't realize what Porter was trying to pull in the beginning. I really thought you might have turned greedy. That you'd give a bad name to the Company."

"I don't know any more about art fraud than you do, Vic."

"I know that now. Mueller straightened me out on a lot of things, but I kept playing along with Porter. For your sake."

Drew believed him. "We'll work it out, friend. Later."

"Will Anzel be all right?"

Drew gripped Anzel's shoulder. "He just saved my life. I'll do everything I can for him."

Vic wiped his mouth with the back of his hand. "Porter didn't plan on Anzel being here or Mueller getting hurt or some woman going over the cliff. He just counted on you taking Smith out for him."

Drew took a final glance toward Smith's body, lying in a thin mound of crimson snow. "Porter got what he wanted. Smith dead and his own career salvaged. But if it cost me Miriam—"

He turned cautiously and passed the cliff with its smooth path over the ledge. Then Drew and the boy went on alone.

❦

Vic knelt and ran his fingers through the scuff marks still visible there. "This trail is fresh," he said. "They struggled here. Poor woman. I'm sure this is where she went over."

"What a horrible way to die," Garret said. "Hey, what's that?"

Wedged against a rock was a colorful Italian pump embedded in the crusty snow. As Vic picked it up, he felt sick. "Garret, do you know whether Miriam Gregory wore this kind of shoe?"

"I don't know. I only saw her that once at the Alpenhof lounge. What's the matter? Do you think Gregory's wife is the one who plunged over?"

Vic stared at the deep precipice, the purple shoe clutched in his hand. "Someone did. Come on, Garret. I'm going to use that radio set after all."

"But you promised Drew—"

"I'm going to call for help. Drew and the boy will need it. Drew can't possibly make it all the way down."

೩೦ಲ

Halfway down, Drew saw Robyn coming to meet them. He hugged the boy and waited. When she saw them, she began running. She was crying and laughing when she flew into Drew's arms.

"Daddy, you're hurt. And you, Anzel." She touched the boy's face. "You look terrible. Are you all right?"

Drew nuzzled the top of her hair. "Anzel's father is dead."

He wanted to shield her from further pain. "Princess, your mother—" With great effort he turned and looked back at the chalet nestled on the mountainside. The sheer cliff beside the house was visible—a well-marked snow path revealing where a human avalanche had spiraled downward. "Robyn, someone went over that cliff today."

She held his hand. "And you thought it was Mother? Dad, don't look so worried. Mother is safe. She's back at the hotel—furious with all of us and telling Uncle Aaron to pack up and get out."

Drew glanced anxiously at Anzel. The boy was motionless, his eyes void of feeling, the color in his cheeks gone. "But Smith said—"

"Dad, whatever he said was wrong. Miriam—Mother is safe."

They cried together, the boy excluded from their embrace. Robyn put her head against Drew's chest. He winced in pain.

"I think I know what happened," she said.

"Ingrid went up the mountain early this morning to confront Smith about stealing the von Tonner collection."

"Then Ingrid is dead, Robyn." *Dead for an art collection,* he thought. He remembered his own blood dripping on a van Ruisdael.

Anzel still stood alone. Robyn turned and spoke softly to him. "Anzel, your mother is waiting for you down in the village."

He shook his head and in a flurry of French cried out, "She'll never forgive me. I'll never forgive me."

She comforted him. "But God will forgive you."

Anzel turned his desperate gaze toward Drew. Drew could offer the boy no hope, no confirmation. He couldn't admit that he wasn't a praying man. Instead he said, "We need to go on down. It's getting late, son."

"Dad, we should wait here. Pierre has gone for help."

"No, Princess. I promised you we'd climb this mountain together."

"It's the wrong mountain."

"Close enough, isn't it? I failed to keep my word, but we can walk down together," he offered.

"You'll never make it. You're still bleeding."

"It's not much further, Princess."

She reached out to support her father's good arm. "Can you really make it? Are you sure?"

"No, but I'll try."

The snow had been left behind on the higher elevation. Now they stumbled and slipped over the rocks and dirt, but kept plodding along, Anzel's footsteps even slower than Drew's. They were a weary trio tripping and lurching along the mountain trail, but inside Robyn felt a quiet peace wrap itself around her heart as she walked with her father.

Finally, she spied Pierre and his friends climbing rapidly up the tangled path toward them with an empty stretcher. "Pierre," she shouted. "Over here. We're right here."

He dropped his end of the stretcher, sprinted the last few yards, and pulled her into his arms.

◈

When Drew awakened, he seemed to be in a hospital bed. The sheets were white and sterile, the smell antiseptic. He realized that he was part of the medicinal odor, and it was his shoulder and chest swathed in bandages. He tried to move and thought better of it. He wasn't certain whether it was the pain or the grogginess that blurred his vision. And then he saw her—at least he thought he did.

Miriam burst through the door looking alarmed, strands of her usually impeccable coiffure flying as she rushed in. He reached out his hand in welcome, but she stopped at the foot of his bed. "Drew, you gave us a fright. And what were you thinking of taking Robyn up that mountain with you?"

His hand went limply to the bed. He felt like a ruffled mess as she looked at him. He wondered where his contact lenses were, whether he had a comb to run against the cowlick in his hair, where he'd find a razor to tackle the shadowed beard that darkened his skin. He made an effort to swing back the sheets and discovered he was immodestly dressed in a blue-checked gown.

"Answer me, Drew Gregory. Why did you take Robyn with you?"

"He didn't take me with him, Mother."

Robyn's voice. She was somewhere in the room, part of the sounds that danced across his mind. What mountain was Miriam fretting about? Heidi's mountain? No, Smith's mountain. *Smith was dead.* That picture was vivid!

"Where's Anzel?" he asked.

Robyn was at his bedside at once, Miriam on the other side—both reaching for his hands. Their faces seemed distorted through his blurred vision.

"Daddy, the doctors are with Anzel."

"And the *polizei,*" Miriam said in disgust.

"They have to talk to him, Mother. The boy killed his father."

This time Drew held tight to Miriam's hand to keep her from spinning and falling. He tried to explain, but it was Robyn's words he heard. "Mandel Reynard was more than willing to tell them what happened. He said Anzel was protecting you, Dad."

Drew actually felt Miriam's hand press against his. Gently, he said,

"Miriam, we were meant to be together. The three of us—a triple braided cord. We were never meant to separate."

He saw pleasure on Robyn's face and a flicker of hope cross Miriam's, but then she said, "Robyn, your father is still sedated. He'll be horrified when he realizes what he said."

He tried to tell them he was awake. He was awake enough to see that Robyn was wearing the forest-green sarong and the silk blouse. "You look beautiful, Robyn," he told her.

She twirled around. "I do, don't I? I love the outfit."

"I used to buy my mother dresses from Steinman's store. She always loved them."

Miriam still hadn't pulled her hand free when Robyn leaned over the rail and kissed him. "I'll leave you and Mother alone. Pierre is waiting for me."

"Don't go. We must make plans to climb Heidi's Alps."

She smiled. "Do you think we ever will?"

"I was wondering about this weekend?"

❦

For the next several hours, Miriam sat beside Drew's bed, watching him slip in and out of consciousness. Slowly, the anesthesia wore off, and he awakened, pleased at seeing her. His smile turned to a frown when the room phone rang. His conversation was brief, his expression angry, his answers monosyllabic. She knew without asking him that the call had come from the Company, from someone within its ranks. She remembered those phone calls from long ago—calls that would send him to places around the world without her.

As he talked, she toyed with three strips of gauze from his bedside stand. Absently, she braided them.

When he cradled the phone, he said, "Miriam, I need to shower and leave here."

"But they're keeping you here for two or three days."

"No, I have things to do, reports to write."

Sadly, she placed the triple-braided gauze on his pillow. "So your cat-and-mouse game goes on?"

He cupped her chin. "I've been after this one a long time."

"You've been chasing answers all your life, Drew."

"It's different this time. I have to know who set you up back at the gallery. And if Aaron tried to destroy you, I'll—"

"Have you talked to him yet, Drew?"

"I've tried. He refused my phone calls."

"But you're brothers."

"That won't matter if he's behind this art fraud business."

"Robyn and I will be fine once we get back to Los Angeles."

"But she may be staying in Europe to marry Pierre Courtland."

"No! She can't do that! They barely know each other."

"Pierre argues that you and I had a short courtship."

"And look where it got us? You walked out."

"Your choice, Miriam. Not mine."

She remembered him begging her to come back into his outstretched arms. She heard him echo the same words. *"Don't turn away from me. Look at me, Miriam."*

She turned back as he said, "We can't let what happened to us sixteen years ago destroy Robyn's chance for happiness."

"I don't want her to make the same mistake."

"We were happy in the beginning, Miriam." He tried to take her hand again.

She pulled away, her eyes on the braided gauze on his pillow. "It's too late for us, Drew."

He glanced at his watch. "Yes, it is late, isn't it? That phone call moments ago gave me my marching orders, Miriam. Swiss Intelligence doesn't want me linked with Smith's death or the carnage on the mountain."

"You're leaving without telling Robyn?"

"I have no choice."

"A few hours ago, you promised to climb Heidi's mountain this weekend."

Drew took her rebuke without wincing. "Miriam, Smith is dead, and Stapleton and Sigmund Valdemar in custody."

"That's as it should be."

Patiently he said, "Smith has friends who won't let his death go unanswered. And since picking up Valdemar yesterday, Germany is boasting a real Stasi treasure. They've been looking for him for a long time."

"That has nothing to do with your promise to Robyn."

"But it does. Valdemar has friends too. Everything blew up for them yesterday—no art collection to sell, so no money for weapons. Langley thinks they'll come after me."

"I'm sorry."

"But not just me." He paused. "You and Robyn will be targets too. You'll be safer if you get out of Zurich. Go home, please, Miriam. And take our daughter with you." He threw back his covers. "Vic Wilson is waiting for me. I'm going away to protect Robyn and you because I love you both."

"And this is the way you show your love," she whispered. "By leaving us again?"

Epilogue

Robyn didn't wait for the lift. She ran down the flight of stairs, out the lobby door, and straight into Pierre's arms.

"I couldn't have asked for a better welcome," he said.

"Oh, Pierre! I'm sorry. I'm on my way to see my father."

The smile that had beamed across his face crashed. "I thought we were going to the Jungfrau today?"

"Some other day. Dad needs me now. *He* really does."

"Robyn, I'm going back to Geneva in the morning."

"You can't—I mean, your holiday isn't over until Monday."

"I want to spend some time with the baron first."

"Are you going to tell him about Ingrid?"

"Someone has to." He looked away, grabbing at strength, she supposed, with a quick little prayer. She pictured Pierre cradling the old man in his strong arms, comforting him like a small child—as Pierre sometimes comforted her—and telling Felix the bitter truth.

"It will be easier coming from me. I know how much he adored her. If he thinks it was just an accident—"

"Maybe you shouldn't tell him at all."

"I've always been honest with the baron. He's bound to ask about the mansion. That's one of the things I want to look into before I go back to work on Monday. The baron owns the grounds, the stables, and the paintings. Even the tunnels are legally his."

"He's so ill—what does it matter?"

"It matters to me. I've called my uncle—he's lining up the best of lawyers. It may end up in the courts for a long time to come, but we're hoping to work out a deal with the government."

She looked up at the strong, honest face before her, his eyes tender as he looked at her. "Are the Klees part of the deal?"

"The Klees would be good to Felix." Pierre stood by the curb, massaging his jaw, running his fingers over the mole on his cheek, over and over. "Kurt thinks I'm crazy, but I'd do anything to get the baron back to the mansion."

"But you can't make Felix well," she warned.

"I can make it easier for him to die. And maybe—maybe he'd be ready to listen to me about eternal matters."

She caught his hand and caressed it. "You're so good to Felix."

"I love that old man like my own family."

"You are family."

"I wish the courts thought so," he said. "Ingrid left no will concerning the mansion, and the baron is no longer capable of making a new one. Rather than let it sit idle during court battles, I'd like to see it open as a museum so everyone can enjoy the baron's collection."

"You're like Felix's son. Could you claim the paintings yourself?"

Longing shadowed his face. "I'm a friend, not an heir. What would I do with all those pictures? My living quarters are small. And I don't know the first thing about cataloguing them."

"Would you like a lady curator?"

"Definitely. You'd have to stay in Europe for that."

"I love it here." *And I love* you, she thought.

"You'd have a long commute back and forth to Geneva."

Blushing, she asked, "Why Geneva?"

"That's where I live and work"

"Not a good idea. You said your living quarters are small."

"I'd get a larger place for my wife."

Her blush deepened. Shyly, she said, "It might be a long time before you can turn the mansion into a museum." You *need to go home and sort out your holiday feelings. And I need to go home and find my answers in Andrea Prescott's Book.*

As she lifted her hand to flag down a taxi, he grasped it. "Don't go. I want you to spend the day with me. There are things we should talk about before I leave for Geneva."

"About what happened up there on the mountain yesterday?"

He hesitated. "It's not a pleasant picture."

"I know how Ingrid died, Pierre. It's inside—" She tapped her breastbone gently. "She didn't believe anything, did she?"

"She believed she could make it without God. Arguing got us nowhere, and now there's no time left to tell her." Their fingers locked.

"She knows now, Robyn, that there was—is a *God*. I find it strange to think of Ingrid's knees bowing and her tongue— dry and parched as it must be—confessing that she was wrong."

"Have I waited too long, Pierre?"

His grip tightened. "No, but you've waited long enough."

"Can you show me what you mean in Andrea's Book?"

He couldn't stop the smile or chuckle; they came as one. "It's not just Andrea's Book, Robyn. It's God's Word." Pierre whipped out his pocket Testament. "Could we go have breakfast somewhere?"

The thorns of other things began to choke her. "Later. I really must see Dad now." She saw his disappointment. "This afternoon I promise. We'll talk then."

"If your afternoon gets cluttered, promise me that when you get back to Los Angeles, you'll talk to your friend Floy and start going to that little chapel. Don't just run by ever again."

"Nothing's going to happen. I phoned Floy last night. I told her about everything—including you and Andrea and her Book." She sighed as she saw another taxi. "I must go. Dad is waiting."

Pierre's face clouded. "He's probably raising a ruckus. I feel sorry for any man in an open-back nightshirt kowtowing to nurses."

"Dad was fussing about that when I left him last night. Why don't you go with me? Help me convince him to cooperate."

"I guess it's the only way I can spend the day with you."

They held hands as they walked up the steps to the clinic. Robyn felt jubilant until they reached Drew's room. It was empty. They hurried back to the nurses' station.

"We're here to see my father, Drew Gregory, but his room is empty."

"Your father?" the nurse asked pleasantly.

"Room 211. He was admitted last evening."

The nurse searched the charts in front of her. "There's no Gregory. No one was admitted by that name—last night nor today."

Robyn's throat constricted. "That's impossible. I was here with him. You were on duty. Now you tell me—where is he?"

A frown replaced the pleasant smile. "Let me call the supervisor. You can speak—"

Robyn ran wildly back down the hall. Pierre caught up with her at the door to 211 and tried to calm her as she stared at Drew's empty bed. The starched nurse was behind them now. "Please. This is a hospital. I told you there is no one here by that name."

"Where is my father?"

"I'm sorry, Miss Gregory. You really must go. It's best for everyone. We'll be admitting a patient here shortly."

"But...my father..."

Pierre held so tightly to her waist that she thought he might crush her. "Sweetheart, they've told you. He's not here."

She ignored him, crying, "Daddy, don't go away again."

"Robyn—sweetheart—maybe your father planned it this way. Maybe they whisked him away to protect him."

"He walked out on me...again...oh, how could he, Pierre?"

"He must have had a good reason for leaving."

"Did he, Pierre? I still don't know why he left the first time. Mother's been right all along. Dad always runs out on us."

She broke free from Pierre's firm embrace and pounded on his chest, crying uncontrollably. "I'm going back home, today! At least Mother still wants me around."

"What about me?" he demanded. "Haven't you heard what I said these last few days? I want you to stay in Switzerland with me."

"For a trip to the Jungfrau? No, I'm going home." She ran outside. "I never want to look at Heidi's mountains again. Ever."

He stopped abruptly.

She turned and winced when she saw his wounded expression. "I'm sorry, Pierre. I can't stay—not now."

"Robyn, I told you once I would never run out on you. Don't run out on me. I'm not your father. I'm the man who wants to spend the rest of his life with you."

"Don't, please. I have to—"

"Go back to your mother's art gallery? Is that what you want? What happened to those plans for a career of your own?"

She bit her lip and fled. This time he didn't follow.

❧⚜❧

The last of summer and early fall slipped away; late autumn came in bursts of glory. In Switzerland the Alps were already covered with deep blankets of snow—the blue thistle and the colorful alpine pansy and asters gone until another July. In Geneva, Pierre had obviously escaped into a mountain of work—too proud to write letters to Robyn, too stubborn to call.

For Robyn in Beverly Hills, the seasonal changes blended. She barely noticed the nip of a chilly fall. Temperatures stayed in the mid-fifties and sixties; only her heart dropped below zero every time she thought about Pierre. For several weeks she jogged past the little white chapel, not even stopping to listen to the music. On her fifth Sunday home, she decided to go inside.

The congregation was singing when she slipped into the back pew. Smiling, the woman beside Robyn handed her an open hymnbook. But Robyn remembered the words: "Because He lives..." *Yes,* she thought, *Pierre was right. I can face tomorrow. Tomorrow is not dependent on my father coming back.*

She brushed furiously at her tears, but they kept flowing that afternoon when she knelt by her bedside, alone. She felt frightened and unsure. But later she rose, confident and joyful. The pages of the Book that Andrea Prescott had given her were alive with promise and a future hope. But she knew more than Andrea's Book; she knew Andrea's Savior personally.

❧⚜❧

Two weeks later, as Robyn placed a seascape on the easel, the art gallery's melodious chimes rang. She turned to the customer with a smile. "I came for a Rembrandt," he said, the smell of his cologne heady, his shining sable eyes intent and caring as he looked at her.

She could hardly find her voice. Was she dreaming? If she spoke, would he vanish? "I have no Rembrandts to show you."

"Anything will do," he said. "I'm not very good in the art world.

I'll trust your judgment."

She couldn't trust her emotions and made no answer. He crossed the room swiftly. "Robyn, my life hasn't been right since you went away."

She wanted to reach up and straighten his seashell tie and touch his face—that wonderfully strong face, too square, not quite handsome, everything she remembered. That irresistible grin tugged at his mouth.

"I missed you, Robyn."

She nodded, tears brimming in her eyes. The chimes rang again. She didn't even look over to check the comings and goings in the gallery. Floy Beaumont slipped past them, welcoming the customers cheerfully, "Good morning. It's a lovely day. How may I help you?"

"Pierre, what brought you here?" Robyn asked.

"You."

She knuckled a tear from each eye. He brushed the next ones away for her. Catching his hand, she impulsively brought it to her lips. "I'm so glad you came."

He responded with lips touching her knuckles and then he leaned down and his kisses progressed to her mouth— gentle, convincing. The door chimes sent him upright again. "Can we get out of here?"

"I'm working."

"Close the shop."

She laughed. "It's bad for business."

"It's important for us."

She led him over to the van Gogh and Monet paintings. "This should be private enough," she said. "For a few minutes."

"It'll do."

"Why did you come to the States, Pierre?" she repeated.

"To attend a reunion at the military academy."

"But you hated that school."

"It was my excuse to see you again." He kept his honest gaze locked on hers. "I came to take you back to Switzerland with me."

"You know I can't go—not now. Not yet."

He glanced around. "Business looks good. Is it?"

"In two or three years, Mother will have the best gallery on Rodeo Drive again—and the humiliation of lawsuits behind us."

"Must you wait that long?" he asked.

"Would you want me to leave her when she's still grieving over Ingrid? At least she talks about their happier days at Radcliffe now, but she won't allow herself to speak of Ingrid's body crushed at the bottom of a mountain. Mother doesn't even talk about Uncle Aaron—and he's still alive."

"Your uncle tried to destroy your mother."

"He almost succeeded. But Mother refuses to implicate him. Let's not talk about Mother. We'll end up quarreling. So tell me about your trip."

He managed a warm smile, his gaze daring. "I called Sauni Breckenridge from the academy."

She choked, saying, "The older woman? Why?"

"The old political problem about Luke is festering in Washington again. I advised Sauni to forget it and fly back to Schaffhausen...*and I told her about you, Robyn.*"

She tried to keep it light. "Did you tell her about Gino?"

"Sauni wouldn't be interested in Gino. But she told me to take you back to Geneva with me—and not to take no for an answer." He caught her hand. "I love you, Robyn. And—oh, no. I almost forgot. I brought you something."

Don't, she thought. *Don't give me a ring. Not yet. Let me work it out first.*

He took a large box from his briefcase. "Someone asked me to give this to you."

She tore the ribbon and wrappings away and stared down at a gold-bound copy of *Heidi.* Inside it said, *To the girl who loved Heidi's mountain. To the young woman who will climb it with me.*

"From my father?" she whispered. "He's safe?"

"Yes. And he wants to see you again. Soon."

"Then why did he go away, Pierre?"

"He couldn't risk staying in Zurich." Pierre lowered his voice, turning now and then to comment on a nearby painting whenever a customer wandered near them. "Your safety was your dad's priority. Can you understand that, Robyn?"

"Not really. How can I?"

"Porter ordered your father out of Zurich—he wanted no link with Drew and the carnage at the chalet."

"Dad was already safely away from it."

"Porter wasn't satisfied—even with his old friend Smith dead and his own career safe. Swiss Intelligence agreed. They wanted Heinrich Mueller back at his *zimmer frei* as quickly as his wound permitted, and they wanted Drew out of Zurich. Porter and Swiss Intelligence were worried about retaliation from Smith or Valdemar's friends. That's the way the game is played. Drew bargained your safety in exchange for his own disappearance."

"I'm not something to be auctioned off at Altman's."

"At that moment they still weren't certain if you and Miriam were involved in the art fraud—or for that matter, where I stood. Drew knew that if he left the hospital without seeing you again, you'd go home. Heartbroken, but safe. Safe perhaps even from me."

"Pierre, Dad trusted you."

"But Porter Deven didn't."

"Dad tried to persuade Mother that it was okay for you and me—" She couldn't finish. Her eyes were on the bound copy of *Heidi*. "Pierre, will I ever see my father again?"

He ran his fingers over her eyes and mouth, outlining her features. "You'd have a better chance in Switzerland. Your father still believes a cord of three strands is not quickly broken. He may not know that Solomon said it, but he believes it. Drew is more than willing to see the frayed cords of your family mended."

"Mother and Daddy getting back together? The three of us?"

Pierre nodded. "Isn't that what you want?"

"Mother will never agree to that."

"Miracles still happen, Robyn."

"Yes." She thought of the little white chapel and the comfort she had found there. "But it's too late for Mother and Daddy."

"Is it too late for us?" he asked.

"I hope not."

෴

That night Pierre stood in the shadows of the Gregory hallway, the living room lamp casting a faint glow on his face. The twinkle in his eyes had dimmed. He picked up his briefcase, reluctant to leave for the airport.

"Pierre, Mother said to tell you good-bye."

"Go with me, Robyn. We can marry in Switzerland."

"It's too soon—but Mother knows I'm going to leave someday and work in a museum cataloguing the famous old masters perhaps."

"There are museums in Europe, Robyn."

"I know. Even in Geneva."

"And you speak German fluently."

"That's what worries Mother. She knows I'd gladly move there."

"How long will you put your mother's career first?" he challenged.

"Until things are going well on Rodeo Drive."

"Please don't make me wait two or three more winters. Your mother can make it without you. She has Floy Beaumont. She could have had your father. Robyn, come with me now. I need you."

"Mother would never forgive me—"

A sad, crooked smile formed at the corners of his mouth as he took a plane ticket from his coat pocket and laid it on the hall table. "I bought two return tickets. Just in case! In case you change your mind, I'll be at Los Angeles International. The plane leaves at 10:55." He touched her face tenderly. "I love you, Robyn."

She leaned against the door as it closed behind him and wept until the taxi drove away. She was still crying when she felt her mother's gentle hand on her shoulder, her voice soft, yet reprimanding, "Did you send him away?...I did that once to someone I loved."

She cried out, "Pierre had a plane to catch."

"So did Drew when I sent him away."

Miriam forced Robyn to face her and cradled her head tightly against her breast. They talked of Switzerland and Drew, of Robyn and Pierre, of shattered dreams and the hope of building them again. Finally Miriam said, "Follow your heart, Robyn."

"All the way to Geneva?"

"If that's what it takes." She touched Robyn's cheeks with her slender hands. "You have dreams of your own—and I'm certain they include Pierre. I'll miss you, but I want you to be happy."

"I can't run out on you while you're trying to get the gallery going again."

"Don't do to Pierre what I did to your father. Don't send him away when you love him." She checked her watch. "Oh, dear. And don't wait to pack your things. There isn't time. Just grab your overnight case and passport. I'll send the rest of your clothes by Federal Express. Or—I'll bring them when I come for—the wedding."

Miriam brushed away tears as she pushed Robyn toward the stairs. "And tell that young man he'd better take good care of you."

❧

Robyn ran down the terminal corridor. She was breathless when she reached the agent and laid her cosmetic case on the counter. Eagerly, she handed him her ticket. "The flight to Geneva—"

He shook his head. "Sorry, miss. That plane is just rolling down the runway. You're five minutes too late."

Inside, her hopes shattered. She dashed to the window and pressed her face against the pane, waving blindly as the jet roared down the runway into the autumn wind. She stood there, the seconds ticking away like a lifetime as the plane nosed upward and became a speck in the billowy night sky.

Everyone else left, their muffled voices dying in the distance. The airline agent scooped up his paperwork. Robyn's fingers went limp; the ticket slipped from her hand and fell behind her. Other jets taxied down the runway, but Pierre's plane had completely vanished.

From out of the painful stillness, she heard a deep, resonant voice saying, "I think you dropped this, Robyn."

She whirled around. For a moment, she stared in disbelief before tumbling into Pierre's arms. He crushed her against him. "I kept hoping you'd come, sweetheart," he said.

"I thought you were on that plane—"

"I was. Seat belt on and everything."

"Then why?"

"I was sitting there thinking, *Oh, God, why? I don't want to lose her.* And suddenly I just knew you were coming."

She cried. He smiled. Her tears fell.

He tipped her chin and wiped them away. "The flight attendant warned me that they had already given the final boarding call. But I had to risk it. I had to get off the plane and look for you." His eyes turned merry. "I even called your mother. She told me you were on your way."

"Did she tell you we have her blessing?"

"She warned me I'd better be good to you. So let's go."

"Where, Pierre? We missed the plane."

"We'll catch another one—any plane as long as it's heading home to Switzerland."

"But your luggage! Your clothes went on without you." He laughed looking at her small case. "And you forgot yours."

"Mother said she'd bring them herself if we want her to—"

"To attend our wedding? I almost forgot," he teased as he dropped dramatically to one knee. "Robyn, will you marry me?"

"Yes," she teased back. "Mother says it's a good idea."

He couldn't stop smiling. "Then I'll buy you a closet full of clothes when we get there—for a wedding present."

As he stood and hugged her, she asked, "Would you laugh at me if I asked to be married at the foot of Heidi's mountain?"

"On top of the Alps if you want."

"The Prescotts could stand up for us—"

"And your father?"

"Someone has to give me away."

The European Connection
Fast-paced international romance thrillers

Doris Elaine Fell

Assignment in Paris
Encounter in Zurich
The Spanish Connection
The Phoenix of Sulzbach
Deception in Prague
Conspiracy on Corfu

"Doris Elaine Fell has become one of America's favorite storytellers."
—**Karen Kingsbury**

"Doris spins an intriguing tale."
—**Robin Jones Gunn**

"Doris Elaine Fell writes with a tender heart. You won't want to miss this one!"
—**Angela Hunt**

The European Connection
Fast-paced international romance thrillers

Assignment in Paris
Doris Elaine Fell

**The fashion circuit in Paris
is a coveted assignment,
but it might cost Andrea her life.**

Fashion journalist Andrea York is on the fast-track to success at *Style Magazine* in Beverly Hills, but she dreams of having her own designer label. Right before she is to travel to the City of Light, her beloved grandmother, Katrina, falls desperately ill. As Andrea searches through treasured mementos, she finds her grandfather Conrad's watch—hands stopped at his death on the beach at Normandy—and some faded photos of men under his command. She remembers Katrina's whisper: "Conrad believed there was a traitor in his unit."

Sherman Prescott's life changed forever the day his wife drowned. The CIA told him it was a simple accident, but Sherm is convinced she was murdered. The file on Melody is sealed now, but he won't rest until he uncovers the truth. Then he receives a phone tip that the last person to see Melody alive is in Paris....

www.oaktara.com

The European Connection
Fast-paced international romance thrillers

The Spanish Connection

Doris Elaine Fell

Sauni can believe her ex-husband died in Vietnam. But it will take more than a military report to convince her he betrayed his country.

Captain Luke Breckenridge, a decorated Marine, died in Vietnam while on special assignment, yet his name is missing from the Vietnam Memorial Wall. The U.S. government claims he sold secrets to the enemy, but the man Sauni knew was a superpatriot. To put the ugly rumors to rest and clear Luke's name she needs the help of someone inside the Central Intelligence Agency.

Veteran CIA officer Drew Gregory knows finding out the truth about Luke Breckenridge won't be easy. The Vietnam War has been over for twenty years, Luke's files have been sealed for nearly that long, and someone high in the ranks wants to keep it that way. Then Drew infiltrates a mercenary camp in Spain, and the tangled facts start to unravel.

www.oaktara.com

SAGAS OF A KINDRED HEART
Experience the romance, the adventure, the intrigue....

Doris Elaine Fell

Blue Mist on the Danube
BOOK ONE

Willows on the Windrush
BOOK TWO

Sunrise on Stradbury Square
BOOK THREE

"Doris Elaine Fell has become one of America's favorite storytellers."
—**KAREN KINGSBURY**

Doris Elaine Fell is a masterful storyteller who emblazons her literary landscapes with unforgettable characters and exotic locales.
—**CAROLE GIFT PAGE**

"Doris spins an intriguing tale."
—**ROBIN JONES GUNN**

Filled with living, breathing characters who remain in your heart long after the last page is turned.
—**DIANE NOBLE**

SAGAS OF A KINDRED HEART
Experience the romance, the adventure, the intrigue....

Blue Mist on the Danube

BOOK ONE

Doris Elaine Fell

**A deep betrayal. Unfathomable love.
Two decades of secrets.**

Kerina Rudzinski, one of the world's greatest violinists, has always found refuge in Vienna, a city as beautiful and mysterious as she is. Here she can lose herself in the music she loves. But though the blue mist above the River Danube comforts Kerina, it cannot completely veil her past. Memories from another time, another place pierce her heart.

American Ashley Reynolds is haunted by a night in the little town of Everdale, and a promise she gave without realizing the consequences. Now, years later, her marriage crumbles under the weight of her secrets.

An ocean lies between the two women, but their destiny is intertwined...with each other and that of an extraordinary Army lieutenant on medical leave.

www.oaktara.com

SAGAS OF A KINDRED HEART
Experience the romance, the adventure, the intrigue....

Willows on the Windrush

BOOK TWO

Doris Elaine Fell

**Secrets lurk behind the doors
of the English mansion...**

Sydney Barrington has it all—success, wealth, and beauty. But something is missing. Jarred from her routine by the unexpected inheritance of Broadshire Manor in the Cotswolds of England, Syndey soon finds herself pulled between a prosperous businessman in America and a dashing Lieutenant Commander in the British Royal Navy.

When Abigail Broderick, the dignified woman in charge at the mansion, and a shadowy attorney insist Sydney has no claim to Broadshire Manor, she determines to unlock the mysteries concealed behind the stately doors.

www.oaktara.com

SAGAS OF A KINDRED HEART
Experience the romance, the adventure, the intrigue....

Sunrise on Stradbury Square

BOOK THREE

Doris Elaine Fell

**She loved him...once.
Might there be a chance for them again?**

Rachel McCully, a university professor, lives for her career, mountain trips, and summer holidays abroad...until a twist of fate propels her to fulfill two promises—one made to her sister, Larea, and one to Sinclair Wakefield, a man who captured her heart nearly a decade ago.

Returning to Sinclair's childhood home in England, Rachel hopes to reconcile with her former love. But circumstances make the timing questionable...and mystery swirls around the mansion in England's fabled Lake District.

www.oaktara.com

About the Author

DORIS ELAINE FELL writes with a sensitive pen, a tender heart, and a spirit of laughter—taking you into a world of adventure touching lives, touching rebels.

Her multifaceted career as teacher, missionary, nurse, freelance editor, and author, has taken her all over the world and inspired her novels. She is the best-selling author of 17 novels with Simon & Schuster's Steeple Hill/Love Inspired imprint, Fleming Revell, Harvest House, Howard, Crossway, and OakTara. Doris was a Christy Award finalist in 2000, a 2003 SPU (Seattle Pacific University) Medallion Award winner, and received the 2004 Silver Angel Award, Excellence in Media (EIM).

Photo of Doris Elaine Fell above taken by the Methow River, the location of one of her novels.

Seven of her titles were published in large print with Thorndike Press, and two books have editions in German, Italian, with another as a special limited edition in Australia. Her short stories also appear in Multnomah's *The Story Tellers' Collection Book 2* and the ChiLibris publication *What the Wind Picked Up*. Doris is also the author of two nonfiction books, *Lady of the Tboli* (Christian Herald Books), *Give Me This Mountain* (Jungle Camp devotional), and articles in mainstream and inspirational publications, such as "Mom and the Talking Bears" (*Focus on the Family*), *Tapestry: Walk Thru the Bible Ministries, Missouri Synod Lutheran Publication, Adventist Review*), "Brat Boy" (*RN Magazine*), "A Seed for Tomorrow" *(Home Life)*, "Bells, Bearhugs, and Mixed Blessings" *(Journal of Christian Nursing)*. And Sunday school publications such as *Evangel* and *Standard*.

Doris Elaine Fell writes from her home in Southern California.

For more information:
www.oaktara.com

Breinigsville, PA USA
07 November 2010
248840BV00001B/10/P